The Blood of a Dragon

The Dragons of Dorwine Book 1

Jack Adkins

Honor Bound Books

Acknowledgments

Writing a book takes a lot more work and a lot more people than I would have imagined when I started this journey in 4th grade with my fabled tale *The Big Wind of Wallingford*. First, and foremost, I have to thank my wife, Alicia, for creating space for me to write, encouraging me, and being my toughest editor. This book is so much better because of the hours she spent pouring over it.

I also want to thank my secret weapon, my Dragon Eyes. These dedicated individuals read the earliest drafts of this book and pointed out its warts and weak spots. My Beta Readers are literary heroes are who largely responsible for the book you are holding.

Finally, I want to thank the old gang. My OG Dungeons and Dragons group with whom I learned to dream of imaginary worlds as we tossed dice and spun tales deep into the night. More than just friends, those young men raised me. The memories we forged so long ago are etched on my heart.

Contents

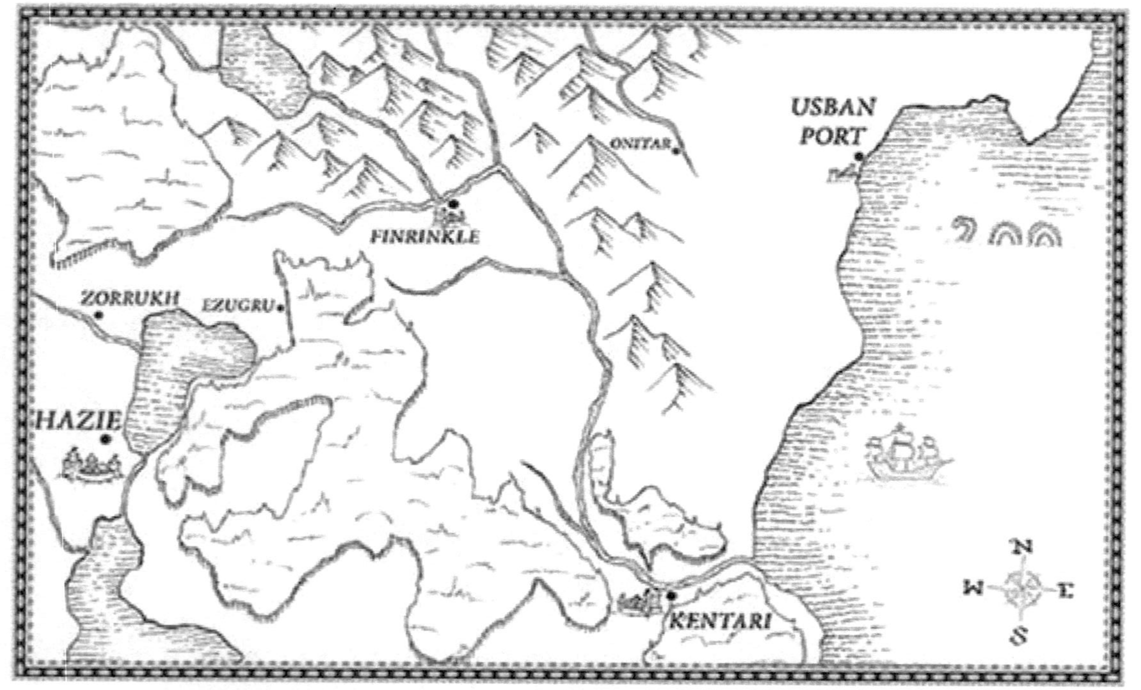

USBAN PORT
ONITAR
FINRINKLE
ZORRUKH
EZUGRU
HAZIE
KENTARI
N
S
E
W

Prologue

The Year 973 Dragon Anum

Screams pierced the air at the report of another cannon. Anuka sat panting, rivulets of sweat streaming down the crimson skin of his face. He glanced up at the crow's nest in time to see cannon fire rip through the mainstay a few feet below the post sending splintered wood and a screaming crewman plunging aft into the churning sea.

Anuka hardly blinked at the carnage. A distant report of pain from his hands echoed in his mind as his pointed fingernails dug into the grimy wood of the main deck.

All around people were leaping into the water, preferring to take their chances with the sharks instead of facing the inevitable capture of their ship.

Anuka considered following them. He could swim, despite his fears. His father, renowned as both a great pirate and respected naval commander, had made sure of that. But he couldn't make himself jump in.

Another DragonsBlood cannon issued a basso thump and seconds later a whistling cannonball blasted through the starboard side of the ruddy old ship just above the water line. She rocked and veered sending those left standing careening hard to the deck. The vessel briefly righted then began listing to port and everyone knew it was over. The ship was sinking.

Wiping the sweat and tears from his eyes, Anuka rose and crawled to the bulkhead. He closed his eyes and bowed his head as his shaking hand grasped the rail. After a pair of deep breaths, he spat out the sweat that had trickled into his open mouth, opened his eyes, and stood on shaky legs.

Mustering all of his strength, he looked over the side of the boat into the tumultuous sea water below. He was small, just over three feet tall, and would likely not be seen by the oncoming attackers, or at least would be mistaken for debris until it was too late to bother fetching him. If he could find something to float on he could paddle west and reach the shore in a day. He had to go now.

Grinding his pointed teeth in frustration, Anuka grabbed the rail tighter and prepared to vault over the side of the boat and into the water below. He looked before taking that desperate plunge and he saw her.

Right below him in the water, he could make out the pleading face and outstretched arms of his mother. His courage drained away like water from a smashed bucket. Anuka's knees buckled and he nearly toppled backward.

In his mind, he could hear her screaming for him as she sank slowly below the surface. She kicked and writhed but continued to descend. Air bubbles burst onto the surface of the water and she was gone.

Anguish crushed his small heart as it raced inside his chest. He opened his mouth to release a building wail but it died in his throat.

He released the rail and sank onto the deck. Screams of fear and battle lust roared around him. Salty spray from the pursuing ship struck the hull and spritzed Anuka's face. He barely noticed.

Anuka no longer cared if he sank to the bottom of the sea to be swallowed whole by Brine, the fearsome dragon that owned these waters. Nor did he care if a bloodthirsty brigand's rusty rapier pierced his heart. Mama was gone.

Chapter 1

To Usban

The Year 983 Dragon Anum

Anuka turned the bone-handled dagger over in his hand. His tiny red legs dangled over the edge of his cot as he frowned at the weapon. The handle was whalebone and carved with designs more commonly found on an Elven dagger than a Goblin weapon. It clearly wasn't Gobin made. The sleek steel blade was more finely crafted than anything any Goblin smith could make. His father had told him it was Dwarven, which meant very old. No one had seen a mountain dwarf for centuries.

He ran a finger gently along the side of the blade, careful to avoid the well-honed edge. Like the dagger, Anuka was also of strange composition. His father was a goblin, a legendary pirate, and a respected engineer. Among other things. His mother was something different. It hadn't bothered him that he didn't know what kind of creature his mother was. Until Papa had disappeared. Without his papa around to entertain him, he missed his Mama more. He thought about the day she drowned a lot more often. Once aboard the *Sea Pocket*, he started having nightmares again about that night.

Having seen some of the world, Anuka sorted through all the creatures he had encountered trying to figure out what type of creature his Mama had been. She sure wasn't a goblin. She was as tall as a human with blood-red skin, like his. Her voice was musical, like the strumming of a harp, and her eyes were dark and deep. He thought she must have been a witch or something like that. Anyone who used magic without using DragonsBlood or actually being a Dragon was a witch or sorcerer. And as good as dead. Her magic hadn't gotten her killed. But she was dead just the same.

The *Sea Pocket,* the rotting collection of boards on which he was crossing the Dragonblade Sea, rocked violently while a handful of passengers groaned. *If we make it to Usban, I'm sinking this heap,* Anuka thought.

Usban Port was the first stop on his journey to find his missing Papa. He needed a boat. Then a crew. And a pile of coins wouldn't hurt either. The coin would probably be easier than the crew. Even though the *Sea Pocket* was crammed full of people, Anuka hadn't yet found one soul fit to serve on his crew.

Most of the passengers were headed to Usban to find work. Usban, like every city in the swamp-laden providence of Zhazie, was ruled by the Black DragonLord Caustimis, or "Bog" as everyone called him. Bog was an enormous Black Dragon who could turn a turd into a mountain of gold. He built massive warehouses where everything from the finest silks to the strongest liquors were made. Those people heading for Usban weren't going to make silk or booze, they were aiming to be sea scavengers. Mostly water-breathers, like Sea Elves or Sea Dwarves would scour the bottom of the sea for shipwrecks from ages past. It was dangerous work, but those who survived were well paid. Dragons paid well for relics of the past, especially weapons. More than half of the passengers of the *Sea Pocket* were likely after that kind of work.

Occasionally, you would meet a Sea Dwarf with a talent for sailor work, but most of those Anuka had met were violent, stupid, and crazy. Not good crew material. Sea Elves weren't much use on a boat. It was too hard to keep them out of the water. There was a Minotaur on board who might be useful on a ship but he had screamed at anyone who tried talking to him. Anuka had also met a High Elf but he had turned out to be some sort of religious nut. A cultist of some kind. Anuka had even seen one big guy that he dubbed Fish Man. But he saw the man talking to dolphins one day and decided against approaching him. Too bad. He could have made an excellent sailor. But based on how he staggered around the deck, this was likely his first time aboard a ship. None of those folk would fit in with Anuka's crew. He looked up in time to see Fish Man walk past an open doorway muttering to himself.

Anuka sighed, slid his dagger smoothly away, and hopped off his bunk. He hadn't yet talked to everyone on board. Straightening his tunic, he painted on his best smile. "Time to go be charming," he said. Then he set off to find someone crazy enough to join his adventure.

———◆———

Kelios stood on the deck of the *Sea Pocket* and was grateful. This was the only passage south he could afford and chose to ignore its many faults. Thoughts of home came on him then, sudden and without mercy. He stood straight-backed with his face in the wind, one hand on the pocked rail of the ship, gazing across the vastness of the sea. Tears streaked back across his temples and into his ears. The knuckles of his pale green hands were almost white as he squeezed the rail. Willing his tears to stop, he swallowed a building sob and opened his mouth for a deep breath of the salty air.

Air. Even after nearly two weeks on the surface he still had twinges of fear that the next lungful would suffocate him. But it didn't. His body was adapting and would continue to learn to use air as naturally as it had water for the first twenty cycles of his life. His body would adapt, but his heart may never.

A pang in his gut reminded him why he left his bunk before the smell of the sea drew him. Splashing from the corner of his eye distracted him further.

Following the ship, just beyond the wake of the crude vessel, Kelios spied a pod of dolphins. They were his favored companions and had shadowed him since the *Sea Pocket* departed the Fareth Tore Enclave. Watching them for several moments, they clacked to one another, leaped out of the water, danced, and splashed. They were showing off for him. He smiled despite his longing for home. *I cannot join you now, brothers, but soon. Soon we shall swim together.* His heart ached for it to be so. He had fled his homeland in haste and hadn't had an opportunity to indulge in a swim. But when possible, he would join his sea companions.

The urge to strip away his ridiculous surface garb and dive into the water was strong. He could almost taste the brine and feel the water washing over his skin as he raced through the dark recesses of the sea. But he crushed those urges. Exhaling, he blew out the mass of longings clouding his mind. Where would he go if he returned to the sea? He was exiled from his family. From his home. What was he without his people? Was he still a Triton? From his encounters so far, he didn't expect to make many friends.

Tossing his head from side to side, he shook his kelp-colored shoulder length hair wildly about, then resolutely took a deep breath through his nose. It still burned a little to inhale too quickly, but he embraced the pain just as he embraced his mission. As much as a grounded bird missed the skies, Kelios missed the water, but his course was set.

"My heart. My people. I will return to you in glory and bring you peace. So I swear." His oath was uttered softly, not meant for random passersby, each word settling deep into his soul.

The spring air was warm and sweet as it caressed her face. Wild daisies and primrose dotted the fields surrounding the cottages she raced over. She cast a massive shadow over the land as she blurred past, wings flared.

A thunderous rumble rolled through her belly as she caught the scent of a large herd of cattle, their blood calling to her. But she was not an undisciplined young Wyrm, impetuous and greedy, so she resisted the urge to circle back for a quick snack.

With one flap of her powerful, leathery wings the ground sloped away suddenly and she was soaring above a verdant valley where rocky cliffs plummeted.

She glided circuitously around the basin to look at the unfolding scene below.

Small hillocks to the right of the burgeoning stream were devoid of trees. Across the stream lay a large patch of wild cardinal flowers, where regal shafts jutted up from the ground, displaying brilliant red flower petals. Though she was still too far away, she could smell their sweet nectar, if only in her mind.

Two more concentric loops and she landed gently among the crimson bed of flowers. Hummingbirds scattered at her arrival.

This was her favorite spot in all the world.

Her eyelids closed over giant serpent eyes and waves of contentment washed over her as she gently hovered above the flowers, careful not to utterly crush them.

No place in the world could match this.

The peace of this place was interrupted by a soft rustle. Totally out of place here, it jolted her out of her revelry. She slowed the titanic billows of her mighty lungs and listened carefully. *There it was again.*

Sudden primal fear struck her but was quickly quashed by the recollection that she was the world's chief predator. Indignation rose, followed quickly by boiling anger, and began to climb her six-foot-long neck, bringing heat to her face. Massive talons flexed involuntarily, carving furrows into the earth as she spun to see a filthy human.

A male, it seemed, carelessly rifled through her worn leather pack. Items not of interest he discarded to the ground and others were set aside for further inspection. His stench was appalling.

The mighty Dragon reeled slightly as two different worlds coalesced, and then divided again into separate realities.

She folded the dream flat inside her mind, tucking it away for another day, and with effort slowly peeled her eyes open.

The dreadful stench of unwashed bodies brought Crenthys fully awake almost instantly. The gentle rocking of the sea reminded her where she was; crammed into a small space. The hardwood under her back was cushioned only by a thin blanket. She was aboard The *Sea Pocket*, headed south to Usban Port on an important mission.

Recalling the dream, she looked around. Someone was, in fact, rifling through her bag.

Her face contorted angrily and violently thrusting herself forward, she slammed her booted foot into the back of the thief's neck.

Crying out in surprise and anguish, he dropped the bag as his face smashed into the bulkhead then ricocheted, and he staggered backward.

Before he could react, Crenthys slid off the bed, grabbed his left wrist in her left hand, and twisted his arm painfully behind him. She wrenched his first two fingers savagely toward the ceiling with her other hand.

He screamed in agony and, as she released her grip, he brought his broken fingers up to his face. He sprinted from the room and Crenthys heard him retching before he had fled ten paces.

She turned and bent down, casually picking up her things from the floor. Both miffed at having her perfect dream interrupted and simultaneously pleased at her handling of the thief, she allowed herself a tiny smile.

Not only had she stopped the clumsy burglar, but now word would spread quickly of what would happen if anyone crossed the wicked little Sea Elf in steerage. Morglun would be proud, she mused and smiled a little wider.

"Are you well?" a voice asked from the doorway.

Crenthys leapt to her feet and whirled around. A roguishly handsome Sea Elf stood facing her. This man obviously had two Elven parents. His skin was a cerulean blue color, lighter than the ocean but darker than the sky. He possessed slender, angular features, like Crenthys. Well, not exactly like her. By her appearance, Crenthys would be called a half-elf. While this Elf's ears were long with a severe point on both the top and the bottom, her earlobes were slightly rounded. His lips were thin and nearly invisible against his skin while Crenthys's were full and thick.

His demeanor was non-threatening, though Crenthys discerned by his shoulder-width stance and the subtle scarring on his hands and arms, that this man was acquainted with violence.

She composed herself quickly and smiled, "Pardon, you startled me."

"My apologies. Are-are you well?" he repeated.

"Yeah, some idiot tried to rob me in broad daylight." She gestured with her bag in one hand and some of her belongings in the other.

"You were sleeping?" the man asked with a chuckle and leaned against the door frame.

Crenthys shrugged and stuffed the items back into her bag. "Yeah, I love the sea at night. So I sit up on the deck while everyone else sleeps and watch the water." That was the answer she had rehearsed to the question she knew would eventually come.

"I know," he said, looking at her, "I've seen you."

Her face must have betrayed her alarm. One rebel eyebrow raised in protest, as it often did in these situations.

"Our people," he said gesturing between them, "we are different. Our joys and our sorrows are different from other people." He smiled at her as he continued. "Besides, who can sleep with all the noise?"

His laugh sounded a little forced, but Crenthys smiled at the attempted humor. That seemed the correct thing to do. "Yeah. That." She slung her pack over her head, settled the strap across her body, and extended a hand. "I am Crenthys."

The man looked at her hand for a moment, then took it in his own. Bowing, he touched his forehead to the back of her hand. The move was very formal, very elven.

She saw that the backs of his ears were both clipped, in the V-shaped notch fashion of a slave, and she became even more intrigued by this man's history. Recruiting new members for the group she worked for was difficult. She was always looking for talented people.

He stood again, still holding her hand, and said, "I am Wave."

A simple name. A slave's name. He spoke so formally for a slave and Crenthys thought about what that could mean. "It is well to have met you, Wave."

"Take care, Crenthys." He bowed slightly, backed into the hallway, and disappeared.

Be careful, she scolded herself. She was running out of time to accomplish her mission in Usban Port and had no use for some flirty Elf.

She looked longingly at her bunk but decided to forgo finishing her nap. There were just too many things to think about right now.

Crenthys adjusted the strap of her bag and silently made her way out of the belly of the ship, up to the main deck, hoping that watching the ocean was the only thing Wave had seen her doing at night.

"So I told him 'It wouldn't be a problem if you'd have left the window open!'" Anuka said, sending the room into an uproar of raucous laughter.

This half of the mess hall was packed with passengers and crew. Most of them doubled-over in red-faced laughter. Tears trailed from their eyes as they leaned on the wall or one another for support.

What a sorry lot, Anuka thought, hiding behind his false mask of mirth as the laughter roared. *My considerable talents are being wasted here,* he mused indignantly. *Probably not an able sailor among them. Not to mention nobody with two coins to rub together.*

He sighed, sensing that the fun needed to end. If he intended to talk to everyone on board it was time to wrap this up. At that moment, the Fish Man sauntered regally into the mess hall.

Anuka wasn't sure what race the guy was but he carried himself like a man with coin. Some kind of sea dweller, he guessed, suspecting the diagonal lines on his neck to be gill slits. He was a big Sum Buck. Not a sea elf but something. One thing he knew for sure; that guy wasn't here to scrub barnacles off the boat or troll for sunken treasure. His clothes looked fairly new and mostly clean. If he wasn't a sailor he would make an excellent mark for a young goblin in need of coin.

The stranger walked all square backed like he had sat on a javelin. From a glance, he might have even combed his kelp-colored hair. Anuka was pretty sure this guy had all of his front teeth. He was perfect!

The green-skinned Fish Man also looked like a man wanting to grab a bite and slip out the back. That would just not do. Anuka's papa always said, *"Suckers grow on trees, you just gotta be willin' to climb up after em'!".*

"Welcome!" he bellowed with all the gusto half-sized lungs could afford him. Every head snapped toward him, including the strangers'.

"Welcome to my mess hall, my ravenous friend!"

Now all eyes turned to the green-skinned man who stood frozen, looking at Anuka. His eyes widened and thin eyebrows rose. "Hello," the stranger said in a deep, watery voice. His eyes darted around the room, then landed back on Anuka.

Anuka's hook was set. He smiled and proclaimed, "Help yourself to whatever you want. We had a ton of fruit and vegetables, salted meat, and fresh seafood but that guy ate it all before we got here." Anuka pointed at the massive middle-aged human sitting nearby and the room exploded in laughter again.

"Yeah, all we have left is that lousy fish soup," Anuka said.

The stranger took one step toward the door, froze and looked at the bowl in his hand. Then he set his bowl on the nearest table and briskly fled the room.

Anuka sighed, rubbed his forehead with one hand and said to himself, "That was stupid. Oh well. Can't hook em' all". He reassigned the fake smile to his face, looked at his audience, and launched into another of his endless stories.

⚬

This wasn't the first time Tabir had been punched by a patient. It likely would not be the last. He couldn't blame the fellow: The only thing worse than having a couple of fingers broken is to have them set in the same hour. There was nothing for it. Tabir didn't dare bring his power, well, Rathune's power, to bear on something as simple as broken fingers. They would regain their function if the poor man followed Tabir's care instructions.

He rubbed at his tender ear where the punch had landed and winced. Too bad the power of healing didn't work on himself. That just wouldn't make sense. Tabir's power required him to exchange some of his own life for the healing of others. You can't pay your debt with coin you don't have. He had whittled away an untold number of his long Elven years to ease the suffering of others. But he didn't dare do that here. In Dorwine, only Dragons could lawfully wield any kind of magical power. While Tabir's abilities originated with Rathune, here the Dragons would consider them magic. He had heard tales of people dying horrible deaths solely for being accused of trying to usurp the chain of magical authority established by the Dragon Council.

Tabir's bunk room on the ship housed twelve beds and he suspected the neighboring room was much the same. He rubbed his hand over the rough-hewn bed frame suspended chest high above the floor of the ship. It was plain, made of unfinished wood that was fairly soft. It had most likely been white when it was new, but now bore the patchy dark stains of frequent use and infrequent cleaning.

Thinking about his childhood bed back in his home city, he smiled. It had been carved from the finest Haylock tree, which has a unique swirl pattern in which five or six different shades of wood twisted around each other. The surface had been smooth and carved with intricate designs. Beautiful flowers entwined and formed borders around elegant birds and regal cats. He had lain in his bed many nights, watching those patterns in the light of the moon.

Gradually, wicked images had replaced the flowers and birds of his childhood. He recalled the faces of hideously twisted demons in bas relief covering every surface of the wood. Carvings of writhing flames hungrily devoured the gentler images on his bedposts. By the time he had reached adulthood, murals of elves and demons, often in lewd poses, marred the surface of nearly every piece of wood in the city. Tabir closed his eyes and shuddered.

How, oh Maker, had he been so blind to it all? For decades before his birth, Tabir's people had been seduced and tormented by spirits of power. An elder among his people had uncovered an ancient teaching that had been previously lost to Elvenkind. This unearthed writing suggested that the bodies of mortals were created to host two spirits instead of just one. Instead of seeking the spirit of their Creator, this elder and his scholars sought to fill themselves with the evil spirits that promised power. The scholars then lured Tabir's people by promises of pleasure and power. These spirits were no harm to the world without a host. But as Tabir's people began to commune with these spirits, the spirits once again were able to influence the world. These demon spirits were intent on building an army for their masters, mortal enemies Keit and Tor, avatars of Rathune, the Maker. But they betrayed Rathune and were sentenced to imprisonment where they await judgment for the wars they fought over control of the world. No one knows when the thousand-year sentence will end, yet when it does, the judgment will come. The resurgence of magic in the world, and the return of demonic spirits, both suggest that the time is fast approaching for the avatars Keit and Tor to be released and punished.

The evil spirits deceived and seduced the elves into allowing them to share their bodies more and more until they gradually reduced their host's spirit to a faint whisper. By the time Tabir and his sister, Analeah, had discovered this, most of the city, many of their family included, were almost entirely under the control of evil spirits.

Tabir was the 10th born son, an impossibility among elves who rarely had more than two or three children. This marked him as a child of prophecy or an abomination. His family had been prominent among his people and some of the first to begin bonding with spirits of power. Tabir, however, was unable to bond with any other spirit. This shamed and disappointed his family. Chosen son, or no, his inability to host a spirit of power had caused his people to drive him out of their city, nearly killing him.

Now he understood that Rathune had graciously protected him by keeping him from bonding with the evil spirits. He bowed his head and whispered a prayer of thanks. Tabir had finally come to understand how his kin had taken their hosts when the spirit of Rathune had overwhelmed him. That filling had protected him but at great cost. Filled by the spirit of Rathune, Tabir returned to his people and issued a stern warning, calling them to renounce the evil spirits they had bonded with or be judged. Some did, but many chose to remain behind and die. Many of his family were among them. He had lived a transient life since.

Rathune judged that city, destroying it and all of the inhabitants who refused to renounce the demons they hosted. Tabir marveled at how clearly the memories came flooding back after so many years and all from touching a piece of wood. Sighing, he put his foot on the wooden handle affixed to the hull and launched himself into the top bunk. A reminder from one of the Slivers of Aracthias, the same writings that his people had twisted to their peril, encouraged him to pray for those who cast stones at him. That would include the one who punched him for setting his fingers. Tabir made himself as comfortable as the bed would allow, for his prayer list was long this day.

Chapter 2

Slight Misunderstanding

When Anuka saw the Fish Man on deck, a place Anuka rarely went, he took a draw of thin ale from the wooden cup in his hand and cheered his luck. Maybe he could redeem his poor handling of the rich-looking stranger after all.

The sound of rattling coins rang in Anuka's mind. He made his way over to the rail where the man stood and cleared his throat. The tall man looked at Anuka flatly but turned to face him squarely.

"Look, I'm sorry if my jokes from earlier were a bit off-color. I get carried away sometimes." Anuka stuck out his hand in the local tradition and saw that the stranger wasn't familiar with the gesture. Right. He was a Fish Man. Retracting his hand, he swept into a low bow and said, "I am Anuka Sandbar."

"Kelios Verromath." Fish Man said with a bow of his own.

Smiling, Anuka pumped a fist excitedly and said, "That's great! Look. I dunno where you're from, or what you're up to, or even what you are, but I can tell you what I've got going on. I'm headed to Usban, I've got some work there. Then I'm looking to put together my own crew. That's right. I'm a captain. In the making. And I'm looking for some lenders for this initial-" Anuka trailed off. He'd lost the man's attention. Anuka followed Kelios's gaze across the deck to a girl leaning on the starboard rail.

Anuka quickly appraised the girl and found her quite fetching. That is if you go in for the tall, slender, buxom, thick-lipped, silky-haired, mixed-blood sea elf type. He certainly did not but the sight of Kelios noticing her put an idea in his mind.

Looking at the forlorn face of his new project, Anuka made a decision. Handing his little wooden cup to Kelios he exclaimed, "Hey, excuse me a minute." He made a quick bow. "I need to talk to somebody. I'll be right back."

Anuka left Kelios standing in confusion as he made straight toward the girl at the other side of the boat.

Being half the size of everyone else put his face even with everyone else's backside. A couple of well-aimed sharp pokes quickly parted the crowd for the little red goblin.

He emerged from the sea of stinking rear ends to find his quarry looking right at him. She was different up close. Dangerous. There was something in her eyes that he hadn't seen across the deck. She looked much less the hapless vixen trolling for affection and more like a plains lion scanning for something small and slow to eat.

No mind. Kelios needed this. Besides, Anuka had handled all sorts in his day. A man of the sea had to know how to handle prostitutes.

"Hey there," he said, straining to keep the natural squeak out of his voice, "I'm Anuka Sandbar. Seaman, swordsman, pirate, merchant, and showman." He swept his worn leather hat from his bald head and bent into a low bow. It probably looked silly on such a small creature, he knew, but he'd seen his papa do it a hundred times and the effect was generally positive.

"Well," she said with a smile. Yeah, she sounded impressed. Thanks, Papa. "Such decorum for a...what are you?"

Anuka straightened himself and grinned broadly to show off his nearly perfect set of mostly clean, sharp-pointed teeth. He had gotten over being the strangest goblin people had met, and loved the effect this had on people. He wasn't disappointed as the young wench's face slipped from teasing to surprise, just a bit. "As I said, I'm Anuka Sandbar. As to my heritage?" He shrugged. "My father is Glamokyn, as your people would say, or Goblin to some other folk. My mother was...complicated."

"Was?" she asked and her face seemed to soften just a touch.

"Was." He nodded in agreement. Tidal waves of anguish beat futilely at the walls Anuka had spent the last decade constructing around his heart; he smiled. And maybe a little sadness crept into his eyes. Just a little.

"And you are?" his change in tone made it clear that the discussion about his mother was at an end.

She pursed her lips for a moment and said, "Crenthys Larin'hul."

I was right, Anuka mused. Human blood, judging by her surname. If you were fool enough to give any credence to the Hierarchy of Creation, like some religious zealots did, you understood that a mixed-blood sea elf was about as close to the bottom as one could get. Anuka wasn't at all sure where he fit on that mythical scale.

"It's a pleasure, Crenthys." He always tried to say their name a couple of times, like Papa did. "Now, let's get down to business."

Ignoring the puzzled look that crawled onto the elf's smooth-skinned face, Anuka slid his arm to her back and, standing beside her, directed her attention across the deck to where an anxious-looking Kelios stood watching them.

"My green-skinned friend there. Do you glimpse him?" Anuka stretched to his tiptoes to see the tall man.

"Yes, I-"

"Good, look, I don't know what he is, either, but I know he's a mess." He turned back to regard her again, smoothly slipping his rough little hand into her delicate one. "He is far from home. Best I can tell, he lives at the bottom of the ocean or something. I don't know. Anyway, he's lonely, obviously out of his element, a little afraid, and lonely."

"You already said lonely."

Anuka smiled. "You're quick. That's where I'm going with this. Look, he isn't terribly hideous and seems in good health. I think the two of you could make a go of it."

Crenthys's eyebrows shot way up, her eyes went wide, and her mouth dropped open.

"I know what you're going to say, and I get it. That's what I wanted to talk about. I'm not exactly swimming in gold right now." Anuka said.

A few seconds passed, then the shock on Crenthys's face melted like wax in the sun, into a frightening look. Slender eyebrows smashed together and her eyes darkened. She seemed much taller and stronger than any Sea Elf he'd seen. Anuka could almost swear he saw smoke trail from her now flaring nostrils.

"I know you probably hear this a lot, but money isn't usually a problem. My dad is sort of a famous captain. Once I find him in Usban I'll be flush. I'm just tryna' help this poor sap out. He has trouble stringing words together and I figured I would..." Anuka let the words trail off. Crenthys looked like she had found an eyeball in her fish soup. It dawned on him that he may have misjudged this situation.

"Get out of here!" she growled through clenched teeth.

Anuka had always been small. He had learned pretty quickly when to keep talking and when to run for it. He suddenly noticed that things had shifted from him holding her hand to her crushing his, so he jerked his tiny fingers free, backed up two steps, and disappeared into the crowd of butts once more.

He had never killed another sentient being in cold blood but right now Kelios wanted to choke the life out of the little red goblin and throw his body overboard. Whatever the little beast had said to the pretty elven girl had been about him, and it had made her furious.

Her icy glare made his stomach churn even harder. Anuka made his way through the throng of people. The girl seemed about to storm off down into the belly of the ship.

Anuka appeared from the mass of people, looked up at him, and simply shrugged.

Kelios expected for him to come hat-in-hand and apologize or try to explain himself but the little creature just shrugged. The desire to toss him bodily overboard surged again.

Walking up to him, Anuka took the cup from Kelios's hand, tipped it up, and drained it to the dregs.

"Whelp, that didn't work." Anuka proclaimed with another shrug of the shoulder. "Better luck next time, eh?" He smacked Kelios, still stunned, on the leg.

Proper words wouldn't pass Kelios's teeth. He tried several times, but his indignation burst like a bubble before leaving his lips.

Anuka looked up at him, amusement on his face as if waiting for Kelios to master himself.

When he finally did, he growled, "What did you do?"

"I rolled the dice, bubby. Sometimes your number comes up and sometimes it don't. We missed."

"*We* missed? What were you aiming to do?"

"Honestly, Kelios. You're tighter than a back stay in full wind. I was aiming to warm your bed, my friend."

"You what? With her? She's a...?" Kelios knew of prostitution but couldn't speak the word.

"Well, I thought so. I might be a couple of coins light on that count." He shrugged again and began filling his little cup at the water keg tap. "Either way, I don't think she'll be warming either of our beds tonight. Maybe I'll try again tomorrow. After she's cooled down." Anuka took a long pull from his cup.

"Try again? No, sir. I forbid it." Kelios spat indignantly.

The little red man smacked his lips. "Suit yourself. But I don't recommend you try it for yourself. I'm pretty good at these things. You know, it might've have went better if I had some coin to grease the deadeyes, if you know what I mean."

"No. I don't know what you mean. And you'll not be using any of my coin to grease anything!" Kelios plowed his way through the crowd toward the pretty elf, intent on making amends.

What insolence! Kelios thought, anger roiling through him. If 'warming his bed' meant what Kelios assumed it meant, it may be best to toss the little red heathen into the sea after all. Where did he get the presumptive gall to secure companionship for him? Kelios thought of beautiful Yoslyn, his intended, waiting for his triumphal return home, and it quelled his burning anger just a bit.

Yoslyn was a princess. Noble, like him. She was beautiful, talented, and from one of the most prominent families in his family's protectorate. She also was the same *species* as Kelios. That was most important to his parents. Their marriage had been negotiated by their parents more than a decade ago. And they had the final say on such things in his culture. Kelios imagined that, had he not endeavored upon this journey, he would have already wed her.

The strange mix of feelings that came with those thoughts made Kelios uneasy. Yoslyn was his wife, in all but the formality of a ceremony. It had taken years for him to come to terms with that.

Yoslyn had never made his stomach feel tight or his head feel dizzy the way the elven girl had from fifteen paces away. Kelios stopped only a stride from the elven girl. She stood, arms folded across her chest glaring at him.

Anuka rubbed his face with his hands and barked out a frustrated noise. He removed his hat and scratched his bald head as he looked around the ship. At the rate things were going, he might as well go talk to the cultist elf again. He spied that elf sitting at the prow of the ship in some sort of meditative pose. It was weird to see a High Elf on a boat.

He was not likely to find any sailor worth their weight in salt or anyone with coin they were willing to part with. It was too risky to chance a burglary on a ship. His gaze strayed to the water but he jerked it back onto the deck of the ship. Closing his eyes to stop his head from spinning, Anuka tried to think of something besides the ocean surrounding him. He needed to go below deck. Panic was sinking in as he struggled to put the water out of his mind.

Usban was only a couple days away. He should have answers there. Maybe Papa had left him a note or perhaps he would get word from an acquaintance near Kentari.

Nearby, Anuka noticed a straight-backed, blue-skinned sea elf looking across the deck. Anuka had seen him strutting around the ship. Apparently, the elf had been watching his encounter with the hooker with great interest. He looked like a personal assistant for someone important. "How many weird colored freaks can there be on one boat?" Anuka muttered under his breath.

"Hey, bubby!" Anuka yelled out as he moved in the direction of the blue man. A full elf he thought as he took in his features. Not mixed like the rent girl and almost every other elf he knew. "Hey, friend." He continued as the man looked curiously at him.

"Are you speaking to me, Glam?" The elf asked in a low monotone.

"Yeah. I'm Anuka. Anuka Sandbar." Anuka gave a small bow.

The elf didn't offer a name. He probably had one of those stupid made up names like "Stick" or "Surf" as sea elves were fond of using.

Elves, even the lowly sea elves, were pretentious in the way they named themselves. A great deal could be learned by an elf's given name alone. It was foolish, in Anuka's estimation, to give away anything about yourself in something as easy to change as a name.

"Yeah, look. Hey man, a word to the wise." He motioned toward Crenthys. "I'd forget the drab if I were you."

"Excuse me?" the man asked, a shade of incredulity woven into his words.

Anuka hooked a thumb and a glance in the girl's direction and noticed she was talking with Kelios. He turned back to the blue elf. "She's nice to look at, and would probably be a real hellcat, but it ain't worth it. We didn't get into price or anything, but I don't think she's worth it. No matter what she's askin'."

The sea elf turned, towering over Anuka like everyone did, and fixed him with a look a shark would give a wounded dolphin. The flat slits serving as the man's nostrils flared into ovals that would have looked dangerous on a larger man.

He had handled bigger people all his life. So it wasn't the size of the elf that sent a wicked shiver down Anuka's relatively short spine. It was his eyes. The dark pupils were so large no white was visible. They were like dark pools of water where a barracuda might be lurking, deep and cold. There was no joy or fervor in those eyes, just emptiness.

A thin scar appeared on his upper lip as the blue hue of his skin deepened into a murky purple.

Anuka's right hand was already curling around the dagger under his vest and his other was inching closer to the rapier at his hip. Before a bloody melee ensued the man deflated like a puffer fish and the purple drained out of his face. He exhaled slowly through his now thin nostrils and offered Anuka a contemptuous sneer before he simply turned and walked away.

When the man was gone Anuka blew out the breath he had been holding and slid his hand out of his vest. Anuka was trying to put a potential competitor off the strumpet's scent, in case Kelios was interested, but it hardly seemed worth the hassle. That girl has everybody torn up. *Beaches. Am I the only one who knows how to properly conduct themselves around a street lady?*

He pushed the conflict out of his mind and started stewing on what to do when they finally made port at Usban. That was when he noticed something wasn't right.

Anuka looked up to the crow's nest and caught a few hand signals the scrawny crewman was passing to the First mate. *Flying Fish Farts.* He looked out over the water port of the bow. In the distance, he saw a tiny, dark speck. *Sum Buck.*

<hr>

"So your servant failed and, what? You thought you would take a turn?" The Elf girl's voice rose with each word and she nearly shook with rage.

"I, no....I mean," his voice trailed off. Even in his own language, Kelios wasn't good at speaking under pressure. So he bowed. It was a deep bow and he held his posture rigid, the way a surface noble might. When he stood again her expression hadn't changed. "I am called Kelios. And I apologize for whatever the little red creature said to you. He does not speak for me."

"His tongue is going to get him killed," she said.

"Agreed. I am debating carrying out that sentence myself."

That softened her scowl and she almost smiled. Almost.

"Kelios. I am Crenthys." She stuck out her hand the way Anuka had done earlier and, on impulse, he took it in his own.

His hands must have felt like a turtle's shell to her. The strength of her grip was surprising. She was a head shorter than him. Though broader in the shoulders than most elves he had seen, she was quite small. He released her hand and stared at the deck trying to think of something to talk about.

"Why are you going to Usban, Kelios?"

He was grateful she had spoken but grasped for an intelligent response. "I don't know." Definitely not the response he hoped for.

"Oh. A world traveler then?" She asked.

What was wrong with him? It felt like his brain and his mouth were in different oceans. "Yes. I am traveling." He did not like to lie. It seemed easier in this case to allow her to believe what she wished. "If I may ask, what is your business in Usban?"

"I'm looking for work inland as a seamstress." She replied.

Seamstress? He would not have guessed that. It was better, he supposed than what Anuka had guessed. As if thinking of the infuriating little creature had summoned him, he heard. "Hey, Fish Man."

Kelios turned slowly to see Anuka striding his way with a concerned look on his face. *Now what?*

"Hey buddy, we've got problems."

"I am busy right now. Please leave." Kelios yanked the hem of his shirt out of Anuka's grasp.

"Well, bubby, this won't keep. Strumpet is gone anyways."

Kelios jerked his attention back to Crenthys only to see her shapely form disappearing below deck. He closed his eyes and exhaled.

"So, like I was saying."

"What could be so urgent?" Kelios barked.

"Well. Not a big deal, I guess. Unless you've got something against being chased by pirates."

Chapter 3

A Dark Silhouette

C renthys made her way back to the deck as soon as she heard the commotion. She didn't like the look of the pursuing ship at all. It cut smoothly across the softly churning sea and held a good line. She didn't know much about sailing but it moved with force and purpose. In contrast, the boat beneath her feet sloshed around the sea like a hog in the mud and never seemed to hold any one course for long before needing some correction.

None of those things bode well for this vessel, its passengers, or its crew. She realized she had been flexing and relaxing her hands subconsciously. Immediately she stopped and looked around to see if anyone was watching her.

The green-skinned man, a Seaborne, she thought, looked at her, wearing a sad expression. Not fear necessarily, which would have been understandable given the circumstances, just sadness. She still intended to kill that little Glamokyn who thought she was a whore, but there was something more mysterious about this Seaborne than she could discern. He had an odd, yet regal bearing.

What is he about? she wondered to herself. *Could he be important to her mission in some way?* From the looks of things that mission was going to need some help, and fast. Of course, he could also be an unwanted distraction.

Standing stiffly against the bulkhead was the Sea Elf. Wave, she thought his name was. Another odd one. Odd and dangerous according to her instinct.

She didn't have time for this. She shook her head. Those pirates were coming and she needed to make a plan. Helplessness gnawed at her and she remembered her years before Apostate. Gooseflesh covered her arms and back. She shuddered it away and reminded herself how she vowed never to be hopeless again. She prayed she could hold to that vow.

Kelios sensed something upsetting the passengers now crowding the deck, but he wasn't sure what. The man in the perch atop the ship's sail alternated between looking off into the distance and shouting things Kelios didn't understand to the crewmen below. Those men dashed about, speaking with either the captain or the first mate.

"There's a ship following us," Anuka said at Kelios's right hip.

Kelios nearly leaped out of his skin. "How do you know that?" He asked the goblin, making it clear that he was still displeased with him.

"I speak the language, bubby." Anuka leaned over the side of the boat and peered intently out over the water. "Stern and starboard. About two leagues."

"What does that mean?"

Anuka shrugged his little shrug. "Maybe nothing. They may be headed to Usban like us. We're only a day or so out of port now, by my guess. Or it's pirates. We're about as far out as you might expect to find them." He glanced up, then around as best he could. "This would be a good spot for a chase."

"Then what will happen?"

"Well, this ship is a piece of dung, the captain is a toothless idiot, and the crew are mostly drunk criminals." Anuka peered off into the distance, squinting. "And that ship keeps getting bigger. I'd say we're shark food. Or worse. Slaves."

Slave? Kelios knew the term. He would be considered a slave among his people, but its meaning among the surface dwellers was very different. Such a barbaric practice. He could not be made a slave. He had a...what did he have, really? Kelios may be floundering but he didn't want to be made a slave. *What could he do?*

"What're you worried about? Can't you just jump in and swim home?"

Kelios shook his head.

"How come?"

"I...I am no longer welcome there. Besides, we are more than fifty leagues from my pod. I could no more swim that than you could reasonably walk that distance."

"Well, that's awful. Sorry, bubby. If those blokes run us down, it's safe to say we'll have a different set of problems." The goblin knifing his finger across his neck was not helpful.

Kelios drew his lips in tight to hold back a salty retort. How could this little creature be so flippant about this situation?

The din of noise grew louder as more and more people became aware of their pursuer. *Surely the captain would make an announcement or address the rumors,* Kelios thought. He could sense the fear and anxiety around them. He briefly entertained the notion that he would try to comfort those gathered on the deck but quickly dismissed that idea. Oration, even in his native tongue, was not among his talents. Perhaps Anuka...He let the thought die when he looked over and saw the little goblin had a finger buried to the first knuckle in one nostril.

Maybe waiting for the captain to speak was the best course.

"Sum buck!" Anuka exclaimed.

The goblin had cupped his hands over his eyes and was looking over the rail at the on-coming ship.

"What does that mean?" Kelios asked.

"It's an expression. Goblin thing."

"No, what are you exclaiming over?" Kelios squinted and blocked the blistering sun with one thick hand. He was drying out and would need to soak soon. While the added shade improved his vision, he still couldn't see what had gotten the goblin excited. A few other passengers chattered excitedly.

"Cannons, bubby. Biguns'. She's a big girl, too. Dang. And she's...Sum. Buck." Anuka nearly screamed that last part. "This is not good."

Others reacted as whatever Anuka had seen became common knowledge. Passengers darted around the deck. Some made for the lower decks while others seemed to be searching for someone. The tension continued to swell and Kelios realized that if he didn't get Anuka somewhere safe he might soon be trampled by a panicked mob.

The Sleek vessel cut a path straight for them as the sky continued to darken. The boat rocked under Crenthys's feet as the helmsman desperately tried to put water between them and the oncoming pirate ship. His efforts were futile. According to what she had heard a man with a scope tell his nearby wife, the ship was called The *Brinery*. The flag flying from the mainstay confirmed that to those with eyes keen enough to see it. Crenthys had heard of The *Brinery*. It terrorized the Seas between the Isles of Fareth Tore and the Eastern coast of Dorwine. It was a slaving ship, a pirate ship, and a gunship that had been given to its infamous captain, Onan Swet, by the Sea Dragon Brine. The pirate ship blasted through the water with a force and finesse the rotten old *Sea Pocket* couldn't muster on its best day.

Everyone was rushing around in a frenzy. Everyone except Anuka. The little Goblin seemed to be elsewhere, even though he was in the midst of utter chaos. He sat on the deck with his back against the bulwark, as the Seaborne, Kelios, explained something Anuka didn't want to hear.

The sound of a thunderclap split the air followed a second later by a resounding boom. A shower of splinters rained down, chunks of wood flew about, and screams pierced the air as the Mast was sheared in two.

Crenthys whipped her head back toward The *Brinery* as devastation continued to rain down on her. A ship as small as The *Brinery* should not be equipped with a DragonsBlood Cannon. But the acrid stench of DragonsBlood, mixed with other chemicals, hanging in the air said otherwise as their ship listed violently from one side to the other. She was flung down onto the deck and nearly squashed as the other passengers around her fell. She rolled to the port side bulwark and pulled herself to her knees. She grasped onto the rail and, pulling herself up, looked across the ever-shrinking gap between the *Sea Pocket* and the *Brinery,* and saw the ship lining up for a second cannon blast. That ship didn't have a DragonCannon. It had two. That was impossible. There would be no hand-to-hand combat or trading of arrow fire as she had envisioned. They could not stand against such firepower. This would be a massacre.

Crenthys intrinsically knew the fight to avoid being captured or perhaps chase off the pirates was already lost. Now she needed to find the best place to be captured to avoid being killed.

Why would anyone waste that much firepower on a ship like this? What were they after? She said a quick prayer that she might live to know the answer to that question. If she did she knew what to do. She had trained for the possibility of being captured and would not let Morglun down. Too much was at stake.

Crenthys took inventory of herself and found no serious injuries. There was a scrape on her left leg from being knocked to the deck and some idiot had stepped on her hand with his crusty bare feet but she had endured much worse. Many passengers had scrambled below deck.

The calm around her was eerie. Her stomach clenched tight and she held her breath. Wind passed silently over the ship since there were no sails left to hinder it. Only a few passengers and crew remained on the deck. Many had plunged into the cold water on the opposite of the boat and others were moving to follow suit. Injured crewmen and passengers scattered across the deck moaned and gasped around her. Someone was crying. Anuka had crawled to the back of the boat and seemed to be pondering a jump of his own. He looked so small just then. All of his brazen arrogance had washed away in a shower of smoke and splinters. He was just another person facing death or capture.

He had an odd, sad look on his face. Despite the destruction raining down on them, something distant held his attention.

She intended to go to Anuka and try to lead the little red man below deck. Blowing a streak of dark blue-black hair out of her face, she started to stand. Then the silence shattered.

The boom and crash occurred simultaneously and Crenthys's feet were suddenly pointed skyward, the boat no longer beneath her.

For a moment she floated in the air as she had back in the grove of her dream, circling slowly above the little valley of soft red flowers. Suddenly, with a resounding thud, her head smacked something solid and blackness enveloped her.

Chapter 4

Boarded

C aptain Onan Swet was the last person Anuka hoped to see. Ever. He had become famous for channeling a brilliant pirating career into an even more heinous position working for Bog and Brine. Anuka's Papa had taken a similar path that landed him captain in the small F.T.E. Armada. Except no Dragons. *And Papa wasn't a bloodthirsty slive*, Anuka thought.

Swet's polished black boot thumped loudly as he stepped over the prow of the majestic *Brinery* and onto the deck of the *Sea Pocket*. He halted after another step and regarded the scene with an exaggerated contemptuous sneer. He looked back at the men securing the lines between the two boats, then nodded once to a nervous young man in an officer's coat. Anuka guessed the officer was to tell the crewman not to make their mooring so tight. They wouldn't be bound to this vessel long.

Swet looked up and to his left at a pair of his men who stood on the forecastle flanking the *Sea Pocket*'s scrawny, toothless, captain. One was a tall, round-bellied human with stringy blond hair and the other was a stout Sea Dwarf with pale skin and a long ragged beard the color of seaweed which was bound together near the bottom. They dragged the battered captain to stand before Swet.

"Cap'n," said the shorter man with a nod, "this'n is Cap'n Roilin of the *Sea Pocket*."

The other man held the blade of a slender scimitar, extending the hilt to Captain Swet. It was Roilin's, judging by his empty scabbard.

"Onan," the *Sea Pocket's* captain said. "We've sailt these same waters many a year, you an' me."

Swet grabbed the hilt and looked with disdain over the filthy rusted blade and turned to regard Captain Roilin. In one quick, smooth motion he lunged forward and thrust the dull blade hard below the man's rib cage and up into his heart. "Former captain," he said.

The men let Roilin sag to the deck, gasping and bleeding. Captain Swet didn't give him another glance. He raised his right hand in the air and snapped his fingers.

Immediately men flooded over from The *Brinery* as if a dam had broken. A half dozen men armed with light crossbows moved to the opposite side of the ship and aimed at the water. Crossbow bolts darted like shooting stars over the bow turning the water crimson everywhere they found their marks. They methodically reloaded and with murderous precision fired another round, picking off those attempting to flee. If any survived the crossbows they wouldn't survive whatever the bloodied water attracted.

More of the *Brinery's* men scoured the ship for useful cargo or anything else of value.

Yet another wave of the *Brinery's* men moved below where they rounded up passengers and crew members and brought them above to the main deck. They savagely knifed many of the crew and threw them overboard. Those passengers who seemed too old, too young, or too infirm were summarily murdered and left bleeding on the deck. So thick was the pooling blood on the main deck, it soon became difficult for the men to walk without slipping.

In the past, Anuka had seen a few goblins tossed overboard for getting rowdy with their captors so he knew he would likely be killed if he struggled. He didn't put up a fight when a dark-skinned human with long stringy hair flopped him onto his back and inspected him. "Yeah, I'm alive," Anuka said, waving his hand back and forth and making a circle with this thumb and forefinger. Anuka hoped the pirate didn't know any goblin hand signs.

The marauder raised a questioning look to the first mate. The middle-aged man looked hard at Anuka before jerking his thumb over his shoulder in the direction of the *Brinery*.

With the main deck secured, the archers filed into the lower parts of the ship and continued to efficiently cull any weak or useless creatures they found. They brought valuables topside, and those were passed over onto the *Brinery*.

Apparently, Kelios had struggled some, Anuka noticed, evident by the bruising on his face and the size of the men dragging him over the prow of the ship. A couple of men began releasing the rigging that moored the two ships together as the *Sea Pocket* began to take on a burdensome amount of water.

Crenthys was one of the last passengers taken over. Anuka had seen her go down hard when the second cannon fired. Now she was putting up enough of a fight to show some spunk but not enough to warrant a beating. *Good for her*, Anuka thought.

Finally, a burly man who stank of urine grabbed Anuka up under his arm and carried him off the sinking ship.

Captain Swet was the last one off of the dying *Sea Pocket*. He stepped over the prow and onto the *Brinery*. Immediately, two of his crewmen leaned over the bulwark and cut the remaining mooring lines. The *Brinery* recoiled and righted herself but the *Sea Pocket* listed sharply onto her side. Crashing waves washed the *Sea Pocket*'s deck free of blood just before swallowing the vessel down into the bowels of the sea. Massive air pockets burped multiple sprays of water as the *Sea Pocket* breathed her last.

Their captors had shut the door behind them, plunging the hold into darkness. They were in the bilge, Anuka discerned. A dim part of him was impressed that his tiny bare feet weren't wet. A dry bilge was the mark of a good ship as any leak would pool there first. As he realized he was naked, that same distant part of his mind wondered why that was the second thing he became aware of. He remembered being searched but being stripped hadn't registered. It didn't matter. He looked around and saw that everyone else was naked, too.

There was no light, save for the thin flicker under the door to the room, but that didn't bother Anuka as much as it did most people, especially the humans. Goblin's eyes were made for the dark. As he looked around he could see others whipping their heads blindly around, eyes agape, desperate to see. All the captives were trussed up with their hands in manacles secured above their heads. Men and women were on opposite sides of the room, bow and stern, though Anuka wasn't sure which way was which. Anuka knew the captives were separated to keep them from fraternizing.

His own hands were manacled to his feet by chains that would have been uncomfortable for a full-sized person. Instead of being affixed to hooks overhead, his were connected to a round metal hook set in the hull for securing cargo. *How special,* he thought.

He saw that Kelios was near the middle of the row of chained men. His eyes were closed as if he was praying or listening to something. Anuka slowly became aware of the din of noise in the room. Sniffs and sobs came from both ends of the boat. A rumble of mixed voices, some hysterical, some angry, buzzed like a beehive. Anuka wasn't sure what Kelios was listening for but he was fairly certain he was as blind as the humans. That seemed odd to him. A man who lived in the inky blue depths of the ocean should be able to see something in the dark. Either way, Fish man was keeping his eyes shut.

A shudder danced along Anuka's spine and he twitched at the thought of water, dark as midnight, swallowing him the way it had his mom. A swell of pain rose inside him like the last gasp of air from the *Sea Pocket* as she sunk. His chest felt tight and tears stung his eyes for an instant but he marshaled them just as quickly. He summoned a well of rage like a roiling ball of all-consuming fire waiting just under his skin and pummeled his feelings into oblivion until thoughts of water, his drowning ma, and his missing pa no longer held him in the grip of despair. His skin began to faintly glow red.

He shook his head violently, streaking his tears across his cheeks and blew out his fear and self-pity in a long breath. That done, he slipped on his invisible mask that so thoroughly hid the fire raging inside him and said loudly, "Well, this is a spoonful of rotten luck, eh?"

The room was suddenly quiet as the mostly blind passengers tried to sort out the new voice.

"Anuka!" came a hoarse cry twinged with relief and desperation. It was Kelios.

"Hey, bubby. We're in it now, eh?"

"Most definitely." Kelios breathed, slumping against his chains and bowing his head. "Why are you glowing?"

"I'm not, bubby. Them Sum Bucks must've hit you on the head or something. He was glowing, but didn't want to talk about that. Anuka found it a bit touching that Kelios recognized his voice and seemed at least a little relieved that he was alive. He couldn't help but smile.

Anuka looked around again to see who else he might recognize. Scanning the faces of the women he saw one or two that he had seen in the crowds on the ship. Finally, he locked eyes with Crenthys. He was careful not to let his gaze slip down past her grime-smudged face. This wasn't the time or place to be ogling her nakedness. He wasn't a total animal.

Her eyes were hard and clear. No tears streaked her skin and, judging by the way her lips were pressed into a thin line, he guessed her jaw was clenched tightly. A stray lock of her hair, mussed during the fray, hung loosely in front of her face. Thin rivulets of sweat ran down from her hair near her ears.

It must be hot in here, Anuka guessed. That kind of thing never bothered him. He didn't get hot, didn't sweat. It was an odd thing but he reckoned it wasn't worth thinking about now. Growing up, his papa was the only person in his family that ever got hot.

On a lark, he gave Crenthys a tiny nod before breaking their stare. To his surprise, she returned the gesture. It showed the tiniest bit of respect and was more than he deserved from her. Somehow he would have to make up for what he had said on their first meeting. He continued his inspection of the survivors.

Near the front of the line of males was a pitifully gaunt High Elven fellow with the palest skin Anuka had ever seen. The cultist, Anuka remembered. He didn't recognize the strange elf without that ridiculous robe he wore all the time. The dark hand-prints on his arms left by the greasy pirates who captured him made his skin seem even whiter. Long wisps of thin white-blond hair flowed around his face like a waterfall and he hung limply against his chains, head bowed. One of the Western Elves, Anuka guessed. Goldenfolk. And pure blood by the looks of him. His ears were pointed top and bottom, where Crenthys had rounded lobes. His ears were pocked with neatly spaced holes that probably once bore many rings. The indentations had not yet closed. The poor creature was murmuring some incoherent nonsense to himself that Anuka couldn't understand. "I hope whoever you are praying to is listening, Goldie," Anuka said to himself before moving on.

Many of the patrons that Anuka had entertained and swindled the past couple of weeks were here, but he didn't know any of their names. He hardly ever remembered someone's name unless they had a lot of coin. That seemed wrong in some nebulous way Anuka didn't understand.

A gigantic creature in the very back of the line was shackled hand and hoof and was covered in sweat-soaked, brown fur. The thing had the body shape of a man but was easily two heads taller than Kelios. His thick broad muscles looked as if they had been fashioned from clay. It had hands like a man, each finger ending in a long, jet-black, nail. The beast, for its similarities to a man ended there, had a giant head that looked like a bull. Or so he was told. Anuka had never seen a bull. If that was what they looked like, he didn't want to see one. A long snout ended in a black nose and nostrils as big as Anuka's foot flared suddenly, sending water and snot spraying all over the poor humans in front of him. A pink tongue darted out and moved over its upper lip as it focused its glossy, angry, black as night eyes on Anuka. A long curved horn jutted out from each side of its head and terminated in a sharp point. Anuka was suddenly thankful for those chains which were probably the only thing keeping that creature from eating him.

The Minothos who yelled at everyone, he thought. Anuka had also heard them called Minotaurs, or bull-men, and saw one once that everyone called *Jake the Steak*. These creatures were really useful on a ship, Anuka knew. They were very tall, sure-footed, and insanely strong. They didn't get seasick or sunburned. As far as Anuka knew, they also didn't talk much, if at all. Every ship he had been on with his Papa had at least one. He wasn't sure where in the world they came from and, by the way the thing was still staring at him, Anuka wasn't about to ask this one.

———⬥———

"The little creep has spunk," Crenthys whispered to herself. She set her mind upon the current situation and thought through some options. There were many ways she could escape but none of them would keep her mission intact. No escape. Allies, then. They would be critical to her survival. Perhaps it was stupid to think she may still wind up in Usban, but she bent her will toward that task.

Crenthys looked around the dark underbelly of the ship and took a mental inventory of potential allies. She wondered why they had stripped everyone naked. It was wise to check thoroughly for weapons or valuables. But to take the time to strip everyone down seemed a bit excessive. Were they just sadistic perverts who took some macabre pleasure in everyone's humiliation? She shuddered when she considered that perhaps they intended to rape some of them. Still, why strip everyone?

Apart from the infuriating little goblin chained to the floor on one side, she could see the sea elf. The full blood. Wave was his name. He might make a suitable ally. Better than the goblin, at least. He didn't seem panicked or overly distressed. There were no tear marks on his cheeks and no mask of despair on his face. Only steely resolution.

She admired him in his nakedness. Layers of thin muscles ran down his arms and shoulders, then across his chest. With his hands bound over his head by a chain long enough to allow him to bend his elbows, she could just make out some scarring on his arms and chest in the dim light of the room.

Her eyes continued their path of slow appreciation when something on his thigh stunned her. Clear even in the dim light that filtered through the cracks of the wooden door, she could make out a fist-sized symbol emblazoned on his mid-thigh. It was a Dragon glyph. A Dragon's slave brand. She knew he was a slave but never imagined he might be owned by a Dragon. This brand was a tattoo. Those were expensive and permanent. It was the image of a rectangle-shaped coin, standing on end, with a vertical slit eye for the stack hole. The other hole in the coin had a leather thong that twirled about the design. Bog. Wave was owned by Metrimion Caustimus. Shuddering again she found herself looking from right to left. She prayed she hadn't said that name out loud. Speaking that name could invite a lot of unwanted trouble, and in her case, could mean death.

When she looked back to Wave their eyes met. He wore the same stoic expression and didn't move to hide what they both knew she had seen. She knew that slavery was legal and common in the Eastern and Northern Kingdoms, but she had never encountered a slave before. Certainly, never a slave like this. A slave to the DragonLords. *What else was he hiding?* she wondered.

Although compassion was evident on her face, Wave's expression didn't change at all. She suddenly felt very uncomfortable and more naked than she had only a moment ago.

A sharp creak like the squeal of an arrow-shot pig stabbed her ears and painful light flooded in from the doorway. Her eyes had been so opened to the darkness of the room the light seemed bright as the sun and stung her eyes. Groans and protests erupted as the door to the room was flung open. She quickly closed her eyes. The last image Crenthys had seen was the silhouettes of two men carrying torches and bolas. She heard them step into the room.

The rows of naked bodies began writhing around, chaotically bumping into each other, and slowly Crenthys's eyes adjusted enough to see two figures approaching them. One held the lazily burning torch on a long thin stick while the other started down the line, roughly inspecting each of the women.

Of course. They were naked so they could check each of them for slave marks. Buying and selling people was perfectly legal but reselling someone else's property was a serious offense. Many slavers became slaves themselves for doing such a thing. The *Brinery's* Captain was being careful.

Crenthys feared for her fellow prisoners as she realized that dead slaves didn't cause much trouble.

She looked again at Wave and saw that two more men were making their way down the line of male slaves with the same rough treatment. Any prisoner who tried to hide or elude the inspectors was swiftly dealt a thump from the bolas wielder. Several prisoners were unchained and led out the door to where more men waited. Slaves.

What would come of Wave she wondered? Would he be killed? Being a pure-blooded sea elf, he couldn't simply be tossed overboard. His gills allowed him to breathe underwater so he would have a fighting chance. Of course, he could be stabbed to death first.

Just then, her attention was drawn to Kelios, whose goblin friend had tried to proposition her. He was being inspected. This was the first time she had noted his strange physiology. His back was covered in a mass of triangle-shaped tiles that reflected the torchlight and cast a sheen. *Scales?* she wondered. When the crewman spun him around she saw on each side of his torso under his arms a row of diagonal slits about two fingers' width apart. Were those gills? A sea elf's gills usually were smaller and located only on their necks. Kelios had them in both places. This was fascinating. The crewmen didn't find a slave mark on Kelios.

They moved on down the line and inspected the other men. Wave was unchained and led away to a fate unknown, much as she expected.

What she didn't expect was what happened when at last they came to the little red goblin.

"You Sum Bucks wanna look at old Anuka, eh? Well, come feast your eyes you sea dogs!" The little half-man spun around and shook his tiny, bright red rump at the men who stared open-mouthed. The room grew a little brighter, and maybe a little hotter, as Anuka waggled his naked rear end at the men. The goblin's skin had grown brighter, possibly even brighter than it had earlier.

The men, still frozen in shock, watched as Anuka spun back around, and putting his chained hands behind his head, began to grind his hips seductively at the men.

Crenthys fought hard to stifle the guffaw building in her chest. An outburst might draw the unwanted attention of the pirates.

"Anuka!" Kelios yelled, breaking the aura of surprise that held everyone in place.

"What?" the goblin retorted while spreading his hands as far as the chains would allow. "They want a peek. I'm givin' them a peek." Then Anuka started to spin slowly. "See, boys? No slave mark on me. I'm a free man!"

That jarred the crewmen into action. "Not for long", slurred the inspector as he grabbed Anuka by the arm and looked him over again. Barely opening his mouth enough for speech, his accent marked him as one of the northern men of the human settlements in the Perdition's mountains. That or maybe from one of the free island trade cities far east of the continent. When the inspection was done, he shoved Anuka against the wall, grabbed the last of their prisoners, a doe-eyed human girl in her early twenties, and led her out of the hole.

They slammed and bolted the door behind them, plunging them into darkness once more.

***

As soon as the crewmen were gone, Kelios whipped his head in Anuka's direction and called out into the blackness. "Are you *trying* to get killed?" There was less venom in his words than he felt. He was surprised to realize he cared about the annoying little creature.

"It's like Papa always says, 'Better to die a legend than live like a coward.'"

"That," Crenthys fired back, "is the stupidest thing I've ever heard."

The lady, Kelios noted, seemed not to hold back her vitriol. Women from his homeland were rarely so bold, except his mother. His eyes were useless as they adjusted to the darkness. Kelios wasn't willing to risk the use of his power just so he could see in the darkness. That would ensure his death. He glanced toward where Crenthys called from, then back towards where he remembered Anuka was.

Anuka shrugged. "Whatever. I'm still kickin'." The goblin's restraints rattled as he fidgeted. "So, are we getting out of here or what?"

"No!" shouted Kelios and Crenthys in unison.

"Sand and shells. You two are no fun at all."

A deep, rumbling growl rose from the back of the line of male captives. The heavy snorts from the bull-man sounded terse.

"Ok. Fine. We'll wait it out. See where it goes. Probably be more exciting that way." The little red goblin's chains rattled again and Kelios imagined him waving his little hands around.

Anuka's confidence wasn't comforting to Kelios at all. Rather, it unsettled him. It would have been better if the little scoundrel seemed at least somewhat frightened. Either he was incredibly brave or a raving lunatic. Which, Kelios couldn't say.

The idea of escaping was appealing, but the reality of its prospects was unavoidable. Unless Anuka had some knowledge or special power Kelios knew nothing of, they would likely be killed in short order or die in the sea. Perhaps, if he could escape, he could swim to Usban. Sea Elves could breathe under water, for a while. Kelios wasn't sure how well a mixed-blood elf like Crenthys would fair. Anuka would be doomed.

He didn't need to see his stinging wrists to notice the trickle of blood running down his elbow and dripping onto his feet. Trying to wipe the blood from the top of one foot with the bottom of the other, he realized that he had never been barefooted during this two-week trip except when he was in his bed. The texture of the boards beneath his thick-soled feet felt at once rough, yet well-worn and smooth from use.

His back and neck ached from alternating between holding his arms up so the manacles wouldn't cut his skin and letting them dangle to rest his weary arms and shoulders. He let himself slump again and grimaced against the burning in his wrists and hands. His head sagged forward and sweat-dampened hair fell across his face. With only half an effort he blew at the hair but it fell right back over his eyes. Futile. He closed his eyes and thought of his brother.

Somewhere in the frigid north, his brother was probably trekking to glory becoming the intrepid hero his mother had predicted he would be. He nearly snorted aloud at the thought. Kelios felt ashamed of his jealousy toward his brother even as he hung from cold iron shackles, most likely destined to die. So be it. His mother had prophesied that he would always be second. So much for her prophecy if he died here.

His people believed strongly in fate. He was a prince by fate, destined to serve them and give his life for them. Fate brought him to the surface to cross Brine's ocean, he supposed. Whether he died in the sea or as a broken slave, years from now, there would be a purpose in his death. Nothing was wasted in the economy of life. *Would those tenets of his people hold true to an outcast? One exiled in shame?* He did not know.

Looking again toward the little goblin, Kelios wondered if that same belief powered Anuka's spirit. The board is set, caution be damned. Faith that fate ruled the destiny of man was a dangerous plank to walk. All of his life Kelios had been taught not to tempt fate. She could be a faithful companion or a treacherous nave to those who didn't respect her power. He had dashed that advice against the rocks when he attacked his brother. And was exiled.

Anuka was not a child of fate, Kelios decided. He was another sort. The sort that defied understanding.

Self-pity didn't serve a man any better than jealousy did. Drawing in a deep breath of dank air Kelios stood straight to relieve the pressure on his arms again and began to set his mind back on the task before him.

Chapter 5

Ill Tidings

P oor guy, Anuka thought to himself, ruefully shaking his head. "He's a fish in a boat and probably doesn't even realize it." He watched as Kelios closed his eyes, breathed deeply and a peaceful smile creased the edges of his thin lips.

It seemed like a very long time had passed since the slaves were carted off though it had been less than an hour. The groaning was increasing from the people manacled to the ceiling. Anuka sighed aloud and reviewed his mental inventory of things to do. One, get myself off this boat or steal it. Two, save the Fish Man from getting filleted. Three, get to Usban and find Papa. Four, go find my boat!

After a few moments, he realized he was sporting a stupid grin of his own. Oh, but his boat! His Papa had spent a lifetime and several fortunes building her. And she was Anuka's! The *Flat Bottomed Girl* was a marvel of engineering and craftsmanship. Or so his Papa had told him. He couldn't remember a lot about it because he'd been young when he'd last seen her. From what Anuka remembered she was marvelous. She was different from any vessel he had ever seen. It didn't look like a boat at all! But Anuka was sure it was wonderful. Papa said so.

When she was his, Anuka would sail the seas terrorizing unsuspecting merchants and beautiful women would fill the docks at every port of call when he arrived.

He slurped loudly, a bit embarrassed when he realized some drool had escaped the corner of his mouth. He looked around to see if anyone noticed.

Anyway. His sails would be full of wind once he found Papa, and the boat that was expertly hidden for him. And he learned how to not be afraid of water. And boats.

He sighed again.

His reverie ended when the door opened again, this time with less force and fewer sweaty pirate types. Here were some nicer dressed folks Anuka hadn't seen before and there was-

"Sum buck! How are you still alive?"

As it turned out there *were* a couple of the sweaty pirates in the group. They were just stacked behind the nice-dressed people. "Shut yer hole you vile little vermin!" One of the smelly types said as he stepped forward and swatted Anuka a couple of times with a riding crop. This one also had a ring of little black keys.

"Oh, bubby! My fault!" he cried, trying to shield his tender parts as best he could. "Ouch. I'm sorry, bubby!"

"Enough." One of the lieutenants said in a flat, bored tone. The crewman looked back to see his superior motioning him to stop the beating and he reluctantly turned away.

Once the whipping had stopped Anuka looked up to confirm his suspicion. Yup. There stood the unfriendly Sea Elf who had been chained up not four strides from him just a few hours ago. And he had clothes! *No justice in this world*, Anuka thought.

The Sea Elf looked carefully over the people in the hole. To Anuka's surprise, the elf humorlessly pointed a skinny finger right at him and said, "That one."

"Right?" said the crewman, still holding the riding crop, incredulity dripping from the question. Anuka didn't understand why these pirates said the word, 'right' at the end of every sentence. So stupid.

"Yes, man. Yes. Right. You heard him. That one." Snapped the lieutenant, who now pointed as the elf had. The way the lieutenant's face screwed up while barking the order put the crewman into motion immediately.

The rough human stank of unwashed body and alcohol as he approached, causing Anuka to flinch away.

"C'mon you." The man said gruffly, yanking Anuka's chain and pulling him closer. The Sea Elf and the officer had shifted their attention elsewhere.

"Fancy man's slave or no, I'm gonna do you good first chance I get. Right?" The crewman's breath was so bad Anuka wished he had drunk more alcohol, or eaten fish entrails. Anything would improve that sewer pit in the man's face. He had gotten close to make the threat and Anuka wished he had one of the knives he usually kept close.

"Right?" Anuka whispered questioningly, using the stupid dialectic phrasing.

"Right. I'ma put my knife in your pointy little ear."

The man's words didn't scare Anuka. He had been half as tall as most men, and the wrong color, all of his life. His entire existence had been one jibe or threat after another. If Anuka was unchained with a blade, he knew whose ear would be sporting a knife handle. But he held back the two or three retorts that would cut this nitwit to the core as he chewed on what he'd said.

Fancy man's slave. Anuka didn't like the sound of that. It was pretty specific, yet it didn't make much sense to Anuka.

"Shaw!" shouted the lieutenant and the smelly pirate unhooked Anuka's chains from the ring on the floor. The foul-mouthed man drug Anuka, none too gently, by the chains and passed him over to another crewman who waited in the doorway.

The vile crewman with the ring of little black keys and the riding crop shuffled over to deliver Anuka. Anuka nodded to himself making sure to remember: Shaw. The man with the keys.

The officer spoke quietly to Shaw. Then Shaw shuffled over and unhooked the pretty prosti-half-elf lady and brought her to stand near Anuka. When she looked questioningly at him, Anuka could only shrug.

"That one." The Sea Elf said, pointing to Kelios. Anuka perked up. Maybe he wouldn't have to bravely rescue the man after all. At least not yet.

As Shaw the Key Man got Kelios freed, the giant bull-man in the back leaped to his hoofed feet, hurled a scream and a powerful shoulder blow at Shaw. Shaw would have been smashed if Kelios hadn't ducked and brought the man down to the deck with him. The two men crawled away from the Minothos's reach.

Anuka shook his head as the creature continued its tantrum. "That was a wasted opportunity," Anuka said with a sigh.

Crenthys looked at him with an indiscernible expression.

"What?" Anuka shrugged helplessly.

Kelios and Shaw hustled toward the exit while Anuka and Crenthys were jerked violently out of the sweltering room. Once they were out of the room, Anuka muttered darkly, "Out of the frying pan and into the skillet."

⸻◆⸻

Anuka realized he should have been afraid, or something, but what they saw of the ship as they were led to a higher deck blew him away. Every door had a handle, some were metal. Every cot not in use was folded neatly or stowed, and everything was so clean. The way the crew saluted the lieutenant reminded Anuka of his Papa's time in the F.T.E. Navy. The *Brinery* didn't jostle and sway the way the *Sea Pocket* had, may she rest in peace.

The room they were taken to was small, likely the borrowed quarters of one of the ship's officers, and was barely large enough for the four of them. A worn hammock with a threadbare blanket on it was slung like a fishing net from hooks on the wall. It seemed to have been stowed in haste because it bulged in the middle with what looked like clothes or other possessions. A small ink-stained desk was mounted to the wall adjacent to the bed.

Crenthys and Kelios were hastily stuffing limbs into trousers and tabards while Anuka stood, still completely naked. With elbows bent, and fists on hips, he stared up at the sea elf. In return, the elf glared down with arms folded across his chest.

"Well?" Anuka asked, drawing out the word and punctuating it with a flourishing roll of one hand in the air.

"Why don't you put some clothes on?" The Sea Elf asked, obviously straining to be patient.

For the first time, Anuka caught just a little of the local Chibering accent coming through. So the Sea Elf man was a local.

Having traveled most of the known world with his Papa, Anuka had encountered a lot of strange speaking folk. He collected accents like he used to collect fish bones. Until his Papa had found his stash. He didn't smile at the thought, pleasant as it was because he finally felt like he was making progress with the smug elf.

"I'm fine." He shrugged one shoulder and pushed his lip out with nonchalance. "What I'd like to know is what's going to happen to us?" Anuka finally plucked up a pair of pants from the pile set out for him and started slowly dressing.

Wave stared at Anuka for a moment and seemed to be deciding something. "You are to be redeemed."

Now it was Anuka's turn to decide something; wait for an explanation, or go for the mostly hidden dinner knife he had spied under the desk.

"Redeemed?" Kelios asked. "That sounds like a good thing."

"Wave?" Crenthys asked.

At least he knew the Sea Elf's name. He didn't know which was more frustrating, learning that they were going to be sold after all or the ignorance of the Fish Man. Anuka let his head and shoulders sag as he blew out a breath.

"Purchased." Crenthys offered with a wisp of reed-thin patience. "We are to be sold as slaves."

Kelios's expression melted from confusion to concern. He returned to trying to tie up his shirt in the front.

"Redeemed, eh?" Anuka remarked, "How do you figure that, and how come you aren't standing here buck nekked like the rest of us?" He gestured to his comrades, forgetting that he was the only one still mostly naked.

"I have arranged for your purchase. I have orders to secure some persons for my master if the opp-"

"Master!?" Kelios warbled.

Before Wave could answer, Crenthys provided, "He's already a slave," as she pointed toward the Sea Elf.

Wave looked at her but said nothing.

Crenthys continued. "The men came and pulled out all the slaves a few hours ago."

"Yeah, to kill em'. Since they can't be sold if they are already slaves." Anuka offered.

"Yes. And, if I am correct, you are a slave of someone very important. Or you would already be dead." Crenthys said.

Wave didn't argue the point.

"How do you know he's a slave?" Kelios asked, finally fully dressed.

"He's got the brand." Anuka pointed at Wave's leg where he and, apparently, Crenthys had seen the slave's mark down in the hole. "Probably has one on the back of his neck to match it."

Wave's hand twitched slightly but he suppressed the reflex to touch the spot Anuka was referring to.

"So, who is this big shot master of yours? Excuse me, ours." Anuka screwed his face up, drawing out the last bit.

"Bog."

Everyone looked to Crenthys when she said it. Anuka pursed his lips and blew out a whistle.

"Who or what is Bog?" Kelios asked.

Anuka spread his hand demonstratively as he explained, "Bog runs the show. He calls all the shots, literally. Zhazie is home to the Black Dragons and Bog is their DragonLord. Bog owns and runs, this whole country. He is god in Zhazie. He's got churches and everything." Anuka swung his arms out wide in demonstration of the vastness of Bog's influence. He was sure everyone knew what his gestures meant.

"Master Bog is the owner of my contract." Wave said flatly. But Anuka's keen ears heard a well-hidden tremor and just a touch of that Chibering again. "But my services are currently on loan to Master Celebris Augmaximitus. Your new master. I am to take you to him."

⚙

"I don't understand," Kelios said softly as he huddled in the corner of the room opposite the small desk where Wave now sat.

"Which part?" Anuka said out of one corner of his mouth, trying to be quiet. "We don't die today. Probably. That's all I need to know."

The knot that had formed in Kelios's gut twisted tighter. Kelios shifted from one foot to the other. "Why are we here? If we are to be slaves why are we not with the other slaves?"

"Oh. That. Well, it looks like we are special slaves. Whoever this Celery Oxminotaur is-" Anuka began.

"Augmaximitis." Crenthys corrected Anuka sharply, like Kelios's tutors used to when he got some point of grammar wrong.

"Whatever. He doesn't want someone to know about his purchase. I'm guessing we are being bought illegally." Anuka said.

"How does that work?" Kelios asked.

The door banged open and Captain Swet strode into the room. He stopped when he reached the middle and cast a dismissive glance at the trio huddled in the corner. Crenthys averted her gaze and Kelios, taking her cue, did likewise. Anuka stared at the captain with his little arms folded, one eyebrow raised, chewing on one side of his lower lip.

The captain let out a disgusted snarl and turned to Wave. Just then a figure in a floor-length black hooded robe glided into the room. The robed figure also stopped in the room and glanced at the three future slaves. His face was a ghastly specter beneath the dark cowl. His skin was ashy gray and his eyes sparkled like the crimson embers of distant campfires. Even in the shadows, it appeared that a wide grin was splitting his lips.

The figure turned fully to regard the three as they huddled together. The bluster seemed to have leached out of Anuka because he now grasped at the hem of Crenthys's tunic as he backed up into her and Kelios. This seemed to please the robed figure more.

He lifted a pair of bone-white hands and slowly drew his cowl back to reveal a milky white face with elven features. His ears, pointed on top and bottom, marked him as a pure blood. Chest-length silky white hair, perfectly straight, spilled out of the cowl. Parted perfectly down the middle of his head, it fell smoothly down each side of his face.

In the dim candlelight of the cabin, his eyes appeared pink and seemed to swim with crimson hues. His teeth were jet black, but not rotten. Indeed, it seemed they were carved from obsidian. His fingernails were long, well-manicured, and as black as polished onyx. They caught the flickering candlelight, revealing no chips or cracks marring their surface.

"Good evening." The elf said in a dialect that was thick and foreign to Kelios. If the others recognized it, they didn't let on.

The moments passed slowly, like fog over a pond. The pale-skinned elf pinned each of them to the cabin wall with his probing gaze. Kelios felt like a fish headed for the stew pot. Anuka continued to clutch Crenthys' tunic.

The eerie elf leered at Anuka and said "Cleave to your friends. What is life without them?" It seemed to Kelios that the pale elf meant to bore a hole through Anuka with his red-eyed stare and black-toothed grin.

"Master Jhaldus." Wave said.

The man straightened, drew his lips to a pucker, and rolled his eyes up as if he was looking behind him.

"Master Jhaldus," Wave began again, a little less timidity in his voice, "the hour grows long and we must depart soon. I'm sure you have other business to attend as well."

Jhaldus looked back at the three slaves and smiled broadly again. "Indeed, I do." He paused for another moment, staring at the trio as a cat might eye a cornered mouse, then he turned, walked over to the desk Wave had just vacated, and sat.

A sigh from his companions told Kelios that they were as relieved as he was. He didn't care for how that strange elf had conducted himself. Not at all.

Jhaldus began leafing through a pile of papers on the small desk before him. After several moments he began making quiet inquiries of Wave, and then the captain. At one point the captain stepped forward and roughly drug a quill across the stack of papers. Jhaldus did the same and then each of them pressed their rings into the wax from the candle, sealing the documents, and presumably the fate of the three new slaves.

"Thank you, sirs." Wave said, giving a small bow. "Captain, with your permission we will take our leave."

"Best be about it, then." The captain said with a dismissive wave of his hand. Then he turned and strode out of the little room.

Jhaldus stood slowly, glided out of the room behind the captain, pausing to stare at the trio for a moment, then pulled his cowl up over his head and glided away like a specter.

"Come." Wave said, "We must make haste." He strode toward the door of the room, gesturing for the others to follow him. They did, though hesitantly.

Wave pointed out some items that were piled outside the cabin. *Our belongings,* Kelios thought. They immediately stooped to inspect them.

"Everything should be in order." Wave said impatiently.

"Scurvy dogs!" Anuka yelled, throwing his small pack to the deck. "Sum bucks stole my dagger."

"We haven't the time for this. We must depart. You can get another dagger." Wave said impatiently.

"No way, man. That dagger was. . . well, it was important to me." Anuka groused.

"More important than your life?" Wave barked. "Than all of our lives? If we don't go now we will miss the tide and have to dock in the main port alongside The *Brinery.* I have no intentions of explaining how I came about three new slaves on a dingy in the middle of the ocean. Even if I can talk or bribe my way past the port master, Lord Celebris will not be pleased."

"Why should I give a deep divin' rip what Calibrate is or is not pleased with?"

"Because," Crenthys began, preventing Wave from launching another tirade at Anuka, and they both stopped to look at her.

She shrugged. "Because Master Celebris Augmaximitis is a Dragon."

Kelios's felt the blood drain from his face. He had just been bought by a Dragon.

•••

"Keit and Tor!" Anuka swore vehemently. "Bloody sand and bottomless oceans!" The little goblin was so red he nearly glowed as he slammed his pack onto the floor.

"Enough!" Crenthys roared back at him. He gave her a hard look but did not respond. She could see by the fire in his eyes that the cursing hadn't stopped but at least it had ceased tumbling, unchecked out of his mouth. She also suspected that some of that vitriol was now aimed at her. They had bigger problems but she couldn't blame him for being upset about the dagger.

Crenthys looked away and watched the crewmen working feverishly to prepare a small boat which, she assumed, they would soon be taking to shore. Being taken as a slave was awful enough. But to be owned by the DragonMan of Shimmer Augmaximitis, the mighty Silver DragonLord, was a whole different level of a problem. One she wasn't sure she had the stomach for.

What would happen when he saw her? Would he recognize her? If so, she would die. For years, she had worked with the anti-Dragon group Apostate. That alone would condemn her. Thoughts like this were dangerous, she knew. Already the old fire began to churn inside her. Dragons had dominated every part of her existence since her first day of life. No one could live on the continent of Dorwine without some cursed Dragon telling them how to live their lives. People suffered under the thumb of cruel DragonLords like Bog, the great Black Dragon, who ruled the swampland of Zhazie. Those frozen souls living at the base of Borman'gariss, the ice-capped mountain of the cruel Red DragonLord, Perdition, also lived under tyranny. But there are also lands controlled by Dragons with metallic scales, who are generally thought to be goodly in nature. Dragons like Shimmer. But are the lives of those living there really any better? Even in the immaculate Elven cities where Druindar, King of the Mortals, walked among his people in the guise of an elf, or in the plains filled with simple farmers ruled by Bormys the Benevolent, the people still lived under the rule of Dragons.

Was a kind taskmaster better than a cruel one if you lived as slaves either way? Maybe for some but ultimately, no. People shouldn't be ruled by tyrants, even well-intentioned ones. She sighed. Dwelling on her past would profit no one. Letting her heart drift back to a better time in her life would be a detriment to her mission. Either way, looking back didn't help. She didn't like the way things were, but at least she understood them.

For a moment she had a pang of fear for the Seaborne, Kelios, she thought his name was. He was so naive that he would be swallowed whole in the grimy slums of Usban. She would try to help him if she could. As long as it didn't endanger her mission. As for the goblin, his mouth would get him killed in almost any city. Still, he had some strength in him. She sighed again as the crew called out for them to load the boat. Perhaps she could watch out for the goblin, as well. Just a little.

Chapter 6

A New Master

Anuka hadn't been this scared since that incident at the Orc brothel in Vuustan. He figured he was a slave now and would likely be branded, frequently beaten, and probably put to work breaking rock or carrying massive logs out of the woods. All of that was fine. But how in the Sun-soaked Sea was he going to get on that tiny boat? A shiver ran from head to toe as he thought about being in that little speck of a boat in the middle of the ocean. He knew being on The *Brinery* was the same thing. But a bigger ship had cargo holds and mess halls he could hide in and pretend there was no sea. Even when on deck he could trick his mind into believing he was safe. Not in that raft.

Kelios stepped into the boat and looked up at him expectantly. Anuka was the last one.

He tried to move his feet, but they weighed fifty stones each and his knees nearly buckled. Anuka was glad for the blazing sun overhead. Without it, everyone would be able to see his skin beginning to glow. His mama had laughed when she told him he was radiant. He couldn't help it. Every time he was angry or afraid, he glowed like burning coals. His mama had said it would happen when he got embarrassed, too, but that hadn't happened yet.

How could he explain this to the others? They'd think he was a coward. It wasn't a fear of water, per se. It was more of a desire to never get wet. On the inside. An absolute terror at the very real possibility that a massive, red-skinned demon might pull him underwater and drown him. Like mama. He squeezed his eyes shut.

He couldn't enjoy the towering spirals of the *Brinery's* giant mast, or the smooth rails painted black and polished to a sheen. On another day, especially one on which this ship was docked, Anuka would have crawled every inch of the magnificent vessel.

"Come, Anuka," Kelios said gently, having most likely seen the fear on Anuka's face but not understanding it. Pretty embarrassing.

With great effort, he slid one foot about a toe's length before an unseen weight ground his foot to a halt.

"Scales!" Wave cursed as he stood in the boat looking at something over Anuka's head.

His eyes clamped shut of their own accord as two pairs of rough, strong hands picked Anuka up and dumped him into the bottom of the little boat.

Still, his stubborn eyes would not open. A sudden jolt threw Anuka off balance. He tried to steady himself as the boat was lowered into the seawater.

A little pain seeped through the blanket of fear that gripped him and he realized his bottom lip was caught between his clenched teeth. He worked his lips free with some effort and tasted blood. That was at the bottom of his list of worries right now.

His head began to swim and he realized he had been holding his breath. He coughed it out and sucked in a mouthful of dank air. He rolled over and anchored his feet against one of the cross planks on the rotten-smelling boat bottom. He dug his fingernails into another plank near his head. There he lay, locked into a crouch, bracing himself for the impact he knew was coming. The boat slammed into the water, jolting belongings and passengers alike.

Anuka heard a couple of unfamiliar voices jeering at him. *Some lackeys from The Brinery must be rowing us to shore. DragonFire find them,* he thought.

He continued to hold on tightly, eyes squeezed shut. *I'm comin', Mama,* he thought. *I'll see you soon.* With all of his heart, he wanted to see his mama again. But his coward's heart wanted no part of death at Sea. He wept for his mama and his coward's heart.

The smell turned foul just after the sprawling hillside city had come into view. Smoke, sewage, and rotting fish clung to Kelios's nose. For the past few minutes he had been breathing through his mouth only, but now he could taste the foul odors.

The sun had mercifully begun setting but Kelios could still see glass bottles, rotting fish carcasses, and various other debris thudding against the hull of the boat as they came ashore just north of the docks.

He and Crenthys joined the two sailors in pulling the boat ashore. The cool water was a balm to his feet and legs. Anuka, the poor creature, had not been able to move, so gripped was he by fear. Kelios never imagined meeting a creature that seemed to be so afraid of the thing he treasured most.

The bottom of the boat scraped on shells, sand, and rocks, and who knew what else, as they pulled it ashore.

"Far enough, right." said one sailor.

"Right. We'll be shovin' off again directly." the second agreed.

Anuka stirred just then, tossed his pack ashore, and tried to climb out of the boat. Whether his muscles were overwrought from holding on so tight or the motion of the boat made him ill, Kelios did not know, but Anuka was struggling to make it out of the boat. Kelios moved quickly to help the little goblin out of the boat. Despite the chill in the evening air, Anuka's skin felt warm to him. Almost fevered.

The goblin nodded his thanks and wordlessly went on wobbly legs to retrieve his pack.

Wave slid a few long, slender, rectangle-shaped coins from a tether and gave them to the sailors. The money was so strange to Kelios. The men nodded to Wave and began dragging their boat around to head back out to sea.

They managed well enough, but Kelios and Crenthys helped them, both eager to be rid of them.

Kelios stood, craning his neck upwards, and took in the city. Beautiful was not the word to describe it, but Usban was certainly fascinating to him.

The entire city was built into the side of a sandy cliff-side dune. At the top of the hill was a stone structure, one of the few Kelios could see, which looked like a fortress or battlement of some sort. It was rimmed with an octagonal-shaped stone wall that was dotted by a handful of tiny silhouettes. Must be the guards lazily walking along the top of the wall.

Below that structure were several single-story buildings of various sizes. Most of them were built from wood of various hues, though Kelios hadn't seen any trees except for the occasional crooked palm tree swaying lazily. He was no expert on surface dwellings but was pretty sure that the palm tree would make poor building material. Nevertheless, small pole structures with roofs thatched from palm leaves dotted the sandy landscape.

From this angle, Kelios could see wide cobblestone roads pouring out from the structures on top of the hill and flowing downward like veins, narrowing as they went. As the width of the road diminished, so did the quality of the homes.

To Kelios's eyes, many of the dwellings he saw were little more than huts. Grass-thatched roofs with mud caked on top resembled lids on top of boxes. The homes and businesses nearest the bottom of the hill did not appear to even have doors.

His keen ears could hear distant yelling and screaming. The faintest traces of various animal voices were occasionally mixed in.

Down the beach, where Wave had set off walking, was a fairway covered with a mixture of rotting planks of wood and patches of cobblestone. Kelios imagined that very little could weather the constant bombardment of the tides.

Long wooden docks jutted out into the water at irregular intervals, though he imagined it made sense to someone. Kelios's ears were filled with the buzz of dockworkers and merchants going about their business. Rough-looking men with clubs wearing tunics and matching leather caps milled about. He concluded that they must be guards.

Hot sand crushed under his feet as he walked along the beach. Crenthys seemed unused to the sand and labored to keep up with Wave as she marched just ahead of him. Anuka, on the other hand, seemed to be returning to himself more and more the nearer they drew to the docks.

Gaining entry into the city seemed a simple enough matter to Kelios. Wave passed more of those long thin coins to a guard and showed him some papers. Then they were ushered through the gate. The foursome passed through two other checkpoints where coins were passed and papers were shown. It seemed that coins and the right paperwork could get you anywhere on the surface.

They passed along a massive fence twice the height of a man and constructed from long poles the size of a man's legs that had been driven into the ground and fastened together with a dark, black cord. The tops of the poles were crudely sharpened to discourage people from climbing over the wall. The poles were a gradient of browns. The darker boards were older and many showed signs of decay. Now

Kelios understood why he hadn't seen any trees. They had all been used on this fence.

During his brief time in the Free Trade Islands Kelios had seen an Orc boy climb a very tall tree just to watch him. He was looking forward to trying that himself.

Coming to a gate with a smaller door embedded in a larger door that could accommodate wagons and such, a few coins were passed, the paperwork flashed, and they entered the city of Usban.

It was the worst place Kelios had ever seen. A large slough of ocean backwash had filled a giant pit. Women of every race Kelios could imagine busied themselves pulling freshly laundered clothes from the water. Only a few strides away, both men and women bathed, heedless of their nudity.

Feeling his face grow warm, Kelios turned away and looked to another open area. There stood a cadre of pitiful creatures in two long lines that snaked up a winding street. At the front of the lines, two rough-looking men in dark robes sat at a dilapidated table, with a mass of papers in front of them. The next person in the line stepped up, said something, and was handed a chit or coin of some type, and had something dropped in a pouch each of them carried, then they scurried away.

"Wage day," Crenthys said casually, noting his interest.

"Wage day? What is that?"

"It's when everybody gets paid, dummy." Anuka provided.

Crenthys fixed a reproachful look on him. "Everyone works for Bog here. Well, for the church. Each week workers are paid a fixed amount on their wage day."

"Minus any deductions for poor work, damage of property, or fine incurred for bad behavior." Wave said without stopping or looking back. "The cost of their food allotment, housing, and basic needs is also subtracted but that is done before the wage is figured."

"What does that leave them with?" Kelios asked.

"Enough to get drunk on." Anuka chuckled. "And gamble. And maybe, if they had a good week, a little trip down to-"

"Anuka!" Crenthys scolded. She was getting good at that.

The little goblin sighed at Crenthys's continued reproach of him. Anuka looked like he wanted to say something else but Kelios was thankful he didn't.

"Basic needs are covered by the church." The half-elf fanned her hands out to the side in a helpless shrug "Protection, medicines, and other services are also provided. Bog even provides recreational materials for his subjects."

Anuka snickered and Kelios's confusion about those recreational materials deepened.

"TWB, baby. That's Tent Weed with some DragonsBlood cooked in." Anuka offered.

"Do you eat it?"

"No bubby, you smoke it in a pipe or rolled up tight in a dried leaf." Anuka said with a grin.

"Or," Crenthys said, exasperation clear in her voice. "You burn it in a brazier like incense. It helps you relax."

Anuka elbowed Kelios and put two fingers to his lips and inhaled sharply. Then he pretended to cough and then started laughing.

Crenthys rolled her eyes at him. "Much of the work in a place like Usban is stressful. It's important to help people relieve their tension."

Kelios didn't understand what his companions were talking about. He looked around and saw overly thin people, gaunt and dirty. At that moment they were passing an infirmary of some sort. It stank of death and illness. Mostly, Kelios saw hopelessness on the faces of the people. Some seemed defiant, or possibly even predatory.

"Is. . . ?" he began, then hesitated. "Does that work? I mean, does this weed make them relax?"

Crenthys smiled a closed-lip smile that didn't reach her eyes. "You'll have to ask Wave. It's his boss." She quickened her pace to move ahead of the Triton once more.

"Master Bog is responsible for the well-being of his people. He provides what they need. Happiness is for them to find on their own." Wave said.

The trudge up the hill was getting steeper so they traveled several paces in silence.

Suddenly, as quiet as death, Anuka was beside Kelios, speaking softly. "So, no. It doesn't work. This place is a pit."

Wave cast a stern look back at Anuka who simply shrugged.

When Wave faced forward again Anuka made a circle with his thumb and forefinger and showed it to Kelios and mouthed the words "pit" and "hole".

Wave had stopped so everyone else did, too. Inns were for people with coin. Inns like this one were for people who walked around with pockets full of DragonsBlood. "Wow," Anuka said. "This is the nicest dump so far." The whole place was made out of pink-colored hewn stone blocks with fancy patterns etched into each one. Each stone was the size of his chest, Anuka noted.

On top of being too fancy for Anuka's tastes, it was also massive. It looked like two stories, plus maybe a cellar. The front of the building took up an entire block of the road.

The roof was slanted and covered with some kind of orange-red mortar. That would be hard to climb, Anuka thought. The front door stuck out worse than Anuka and his group did. It was made of thick wooden planks. The whole door. And this wasn't the spongy wood that grew in the trees along the beach. This was a dark wood. Dark and hard. Unless his eyes failed him, and they rarely did, Anuka believed the L-shaped door handle was made of brass or some other ridiculously expensive metal. He even spied a keyhole.

No one had locking doors on their buildings. You just hired thugs or tried not to leave anything valuable lying around. Speaking of thugs, this Inn had two, and even those were high quality. These two very tall humans flanked the outside of the door, each wearing splint armor and sporting a metal sword on both hips. Anuka wondered who put that kind of cash into their thug's gear. These guys were going to get stabbed standing out here. Besides, that armor's worth more than most people in this town would earn in months.

Anuka fingered the hilt of his rapier, thankful to have it back, and wondered how best to handle both men at once. He missed his dagger. *We can get you another dagger* Wave had said. Idiot. That weapon was irreplaceable. If he had his dagger he could handle these two. Sell their armor, and swords, and then find Papa. The rapier was an okay weapon but nothing special. He used it to set up his dagger work.

Wave stepped up to the guards, showed them the papers, and talked with them at length. Anuka looked around.

Since they had started up the hill, Crenthys had been licking her lips like she had jam on them and rubbing her hands on her shirt. Now she was looking around like she expected a band of Orcs to leap out of the bushes and attack her.

"Boo!" Anuka yelled and poked her leg.

She jumped and smacked his hand hard with lightning reflexes. "Don't!" she said to the goblin through clenched teeth, jabbing a long finger at him. "Don't do that again."

"Easy sister. You're wound up tighter than a lute string. Relax."

"Relax? In case it slipped your observation, we've been sold as slaves. To a Dragon!" The last part she said in a harsh whisper but with no less passion.

"I noticed," Anuka said smiling. "And I noticed that you weren't this nervous when you thought we were all gonna die."

"Leave her be, Anuka." Kelios extended a steadying hand towards the goblin. "We are all concerned for our well-being. Perhaps we can find you some TWB."

Anuka snickered and Crenthys glowered at him. The look Crenthys gave Kelios told him that he had said something stupid.

"Right. My apologies." Anuka said. "Look, Kelios you're going to have to start listening to how people talk if you want to fit in, right?"

Kelios looked from Anuka to Crenthys, and then back to Anuka.

"You're supposed to say 'right'. It's how the locals talk. I finish a sentence with 'right?', puttin' a little question on the end. Then you respond..."

"Right?" Kelios asked.

"Close enough. Oh, here comes the fancy Elf. Looks like it's showtime." With one hand Anuka snatched the wide-brimmed hat off his head and rubbed his bald head with the other. Then he flipped the hat back in place and rubbed his hands together vigorously. "We all set?"

Wave looked at Anuka flatly. Then turning to the others he said, "We may enter. You have a chance to freshen up before seeing the master. I suggest you take it."

He picked up his bundle and strode towards the door. One guard opened the door, then stepped inside to hold it while the other guard eyed the group cautiously, hand on his sword.

This Celibate Axelhound must be somebody important. Everyone was on edge. Anuka smiled as he stepped in to meet his master. What was the worst that could happen?

The opulence of the place made Crenthys's stomach turn with anxiety. All her life she had been a guest in a lot of places like this, many nicer. Memories of her other life stirred emotions she preferred to leave buried.

A row of wooden bins shaped like feed troughs lined the walls on the left and right of the room and held sand-crusted shoes. Several rows of ornate hooks hung at various heights to allow outer garments to be hung up. Everything was made of wood. Haylock, Borch, and Mith wood. All imported and expensive. Flanking the massive sitting area just beyond the entryway were two more mostly human guards, everyone had a bit of elven blood in these parts.

Wave instructed them to remove their boots. Only Anuka protested, but it seemed he did so only to annoy Wave. Her feelings toward the goblin vacillated between murderous intent and grudging respect but were currently leaning towards the lethal side.

A pleasant blend of soothing aromas hung lazily in the air of the beautifully decorated common room. Finely crafted furniture decorated the space, including some huge lounge chairs, obviously made for very large, heavy people. She became aware that her bare feet had sunk into a thick, plush rug and her toes wiggled settling further into the rug of their own accord.

Two men, one of them human, one half-elven, and a lovely young human girl collected their scant possessions and carried them upstairs. They kept their heads down, not meeting the newcomers' eyes. The young girl's hair was pinned into a bun and Crenthys thought she spied part of a slave's tattoo on her back as she disappeared up the staircase. It made her sad. At one time, she would not have thought twice about the girl unless she was slow to carry her things away.

When she looked back, Anuka was burrowing into the rug at her feet, grinning contentedly. He jumped up before she, or anyone else, could scold him.

Wave began the trek up the stairs and they followed. The steps were twice the width of normal stairs which required taking two steps per riser. Made for much bigger feet, she knew. Everything, even the height of the ceiling, was constructed with DragonKin in mind. Amazingly, the stairs did not creak under their weight. On the right side of the staircase, a smooth handrail fastened to the wall was made of highly polished wood about a hand span wide.

Wave stopped at the uppermost landing and regarded them. "Clean yourselves up. I will fetch you. When you speak with Master Augmaximitis, be respectful." He pointed a slender finger at Anuka as he continued. "If you embarrass me or yourselves, I won't hesitate to drag you back to the docks and find others to replace you."

Anuka shrugged. "Look, you need me. I don't know why yet, but I know you do." He held up a tiny hand to forestall Wave's protests. "Don't worry. I won't make a fool of you. Relax. We both want the same thing."

Wave looked at the Goblin with as much disdain as Crenthys had seen from the elf. "I doubt that," he said.

The Sea Elf turned on his heel and stalked down the long hallway.

Two weeks on a boat had left Kelios with the impression that surface dwellers enjoyed living piled on top of one another, or at least did so out of necessity. This room was marvelous. He was accustomed to tightly woven hammocks or wonderfully comfortable Copula beds, which resembled massive jellyfish in his homeland. The beds he had slept on since coming to the surface were paltry in comparison. Only the giant rectangle before him showed any promise. It looked somehow firm and soft at the same time. His sore feet, tired legs, and aching back urged him to flop onto the bed and drift into oblivion. He sighed. *How had he gotten himself into this mess?* Again his mind drifted back to the fight with his brother.

Not yet. There were things he needed to do before he allowed himself such luxury as self-pity and a soft bed. Kelios made his way around the spacious room examining its contents and furnishings. A sturdy-looking wooden chair sat in one corner, with cloth coverings over the seat and back. It too, called him to come and sit, but he moved on. A large rectangular box resembling a treasure chest sat on the floor at the foot of the giant bed. He gingerly opened the lid and peered inside. Kelios found linens and other cloths that, unfolded were as long as a man. Returning the items and closing the lid, he continued his inspection. Opposite the bed, he found an unlocked door that led into a small room with a long metal basin that dominated most of the space. There was a wooden stool near the metal basin with two more of the man-sized cloths folded and lying on top of it. With a timid hand, he touched the metal with one hand and found it cold.

"Would the sir like me to draw him a bath?"

Kelios jumped and pulled his hand back guiltily at the unknown female voice.

"Begging your pardon, sir." She said with a curtsy. She was a plain-looking human girl who appeared to have some elven blood judging by her fine, thin face bones and narrow eyes. Her hair was brown like the sand of the street and tucked under a thin white bonnet. She wore a simple grey smock with a white apron tied about her waist. Her feet were bare.

"I did not mean to frighten you, sir. I only-"

"It is well. I was deep in my thoughts. A bath? Is that what you said?"

"Yes, M'lord. I can bring heated water right quick for your bath. I can have your tub filled up as quick as anything. I'll bring up some soap as well, just mind not to get it in yer eyes, sir. It's quite strong."

"Yes. Of course." He desperately needed to be in water but a heated bath sounded terrible.

She stood for a moment with her head bowed, chewing on her lower lip.

"Was there something else?" Kelios asked.

"Well, would M'lord be wanting me to help him with his bath?"

Why would I need help? He wondered to himself. It seemed pretty straightforward. He looked at the girl for clues and noticed the edge of her slave's tattoo on her neck. His stomach collapsed on itself as he understood her meaning. "No!" He blurted, causing her to lift her head sharply. "I am weary. And, and I am in great haste. I have to meet the DragonLord's emissary this evening."

Something like relief passed over her face but she made a good attempt to hide it. "Very good, M'lord. I'll fetch yer water, right?"

"Right." He said, remembering Anuka's linguistics lesson. As she turned to go, he stopped her saying, "You said hot water?"

"Yes, M'lord. Hot as you like."

"Would it be too odd a request to ask for cold water?" The request made perfect sense to him, but judging by the confused expression on the girl's face, he saw that this was a strange request. "If it's too much trouble..."

"No trouble, sir. Just not something I hear much. Cold water it is."

As she left, she laid a bundle on the bed that contained a full set of clothing. It would probably fit Kelios well enough.

Oceans deep, he thought. Is bedding a woman on the surface as simple as her asking to help you bathe? He feared his virtue would not survive this place if he didn't learn more of its culture quickly. He blew out a breath and looked at the metal basin. "Cold water, indeed."

⚬

A bell rang in the distance and Crenthys figured it was meant for her and her companions. She had washed quickly in the basin and donned the clothes that were brought for her. Her hair had been a shipwreck and repairs had taken some time but everything else was refreshed in short order. Crenthys preferred to wear her hair shorter but it wasn't practical. Too many men would gawk and drool over a woman with long, lush hair. Sometimes that edge made it easier to get information or ask for favors.

She stepped out into the hallway to wait for the others. As she closed her door she saw Wave standing placidly beside it.

"You are ready? Good." His mild port accent laced his formal speech. "Let us gather the others." He stepped past her and moved down the hall quickly but she had seen the approval in his eyes as they scrutinized her. It had been an inspection, she noted. He wasn't ogling her. Just being efficient. It struck her as odd. She was accustomed to men looking lustfully at her shapely form, had come to count on it.

Kelios stepped out of his room after one knock from Wave and wiped his hands nervously on the loose white linen tunic he wore. The sleeves were long and probably on the cusp of being out of fashion, certainly would be by next season, but he wore it well. His trousers were a dark gray, nearly black, and were a little tight on him, which highlighted his muscles. He wasn't muscled precisely like a human, she had noted when they were on the ship, but he was well muscled. His black leather boots looked huge but came up just a little past his ankles, hiding the fact that the pants tucked inside them were probably a bit short. His long seaweed hair was bound with some sort of black tie and looked quite striking. Perhaps the right hand of the Silver DragonLord would not kill them all outright.

Eight knocks later, Anuka came wobbling sleepily out of his room wearing an overlong towel folded and tied around him to look like one of the Black Priest robes. He had even wrapped the face towel around his tiny head to resemble the square cap they wore. He snapped his open palms together as if praying and bowed at the waist to Wave.

Wave's change of color from sea-blue to deep purple was barely enough to keep Crenthys from spewing the laughter trying to launch its way from her belly to her lips.

"Humble Anuka Sandbar, Sea Master, Scion of Swordplay, Absconder of Feminine Virtue, at your service my lord."

That did it. She felt the chortle coming but was helpless to stop it. First came the inevitable snort, then she burst into a fit of laughter. Soon she was doubled over leaning on the wall for support. It was too much. All of their lives hung in the balance of the imminent meeting and Anuka laughed in the face of all of it. So, too, did Crenthys now as she began the second chortle/laughter/snort cycle.

"Take that off!" Wave exploded.

Shrugging, Anuka did as instructed and stood stark naked, save for his little hat, in the middle of the hallway.

"Where are your clothes?!" Wave roared, snatching the wet towel from the floor and thrusting it at Anuka's midsection.

"Well, oh exalted slave handler, someone gave me pants to fit that Minotaur back on the boat. And a shirt three of me could wear at once! Not to mention the boots!" To make his point Anuka snatched the biretta from his head and slammed it on the floor with a splat.

Wave glared down at him with murder in his eyes and, to his credit, Anuka matched his glare. Suddenly, Wave mastered himself. He drew in a deep breath through his thin nostrils, then released it slowly. "Master Anuka, please kindly put your old clothes on and come back immediately." He had to chew the last word off to keep the venom from his words but the ice in his tone cracked through.

Anuka stared for a moment before he disappeared into his room, slamming the door behind him. Wave worked his hands into fists and tried to hide them under the ruffles of his long, loose, tunic. But Crenthys saw.

Kelios stood, looking around uncomfortably, seeming to not quite know what to say or do. So he said nothing. *That was probably best,* Crenthys thought as she composed herself and wiped the trailing streams of moisture out of the corners of her eyes. That little cretin had made her laugh,--guffaw no less. She could feel heat on her cheeks, even now. Her laugh was atrocious and she had lost control and let it burst forth in front of everyone. *Anuka would pay for that,* she made a mental note. She still struggled to keep a smile from her face.

In just a few moments, Anuka reappeared wearing his previous clothes which looked to have been brushed off and shaken out. *The little stinker had them ready all along,* Crenthys thought. He was just poking Wave again. Why? Why would he instigate the one person who held their future in his hands? *He was crazy,* she thought, shaking her head as the troupe walked down the hallway and turned left toward a large double door at the end of the hall.

Wave approached the door demurely and knocked softly. The Sea Elf seemed to slip reflexively into a subservient posture with his head bowed slightly and his hands folded in front of him. Anuka was picking his nose.

The right door opened slightly and a guard peered out. Wave spoke to him and the door opened to a dimly lit room. Wave walked meekly past the guard and beckoned them to do the same. The guard holding the door was armored like the men outside the Inn, but the similarities ended there. This man was on par with the others in size but was a grizzled hulk of a man under the armor. Where the young guards downstairs were smooth of skin this man was covered in coarse hair with a cluster of thin scars across his forearms and knuckles. Even his rough-skinned legs carried the signs of prior abuse. He was probably at least forty winters old and probably had been a warrior for most of that time. His visual inspection of each of them, especially

Anuka, reminded Crenthys of the way a hooded snake decided who to bite first. His light green eyes bore into her. He held her gaze the way another man might grab her arm to keep her in place. She sucked in a tiny breath. His kind was known to her. A killer who thought no more of ending a life than sharpening a blade or double-checking a watch post. Murder was just a means to his objective. This man's goal was to keep his lord safe.

With an effort, she wrenched her gaze from his and walked past him into the massive room. Crenthys hoped no one saw her shudder.

Chapter 7

The Price of Freedom

S *alt and sand*, Kelios thought as he looked at the massive creature sitting on the oversized chair near the hearth. He was bent over at the waist resting his forearms on his knees. He seemed to stare into the roaring fire, taking no note of his guests. It seemed laughable to Kelios that this elegant mass of scale-covered muscle would need soldiers to guard him. By Kelios's best guess this DragonMan was more than nine spans tall and twenty stones or more in weight. Firelight danced over the long ridges of his shiny silver scales. They looked like small puddles of water in the firelight. He had three thick toes on each foot, each culminating with a black claw the size of Anuka's hand. His eyes did not move. They were the deepest of black and reflected the firelight as his scales did. An impossibly large coat made of finely woven dark blue wool covered his arms and torso snugly, revealing every contour. He wore light brown trousers tailored to accommodate his long, scaly, tail.

No one interrupted him. It seemed that everyone in the room was content to let the man sit as long as he wished. This creature reminded him of his father. He commanded fear and respect wordlessly. Without moving, the DragonMan said in an almost lyrical basso voice, "Leave us, Captain."

"Sir?" the guard's inquiry was filled with as much questioning as a single word could be.

"I am well, Terifis. No one here will harm me."

He paused for a moment, then turned and walked out of the room, shutting the door sharply behind him.

The Dragon stood and Kelios knew his previous estimation of this creature's size had fallen short.

"Forgive me. I am unused to being sequestered but my presence in the city would prove...alarming to the citizenry. I grew cold." He looked at each one of the group, in turn, spending much longer on Anuka than the others. The goblin squirmed under the reptilian stare. Then the DragonMan smiled. Or so it seemed to Kelios. It was difficult to tell.

"Thank you, Wave, for bringing them here. Your service is impeccable, as usual."

"I live to serve, my Lord."

"Yes. And Caustimis will hear of your service."

"Thank you, my Lord." Wave said with a bow.

The scale-covered giant turned and took a regal step toward the three misfits, then regarded them, not as one might size up a newly acquired property, but more like a father might appraise his recalcitrant children. More than his size, his wealth, or even the massive political power a DragonLord carried, this Celebris was a creature with tremendous presence. Kelios didn't perceive disdain or superiority in those fathomless black eyes. As he steeled himself and met that glassy gaze he thought he saw compassion. But that was ridiculous. Even though his people lived at the bottom of the sea they had heard much of the Dragons of Dorwine. If the reports were accurate, Celebris wasn't even a mortal creature. He hadn't been born at all, rather had been created by the magic of a Dragon--his master, Shimmer, the Silver DragonLord. He had no soul and could neither love nor care for anyone or anything beyond the desires of his master. The tales held that a DragonMan could not disobey his creator in anything.

"I am glad you are here." The Silver began. "While in my service, consider yourselves my guests."

Guests? Kelios thought the word must mean something other than what he believed.

"I thought we were your property." Anuka offered wryly.

Wave snapped from where he stood and made to cuff Anuka but a raised hand from the DragonMan stayed him. "It's alright, Wave." The massive emissary stooped to consider Anuka and said, "You are quite right."

Kelios breathed a sigh of relief. Conflict with this man was the last thing...

"I thought, Sir Augmaximitis," Crenthys began with a faint hint of frustration and heat in her voice, "That the Silver court neither condoned nor participated in slavery." Her words seemed to teeter between a statement and a question.

The massive silver head turned slowly to regard her and stretched into a semblance of a smile. "You, also, are quite right."

The DragonKin stood to his full height, seemingly looking at nothing in particular for a moment, then began pacing around the room. "Wave," he said pausing to extend a hand toward the Sea Elf, "was returning from an errand to be my host during my time in this city. When peril befell your ship, he acted quickly in the manner he deemed best. I had instructed him to choose some agents to assist me with a special problem."

Crenthys gave Kelios a curious look. Curse this difficult surface tongue. There was so much innuendo and unspoken communication that he did not understand. The language was derived from True Dragon, an ancient language only spoken by Dragons and their kind. It had been devised for the Dragons subjects and was generally a much simpler form of communication. That made it nearly impossible to master for an outsider.

"When your ship was attacked, he did what he had to do. I regret that he had to make slaves of you to accomplish his ends."

"Regret? So you're gonna cut us loose then?" Anuka asked.

Again the giant looked down at Anuka. "I am not."

Anuka snorted and dropped his hands to his sides.

"Both the law and custom of this land, by which I am bound as a guest of Master Caustimis, forbid it. However," said the DragonMan, lifting a massive finger to forestall Anuka's further protest, "I have recourse under the law to offer you manumission."

"Man, you what?" Anuka spat, squinting and tossing his hands in the air.

"He means to free us, legally," Crenthys supplied for Anuka. Addressing the Dragon, she said, "In exchange for what?"

Freedom? Kelios had only been a slave for a few days but was ready to be done with it altogether. But what was Crenthys speaking of? Did this poor girl trust no one? What had befallen her to fill her heart with such distrust?

The DragonMan turned and regarded her again, this time Kelios was sure he was smiling. "You are wise, lady. Wiser, I think, than your scant years of life should allow. Which of your parents was human?"

Crenthys subtly tensed but relaxed in a flash. "My mother. They were in love." She lifted her chin as she spoke, her face gleaming with pride.

"They married?"

Crenthys nodded in reply.

"Hmm. Rare to find mortals wed."

"My father was old-fashioned."

It was the DragonMan's turn to nod.

A single bead of sweat trailed down Crenthys's temple and disappeared down the collar of her shirt. Her pulse throbbed in her neck. Kelios silently cursed himself again. Something was clearly vexing the pretty young woman but he had no clue what it might be. Women were a much greater mystery to him than something as comparatively simple as Dragon politics and the linguistic subtleties of the surface languages.

"Let's return to my problem, shall we?" The question was more of a polite statement indicating that Celebris was ready to move on. The way the DragonMan spoke was unsettling. Kelios suppressed the urge to scratch at his gills, like he did when something made him emotionally uncomfortable. He could almost hear his mother scolding him just for thinking it.

"You know of DragonsBlood, I assume? Even you," he looked at Kelios, "living at the bottom of the sea." The attention made Kelios even more uncomfortable. It felt like his father was questioning him on one academic topic or other.

"The blood of the Dragon is a gift from the immortal to those in their care. By it, you have access to the ancient magic of the gods. All of this you know. You may not know that someone is stealing it."

This drew everyone's attention. Even Anuka, who had been drawing lewd sketches with his big toe in the fibers of the thick rug, looked up sharply.

"Yes," the Silver continued. "And in great quantities. We have traced the source back to Usban, or nearby, and I have been tasked by the DragonLord Council to discover the perpetrators. Quietly." He paused to emphasize the last word.

"So...the church, then?" Crenthys whispered breathlessly.

"I do not believe so. My investigators have spent a week poking, prodding, and interrogating. The church seems in proper order."

"If you have investigators, whaddya need us for?" Anuka asked.

"I have nearly exhausted my avenues of official inquiry."

"Ooooh. Now you need some unofficial inquiry." Anuka quipped.

"Indeed."

"Wait," Crenthys began, "All DragonsBlood comes from the church. Where else could it be coming from?"

Celebris's small smile didn't touch his eyes.

Kelios was beginning to grasp the weight of what the DragonMan was saying. Kelios knew this much from his study of the surface lands. Not only was DragonsBlood incredibly valuable as a great source of power, but it was also used as currency for large purchases like land and buildings. One smear of the stuff was worth more than most men could earn in a year. It was also totally controlled by the Dragons and their priests. If someone was stealing and selling Blood illegally, the Dragons were going to take this very seriously.

"So, what are people doing with this stuff? Getting stoned?" Anuka asked.

Crenthys rolled her eyes and leveled a hard stare at the little goblin. "Anuka, using DragonsBlood to make drugs is like using diamonds for slingshot ammunition." She said incredulously.

"Understand me," Celebris said. "We are talking about massive quantities of DragonsBlood. It is being sold without alchemy. So we do not know what it is being used for. Honestly, any quantity of DragonsBlood in the hands of anyone other than a licensed alchemist is incredibly dangerous."

"Not to mention being hard on the purse, eh?" Anuka asked.

"Mr. Sandbar, the implications reach far beyond the scope of economics. You are aware of the rebel organization that calls themselves Apostate?"

"Vaguely," Anuka said with a noncommittal smile.

"These miscreants are buying DragonsBlood before it is properly distilled. They could cause catastrophic damage to our way of life."

For once, Anuka seemed to decide against saying whatever was on his mind.

"How do you know it is Apostate?" Crenthys asked, her voice thin. Wave stared at her.

The DragonMan sighed. "We do not. But I am being encouraged to make sure that it is them. If you catch my meaning."

"Soooo, what do you want us for, Master?" the sarcasm on Anuka's last word dripped like honey. Even Kelios could not miss it. Wave moved to attempt another swat at Anuka but was again stayed by a look from Celebris.

"What I propose, is that the three of you solve my problem and find the evidence I need to take back to the Council. Evidence to move against Apostate. In exchange, I will free you all. You will have three days."

Suddenly growing excited at the mention of freedom again, Kelios asked, "Why three days?"

"Because," Wave supplied, "The other slaves from The *Sea Pocket* will be held at the dock for three days, while they are processed. Then they will be brought into the city. When they arrive they will be able to identify all of you. The laws protecting slavery in this city are very tough. It would cut Master Celebris's time in the city short if he were accused of buying slaves at sea and smuggling them ashore. Which I did, on his behalf."

"After three days, you will become slaves in earnest." The silver-skinned DragonMan added grimly.

"Why us?" Crenthys asked.

He looked at the woman for a moment. "I can't trust anyone here. There is natural distrust among the Dragons of differing colors. While Master Caustimis has been faithful in his dealings, many of his people aren't as helpful as they could be." Celebris looked at the others in turn before continuing. Kelios saw twin reflections of himself in the DragonMan's shiny black eyes. "Perhaps you will betray me, perhaps you will not. The risk is great for you if you betray me. My reach is long. I think you should take my offer, find the evidence I need, and be on your way. My trust is not offered lightly."

"But these are Bog's people, are they not bound to offer you full cooperation?" Kelios asked. The layers of treachery were making him dizzy.

"Some are. Most, even. All of them care more for their Master than for an agent of the council. I do not accuse Caustimis of any involvement but securing full cooperation from some of his people has proven difficult. Wave's excellent service excluded. We are on the brink of a war between Dragons. It is closer than most know. And while no one wants that, everyone seems to be willing to get as close to that precipice as possible. I am not. My Liege Lady is not."

That made sense, Kelios thought. Could his mother have been mistaken? He was not the chosen brother, yet here he stood poised to help prevent an unimaginable catastrophe. His gut twisted as he saw the massive cogs of fate turning. His mother was a True Prophetess. She had never been mistaken. But she wasn't here and a sudden impulse gripped him. He would do as he pleased. It was a simple thing, but at once he felt excited and ashamed for his rebellious thoughts.

"What do you want us to do?" Crenthys asked, seeming to have found her courage.

"Inquire in the places my people cannot go. Or places where they find no answers, at least. I will send you with a token of my authority but I recommend that you use it only in the direst need. The fewer people who know you are my agents, the better things will go for you."

"Sign me up!" Anuka said enthusiastically, surprising everyone. "Let's go. This sounds great." He put his tiny hands on his hips and looked around.

"I agree. This is a noble work and it must be done with care." Kelios said, drawing a single nod from the goblin.

Crenthys seemed to have reservations but nodded her head in slow ascent. "Yes. I agree to your terms, as well."

"Very well. Master Wave and my secretary will put everything in order. You can begin immediately. I can provide a guide for you."

"I know the city." It was Crenthys's turn to be the subject of everyone's stares. "This isn't my first time in Usban." She continued a bit defensively.

⸺◆⸺

Anuka carefully rolled the ornate metal rods inside the fancy shirt they had given him and tossed the candles they recently held aside. The small shoulder bag he carried was bulging but it would do. Hopefully, it wouldn't matter soon enough. He glanced around the room checking to see if he had left anything valuable behind; his or not. Reflexively he checked his left hip and cursed again. "Sum bucks stole my dagger!"

Creeping to the door, he reached up, grabbed the handle, and gave it a yank. Crenthys stood in the hallway. He eyed her suspiciously. He'd seen plenty of Elves and half-elves and this one didn't move quite right. She moved more like a human. Like a male human, even. *Maybe it's her heritage*, he thought. Her eyes caught him staring so he closed his door and moved down the hall.

"You all set?" she said.

Anuka pasted a wide smile on his thin red lips "Yup!" he answered with as much spunk as he could muster. *Maybe that was overdoing it*, he thought. He caught her doubtful eyes boring into him. "Let's go find them Blood Letters."

Crenthys looked at Anuka. "Blood what?"

"You know, Blood Letters? Somebody letting DragonsBlood into the streets..."

Crenthys continued to glare at Anuka.

"Nevermind." Anuka said.

The moment was broken when Kelios stepped out into the hallway wearing his pretty-boy outfit the Dragon gave him.

"You are ready?" Crenthys asked him.

Kelios nodded and asked, "So, what is our plan of action? Where are we to go?"

"Let's figure that out on the road," Anuka said. As he walked between the pair, he grabbed hold of each of their tunics and began dragging them along with him. Crenthys smacked his hand free from her shirt and he stopped and looked at her, hands on hips. Biting back his first retort he said, "Time's a wastin'," then led them toward the stairs.

Anuka glanced back in time to see Crenthys and Kelios exchange a look. The Seaborne shrugged and gestured for Crenthys to go in front of him. *There may be hope for that boy yet*, Anuka thought.

Outside the Inn, the street flowed with a sea of people. They were mostly servants, some pushing carts, some carrying fresh water, others delivering messages. *Oh yes,* Anuka thought, a wry smile splitting his face, *too easy.*

The other two joined him and they all started walking down the hill. They passed outside the thick wall that separated this ward of the city from the lower ones and began moving west. The farther they moved from the wall, the more it seemed like a totally different city. The buildings gradually looked more like huts. The ones fashioned of wood looked worn and dirty. The streets were lined with clumps of sandy mud, piles of animal dung, and other detritus. The air stunk of fish and sweat. In the upper wards, the servants wore clean, though simple, clothing. Here the people were mostly naked. The men wore short pants rolled up past their knees and no shirt. Many wore square hats made of straw or pieces of cloth tied around their heads to protect them from the sun. The streets were loud and crowded.

Anuka looked at his companions whose long legs carried them several strides ahead of him. Their clothing made them stand out here, and they looked hot! Anuka stopped to peel off his tunic and stow it in his bag. He donned just his vest. Fish Man noticed that he had stopped and signaled Crenthys, who looked back impatiently just as Anuka finished dressing. "It's hot!" he yelled. She gave him a flat stare. He flexed the taught muscles in his little arms and motioned at her with his eyebrows. She turned and started walking again, Kelios in tow.

As they continued downhill, closer to the next wall, the houses became businesses. Wood shops, mills, textiles, and even a smithy or two were crowded together along the narrow streets.

At the next wall Crenthys showed the guards the papers Wave had given her and the threesome passed into the place Anuka had been waiting for. The market.

People were everywhere. Big people. Small people. Human people. Elf people. It was a dream come true for Anuka. Crenthys moved over to a little cubby and motioned the other two over. "This is what we should do..." she began.

"Look," said Anuka cutting her off. "It's been great working with you two, but I've got places to be."

They ogled him like octopus tentacles had suddenly sprouted from his nose.

"I'm done. I've got stuff to do. Good luck to you both."

Crenthys grabbed his vest as he turned to go and this time he swatted her hand away. "Get off me!"

"You can't just go, we have orders." Kelios lowered his voice and continued. "That dragon will hunt you down and have you killed."

"Nah." Anuka gestured at the crowd. "Three heartbeats and I disappear. I'll find a boat going...somewhere, I don't really care. Then I'm going to find my Papa." He hated being so glib but they wouldn't understand. They were nice enough and he genuinely wished them well. But nothing came before Pops. This was his best shot at getting back on his trail. He had to take it.

"The fate of the world is at stake here. Don't you care about that?" Kelios asked.

"No, he doesn't," Crenthys answered the Seaborne.

Anuka shrugged. "Like I said, it's been fun. But I've got things to do." He gave a little bow, backed into the throng of people, and, true to his word, disappeared.

Chapter 8

An Old Friend

C renthys hadn't been lying. She had been to Usban Port before and knew it well. But that had been a lifetime ago. Few people here knew her now. Frowning, she wondered if that would be a good thing. Morglun had sent her, or was planning to before she ran away, to make a few things right in Usban and she still meant to do that. When or how exactly, she wasn't sure.

She and Kelios wound through the city streets dodging people all along the way. Kelios would be much better at cutting through the crowds if he weren't so new to surface life. City life especially. In a lot of ways, it was like traveling with a child. She had to show him how to stow his purse so it wouldn't get cut. She taught him not to look at merchants too long, and not to look at guards at all. She sighed. No time for pity. You work with what you have. It was nice to have a large, odd-looking, escort. Kelios garnered a lot of looks.

It could have been worse. They could have been dragging that whiny little red-skinned weasel along. She was both angry at him for leaving and glad he had. He was as good as dead to her now. If she couldn't figure out who was really stealing the DragonsBlood, she supposed they would all be dead soon. Pushing her grim thoughts away, she focused on the bazaar around her. Rows of structures, some more temporary than others but all able to be packed up quickly, lined every street in this section of Usban. She knew generally where she was going but so much had changed, and not for the better.

These poor people looked so defeated. Yells and curses outnumbered laughter ten to one.

There were few children. That much hadn't changed. Bog had a very strict policy on how the children of his kingdom were to be educated. Once they were able to walk and talk well enough, all children were sent to the capitol city of Zhazie for what the old Wyrm called *Life Training*. Some of the children returned as teenagers trained in a useful skill and worked in their town or village. Some returned as haunted shells of themselves, likely having been victims of abuse at the hands of a strict teacher or devious student. Still others never returned at all.

It sickened her to think that so many on the Dragon Court applauded Bog's efforts to care for the needs of his people. If they saw what it did to the people they wouldn't believe as they did. *Surely Celebris saw this?* she wondered. More grim thoughts invaded her mind.

The bombardment of scents pulled her from her thoughts as they shuffled along the sand-covered cobblestone streets. The sweet smell of Beachwood smoke, no doubt from a meat vendor roasting fish or some other animal, wafted through the crowd triggering memories for Crenthys. Many of those she did not want to recall. Some she did.

The strong smell of stale urine baking in the hot sun overpowered them each time they crossed an intersection. At the aroma of spices native to the Eastern Coast of Dorwine, her mouth watered, making her think of the delicious foods she had enjoyed here years ago. *Seas,* but she was hungry. They would deal with that later.

She knew they were close when the street opened up to a massive semi-circular amphitheater. A long train of wagons circled the top rim of the theater behind the seats that had been built from large stones. She guessed they had been quarried from a nearby cliff-face and cut to look like stairs. Each wagon had a large cage on it that contained some sort of animal. The smell of fresh animal dung stung their noses, but the cacophony of sounds the beasts made brought them to a stop. Kelios was curious, too, it seemed. He stood transfixed, watching a group of men unhitch a wagon, then wheel a single cage down the ramp between the long rows of seats to the center of the amphitheater.

"What is this?" Kelios questioned, his mouth agape.

"It's a beast collection. The beast masters will set up the cages and charge people to come and see their animals."

"Why are they in cages?" Kelios started walking toward the line of wagons. Crenthys followed him.

"So they don't escape and hurt anyone." She said, amused.

Kelios strode up to a cage containing a massive brown bear and stared.

"I don't understand." The poor man sounded lost.

"Kelios," she said putting a hand on his shoulder as she came up beside him. "They are exotic animals. Creatures from other lands. These men travel around with them and show people in towns across the land what beasts from other lands are like. They are just animals."

Moisture rimmed his eyes as he turned to face Crenthys. "A few weeks ago I lived at the bottom of the ocean, breathed water, and could swim faster than any man or elf could run. Should I be in one of these cages, too?"

Crenthys regarded him, mouth agape, not knowing what to say.

"You are right," Kelios said and turned back toward the way they had come. "We have a mission to complete." Crenthys followed after him wondering what the incident with the bear was really about. He had conceded the argument but she doubted he had changed his mind.

Soon they came to the place she remembered. She stopped and pulled Kelios off to the side of the street.

"Kelios, some of the places I need to go to, I have to go alone."

Kelios tilted his head to one side and furrowed his thin eyebrows.

"What do you mean?" he asked.

"I know people. Dangerous people who rule their own little gangs in these streets. I need to speak with them, alone."

"If they are dangerous, then I must accompany you."

"They won't be dangerous to me. Not really. But they don't know you and will not tell us what we need to know if you are with me."

"How am I to protect you if you leave me behind?" he asked, sounding hurt.

"Protect me? Kelios, I don't need protection." Why did he think he needed to protect her? Was every man this way? Did they all judge her stature and shape and immediately think her to be vulnerable?

"I-" he began, then thought for a moment before trying again. "I don't know what else to do. I don't understand this place, this city. There is so much intrigue and innuendo going on and I feel I don't understand the language at all. What is my role in this mission?"

She honestly didn't know. He was like a fish in a boot. Crenthys had known from the beginning that she would have to go into the Helmer's lair alone. Kelios would say something to get them all killed or Anuka would wind up the Helmer's lover.

"Stay here and watch for Celebris's men."

"Celebris's men?" Kelios asked.

"Yes. I'm sure he is having us followed. See if you can spot them. I won't be long." She hated lying to Kelios but he could not follow her. If Celebris had men watching them, the Seaborne would never see them.

He nodded reluctantly.

"This is helping. Watch my back and stay out of trouble," she said as she turned and went down a small alley.

Kelios wandered back to the caged animals. How could a society be so cruel to find entertainment in caging animals? They looked so sad as he looked from cage to cage across the courtyard. Was this how Crenthys saw him? Was he just another animal to her? He flexed his webbed toes inside the ridiculous boots he wore. Crenthys certainly didn't find him very useful. Who was he kidding? He wasn't useful here. Since his first lungful of air, he had been bumbling about trying to find his way. He needed to understand the surface world better if he had any chance at surviving. He looked across the courtyard at the bear's cage and started toward it.

This was foolish, he knew, but he was tired of being useless. He could help someone and perhaps get a new perspective.

No one was watching as he approached the bear's cage. He knew the physiology of many surface beasts from his studies. This beast was massive, every inch of it covered in thick hair. It eyed him suspiciously. Kelios drew in a deep breath to relax his mind and stuck his arm, palm down, through the bars. The bear bristled and stood on its hind legs. Kelios stared at the animal. It was so tall, it couldn't stand up fully inside the cage. Kelios closed his eyes and bowed his head. The cage rocked as the bear returned to all fours and approached him. The bear issued a low and dangerous growl as it approached. Then he felt it approach.

A shock of knowing went through his arm as the bear nuzzled its head under his hand. The fur was thick and coarse. It was a she, Kelios understood, as his spirit moved into the beast. Crenthys was right, in a sense, that this was just an animal without a complex spirit like a man. But it teemed with life and intelligence and emotion all the same. The massive pumps of the animal's heart were alarming to Kelios. Never since melding with a small whale had he felt such a heartbeat. And so warm! He had not communed with any of the surface creatures since coming ashore and was surprised at how much warmer this creature's blood was than his own.

It had a name. It could not be pronounced or translated into anything mankind would recognize, but it was a unique creature no less. Both he and the bear had their eyes closed, but Kelios could feel her watching him as his spirit moved about her consciousness with rapt curiosity. In a space between her head and her heart Kelios stopped.

There was a well of great sadness that almost overwhelmed him. He could feel the tears on his cheeks and the sobs wracking his own body though they seemed to him to be very far away. He felt also the tugging of his body. It was gentle and matched the strange words he heard being spoken to him, though he did not understand them.

Then he realized someone was shouting and began drawing back to his own body. He was stopped abruptly as the emotional center of the bear pulled at him. She wanted him to stay. She was so lonely. When he told her mind that he could not stay, she understood but her sadness grew somewhat.

The world around Kelios came back in a rush that nearly overwhelmed him. His body felt so heavy. He staggered about, groping for something to steady himself.

"Git yerself back!" he heard a man shout. He turned bleary eyes upon a portly, middle-aged, human man with a thick mustache pointing a weapon that looked like a trident at Kelios. Kelios's mind registered it as a hay fork.

"Thot ent his bear. He got no bisness foolin' about wit it. Fin' to get killed, he is. Now you lot get on from here." The man held the tool in shaky hands.

Kelios had a memory that wasn't his flash through his mind. Before he knew what he was doing he stepped up and roared a primal scream in the man's face. It was echoed by another roar from the bear that put the man on the ground. He looked up at Kelios, then to the bear and back. He stammered but failed to say anything. Kelios stalked past the man and the crowd parted before him.

He didn't know where he was going, but he didn't care. The bear was still inside him, raging in his mind. Kelios stomped his way down an empty alley trying to clear his mind.

Crenthys could feel eyes on her as she moved out of the alleyway and into a crowded street lined with shanties in ill repair. The wind and rains barely touched this section where buildings were right on top of one another and all connected by bedraggled awnings. Between the buildings were impromptu tent shelters sparsely covering bedrolls, piles of tattered blankets, and equally worn occupants. People were crammed anywhere and everywhere here. Despite the multitude of buildings and volume of people and noise along this corridor, few stirred save for the handful of guards lounging around on the corners, watching but pretending not to. What would Morglun think if he saw the squalor his people lived in?

She caught the eye of a young human boy whose age was hard to guess. He was gaunt and dirty with a short crop of greasy brown hair and hard eyes. Out of the corner of her eye, she could see the urchin slipping a hand slowly to his back where she knew a knife or dagger would be waiting. Slowly, she raised her right hand just above her waist and tucked her third finger to her palm with her thumb, and curled her first two fingers like claws, the pinky she stuck out stiffly at an angle. The boy saw the odd gesture, quickly pulled his hand away from his back, and stood. He motioned with his head for her to follow and he disappeared behind a sheet that covered a doorway nearby. She followed.

Cautiously, she slid the makeshift curtain aside and stepped into the dilapidated building. The windows were covered with scraps of boards but streams of light filtered through the cracks and glittered like stars as motes of freshly disturbed dust flitted around the room. Behind a countertop made of old barrels and rotting planks, the boy disappeared into the darkness at the end of the hall. Again, she followed. At the end of another hall, she found the boy standing in almost total darkness, waiting for her beside a closed door. Her ability to see in the dark wasn't half as good as she pretended it to be and her eyes were still slowly adjusting.

The boy put a thin, dirty finger to his lips warning her to be quiet. The boy was so young. He opened the door and stepped in pausing just inside the doorway. When he stuck his head back into the hallway, he again motioned for her to follow. This was another hallway with doors staggered down both sides. She heard distinct sounds of a carnal nature coming from one of the rooms but pretended not to notice. At the end of the hallway, she saw a short man though none would mistake him for a child. His head came to Crenthys's chest but he was twice as broad. His hair-covered arms were exposed and she noted blotchy green and blue skin with mottled patches of white coloring his arms. All of his exposed skin looked the same. He was bald but had a long blue beard braided into a single tail that hung below his waist. The skin of his face was weathered and hard like the leather on an unused saddle and his eyes were as clear blue as the sea. The aforementioned hairy arms were crossed over his ample chest and he leaned casually against the wall, staring at her. Sea dwarf, she recognized.

His people had abandoned the mountains centuries ago in favor of a life at sea. Today many were hired or enslaved by the Dragons for their unique ability to find lost treasure. Sea dwarves were still a necessary part of any salvage crew that scoured the sea along the coast, and there were many of those crews. This one had the look of a man with a different set of skills. A slender, curved-blade scimitar hung from a hanger on one hip and a long-bladed dagger rested in a leather sheath on the other. She noticed at least two throwing knives secreted about his person. And she noticed him noticing her.

She kept her expression cool as the boy reported the little he had to report and then took his leave back the way they had come. The dwarf never took his eyes off of her. When the boy was gone the dwarf smiled at her. He was missing four top teeth on the right side. The pale jagged scar that ran across the same area of his lip gave her some idea of what might have happened to those teeth. "What've you got then?" He asked. Raspy and reed-thin, the words sounded as if they required a great deal of effort, but there was no strain on his face.

"I'm ta see the Helmer if I can."

"Right?"

"Right."

He studied her another moment. "What business? Buyin'? Sellin'? Or Workin'?"

"None a dem. My business is my own."

"What. Business?" he repeated menacingly.

She sighed, untucked her long, loose tunic from her trousers, and showed him the mark tattooed on her ribs under her right arm. It was a reptile eye and a long-bladed dagger, much like the one the dwarf carried, stabbing the eye with blood dripping down. She hated showing that symbol. Not that she was ashamed of what it represented, but revealing it always made her feel vulnerable. Luckily, no one noticed it aboard the *Brinery*.

"Right."

"Right." She agreed.

Slipping a key from inside his belt, he turned around and fidgeted with the lock on the door, then it opened. A plume of blue-gray smoke billowed out of the room and hit Crenthys in the face. She coughed once. It was TWB: Tent Weed and Basilisk blood. Strands of three different types of intoxicating plants were dried and sprinkled with a little dried DragonsBlood. Then twisted together like tobacco leaves and soaked in honey. Then it was dried again and plugs were cut and smoked in a brazier. Crenthys was immune to the mind-numbing effects but one plug could keep a room full of people stoned for days. The smoke burned her eyes and she blinked away tears as she stepped into the hazy room.

Just inside the door to the right, a long wooden table had been shoved against the wall with an identical table stacked on top of it. Stools and chairs were roughly piled nearby. The rest of the room was clear. Except for the half dozen nests scattered throughout the room. In the center of the room stood a large heating stove whose iron door hung open. Each nest was occupied by two or three people. Each of them was writhing, reclining, or giggling. Some were...doing other things. Everyone attending this party was scantily clad. To be fair, the little stove was heating the room pretty well. Everyone was glistening with sweat but that was also one of the side effects of the intoxicants they were breathing. There was a guard in the room but he sat on the floor near the tables with his back against the wall, staring at nothing.

Crenthys stepped up near the stove. With a booted foot, she gently closed the stove door, stifling some of the smoke. Three strides away, languidly sprawled on a pile of blankets lay the Helmer. She was a large woman, for a human, with a wild shock of curly red hair that had faded with age to light rust. The same curly red hair sprouted liberally from each armpit, visible because her thick, soft arms were cast over her head in a random array. She wore a dirty yellow sleeveless shirt that had, either by design or circumstance, crept up her ample belly and was tucked under her breasts. Her head bobbed slowly as she raised it enough to try and focus on Crenthys. "What's sizzlin' Tamris?" Crenthys asked the prone woman.

"Brinka?" the woman slurred. "I thot yous dead."

"We need to talk, Tam."

That seemed to sober her up a bit. As she sat up, she shoved the young half-elf off of her legs. With effort, she rose to her feet and looked Crenthys over from head to toe. The others in the room paused their revelry to watch the two women.

"I thought you was dead." Tamris said again, this time with an edge of hardness and a little more clarity. "What is this?" she asked gesturing at Crenthys's clothes.

"A lot has changed. I'm working on something serious and I need some help."

"Right?"

"Right."

"Well, talk," Tamris said.

"Not here," Crenthys replied. Stoned or not, Tamris understood her meaning.

"These are my people, Brinka, *our* people. It's you I don't know if I trust."

"Fine," Crenthys said through clenched teeth. *So much for subtlety.* Tamris could be impossibly stubborn. "We need to talk about DragonsBlood."

"Well, we don't know nothin' 'bout DragonsBlood. Whoever you are." With a flash, Tamris had a curved-bladed hunting knife in hand.

Crenthys sighed. "Why does it always come to this, Tam?" She snapped a quick kick with the toe of her boot into Tamris's hand. With a cry, the blade went flying. Crenthys grabbed her wrist and twisted the woman's arm behind her back. Tamris gave another pained cry as Crenthys worked her into an efficient headlock.

"Now, Tam. Let's talk about DragonsBlood."

Kelios was pacing in a wide "T" shape, checking each street of the intersection. He couldn't shake the feeling that the men who had caged the bear would come looking for him, and Crenthys had tasked him with watching for Celebris's men. Neither group was visible so far. Relief flooded over him when he saw Crenthys striding out of an alley. It may have been the same one she went up. They were all so similar he had trouble keeping track. For the tenth time in a quarter-hour, he rubbed his sweaty hands on his shirt. He felt sand squish between his toes inside his boots as he moved toward her. She stopped and waited for him in a little cubby just off the main intersection where he had been pacing.

"Are you well?" Kelios asked with a little panic in his voice.

She nodded. "Well. And I learned some things. Let's go back to the Inn and I'll fill you in on the way." She started back the way they came and Kelios grabbed her arm.

She looked at his hand, then up at him questioningly.

"Not that way. That is-we should go back another way."

She pulled her arm away and looked down the street in the direction she had been heading. She looked back at him. "Kelios?"

"Some men are looking for us that way. Well, for me."

"Kelios?" Crenthys said again, her question growing sterner. "What did you do?"

He looked her in the eye and said with resignation, "I went back to see the bear."

"What happened, Kelios?" Her hands were on her hips, her lips drawn tight.

"I-I spoke with the bear. And I screamed at a man. The bear got upset. After they calmed her down they started looking for me. I've been down here ever since."

"What do you mean you spoke to the bear? Did you yell or something and get her upset?"

"No, Crenthys, I spoke with her. I stepped into her mind to try and find out why she was there."

"I don't understand. And why do you keep saying 'she'?"

"*She* told me." He offered a mirthless smile. "Some of my people have an affinity with animals. It is said among the elders of my people that before the Trial of False Gods all people of this world could do as I can. Now, none of the natives to these lands can."

"Kelios, I didn't know...any of that. It seems like magic, to me."

"It is, after a fashion, though not magic from the Dragons."

"All magic comes from the Dragons." She said matter-of-factly.

He smiled in reply but said nothing. As silent moments slipped by he saw her confidence in what she knew about the world begin to crack. It pained him to see her long ingrained notions falter. "It does not matter," he said with a little sadness in his voice. Proving he was right would be a simple matter but he didn't need to be right. "We have a mission and we should be about it."

She looked at him and seemed to be trying to decide something. Perhaps she was deciding whether or not to believe him. Or was she now afraid of him? Did she mean to leave him, as Anuka had?

"Kelios." Her recent unease had suddenly shifted to concern. She looked around the alley and lowered her voice. "This thing, you can't do it. It's illegal here. More than illegal. If you are caught using magic that isn't authorized they will kill you."

"She has young," Kelios said.

"She what? Who has young? The bear?"

"Yes. She had two cubs when the men took her. She doesn't know if they yet live or if she will ever see them again."

"Kelios, I don't think you are listening." She grabbed him by his sweat-slick arms and squeezed them. "Believe me, they will kill you and not ask any questions."

He didn't say anything so she continued. "I know this is important to you, and it's awful that they have put her in a cage, all of them. But we can't change that. There are other things we *can* change. But right now we have a mission, remember? And it's important."

She was right. The fight for the bear wasn't one they could win and they had a duty with a deadline. He exhaled slowly and looked at her. "Did you find the evidence against this Apostate?"

Her face changed again, eyebrows tenting together. If the subtleties of this surface language were confusing, the faces Crenthys made were positively befuddling.

"No, Kelios, it's not them. Something else is going on here."

Now he was confused. "I thought it had to be them. Aren't they the rebels inciting all the trouble in Dorwine? Fighting Dragon rule, and all?"

"It's not as simple as that. They aren't doing this. They may be guilty of many things, but not of this."

"Then why is Celebris so anxious to prove it is them?"

"Because it's easier for the Dragons if it's them. They are established enemies. Pin this mess on them, crush them, and everyone is happy."

Surface politics made no sense to him. In the sea, a matter was judged by Elders and done with. "If these Apostate people truly are rebels against the lawful rule, and are guilty of crimes, why do you care if the Dragons crush them?"

Crenthys stomped a foot on the ground and her face twisted with anger. She stepped close enough to touch her nose to his and said through clenched teeth "Because it isn't right." That was more vitriol than he had ever heard from her.

He stepped back and looked at her quizzically. "Crenthys. Why do you care?"

Her stare was as hard as granite and her chest heaved as she breathed in and out through her nose. Stepping in very close again, she whispered, "Because I am Apostate."

Chapter 9

Missing Pieces

Anuka squeezed the coins tighter as he dodged and wove his way through the crowd. The cries of the men he'd taken them from were growing fainter but he wouldn't take any chances. He hadn't expected them to be so persistent over a few coins. Besides, if they didn't want to get ripped off they should've let him in on their dice game. No one would front him a few seed coins to play with and now look at 'em. Broke. Darting into a small store full of barrels he ducked down, counted the coins, and frowned. He was all but broke, he realized.

"Pennies." He grumbled, standing up from his hiding spot. Looking around, he snuck out the side door and rejoined the crowd. He thought he had been heading West but wasn't sure. If he could find a wagon to climb up on he could know for certain. There was a huge temple to Bog near the West end of the city but his stature and the throng of people made it impossible to see anything but hind ends. Sometimes he wished he was taller. It probably smelled better up there. Thinking about such things was a waste of time. *Boat. Crew. Papa.*

Pushing aside problems he couldn't fix, he looked around for solutions to problems he could. Namely his financial situation. The farther he walked the more the shops and wagons and stupid people thinned out. Well, these people all looked pretty stupid but at least there weren't so many of them. The first Inn he saw looked like a laborer's tavern. That wouldn't do. Poor stupid people in there.

The next two were much the same. Anuka was about to give up when the cobblestone road gave way to a well-manicured dirt path. Each side of the path was festooned with cute little bushes no taller than Anuka. The shrubs were spaced evenly and seemed to be well cared for. He picked up his pace and followed the path up a sandy little knoll. He saw the stern of a huge scavenger boat sticking straight up in the air.

"Whoa!" he exclaimed, pumping a fist in the air, "This should do." He raced up the path to take in the whole of the place. A cleverly designed, nicely painted sign that looked like a sail hung from a mast pole that read *"Lucky Toss"*. The front of the Inn looked like it had been tossed from the sea and landed here, bow first, half-buried in the sand. The windows looked like cannon ports, replete with shutters fashioned after gun ports. A lively crowd could be heard inside, along with some kind of stringed instrument. The music didn't sound like much but it was like Papa always told him, *son, you don't always get to pick which idiots you work with.*

Every city had a place like this. Sometimes two. It had a nice facade but it was full of dangerous people. Killers, thieves, solicitors, priests, all the worst came to places like this. Even as the thought entered his mind, he saw a big ugly human and that creepy pale-skinned elf from The *Brinery* step out of a fancy covered wagon and enter the inn through the back of the building. "Sum buck!" Anuka exclaimed. If that human wasn't the slave-making Captain Swet, Anuka was a sea dwarf.

He quickly realized that attracting that man's attention was a bad idea, so he hustled up the path to the front door. There was a stone well in the small courtyard with a wooden pail hanging from the rope that wound around a cranking mechanism. Anuka took in some details. It's important to know some good hiding spots when you're going to rip off dangerous people.

Grabbing the handle, he opened the front door and let the revelry wash over him. A blast of hot air hit his face like waves on the shore and he drank it in. The fire was roaring. The room was an oven. Anuka loved it. He had always preferred the hot over the cold. Papa said it had something to do with mom but he figured it had more to do with standing on the decks of ships under the mid-day sun in the middle of a giant ocean most of his life.

The place stank of sweat mixed with the smell of mead in various stages of fermentation. Anuka hated mead but was happy to see the sweaty patrons enjoying it. *What a bunch of freaks!* he thought joyously. There were sea elves, sea dwarves, humans of every shape and color, and a few that seemed to be mixes of several things. He even spied a grumpy-looking goblin in a filthy apron ferrying drinks to the tables. The old fellow had the typical green-colored skin common among the Glamokyn. Anuka frowned. It was like he kept expecting to see another red-skinned goblin but it never happened. He was also a freak. He sighed and stepped in a little farther.

The place was packed and he didn't want to draw attention to himself by being a bashful door lurker. So he raced to the front of the room and, skidding to a stop in front of the blond human playing lute, yelled, "Ho you salty scumbums! Anuka is heeeeerrreee!"

Startled, the flutist fumbled a chord and stopped playing. Anuka looked back and gave him a reproachful look. "Make that thing cook." The boy, he was probably less than twenty, looked at Anuka for a few seconds, mouth agape. "Play something with some fire or give that scrap of kindling to me and I will."

At the challenge, the boy clamped his mouth shut and twisted his face at the insult. Then he did what Anuka said to do. He launched into a passable rendition of *Fire in the Galley* and Anuka began to nod his head and clap to the rhythm. The rest of the room had quieted some and many of the patrons eyed Anuka warily. When the chorus came Anuka danced for all he was worth. He had learned a few steps in the Free Trade Isles, as well as some other seedy ports of call. Anuka thought he did many things well. Some things not so well. Dancing was something he did very well.

The room immediately erupted into laughter and cheers at Anuka's odd gyrations. He never missed the beat and punctuated each crescendo and key change with a corresponding shift in movements. Anuka gave himself to the music. The young player had a decent rhythm and knew a handful of popular tunes. Anuka moved like a frenzied shark but did not sweat a single drop. After just a couple of minutes, his muscles began to protest but he pressed on. Anuka was made for this. The energy of the crowd clapping and laughing, either *for* him or *at* him didn't matter. He loved the feel of his body drawing the stress from the crowd. Maybe one of these louts had to kill someone tomorrow they didn't want to. Tonight he wouldn't worry about that. Perhaps the fat little merchant to his left, who tried to dress like a commoner, owed money to the gigantic human in the back. *Sum buck!* Anuka almost faltered at the sight of the massive man sitting casually at his table, draped in weapons and armaments. He kept dancing and tried to adjust his plan to prevent his death at the hands of that monstrosity while using him in his quickly forming scheme. He needed to work these guys up and siphon some coin off of them. Papa needed him.

Anuka could sense that the end of the song was coming but he knew he had the crowd. The watery-eyed old goblin bartender had even stopped his work and was watching. Anuka's cartwheel landed him in plain view of the giant warrior. Sands that sucker was big. Anuka imagined his whole foot could go in that man's left nostril. Anuka didn't like the smug look the ham-fisted man gave him. He could feel the condescension in the man's sneer. It made him feel small and that smug Sum Buck knew it. Anuka hated bullies. Papa always said there was one in every crowd. Anuka decided to turn this guy into some coin. Starting a tavern brawl was delicate work, but Anuka was well-practiced.

The song ended with a flourish and Anuka landed the last chord in the splits. The cheers and table slapping were thunderous. He leaped to his feet to bow and thank his adoring audience. The smooth-faced human kid behind him was drenched in sweat. He looked like he fell off a boat.

"Thank you all. Let's beat on the table and scream like idiots for my friend on lute..." Anuka waited just long enough for the boy to realize he was supposed to provide his name and continued, "Ah, who cares? I am the illustrious Anuka Sandbar!" The cheers peaked and started to die so Anuka jumped in. "Ok, cut that mess out." He waved for them to stop. They laughed more. He was just a little off-pace so he jumped right back in. "I just hit Usban tonight. I told the harbormaster that I wanted the place with the best ale, prettiest women, and the loudest crowd and he knew right where I should go. But they were closed, so here I am." A couple of guys were cackling but they seemed the sort to spend the evening laughing at one another's farts. "I'm fresh off the boat from the Free Isles. So, you've got Dragons, eh?" Anuka looked around the room and pretended to whisper, "No Dragons in here are there? No? Good! I have some questions." Everyone erupted at that one. Anuka smiled. This was gonna be a good night.

"Honestly, have you ever wondered where baby dragons come from? I mean just tryna puzzle out how they..." Anuka made a gesture with his hand, "I can't figure it out." Another eruption. The old goblin was laughing now. Another joke or two and Anuka was ready for the kill.

⚫

"Why don't we go back and check in? At least."

Crenthys was shaking her head. Kelios wasn't getting it. "It's too soon. We don't know anything yet. If we go back now the Silver will think us incompetent."

"I think we do know something. Or you do, at least." His face was less placid than normal and she saw what could almost be anger on his face. Good. Let him be angry. Angry and distracted.

"I told you, Kelios, I got a lead. A good lead from some bad people. We're going to check it out."

"Yes, and if you would tell me where we are going maybe I could do something useful."

Crenthys halted her military march and spun to face him. Yes, that was anger she saw.

In a firm but controlled, quiet voice she told him, "We are going to the back room of a seedy tavern that serves as a front to a fencer who sells DragonsBlood. My contact said he has been selling a lot more lately. I'm going to try to buy some with the coin the Silver gave us and I'm going to ask some questions."

"And what am I to do?" Kelios tented his hands on his hips and stared at her.

He's sincere, she thought. *I should have sent him back to give a report and done this myself.*

As if reading her thoughts, Kelios said, "I understand that I am a liability here. I don't know the intricacies of this language yet and much of this intrigue that everyone seems to understand passes by me like an eel in the dark."

The weird expression and the odd, warbling quality of his voice together were almost comical. She almost interrupted but decided against it.

"I also understand that you don't need my protection. But I want to help. My freedom is on the line here, just the same as yours."

Things would be simpler if he didn't have a point. She sighed. "Yes. You're right. I don't want any of this guy's men to interfere with our meeting. If you see someone or something suspicious yell for me. Or...something."

He smiled broadly.

"Now come on. Let's get this over with." *Wow,* she thought, *this Seaborne is easy to please. I tell him I need him to do nothing and he gets all excited. What a strange species he is.*

She was avoiding the probability that she would need to ditch Kelios. It occurred to her that Anuka had done that same thing. He ditched them for the sake of his own mission. The way he did it, so flippantly, is what upset her most.

With the scant information Tam had given her, Crenthys was starting to piece some things together. Morglun had learned of an associate named Coryn interfering with the business Apostate had in Usban. He knew little else, but Crenthys believed that this Coryn was involved in the DragonsBlood matter. Morglun would want her to find this man and quietly resolve the matter. That was before the DragonsBlood problem was on the table. Now Crenthys would have to sort this mess out on her own. Apostate was always so careful. People's lives depended on them being so.

The directions the Helmer had given her were simple enough but this place seemed a little out of the way. Probably for the best. The fewer people they encountered, the better. The building was easy enough to spot, once they were in the right part of the city. The Helmer had warned her about the Inn but the odd structure was still surprising. Two armed men wearing scowls interrupted her inspection of the building. One was a massive shirtless human with folds of skin and blubber covering considerable muscle. His head was shaved and sweat was pouring down into his eyes. The second man was a contrast in size. He was short and rail thin with beady dark eyes and long strands of greasy black hair. Each of them wore a cudgel, since carrying bladed weapons bigger than a fish knife was forbidden for all but guards and DragonKin.

Crenthys held up her hands reassuringly and said, "We've come to see the Fisherman. The Helmer sent us." The two men shared a look. When they looked back Crenthys had fanned three of the long, glinting dragon coins for them to see. The smaller guard reflexively ran a tongue over his two remaining top teeth and eyed the coins.

"See about it, Raj, right?" after a few moments, the greasy-haired guard threw an elbow and a nasty look at his sweaty companion, who was also gawking at the coins. "Right?"

"Right!" The sweaty guard answered incredulously as Crenthys snapped the three coins back in a stack and made them disappear into her shirt pocket. Reluctantly, the shirtless guard turned and climbed the trio of wooden stairs leading into the back of the building. Crenthys noticed the bulge of a curved-bladed knife sticking down the back of the bulky man's trousers, a dirty wooden handle bobbing just above his waistband as he loped toward the entrance. *So much for weapon restrictions.*

The guard was gone longer than was necessary, Crenthys thought. That was never good. She noticed she was fidgeting again and willed herself to stop. Like all plans, this one would likely fall apart soon after she stepped inside. If she got inside. Knowing that didn't stop her from going over her plan again in her mind.

It was then that she noticed Kelios and the greasy guard trading threatening looks. He was going to get them both killed, she was sure. It looked like some kind of primal dance between two plains lions. The idiot still thought he needed to protect her. She could almost smell the stupidity leaking out of him.

Her mouth was half-open to speak when the door banged open and the sweaty guard stood looking at them from the doorway. "She goot." He said with a clipped accent punctuated by some sort of dental problem, Crenthys thought.

"Right?" the greasy guard asked, a little surprised.

"Right." The solemnity in the sweaty guard's reply twisted the knot in her stomach even tighter.

Stop that! She scolded herself. Reminding herself of who she was and what she was capable of, she took a step toward the bulky guard, and Kelios fell in behind her.

"Jus her." The fat guard said, pointing a plump finger at her that looked like another, longer, thumb.

Crenthys stopped and turned, putting a hand on Kelios's chest to stop him from protesting. They had talked about this, her soft glare told him.

He returned the glare but relented.

Crenthys turned and stepped into the dark building to buy some DragonsBlood.

⸻ ◆ ⸻

Tabir was finally given clothing. The remaining passengers of the *Sea Pocket* were led ashore and they were each provided with a pair of thin pants made from rough cloth akin to a grain sack. They were cinched at the top with a brittle piece of twine that frayed on each end. The legs of Tabir's pants were tattered above his ankles.

Hot sand burned his feet and the midday sun was cooking his scalp but he was glad to be ashore. He stood in line, if it could be called that, with the other passengers. Since The *Brinery* had docked, other ships had slowly filtered into the large cove where Usban Port was nestled. Tabir was sad to see clumps of naked slaves being processed on the decks of those other ships. Why were there always so many slaves?

Tabir's elven eyes were very keen. He hadn't appreciated how good his eyesight was until he had met those from other races. Beyond the end of the long pier, Tabir saw rows of bodies along the shoreline. Pairs of men were dragging the corpses into the knee-deep water and tossing them into a shallow-hulled boat. A burial boat, Tabir guessed. He had seen such vessels take victims of plagues or massacres for burial at sea.

He couldn't see well enough at such a distance to determine much about the bodies but a sinking feeling in his gut told him why there was such a great need for a new crop of slaves.

Bog was famous for his harsh treatment of his subjects and slaves were just property to him. The Black DragonLord's cities were built for commerce. Goods flowed liberally in and out of Zhazie ports and clamored along the rough roads connecting the cities spread throughout the massive swamp. For their troubles the slaves were given enough food and shelter to live, enough coin to get drunk on, and reasonable protection from the criminal element that such a society breeds.

Churches of the Black DragonLord were more akin to banks. Priests were just accountants and law scribes. Veneration to Bog was paid by earning coin for their "god". Tabir assumed that when one could no longer produce coin they wound up like the poor souls being loaded into boats for burial at sea.

Now he was poised to join them.

The hallway was dark and continued for another fifteen feet or so. Crenthys paused to let her eyes adjust to the low light.

A fat finger jabbed her ribs and she turned and smacked away the hand before she could stop herself. The big guard stared at her, mouth agape, a stunned look on his sweaty face.

"Don't touch me." She curtly commanded before slowly turning back and walking to the door on the left that was slightly ajar. The light escaping from the opening flickered, making the glow dance across her face as she stopped to peer in.

A grunt and nod from the chunky guard encouraged her to go in. Putting her hand to the door, she gently pushed it open.

The room inside was larger than she would have guessed. Most likely because of how sparsely furnished it was. A single table with two full-sized chairs occupied the outside wall. Light emanated from a single, half-burned, wax candle in a simple wooden stand in the middle of the table. A board on the floor creaked as Crenthys stepped into the room. A shiver ran along her spine followed by a trickle of sweat. The rest of the room was nearly empty. Wooden planks covered the walls of the room, split and bowing at the ends from age. On the same wall as the table, nearer to the center of the wall, was a window that had been boarded up from the inside. She recalled seeing decorative shutters covering the windows on the outside of the building.

Behind her, the door was pulled shut by the fat guard and immediately the room seemed to shrink. She didn't think the windows could be easily used as an exit if necessary. The chairs seemed sturdy, despite being at least as old as the boards on the walls. At one time, this must have been a very nice place, she decided. There was work to be done here. Usban was a mess. Tam was...well, she was Tam. To the extreme. How could she let herself go like that? Morglun would have her flayed when he found out just how bad things had gotten. *Could I rat her out?* Crenthys wondered. When things were bad for Crenthys, right after... She pursed her lips together and closed her eyes, willing away the tears that threatened.

Tam had been there for her when she was in free fall, and soon after Morglun had taken her in. Crenthys would do the same for her old friend, she decided. After all this mess was sorted. She turned and began to pace around the small room and nearly screamed. One of the chairs had suddenly become occupied by a white-skinned elf with pink eyes who sat smiling sweetly.

"Why, hello Crenthys." He mumbled in a slurred approximation of the common tongue. "I was surprised to hear you were at my door. But pleasantly so."

Crenthys couldn't help the shock and horror that was frozen on her face. She had picked the inn owned by Jhaldus. The slaver who had sold her and her companions to the Silver aboard the *Brinery*.

Chapter 10

Tightening the Strings

T he mottled blue, green, and tan-faced dwarf at the table closest to Anuka looked like his heart was going to explode. Perfect. The peals of laughter were chained together and rolled like waves washing over the little goblin. Everyone was fighting to breathe and Anuka loved it. Well, almost everyone.

The big human in the back was no longer lounging back in his chair. He was now sitting forward, one arm on the table, looking hard at Anuka. He didn't get it. Everyone else was dying from laughter. This guy looked like he wanted to launch daggers from his eyes and skewer Anuka.

Apart from the turd in the milk bucket, this is going better than I imagined, Anuka thought as he spread a wide grin across his face showing most of his teeth. The patrons didn't notice the human, else they were too afraid of him to even glance back at him now. "I have a few daggers of my own, shovel-face," Anuka muttered to himself as the laughter died down.

"Dragons!" he bellowed to get the room focused back on him. "Man! What's a goblin to do?" He tossed a wink at the old barkeep who startled. The crook-nosed goblin looked around as all the eyes focused on him, quickly turned, and shuffled back to the bar. "Dragons are like Cerellion Nether Rot. They burn your bottom, always need attention, and show up when you go places you know you shouldn't."

More laughter exploded from the room full of juvenile men. Crooked men, all. Wealthy, dangerous, or both. Anuka shook his head slightly and watched the severe human straighten in his seat, take his wooden mug in his giant hand, and crush it to kindling. Drink squirted out the top in a geyser of brown liquid that splashed on a nearby table. The man never stopped staring those daggers at Anuka.

It made Anuka's next swallow a little harder to get down.

Kelios's tension didn't ease when the big guard came out alone. He came outside and stood on the top step, fanned his arms out wide, stretched, and issued a long yawn. The big man smacked his lips together and looked at his greasy companion. They both turned to look at Kelios.

For some reason, their stares made his hackles rise. Perhaps it was the emotions of the great bear still stirring inside him but their gazes seemed predatory. Deep in his gut, Kelios could feel the echoes of a primal response. It chilled him. Sniffing, he forced those feelings down deep and turned away. Starting a fight wouldn't help the mission and certainly wouldn't help Crenthys. He pretended to be inspecting the outside wall of the building in hopes that the two guards would find their amusement elsewhere. The boards were well weathered and seemed to have been treated regularly with some sort of red paint that extended their life. As he ran his hand across one of the boards the urge to smell it grew very strong. Stop! He chided himself.

It wasn't uncommon to have some lingering psychic side effects after touching a creature's mind but this was abnormally strong. Perhaps it was because the beast was so foreign to his mind. Or maybe because its will was so strong. He could smell stale sweat, mixed with a twinge of fear and excitement. That, he knew belonged to the two guards. He closed his eyes and sighed.

"Say, what manner of creep are you, anyhow?" the voice belonged to the smaller of the two men, Kelios discerned, but he sensed both of them moving towards him. Better to face them head-on. He turned and slowly looked the two men over. "You some kinda Sea Elf or summat?"

"Don't look like no Elf." Raj chuckled from over the small guard's shoulder.

Praying Crenthys would be quick, Kelios pasted on a thin smile and said, "I am what your people call a Seaborne. Or Fish Man. Maybe Merfolk or Merrow."

"Right?"

"Right," Kelios answered the greasy little human.

They were slowly advancing on Kelios so he stepped back one step and felt the wall at his back. *Great*, he thought.

The smaller man stopped and considered him.

Kelios did his best to seem unafraid yet non-threatening at the same time. He seemed to be failing at pulling off one or both of those looks.

The greasy-haired guard ran his tongue over his remaining teeth as he had before. Then he showed off that handful of rotten gems with a huge smile. "Got any more of that gold like what your girlfren had, Merman?"

———— ❖ ————

"Please, have a seat." The elf, Jhaldus, gestured one of his long-nailed hands to the vacant seat at the table beside him.

How had he gotten in here? Her mind screamed. She hadn't heard the door. *And what does this mean?* she wondered. Did Tam betray her? She thought of Kelios, then the mission, and began to summon hefty doses of calm and poise. She glided cautiously across the tiny room, daintily sat in the chair, and elegantly crossed her legs as she thought an Elven lady would.

"You must feel like the mouse now, caught by the cat?" He smiled, revealing those awful ebony teeth. Crenthys tried not to shiver. Barely succeeded.

What could she say? He was quite right.

"When I saw the slave buying other slaves, I knew a great mystery was at hand. I am so glad to be in a position to unravel some of this puzzle. Won't you tell me? Why do you want to buy DragonsBlood? Buying DragonsBlood is illegal, yes? A slave found with a single drop would be killed. No questions."

She didn't like being the mouse. She didn't like his smile or the way he was leading the conversation. Crenthys had brushed up against some of the most depraved creatures known to the world. What's the worst he could do? Kill her? He was some criminal despot trying to claw his way to the top of the political sewer of Usban Port. So be it. She would be circumspect and see how much he knew and perhaps learn something.

"Someone is pouring a lot of DragonsBlood onto the streets of Dorwine and it isn' the church. No Alchemy. Totally pure." the pale Elf said smiling so broadly his eyes twinkled.

She found herself suppressing a shudder. *Ok, he knows about the DragonsBlood.* She figured he did.

"So much wealth. Someone is going to get themselves killed. Why do you care?" the Elf said.

With difficulty, she bit off a couple of snarky retorts before deciding to remain silent. *So, he probably knows about Tamris and likely Apostate as well.* She prayed he didn't know about the Silver.

Still smiling, the Elf rubbed at his right hand with his left. "I see. Why are you here, in my building, child of the sea?"

Crenthys felt unsure. How much did he know? *More than me,* she mused. So much for subtlety.

The Elf's smile switched suddenly to a contemplative look that ended with a sigh. "You mus not be too hard on your old friend." She looked up at him as he continued. "The thing about DragonsBlood is, once you make a customer they become quite loyal. So much wealth, you see?"

"So, you are the source?" Crenthys asked, trying a more direct approach.

"No. But very little happens in Usban that I am not aware of."

"If not you, then who?" she asked. The creepy elf seemed surprised and then disappointed. "Why not satisfy my curiosity? You've told me too much already. You can't let me live now."

He smiled again, unconsciously rubbing his hands together once more. "I know much about you. But you surprised me some. And you are clever, Brinka."

Crenthys's stomach clenched when he spoke the name no one should know.

⚬

"Dragons!" Anuka roared over the crowd. "We all love 'em, really." He waited, to let the laughs die down and the tension build just a little. "But DragonSpawn? What's that all about?" He paced around waving his hands dramatically. "I mean, whose idea was this? Let's make dragons that look like people. How does that make any sense?" He put his hands on his forehead and flung them out dramatically as if his head were exploding, while he simultaneously pursed his lips to mimic the explosion. "I don't get it. And someone answer me this; why do some look like boys and some look like girls? They can't have DragonMan babies!" The laughs came but a current of nervousness and uncertainty was apparent now. That was odd, he thought. Anuka started to pace back and forth on the scuffed wooden floor on the front of the little stage, eyeballing random patrons as he marched.

"I mean, the boy DragonSpawn has the big muscles and chest like a tree trunk." He poked his little chest out and let his arms dangle loosely at his sides as he paced about with his bottom lip poking out and his brow furrowed. "And the girly ones have all the right curves." Anuka stopped to pantomime the outline of a woman's curvy figure with his hands. "But they ain't got the right equipment." When he pointed at his nether region the laughs kicked up a bit, still underscored by nervousness. Anuka wasn't sure what was going on. This should be building to a big laugh. "I mean, I bet this guy," Anuka said, pointing at the goblin bartender who had just wandered back to watch the show, "Has more down there than any DragonMan" Suddenly, the hulking human exploded from his seat. His table flew to the side and crashed into a nearby table knocking a handful of patrons, and their drinks, to the floor.

"YOU GO TOO FAR!" The big man yelled pointing his finger at Anuka. A finger that was inexplicably tipped with a great talon. The room let out a collective cry as the pale white skin of the human transformed into thick, red scales. The human's dumpy face stretched into the leathery snout of a Red DragonMan.

Oops. Anuka thought.

The room instantly became silent, save for the panting of the DragonMan. Every patron looked from the DragonMan to Anuka, then to the fallen patrons, and back to the DragonMan.

Just my luck. Anuka chuckled madly and said in a low voice, "Well, here we go."

Chapter 11

Changes

K elios could smell more than his mind could handle. Sweat, rancid breath, clothing that had gone days or weeks without being washed. He could even smell the residual sweet stink of herbs that his subconscious mind somehow knew. Every scent was so powerful Kelios felt nauseated. The guards pressed in on him. The lingering effects of the bear made his senses sharper than he would have liked but he had other things to worry about just now.

"I don't have gold." Kelios patted his jacket and pants pockets in demonstration.

"Oh, I'll bet you've got plen'y werf sump'n, right Raj?"

"Right." The larger guard agreed. His eyes seemed to disappear under his furrowed brow as he concentrated on Kelios.

The arm holding Raj's cudgel still swung low but the big man flexed his meaty hand on the handle.

Kelios's skin crawled with the sensation of hair on his arms suddenly standing. But he didn't have hair on his arms. Kelios pushed up his sleeves and ogled his arms. "Oceans deep...". Tufts of dark brown hair sprouted from various points on his forearms.

If the room were any more silent it would have made a graveyard seem like a Dragon Day parade. *Might as well go all in,* he thought.

Anuka deftly climbed up on the closest table, kicking aside an empty mug. "What the matter Red? Scales too thin for a few jokes?"

The red-scaled DragonMan blinked slowly and a slender tongue flashed over his reptilian lip. He stared at Anuka with the red-flecked eyes of a snake, and said in a deep, raspy voice, "You. Go. Too. Far!" The last word flew over his forked tongue like a ball of lead from a Dragon cannon.

"That's enough!" rasped a garbled voice that sounded like it came from someone being choked. Who also had rocks in their mouth. Every head, including the big red Dragon's, turned to regard the wrinkled old goblin barkeep who, to his credit, didn't wilt under the stares this time. "Everyone settle down." He looked at Anuka as he spat the words. "No fights tonight. We can't have this place full of Nobs. Not tonight." Nobs was the local name for the peacekeepers in the city. They were from the Temple of Bog and didn't like to be bothered. If they showed up, they would exact a great deal in "taxes" from everyone. If a fight broke out there could be beatings and maybe even a hanging or two.

No DragonMan was getting beat or hanged, that was for sure. He'd have to back off. Why had he gotten so carried away? He was getting more desperate each day his Papa was lost.

"Why don't you stick a fish in your face hole and sluff off! I wanna see the Dragon eat the little guy!" The cry came from the other side of the room, opposite the barkeep, near the door, and was echoed by a chorus of cheers.

Great.

Panic shot through Crenthys and she looked at the door. She mastered herself at the last moment or she would have fled. When she looked back at the ivory-skinned elf, he wore that awful smile again. The fat guard was probably at the door, she reasoned. Getting by him wouldn't be a problem but if the door was locked or the tubby guard was leaning on it, she might not get out before Jhaldus attacked her. The thought of exposing her back to that one, even for a moment, brought another wave of shivers.

"I heard a surface man say once that it isn' the tales of bards, but the secre's a man keeps that make him. The same could be said of a woman, I suppose."

How did he know that name? *Idiot.* Tam betrayed her completely. But why? What did this creature have that could hold Tam so strongly she would betray Cren's secrets? It was more than a drug addiction. Tam wouldn't betray so much for Tent Weed.

"What do you want?" she asked with as much venom as she could muster. It wasn't much.

"I want what every surface man wants. Live in peace. Make a good living. Enjoy the pleasures of life."

"What do you want from me?" Crenthys said.

A faint, rosy color crept up the elf's face, stark on his pale skin, and he lost his composure for a brief moment, then said, "I make my way on information." He smoothed the dark leg of his silk trousers, though it lay perfectly smooth already, and looked at Crenthys with that same eery, lurid mask he had been wearing. "From what you have said, I can guess that the old Silver doesn't know who is behind the DragonsBlood. Or he hasn' told you. My guess is that the Dragon Council wishes to lay the blame on a convenient enemy. You are here to make firm that story. But he doesn't know what you are."

She needed to go. Now. She glanced over the slender elf's person with the detached professionalism she had been taught, lest she become nauseated, and didn't notice any armor on the elf. And, unless they were secreted very well, he carried no weapons. Could she break his slender neck before that guard came in with his cudgel and cracked her skull? Not likely.

"Your options aren't so many as you imagine."

She hadn't realized that she had been coiling to strike and she settled herself back down in the chair, feeling caged. "What do you want from me?" she asked again.

Jhaldus unfolded his slender legs and, leaning forward, rested his arms on the table. His thin lips parted, revealing his onyx teeth and he paused to consider his words. Then in a rush, he said, "Work with me. We will send that Merman back to the Silver with some proof and tell him you ran away. When the Dragon leaves you will work for me. If half of what Tam has said about you is true, you would be a great help in my work. When politics settle down once more you could even take Tam's job. She is old and useless to your group now. Brinka, come work with me."

A bestial roar split the tension like a knife. Both Jhaldus and Crenthys jerked their attention toward the window.

Chapter 12

Predator or Prey

K elios stood panting, his throat raw, as the pair of prone attackers gaped up at him from the ground. This wasn't right. Everything felt wrong. Somehow a sliver of the bear he had communed with earlier had gotten inside him and was clawing its way to the surface of his mind. Always before, the change had been directed by his own will. But this beast had batted aside his attempts at control like a whale thrashing a schooner. His ears rang and his mind buzzed with information all while his body screamed in protest to the changes. The shock and pain of his bones stretching and thickening, his skin hardening and sprouting patches of dark brown hair from every pore, washed over him. Those seemed a distant problem compared to the horror of understanding what the bear had planned for the two on the ground.

"Dragon's breaf. Wha.." The greasy one sputtered as he tried to scurry away backward like a crab.

I love crabs, the bear inside him thought. Kelios was terrified as he felt his face finish stretching into a bear's maw and yet also into a wide grin. Horror gripped his mind because the thoughts he was having were no longer his. He roared again and pounced on the skinny little thug.

Anuka hunkered down under a table that he thought was very sturdy until two brawling patrons crashed atop it and it sagged with a crunch. He scurried away under another, sturdier-looking, table. This was totally out of hand. Just the way he liked it. Nobs would show up but, hopefully, he'd be long gone by then. The sea dwarf merchant rolled across the top of the table he was under and slammed hard onto the ground next to him.

Anuka scurried over to check him and was relieved to discover that he still carried his purse. Cursing again, for lack of his favorite dagger, Anuka pulled his substitute blade out, slickly severed the leather thong holding the man's coin stack pouch, and slipped it into his own.

He risked a quick look to see chaos still reigned. Everyone was fighting, hiding, or unconscious. He didn't see the DragonMan, but last he'd seen him, he was wrestling with three patrons. Anuka did see the door and, with his bearings back, scurried after it.

Only stopping once or twice to snatch up a coin stack or two, Anuka saw the door. It was cracked open! Luck was running with him tonight so he didn't hesitate. Rising to almost full height, he dashed for the door and was a mere two strides away when a blur and a crack snapped the door shut. A handaxe Anuka could only wield with both hands was embedded in the door with part of the head buried in the door frame also.

Turning, Anuka saw the Red DragonMan, his right arm still extended from the throw. Without taking his eyes off Anuka, the DragonMan casually tossed the human he had by the neck to the ground. Was he smiling? It was sort of hard to tell as Anuka watched him advance. Anuka slowly backed up towards the door. The creature didn't stop until it was two strides away, one stride for the Dragon.

The massive DragonMan leered down at Anuka, reached his right hand over his head for the sword hilt behind his back, nearly scraping the ceiling with his hand, and stopped. Reconsidering, the Red brought his hands around and held both up for Anuka to see. With a flexing motion, the scaly skin around his razor-sharp claws effaced, exposing more of the deadly talons.

Then came the roar. It was the second roar, but no one had heard the first one over the noisy brawl. In the silence before Anuka's bloody murder, everyone heard it.

The DragonMan dropped his hands and whipped his head in the direction of the sound.

Without sparing a moment's care for the bestial cry from beyond, Anuka sprinted two steps, leaped onto a chair, and vaulted gracefully through the ornate shutters covering the window.

⎯⎯◆⎯⎯

Jhaldus looked sharply at Crenthys and she thought that he blamed her for the noise. It had come from the general direction of where she had left Kelios. She hoped he hadn't done something stupid.

A soft click at the door had Jhaldus on his feet, spilling his heavy chair onto the floor. The door slid open and a slender figure, cloaked in shadow, draped almost entirely in dull black leathers, glided slowly in the room. Shock and horror seemed to grip Jhaldus. He staggered back against the wall as the figure gently snapped the door shut behind him. With a violent jerk, he wrenched the slender handle free of the door and dropped it to the floor with a clang. The figure hadn't seemed to notice Crenthys yet, who still sat, frozen, unsure what to do.

The intruder was covered in black except for a small slit for his eyes. Those eyes. Pink, but not the creamy color of Jhaldus's. This man's eyes were bright and angry looking. Where Jhaldus's eyes swam with streams of white, this creature's orbs ran with rivers the color of blood. The figure reached up to the bit of his outfit that covered his face, pulled it down below his chin, and revealed milky-white skin. Then it spoke.

In words Crenthys could not understand, and in tones that tumbled over one another in a strange way that was violent yet flowed melodically, like jackals bringing down a gazelle, the intruder seemed to be chastising Jhaldus. Shaking his head, Jhaldus responded with a torrent of words in the strange language. The words tumbled smoothly out of his mouth like water from a pitcher. There were no hard or rough sounds in the language and Crenthys suddenly understood why Jhaldus struggled with the "T" sound in the Low Dragon tongue.

Crenthys couldn't understand the words but she thought she understood what was being exchanged. Very slowly she began to rise from her seat. Without turning to regard her, the intruder pointed a slender gloved hand at her, so she settled back down. This was very bad. She saw two daggers on his side and had spied the hilt of a slender sword on the other.

Jhaldus seemed to find his spine and screamed a retort at the stranger, jabbing a bone-white finger at the man.

In a flash, the other elf had drawn yet another dagger she hadn't even noticed.

Then came the second roar.

This one was more than the first: More volume. More fury. More terror.

Everyone froze. The newcomer had a curious look on his face. The arm holding the dagger threateningly at Jhaldus sagged just a bit. Then the slaver slapped one hand to something hanging on a chain about his neck and the lights of the room winked out.

Crenthys had seen darkness. She had walked from the bright sun into a dark room and remembered the stab of panic as her eyes adjusted. Only this time there was no adjusting. Just blackness. Complete and total darkness.

A thought later, the table rammed into her gut and sent her, chair and all, tumbling backward to the floor. She rolled away ungracefully but managed to end up in a crouch. Crenthys discerned the sounds of furniture being shuffled about, mixed with curses and struggling, even the unmistakable whoosh of a blade quickly whipping through the air. Her heart pounded in her chest as the men scrambled about. She fell forward and planted her hands on the floor, then she stopped and listened. Only one set of feet shuffled around the room, which suddenly seemed smaller.

As quietly as possible, she scooted to her left until she found the wall and slowly crawled along it. The shuffling sounds were punctuated by the violent swipe of a blade. It was the intruder, sweeping the room. The tenor of the blade cutting the air had changed and she guessed that he had switched to his slender sword. He was going to find her. Somehow, she had to get past him. As quickly and silently as she could, Crenthys crawled to where she guessed the table had been.

Her hand jammed painfully into one leg of the table, audibly cracking several knuckles and nearly taking her breath. The shuffling stopped. Nothing to do but seek shelter. She moved with more speed and less stealth and could almost feel the intruder change direction. She knew the strike was incoming.

Then an inhuman terror-filled wail pierced the air, followed by growls and a third roar.

She had to get out of here. Lurching forward, aiming to go under the table and make for the door, Crenthys felt confident she could splinter it open once she gained her feet. Instead, her left hand found open air, and she plunged headlong into a hole she hadn't expected. Her belt slowed her fall a bit and served to turn her into a flip. Her heels slammed against the rim of the trapdoor before she plunged into a free fall.

Chapter 13

Beyond Your Control

K elios felt like the passenger on the back of the massive bear. The bear that had just mauled a screaming human and was now chasing down another human who was bald, fat, and had just gained his feet. This ride would not end. The worst part was, Kelios loved it. He felt pure joy surge within him. As his quarry began to run, he sprinted after, bloody tongue flapping gleefully out one side of his mouth.

Suddenly, Kelios understood why bears were in cages. The beast's primal urges pumped through his veins and Kelios was helpless to stop the rampage. Worse still, he had heard some ruckus from inside the bar and it sounded like those inside might be coming outside.

The tubby guard grabbed at the far corner of the building in a desperate attempt to make the turn and get away from the marauding bear. But it was pointless. Kelios dug his giant claws into the earth and slid his massive form to a near halt, then he pulled two sets of claws free and propelled himself after the fleeing man. One hard push on his back legs and he was close enough to taste the man's fear. The bald guard glanced over his shoulder, astonished and terrified that the beast had gained so quickly, and stumbled forward as if the strength had drained from his legs.

Kelios pleaded with the bear inside him to spare the man, but the bear ignored him. Kelios knew he could leave no witnesses to his transformation but he didn't want to kill the pleading guard. All the bear's pent-up rage--of being captured, the fear for her young, and the sheer primal desire for slaughter--mixed together to make the bear's will as hard as iron. She didn't even hear Kelios's plea.

"Ima, ima, ima..." the fat man panted. "Jus lemme go. We ain't mean nothin by it. I'm sorry. I'm..."

The bear stood to her full height and glowered down at the man then bellowed forth a final roar of victory. It was the last thing the man heard.

"Sum buck!" Anuka swore in a hushed tone as he brushed away the tiny stones buried in his arm from landing on the ground outside the window. He was already moving when he heard the door bang open and people started bustling out. He snuck around the back of the tavern. That had gone way better than he'd expected, but where in the storming seas was the roaring coming from? The last thing he wanted was to be caught between a DragonMan wielding a long-bladed sword and some feral beast. He peered cautiously around the next corner and saw a couple of figures at the far side of the back of the building. The back half was more of a small warehouse than anything else, Anuka reckoned. His eyes were still adjusting to the low light but he was pretty sure he saw two figures. One sat with his back against the building, knees tented up, head in hands, and the other lay on the ground.

His hand went to the handle of the sorry replacement knife he'd been given and he slid it silently from his sheath. Cautiously he approached the scene. As he drew nearer, he thought he heard weeping coming from the sitting figure. The longer Anuka looked at the scene, the less it made sense.

There was a half-eaten human on the ground. Looked like he'd be fat if you could put all the pieces back together. And Fish man sat there, covered in blood, crying like a baby, looking pretty guilty. "Hey, bubby," Anuka said, slipping the knife back into the sheath but keeping his hand close.

Kelios's head jerked up in surprise. His face was a wreck. But not just his face. All of him, really.

"Anuka." Kelios gasped getting quickly to his feet. "How did you find me?"

Anuka shrugged. "Oh, you know. I was just kinda wandering around. So, what happened here?" Anuka pointed to the remains.

"Bear." Kelios stammered a bit too quickly. "There was a bear."

"Yeah..." Anuka said, rubbing his chin with a hand. "I heard that. What the shells is a bear?"

"Oh. It's a giant creature. Similar to a dog, only much larger. Bigger than a man. Covered in hair. Rife with teeth and claws."

"Giant dog, eh? Nasty." Anuka said with a shudder. "Oh, hey man, we need to get out of here. There are about thirty angry drunk guys and a Red DragonMan around here. They might be looking for me. Oh, and Bog's people will be comin' to beat and hang people." He grabbed the only clean spot he could find on Kelios's shirt and pulling him along, headed away from the tavern.

Kelios pulled free. "Wait. Crenthys. We have to find her."

"The hoo- eh... heroic Sea Elf? Maiden. Woman."

"Yes. She is in that building." He strode past Anuka with a head full of steam. He stopped suddenly at the sound of voices and flattened himself against the wall of the building. He looked back at Anuka who had already padded back the way he came, motioning for Kelios to follow. The seaborne caught up with Anuka in short order and grabbed his arm. "We can't leave her!" He barked in a harsh whisper.

"Relax, bubby. There's a door down here. And bad guys back there. Come on." *Sheesh*, Anuka thought. *This guy is wound up.*

They got to the end of the building, slipped around the corner, Anuka acting as a scout, and trotted up two rotting steps to a door that appeared to get little use. It was either locked from the inside or stuck fast. Anuka's pointed ears perked up. He could have sworn he heard people coming around the building from both directions.

"Step aside, my friend. We are out of time." Kelios had a weird, calm look on his face so Anuka stepped out of the man's way. With a resigned sigh, Kelios wedged his fingers around the bottom of the door and simply ripped it open.

"Shells bells," Anuka whispered. *Boy been working the anvil or something*, he thought. Then he noticed tufts of thick black hair on the back of Kelios's neck gradually sinking into his skin. *What the...?*

———◆———

The fall was terrifying. But brief. Crenthys flipped head over heels a couple of times, then landed on her hands and knees on hard ground. The force of the landing jarred her joints, and her teeth banged together hard. But she could see. A little at least. Very faint light illuminated a corridor that seemed ancient. Massive square pillars supported thick crossbeams all along the path, fortifying this passageway. It looked like one of the ancient Dwarven mine shafts she had seen in Khilis. The thought made her shudder.

Above her, she heard shuffling and remembered what had just happened. The elf that tried to murder Jhaldus was still up there. And Jhaldus was down here, somewhere.

The hole she had fallen into was pitch black but she hit her head on the edge of a trap door as she fell.

Once her eyes adjusted, she glanced around and found a short stick that felt like a tool handle with a hook on the end. Using the hook end she gently pushed the trap door shut until it clicked. She didn't know how to open the door from the room above and prayed the assassin didn't either.

A dim light glowed from down the hallway. Crenthys peered that direction, then slowly crept along the hard dirt path, her feet crunching on the tiny bits of loose earth and rock scattered along the corridor. She didn't fancy herself much of a tracker but squinted in the dim amber light in search of tracks. She couldn't see any. The silence was so profound her ears ached with the strain of listening as she moved ten slow, quiet strides along the tunnel. On the left side of the corridor, about ten more strides ahead, Crenthys saw a half bowl-shaped fixture mounted about head-high on the wall. Steady yellow light came from there. It did not flicker as a torch would. Gingerly she crept along, aware that the light would reveal her presence much more than any noise she might make.

She touched the bowl carefully and nothing happened. Carefully, she slid her hand over the top of the bowl and felt inside. She expected heat but there was none. Her fingers brushed something that felt like a smooth stone and she jerked her hand free of the fixture. Light scattered about the hallway and she heard something roll around. *Come on, Cren,* she reproved herself. Then she reached back into the bowl and fished out the light source.

It was a stone. Oblong in shape, like an egg, only not so big around. It wasn't bright but it also wasn't pleasant to look at for very long. *Dragon Magic,* she thought. Used in something so simple. That kind of extravagance was rarely seen outside of a Dragon's Keep.

The urge to pocket it, even to turn it in to the church, was strong. But that was stupid. Was she going to go to the church and turn Jhaldus in? The thought of Jhaldus reminded her of her current situation and she dropped the light stone back into its sconce. Then she peered around for a pair of eyes looking back at her.

A short distance ahead she made out a door frame on the left with the corridor continuing on past that. She knew that her eyes were greatly inferior to those of the pale-skinned elf she suspected was lurking down here. His people made their homes in the light-less caverns that sprawled far below the surface. It was said that his people would be nearly blind in the light of a sunny day but could read the pages of a tome in almost total darkness.

She wasn't worried about Jhaldus reading her a nighttime tale. She was afraid he would slip a dagger between her ribs. As far as she knew, he was unarmed. And she never was. So, drawing in a breath of cool, stale air, Crenthys began to slip along the wall towards the door, glancing over her shoulder. As she stared into the darkness, Crenthys couldn't shake the feeling that something she couldn't see was staring back at her.

⁕

Kelios felt different. Still carrying traces of the bear in his mind, Kelios took in a plethora of odors. Strongest among them was the stench of ale, reed-thin and stale. Layered on top of that was a mixture of fresh blood and old sweat. Stepping further into the small hallway, mostly so Anuka could squeeze in and shut the door behind them, Kelios thought he also caught the faint scent of smoke and something he didn't understand. He knew the smell but wasn't sure which part of him knew it; Triton or Bear. It lingered like perfume and was sweetly enticing to his more primal nature. It made him want to chase something. A scent the bear knows, he decided and nodded grimly.

He jerked when Anuka swatted his leg. The little goblin had been trying to get his attention. When Kelios looked down, the little guy wore an impatient look and tapped his long ears. Kelios had been so wrapped up in the scents of the place that he had forgotten to listen. The sounds of slow, deep, muted snoring floated through the wall to their right. Somewhere he heard sobs and the sounds of glass being swept up. It was an odd sensation to have ears stronger than his own hear a sound and then have to funnel it through his own experiences to identify it.

Kelios turned to motion Anuka to follow just as the goblin blew past him. Sighing, he followed the little Glamokyn down the left fork of the hallway.

It only now occurred to Kelios that he wasn't properly mystified by Anuka's re-appearance. Shouldn't he be halfway back to the Free Trade Isles by now? Why was the goblin still in the city?

His heart was pounding and he flexed his hands unconsciously as they moved along. Up ahead Kelios saw the door Crenthys must have entered through from outside. He was almost sure of it. Anuka stopped outside a different door that was slightly ajar and peered inside. The scent of Crenthys wafted down the hall as Anuka gently pushed the door open.

Kelios found himself tensing even further. Anuka stepped inside with no thought of stealth. The room was nearly empty but there were signs of a struggle. Both chairs lay on their backs on opposite sides of an old, thick wooden table that had been turned askew.

"Sum buck!" Anuka breathed, spinning a circle as he walked around the room. "What happened in here?"

"Crenthys was here."

"This look like her handiwork?"

He dare not tell Anuka about the bear. "I saw them enter here. And I, I heard her yelling through the wall." Kelios didn't look at Anuka but could feel his eyes on him.

"Okay. Then where did she go?"

"I don't know. I didn't see her leave." Kelios said peevishly.

Out of the corner of his eye, Kelios saw Anuka pacing.

"What's this then?" Anuka asked.

Annoyed to have his search interrupted, he spun and lowered an exasperated glare on Anuka who stood with an index finger jammed into a fresh gash in the wall. Withdrawing his finger and fussing with a splinter, the little goblin moved aside, which allowed Kelios to get a look.

Grabbing the low burning candle that sputtered on the floor, Kelios moved closer to investigate. It looked like a slash from a sword of some sort. Tracing along the wall he noticed several more. *What had happened here?* he wondered. *And where had Crenthys gone?*

"Master, is that you?" croaked a voice from the hallway, nearly causing Kelios to drop the candle. Anuka was suddenly at the door, holding his long knife down at this side. Kelios fell back as an ugly little goblin with white stringy hair pushed the door open and stuck his head inside. "Master-"

In a flash, Anuka pounced on the poor old creature and rolled him onto the floor. Somehow, Anuka wound up on top of the old goblin, pinning him to the floor with his feeble little arms bent painfully at his back. In the next instant, Anuka had the knife at the terrified Glamokyn's yellow eye.

"Hey, friend." Anuka rasped in the creature's ear. "Remember me?"

The old man tried to struggle but Anuka had him. He gasped out a string of spit and lay still. "What do you want?"

"Me? Lots of things. My own boat. Chest full of rubies. A well-stocked harem." Anuka picked the old man up and slammed him back to the floor, quickly putting the knife where it could be seen. "Right now, I want to know where my friend is!"

Kelios didn't know what to think. He was sure Anuka was going to gut this old goblin right there. His desire to explain to Anuka that it was wrong to kill was tempered by shock at the bear's thrill at eviscerating the poor fat guard. A shiver of revulsion rippled through him. He was a murderer.

A scent, dirty yet sweet, hit Kelios just after he caught a flicker of movement in the hallway. It was the same scent he had caught when they first came in.

"Who else is here?" he asked breathlessly as he stared into the mostly dark hallway. Finally, he looked back at the two goblins and repeated the question.

"M-master is here. Or was. The freak chased out all the guests-oww!" he howled, sending a fresh spray of spittle to the floor as Anuka wrenched his arm further.

"Anuka!"

The red goblin's gaze snapped to him and Kelios pointed to the hallway.

"Who else, friend?" Anuka asked, leaning back down to speak into his captive's ear.

"Master's guests." He wept and seemed to slump even further into the floor.

Out in the hallway, they heard someone trying to open the door leading outside.

"We have to go," Kelios told Anuka. The red half-man stood abruptly and the knife disappeared. Without hesitation, the two left the old barkeep sobbing on the floor.

Chapter 14

Into the Darkness

The metal handle on the door felt cool to the touch but wouldn't turn. Locked.

Gazing down the hallway past the door she saw her shadow stretched long into the empty darkness. She wanted to find Jhaldus but wasn't sure why. The smart thing to do would be to find a way out. To get away as fast as possible. *Dragonsbreath*! What had happened to Kelios? She had to trust that he had somehow gotten away in all the commotion. It seemed likely that he may have been the source of the commotion, whatever it had been. Hopefully not the victim of whatever had happened.

Nothing for it now. She had to get herself out of this mess first.

Deciding it was a bad idea to leave an unchecked room behind her, she glanced around in both directions, then grasped the handle firmly with both hands and leaned.

The mechanism was solid and it barely budged against her weight. She closed her eyes and drew in a deep breath. In her mind, she formed an image of her breaking the lock. Releasing her breath she leaned again and slowly began to increase pressure. The part of the handle nearest the door began to warm. With a sudden groan, the handle gave way and Crenthys stumbled into an unlit room.

Her breathing was labored and her arms shook. Tapping the power buried within her was taxing. She quickly took in her surroundings. The floor beneath her feet was smooth, flat, and surprisingly clean. In the corner to her left, she saw an Erstyme stove. Instead of burning wood or coal, it was heated by a chemical mixture containing DragonsBlood. It likely cost as much as the tavern above. Spotless shelves lined the wall near the stove with matching metal pots and pans stacked neatly by size. A set of knives with honed blades so polished that they reflected the dim light lay on one shelf. Again, perfectly arranged.

Glancing around she noted a small table made from dark, polished wood was against the wall opposite the door. A thin chair, made from the same polished wood as the table, was tucked neatly at the table. A thick wooden bench was nestled against the table across from the lone chair. It seemed a lonely existence to Crenthys.

A simple, sturdy broom was perched against the wall to Crenthys's right behind the solitary chair. Between Crenthys and the broom, she saw a single painting mounted in the middle of the wall about head-height. Curiosity peaked, she stepped further into the room to look at the painting. It was the most grotesquely horrible portrait she had ever seen. From a distance, it resembled an Elven lady with pale-white skin like Jhaldus and the assassin. Up close she saw that the woman's hair was painted starkly with snakes whose tails sprouted from her scalp and the ends were snakeheads. The eyes were scorpions, painted red. Her teeth were swords, knives, and daggers of various types. The one visible ear was studded with a glossy, purple spider hanging from a strand of webbing.

Crenthys finally tore her eyes away from the terrible painting only to discover she still saw the images seared into her mind as she looked into the darkness of the next room.

⁂

A quick glance over his shoulder confirmed his fears. Sum Bucks were coming back. They had passed the back door they'd come in when Anuka saw the door slowly pushed open. He quickly opened the nearest door, which happened to be where the snoring was coming from, and smoothly stepped inside. He hoped the fish man was on his tail but he didn't spare a glance. On a padded pallet in the room lay a barrel-chested man in his late middle years, and a young woman with red curly hair, sleeping. As Anuka moved toward the pallet, the man sat up but was instantly smacked between the eyes with the pommel of Anuka's borrowed dagger and dropped immediately back to the bed, unconscious.

The woman jerked up and fell backward off the bed, naked arms, legs, and everything else flailing wildly. She hit the floor with a thump then came up screaming and clutching for the blanket to cover herself.

Anuka gave a very shocked Kelios a dubious look. "I thought you knew what to do for this part," Anuka said before sighing and flopping his arms helplessly. "The hard way, then. Get ready."

The little goblin made his knife disappear again and simply jerked the door open. A scrawny mixed-blood elf wielding a short-handled scythe fell headlong into the room. He landed comically in a pile atop the unconscious human, the elf's long dirty-blond ponytail slapping the man in the face.

Anuka gestured at the elf who was trying to regain his feet and nearly yelled over the top of the still-screaming woman, "Well?"

Blowing a terse breath through his nose, Kelios squared up on the elf as he tried to rise and, with a grunt, launched a brisk hay-maker into the attacker's jaw that sent him flying back atop the unconscious man in the bed.

Anuka nodded his appreciation of Kelios's work. Then he swiped a fine-looking hat from the dresser near the door. Anuka took a closer look at the human on the floor. He was definitely Swet, the Captain of The *Brinery*. "Not bad. Let's go."

With a glance down the hallway, Anuka noted that someone had gained entry at the far end of the hall. So he sprinted through the nearest doorway which brought him back into the common room of the bar. The devastation was beautiful.

"What in the blazing sun happened here?"

"I did!" Anuka beamed. Footfalls from the hallway ended his revelry. "C'mon!" he urged Kelios and they darted for the front door of the bar.

The fleeing crowd had nearly ripped the door from its hinges when they fled earlier, so when Anuka crashed into it, he nearly fell on his face. Kelios was right behind him. As they burst into the courtyard, Anuka looked around frantically for some escape. He considered running to the south but heard a different set of voices growing louder from that direction and decided against it. The sounds on the other side of the building were getting louder also, and he guessed the patrons from the bar were headed his way. His gaze landed on the ornate well in the center of the courtyard. Fresh out of options, he sprinted toward it.

Leaning over and looking down the gaping hole, Anuka could not see the bottom. The rope mechanism at the top of the well appeared to be non-functioning. Anuka tugged at the rope. It didn't budge. He looked to the side and gave Kelios a mischievous grin.

"Papa always said 'you're only as stupid as the people you follow'." Anuka climbed up on the short stone wall of the well, and grabbing the rope, began to shimmy down. He paused a few seconds later, looked up at the horrified Kelios, showed him that grin again, and descended into darkness.

⸻ ◈ ⸻

Perhaps the creepiest thing in the room was the presence of a second bed. She didn't know much about the odd elf but she couldn't imagine that Jhaldus had a wife or any kind of lover. Shivers of revulsion ran down her spine.

She didn't want to enter the room, especially since all the locks for the door were on the outside. Gently closing the door, she backed into the narrow hallway and continued to look for things of interest.

On the wall to the right of the door hung an odd picture frame with an image of a man changing into a spider. Or perhaps the spider was changing into a man, she couldn't tell. It was the only thing in the lair she had seen that wasn't perfectly straight. She reached up to straighten it and the picture slid to the left, revealing a previously hidden hole in the wall behind it.

She slid the picture out of the way and saw a peephole just big enough for her to stick her head into. Moving her face closer, she strained to look through the portal. It gave a view to the hallway she had been in a few minutes back. Farther down that hallway she saw the bottom of a pair of double doors made of dark wood. She almost gasped aloud when she saw a shadowy figure pass by.

Instantly she thought the figure might be able to see her if it were to look in her direction. But then she noticed there was some sort of film covering the outside part of the hole that made Crenthys think that would be unlikely. With terrified fascination, she pressed her face closer to the hole again and watched the figure skulk away toward the doors. *The assassin!* She thought to herself. He had found his way down and was looking for them. Well, Jhaldus at least.

She was familiar with the axiom that the enemy of my enemy is my friend, but doubted it applied in this case. Part of her believed the other elf had wanted to kill them both. Another part of her instinctively knew that if the elf had wanted her dead, she would be.

She pursed her lips at that thought and looked back out the portal. If she met the assassin on even terms he would discover she could not be so easily killed.

The figure stood, carefully inspecting the doors. Crenthys could barely make him out in the darkness but she saw his thin fingers tracing along the seams of the doors. Then he rifled through his pockets and produced some sort of instrument. After a few moments, the elf slowly opened one of the wooden doors and peered inside.

Before the assassin opened the door completely it was flung open with a screech and a bang. A red-scaled DragonMan came roaring through the doorway, long-bladed sword held high.

Crenthys couldn't stifle a gasp and she jumped back in surprise. Roars, grunts, and the clanging of metal tempted her to continue watching the sudden fight. Good sense told her otherwise.

Jhaldus must've gone through those doors also, she reasoned. She hadn't found him in here. The best thing for her to do was to go back the way she had come, find Kelios, and get back to the Inn. The faintest sound of wood creaking froze her in her tracks.

Not wanting to make a sound of her own, she slowly turned and looked back through the hallway between her and the trap door.

Jhaldus stepped from the shadows. He held some sort of miniaturized crossbow the likes of which she had never seen before. And it was pointed directly at her. "I don't want to disturb your voyeurism but we are running out of time." Although she could still see lines of fear etched on his face, he mostly seemed excited. His red bloodshot eyes danced gleefully as a thin grin spread across his face. "We clearly are not the only ones down here."

Crenthys's mind raced as she tried to find some way to escape. The distance between her and Jhaldus wasn't great. He couldn't get off more than one shot, but she didn't know what the weapon was capable of, or how good his aim might be. She thought of Kelios and what sort of trouble he might be in and decided she needed to act.

Before she could take a full step, the weapon fired and a tiny dart shot into her chest just above her left breast. The wound burned like fire.

She reflexively reached to pull out the dart but her hand was growing numb, fingers unable to close into a fist. Her legs also seemed to be failing, so she reached her other hand out to brace herself on the wall, but missed.

She saw Jhaldus lunging toward her as the room suddenly lurched to one side. The elf made to catch her and the two of them went down hard on the floor.

Her last coherent thoughts were of the two of them in a tangle on the floor, Jhaldus cradling her head and stroking her hair gently. "Hush now, *meleth*." He hissed in a soft voice. "Sleep now. I will arrange everything."

Blackness enveloped her.

Chapter 15

The Only Way Forward

The cold iron rungs of the ladder leading down the well were slick despite the texture of the rust on the surface. Kelios thought about how great a fool he seemed. If his brother saw him now, following a guileless half-goblin down a barren well, he would laugh himself silly. His brother was probably perched on the prow of a mighty warship bound for the Dragon Kingdoms of the South to bargain for continued peace while Kelios rotted in a hole.

"Ho bubby!" Anuka cried. "Uh, we got problems."

Kelios released one of the rungs and pivoted around to see what Anuka was going on about. The goblin stared up at him wide-eyed as if he had just seen a Kraken crest the water below. Kelios saw nothing.

"What is it?" Kelios asked and cringed a little as the sound of his voice echoed off of the stone walls and the water below.

Anuka pointed down to the water. "It's water, Bubby. Go back." The goblin started climbing up the ladder again but stopped when he noticed Kelios wasn't moving.

"Anuka, it is just water." He peered at the water again. The shifty little goblin was growing more agitated by the moment.

Undaunted, Anuka continued to crawl upward and managed to get between Kelios and the ladder.

Anuka is an imbecile. Relenting, Kelios released his grip on the ladder and leaned back, supporting himself with one hand on the opposite wall, and let the goblin pass. "What are you doing?" Kelios said as loudly as he dared.

Anuka skittered up the ladder like a spider, then looked back expectantly at Kelios.

What is wrong with this creature? Isn't he supposed to be some great pirate? Anuka's fear of water made no sense to Kelios. Kelios sighed when he realized he would have to be the one to investigate the water below. He fell backward off of the ladder and plunged smoothly into the pool.

The water was cool, mostly clean, and only about ten strides deep. Kelios looked quickly around to see what had spooked Anuka but saw nothing. The bottom of the well was piled with fist-sized stones covered in a layer of silt from which had grown some green vining plants that were swaying to the current of the freshly disturbed water. There was also a hewn stone doorway leading East.

He paused for a moment and considered his options. Anuka was unpredictable. Spooked as he was, the goblin was even more volatile. Kelios feared that Anuka had already crawled out of the well and was being beaten to death by a mob of drunken bar patrons. On the other hand, the doorway might be a means of escape for both of them. Cresting the surface of the water he saw Anuka most of the way up the ladder.

"Anuka," Kelios said in a coarse whisper.

The goblin looked down the shaft and Kelios motioned him down. Instead, the infuriating little creature started back up. He had only gone a few rungs before angry voices turned him back. He turned and descended quickly, but stopped about ten feet above the surface of the water.

"I found something down here, come on," Kelios said.

"Man, I don't care if you found a wagon full of boobies, I ain't gettin' in that water."

Why does he have to make everything so difficult? Kelios let out an exasperated sigh as he treaded in place. "Look, there is a doorway. Just there." He nodded towards the water with his head. "I am going to inspect it. It could be our way out."

"Or it could be the most awful way to die imaginable. Either way." Anuka quipped with a serious look on his face.

"Just don't wander off until I get back." Then, barely making a splash, Kelios plunged headlong into the water.

⸻ ◆ ⸻

Crenthys opened her eyes slowly as if waking from a dream. The room lurched oddly from side to side and she thought she might be sick. Hearing low voices nearby, her blood pumped in her ears as she struggled to sit up. Her body simply would not obey. Absolute terror gripped her and she began to panic. Her eyes parted languidly but she could move nothing else.

"Gently, Pazzix, you musn' damage her. She is perfec." The hungry tone in his words and strange manner of speech left no doubt the voice belonged to Jhaldus. She saw Jhaldus's hand stroking her hair, though she could not feel it. When she strained to cry out the words would not form. Even her tongue was paralyzed.

She heard more movement and realized that someone, obviously a very strong someone, was carrying her. Whoever it was growled a curse in a tongue she hadn't heard in years. High Draconic. The Red DragonMan. His name must be Pazzix.

Crenthys was sure her heart would fail if this nightmare got any worse.

As she was carried along, she noticed red scales on a massive three-toed foot. Her life was forfeit. Her only hope was that Kelios would find her. But as sincere as his intentions were, he would be little use against a Red DragonMan.

DragonMen. DragonKind. DracoSpawn. There were many names for them. Whatever you called them, these were the creation of a True Dragon. A creation that required an enormous amount of skill and effort. Each one carried a fragment of their master's power, including access to incredible magics. DragonMen were stronger, faster, and more cunning than most mortals. DragonSpawn were magically bound to their masters by shared blood and were loyal unto death. In the unlikely event that a True Dragon died, their creations usually followed soon after because of their blood bond.

It was a bad omen for Crenthys, and her mission, that Jhaldus had a Red DragonMan in his service. The Red Dragons were among the most ruthless and powerful of their kind.

It struck her as odd that she was still thinking of her mission. When they found out who she was, surely they'd kill her. Barring some miracle, her mission, and her life, had reached their end.

The DragonMan stopped walking and she heard Jhaldus open the doors. The Red, cradling Crenthys like a baby, carried her through the door. Jhaldus followed.

An odor hit them as they entered another room and Crenthys felt like coughing. Her eyes were dry and she closed them tightly. She moved her eyelids! A dam of elation broke over her. It was a small thing but confirmed she wasn't paralyzed permanently.

"Grik'chs!" Jhaldus said brusquely in the Elvish dialect he had used with the assassin. Using other languages was forbidden in the Dragon lands. Unless you were a Dragon. "This place reeks." He continued. "These little vermin aren' doing their jobs!"

Pazzix growled indifferently, then strode to a section of wall where he laid Crenthys on a bench. Taking in as much of her surroundings as she could, Crenthys saw cages built into the opposite wall. Her captors wandered off a few paces and were having a discussion she could not hear. Some of the cages contained something or someone inside. Outside of the room, just beyond the dark doors, she saw the broken body of the Elven assassin on the ground. *Dragonsbreath.*

She blinked again, though still with great effort. Still unable to turn her head, she rolled her eyes up as far as she could. Crenthys saw what looked like a man, only half as tall as most with a full-sized head, inside one of the cages. He was a Hob. At least that is what her people called them. Hobs were shorter than dwarves with heads too big for their bodies. She had only seen a dozen in her life. He was gaunt and dirty, with an unkempt beard that grew from a neat goatee.

The next cell held two humans who looked like brothers. They were in much better shape than the Hob but they stared fearfully at Jhaldus and Pazzix. One clutched the other's arm and they crept to the back of their cell.

The prison cells were lined up all the way down the hall beyond what Crenthys could see. She was still unable to roll her head, even to the side. In the last cell she could see, a strange creature melted out of the shadows. It walked like a man, but had the grace of a cat. Its clothing covered most of it but Crenthys imagined the short, coarse hair on its face, hands and feet covered its entire body. The hair on its chin and neck was mostly white and cleaner than everything else she'd seen here. The creature's face was a speckled weave of orange and amber colors. It was quite beautiful. Pale green feline eyes stared at her as it crept closer to the bars. She saw compassion on its feline face.

"It will be okay, sweet." It said in a soft but masculine voice. It spoke in perfect Low Draconic. She would have gasped, had she been able. Crenthys had heard of the cat people. Malkin or Felis, as the Dragons called them, but had never seen one. They came from a land outside of Dorwine and were not known to travel. This creature must have been captured, she reasoned. His stare lingered and deepened until Crenthys started to feel that the Malkin was more afraid for her than for himself.

"You're crazier than fifteen layers of Tor's Abyss if you think I'm gettin' in that water. Let alone under it." Anuka waggled a finger at Fish Boy. He drew his hand back when he noticed it was shaking. It was probably rage. That's why he was shaking. This pebble-brained Seaborne had a head full of sand.

"Anuka, it's ten strides at most."

"Well, since you stride underwater I'm not sure how far that is. And it doesn't matter. I'm not doin' it."

"You don't have to do anything," Kelios argued with a shrug as he floated in the water. "I can easily pull us both. Just hold your breath for a few seconds."

So there it was. The hard truth. Anuka was terrified of water. He knew it, and he guessed that Crenthys and Kelios knew it too, but he'd never had to face it like this. He'd always had a good excuse for not pulling oar when mooring a small vessel, or taking a turn on a scrape to clear the ship of barnacles or other trash. He didn't have a good excuse now. He would rather eat his new hat than stick a toe in that water. It will be fine, he told himself. Then he saw a flash of the image of his mother sinking away...

"Nope. Can't do it, Bubby." Anuka finally said. He turned to head back up the ladder and take his chances with the angry mob. That was when he saw the three men looking down the well at him.

It took a second for it to register why three men would be looking down a well. He leaned his head forward to rest on the rung he clung to and felt his stolen hat push back off his head. He sighed. "Sum buck," Anuka growled and slammed an open hand onto the hard metal ladder.

"Anuka!" Kelios yelled.

He looked up just in time to see a stone come careening down the shaft. Anuka ducked and the stone clanged noisily off of the ladder near him, splashing into the water below.

"You Sum Bucks!" Anuka cursed at the men. Then he looked down at Kelios and growled, "You'd better catch me!" Without warning, he let go of the ladder and fell.

The water was like ice and he sucked in a breath at just the wrong time. He gasped, sputtered, and flailed his arms wildly. He wasn't helping Kelios keep hold of him, but Anuka could only think of escaping the water.

"I have you! I have you! Stop hitting m-" An accidental backhand flopped into Kelios's face. Anuka was aware that Kelios had hoisted him out of the water so he could breathe. He stopped wind milling his arms and coughed once or twice to expel what little water he had taken on.

"It's ok," Kelios assured him, as another rock tumbled down the shaft. This one came close to striking them, splashing just three feet away. The men up top had taken to simply dropping stones instead of trying to toss them down. That was proving much more effective. "Why are you so hot? You are burning with fever."

"No." Anuka gasped, then burped. "It's-I'm ok. My skin does that when I get...angry. It's a goblin thing." He was going to say when I get scared but decided he was probably more angry than scared right now. Yeah, he was sure he was.

The look on Kelios's face was grim and Anuka didn't like it. "We are going to have to go through that door," Kelios said.

Anuka didn't need another rock crashing down to know he was right. This was the moment, Anuka told himself. Either he was fated to be a great sea captain aboard the *Flat Bottomed Girl* or he would die here and everything he'd been told growing up was a big floating whale turd. He sighed, suppressed a shiver, and decided that either way, he wanted to get it over with.

"Ok, but if you drown me, you Sum Buck, I'll haunt you to the bottom of the ocean!"

"Take three deep breaths," Kelios instructed.

Anuka did as instructed, then Kelios plunged them under the water and into darkness. Anuka's held breath escaped almost immediately.

Chapter 16

Shadows in the Dark

The cat-man flinched as Pazzix slammed his armored forearm against the bars. "Get back!" the big Red said with a hiss. Crenthys flinched inwardly when she heard the Draconic tongue. While it was a language she was familiar with, those memories would take her to an even darker place that Crenthys couldn't afford to venture right now. If she wanted to survive there was no time for self-pity. *Do I truly want to survive?* She should have died years ago. No. She wouldn't go down that path, either. Against all odds, she had survived and found purpose with Apostate. They still needed her. Dorwine still needed Apostate, regardless of what the Dragons thought. There just had to be another way for people to live, without Dragons. First, she had to survive this setback.

Jhaldus appeared and, bent down to look at her. "Have you been making friends?" He stroked her face with one hand and she was grateful she couldn't feel it. "Never mind tha' one. He will go to Zhazie soon." Jhaldus looked over his shoulder at Pazzix and said, "We musn' linger. Get what we came for and we mus' go."

Growling curses as he went, Pazzix stalked off. Jhaldus looked around the room anxiously. She didn't know how long she lay there but it felt like an eternity. Small tendrils of sensation were coming to the tips of her fingers and toes.

Pazzix returned carrying a long metal box that, even in his massive hands, seemed heavy. He set the box down on the ground near the bench where Crenthys lay and scooped her up. The big DragonMan laid her across his shoulder like a sack of grain and stooped to pick up the metal box with his free hand. She marveled at his strength.

Crenthys's view was mostly of Pazzix's backside as they bobbed along. They left the area where the captives were being held and entered a room that didn't smell any better. She heard the high-pitched cheering of creatures she recognized as Kobolds. They were sycophants of Dragons, claiming to share Draconic blood. But they didn't possess any of a Dragon's blood or powers. Pazzix gave them clipped instructions in the Dragon language. He didn't bother to mince words because he probably assumed Crenthys didn't understand what he was saying. The DragonMan told them to keep feeding the slaves and to be sure to feed the beasts.

She heard the Kobolds scurry off to do Pazzix's bidding. Jhaldus led them into a room with a thin ornate rug of red and gold that covered most of the floor. Once the door was shut behind them Crenthys noticed this room smelled much better than the previous two. Out of the corner of her eye, she saw dark wooden bookshelves. This room had the faint aroma of sweet-smelling smoke.

Crenthys was still unable to see much apart from the DragonMan's behind, but she heard Jhaldus open another door and the three of them stepped into a darkened hallway. They moved along the hallway with Pazzix grumbling and stumbling in the dark. Jhaldus admonished him to be quiet and follow. But the box the Red dragged behind him made that impossible.

As they stepped through yet another door at the end of the hallway, Crenthys thought she heard a commotion from the other side of the door they had just come through.

⸺ ◆ ⸺

Ember watched from inside his cell as the DragonMan, slaver, and paralyzed Half-Elf disappeared through the door opposite the prison.

He had read many books about the curious pale-skinned race of elves. He desperately wanted to follow the man and see if what he had read was true. These Dark Elves, the name seemed ironic because of their pale skin, chose to live underground. Ancient texts indicated those elves fled from the duties the creator god, Rathune, had given them, therefore they had been excluded from his blessings. So he had read.

Ember glanced at Offund in the adjacent cell. He had yelled some epithet at the departing party. If he continued to run his mouth, the little Hob would likely get himself killed. His race of beings were temperamental by nature, or so he had read.

Ember unconsciously stroked the fur on his left forearm with his right hand and scolded himself when he noticed. This place was filthy and its proprietors were likely on the run. He needed to escape so he set his mind on doing so.

He heard the two human males chattering in the cage down the row once the slaver was gone. They were siblings, Ember decided. They behaved like siblings. Ember would know. He had nine brothers and four sisters.

Ember spent the first day of his captivity believing that those humans were going to be rescued and was counting on the same happening to him. That had not yet happened. For the past four days, the humans had said much and done little, apart from having conversations with the other captives.

There was an elven lady, and perhaps a few more humans, besides Offund and himself. Offund had been here the longest and it seemed unlikely he'd be released soon. Ember wasn't sure what being taken from this place involved, but he doubted that anyone was being freed. People were likely ransomed or sold as slaves. The humans seemed to be sailors of some stripe and claimed to be quite wealthy. The elven lady was a mystery but she spoke like a person of education, or of wealth, perhaps. Offund was complicated but, unless Ember had missed his guess, the little Hob had some sort of magical talent. He was not a Dragon and that was the problem. Non-Dragons, even those with DragonsBlood in their veins, were forbidden from using magic. Using magic without being a Dragon, or without the aid of DragonsBlood, was a challenge to the Dragons who claimed that to do so was impossible. Dragons were possessed of incredible hubris and did not share their power lightly. Such a revelation would also be devastating to an economic system centered around the magical properties of DragonsBlood.

Ember had a similar problem. He didn't think Jhaldus knew exactly what Ember was, or what he could do. Malkin were so rare Jhaldus may have captured him just to sell him as an oddity. If Jhaldus knew of the myriad of magical glyphs that were hidden under Ember's fur, the elf likely would have a different clientele in mind. Probably a Dragon.

He shuddered at the thought and noticed that he was stroking his fur again. He forced himself to stop. A Dragon of any color would quickly execute someone practicing magic outside of their control. Or so he had read.

⚬

Anuka fought his rising terror as Kelios dragged him by his collar through the murky water. His lungs screamed for air. It took all his will to keep his lips pressed together. The trip seemed to take forever though Anuka knew it had been only moments. He could not dismiss the plaguing images of his drowning mother from his mind.

He opened his eyes and strained to see. He made out a rough stone ceiling covered with moss and lichen. Behind them, he saw a faint, rapidly disappearing light.

Finally, Anuka felt they were ascending. At last, Kelios broke through the water and heaved them up onto a mud-covered stone bank. Anuka gasped and greedily filled his lungs with air. He rolled to one side and noticed his hands were shaking. They were glowing red, little tendrils of smoke wafting from them. Making fists, he closed his eyes tight and tried to focus on breathing steadily. Kelios scurried back to the water and plunged a hand in. Anuka looked up to see what Kelios was about.

"You burned me," the Seaborne said.

"Sorry," Anuka replied.

Anuka was content to lie there awhile longer but Kelios withdrew his hand and moved to inspect the nearby tunnel. It was no more than a couple of seconds before Kelios was yelling back to him. "Anuka, I found a door."

Anuka sighed, pushed himself up into a sitting position, spat into the water, and slowly stood up. "What is it now Fish Man?"

"I don't know why you insist on calling me all these different names. I have a name. Where I come from I am essentially a prince." Kelios gave him a slightly peeved look as Anuka waddled over to him. "You are welcome, by the way."

Anuka sighed again and looked up at Kelios. He must have burned him worse than he thought. "Yes, thank you. We did not drown and we didn't get our heads smashed with a rock. Thank you very much, bubby. Happy?"

"You are impossible to get along with sometimes." Kelios looked disappointed.

"Look, I'm sorry. Can we just crack open this door and see what's on the other side? Maybe we'll get lucky and whatever's on the other side will kill us both."

Kelios sighed but turned to the door, knelt, and looked at the complicated lock. "This is different than other locks I have seen." He rubbed a finger over the keyhole and looked at Anuka.

He came over to inspect the lock beside the Seaborne.

"Well, this wasn't made for a door," Anuka said as he moved Kelios's hand out of the way and looked into the keyhole from an angle. "I need more light."

Kelios got up and walked over to a sconce on the wall and withdrew a decrepit torch from it. "Do you know how to light this?"

"I guess you don't have a lot of torches underwater, eh?" Anuka sighed and took the torch from Kelios. Despite being a little wet, it was mostly intact. Anuka raked out the cobwebs and broke off the burnt tips of the torch. He dug into the small pouch on his shoulder bag and produced two small stones. Holding the torch between his legs he began to strike the stones until a small spark lit the torch. Then he blew gently on the torch until it came to life. Satisfied, Anuka handed the torch back to Kelios. Anuka smiled at Kelios who simply shrugged.

"First of all, never look straight into a lock hole," Anuka said. "You never know if it has a needle trap or something else really nasty in there."

Kelios brought the light near the door, then turned to the side a little, heeding Anuka's advice.

Anuka pulled a soaking-wet folded cloth from his pouch. It was a dinner cloth from the Inn where the Silver was staying. He unfurled it in his hand, revealing a small knife, an eating utensil, and two pieces of wire. Anuka grinned as he looked up at Kelios who seemed a little taken aback. Anuka took one piece of the wire and wrapped it around the utensil. Then he bent one end of the wire and rotated it back and forth in the lock until they heard a metallic click and a dent blistered up on the backside of the utensil. Kelios and Anuka both jumped in surprise. Anuka chuckled and moved the utensil aside to reveal a once sharp needle angled crookedly in the keyhole.

"See, I told you," Anuka said with a smile.

Kelios just stared, his mouth agape.

Anuka motioned for Kelios to raise the torch and the Seaborne complied. He nodded thoughtfully and picked up the slender knife. Then Anuka wedged the knife into the keyhole beside the needle as far as it would go. A few seconds later they heard another metallic clank. Anuka looked at Kelios.

"Reloader," Anuka said as he ran his tiny fingers over the surface of the door.

"What are you doing?" Kelios asked.

"That isn't the lock to the door," Anuka said. "Step back." Kelios did so and Anuka pushed on a spot on the door. The smooth metal of the door sank in about as deep as Anuka's first knuckle and he heard another metallic sound. With his other hand, Anuka pushed the door open, then looked back at Kelios and offered one of his mischievous smiles.

Kelios just shook his head and, with a grin of his own, stepped through the doorway.

Anuka followed Kelios into the room, squinting against the light of the torch the Seaborne still carried. Anuka could see better without it but he still wasn't sure how well Kelios could see in the dark. He shielded his eyes from the torchlight and looked around. A box that looked like a pig trough was filled with dirty, crooked sticks about as long as Anuka was tall, each with a sharp point on one end. In a disheveled pile on the opposite side of the room lay a dozen or more pairs of small leather boots. That explained the putrid smell Anuka had noticed when they entered this place. In one corner of the stone-walled room, several round wooden shields were stacked haphazardly.

"Burning sands." Anuka cursed, "A Kobold armory."

Kelios looked at him doubtfully. "Not goblins?"

Anuka stooped and picked up a thin husk about the size of Anuka's thumb and showed it to Kelios. "Nope. Kobold scale."

Anuka's stomach clenched as he looked over the small piece of scale. "Sum buck." Where there were Kobolds, there were Dragons. Or DragonMen. Kobolds worshiped Dragons and their Spawn like gods. Technically, Dragons *were* gods. At least that's what they claimed. But Kobolds groveled and slobbered all over the Dragons, killing each other just for the chance to please one. It was pretty pathetic. No respectable goblin would do such a thing.

Anuka thought back to the big red DragonMan he had incited in the tavern and prayed to every god he could think of that he wouldn't see that one again. His plan to anger the big buffoon had worked out pretty well until he turned into a DragonMan. Anuka's hand went reflexively to his coin-filled pouch. He hadn't figured on the big idiot being a Red but stuff happens. Hopefully, that moron was still up top chucking rocks down the well with the other idiots.

He tossed the scale aside and, looking up, saw Kelios carefully opening the next door.

Light spilled in around the crack as Kelios poked his head through. The Seaborne opened the door and stepped through, into a large room.

The stench of sweat and filth worsened with the open door and Anuka hustled to follow Kelios. The room they stepped into was huge. Another shabby wood door was positioned directly across from the one they had just entered. Anuka looked to his right and saw a less shabby door on the center of a wall about fifteen strides away. The ceilings in this room were taller and were hewn from a smoother stone than the previous areas. The stonework looked newer. Anuka also noticed an animal smell that he couldn't place.

Kelios turned to Anuka and had opened his mouth to speak when the door to their right opened and a tiny, orange-skinned Kobold entered carrying a dented metal bucket. Each of them froze. Kelios stood, mouth agape, only a moment before he exploded into a sprint toward the Kobold.

The bucket clanged to the floor and the little creature darted back through the door before Kelios could reach him. Anuka set out to follow but was stopped by a loud bang behind him. He looked back to see the remaining door flung wide open. A nasty little Kobold stood holding a whip with a short, wooden, handle. The Kobold grinned deviously at Anuka.

Chapter 17

DragonMen and Their Pets

C renthys heard water lapping in the distance well before they got to the shore. The smells of brine and dirty sand were as strong as the DragonMan. He labored through the dry sand, still carrying her over his shoulder, and dragging the heavy box beside him. Their combined weight was taxing him. Sensation was slowly returning to Crenthys's body and she could now feel him squeezing her waist to keep her in place. She could turn her head a little now, side to side, but she didn't want her captors to know that. Based on what she could see she estimated they were several hundred paces south of the docks. The lights on the pier illuminated a few figures scurrying about the docks but her group would be invisible to most in the fading dusk.

The big DragonMan stopped and set the box down while Jhaldus went ahead. The pale-skinned elf chatted softly with someone Crenthys couldn't see. When that conversation was over, Pazzix resumed his trek through the sand. Crenthys caught a glimpse of someone new but couldn't make out much in the dark.

Pazzix splashed into the seawater and laid Crenthys roughly in a narrow skiff. She took satisfaction in his huffing after he set the metal box inside the boat, also. Jhaldus stepped into the boat, holding his hems up to keep the folds of his robe out of the water. He took a seat near the rear of the boat where Crenthys lay. Once rested, Pazzix and another man gave the little boat a shove, then heaved themselves aboard as yet another man started rowing. The other men were humans, or at least near to it, Crenthys surmised from her brief glimpses of them. They briskly set to work, speaking only in terse bursts. Crenthys sensed they were uneasy.

Once underway, Jhaldus turned his attention to Crenthys where she lay at his feet. Stooping down, he took her face in his hands and inspected her. "I suspec' you are gaining some feeling back by now. Don' worry. It will be hours before you are strong enough to move much." His smile told her he understood the poison far better than she did and he would not be fooled by an escape attempt.

She tried to fix him with a look of defiance but barely managed a frown.

That made his smile even wider. Before long, the night air grew cooler and Crenthys felt the cold seeping into her bones. Jhaldus must have noticed the quiver of her lip. He dug a pair of blankets from a dented trunk on the tiny boat. He put one blanket under her head. The other he draped over her. She was grateful for the warmth. The pale elf took extra pains to tuck the blanket under her body as the wind from the sea fought to carry the blanket away.

⸺◆⸺

Kelios almost had the little Kobold in hand when he heard a snarl from behind him, followed by Anuka yelling, "Hey, Fish man!" The Kobold escaped Kelios's grasp and the door banged closed behind the creature. Kelios spun and saw a trio of repugnant-looking creatures stalking out of the door across the room. The beasts resembled what surface dwellers called dogs but their backs were covered with mottled patches of scales. Each foot terminated in three wicked claws. Their lips parted, revealing foul, blackened teeth with sharp points. Long strings of drool oozed from their mouths and dangled near the floor.

Their eyes were as black as the ocean floor and reflected the room's flickering torchlight like pools of inky water.

Another Kobold, holding a wicked riding crop, stood behind them goading the beasts on.

Kelios had been taught to speak with animals and befriend them. But these animals didn't seem like natural creatures. Their minds were closed to him. These pitiful beasts looked like they had been tortured relentlessly by something evil. Kelios could almost taste the violence brewing in the air. He spared a glance at Anuka who stood a pace or two in front of him, the small knife tucked in his belt. Kelios stepped forward and pulled Anuka behind him.

"Them ain't no puppy dogs," Anuka said. Kelios didn't look back at him. The bestial dogs stood three abreast and were slowly advancing on Kelios and Anuka. Violence never brought about the best result, but he knew sometimes it was necessary.

"Whatever happens, stay behind me," Kelios said over his shoulder resolutely. Then he turned and stepped toward the dogs. Perhaps they could sense his decision because all three bared their teeth and issued low growls. Chest heaving, Kelios snarled and released a ferocious roar that shook the room.

The familiar feeling seized Kelios as he felt the change come over him. It was both ecstasy and agony. Kelios pushed down his fear of becoming the bear. His mind blossomed with a myriad of sensations and his body erupted with power.

Kelios felt himself falling forward and landing gently on paws instead of hands. The aftershock of the change washed over him but he pried his eyes open and looked at the three beasts through blood-red lenses of anger. The dogs seemed less confident than they had been only moments before.

Kelios could barely make out the stream of curses Anuka released from somewhere behind him and he ignored the shrieks of terror coming from the Kobold. His focus was now on three masses of scale, teeth, and claw.

With another primal roar, Kelios lunged forward and swatted the middle dog on the maw with a savage claw capable of decapitating a man. The dog yelped as it somersaulted backward over the beast to its right. It landed in a roll, shook its head a moment, slowly stood on wobbly legs, and staggered back to the fight.

———◦◦◦———

Sum buck, Anuka thought. *We're in it now.* "What in the nine shades of blazing torment happened to Fish man?" the little goblin cried. "Bear ate him. Sum buck." This was more than he could stand. Anuka had seen Dragons show off their magic to impress their underlings but this was his buddy, Fish Man. He never even learned how to say his name. His mind raced as he tried to decide what to do about the bear once it finished killing the dogs. Or the other way around, if that's how things worked out.

Anuka caught a flash of movement from behind him and spun in time to see the previously escaped Kobold leveling a bow at the bear, er Fish Man. Quick as a minnow, Anuka loosed his dagger at the Kobold's eye. The hilt smashed right into its nose. The little orange creature shrieked and dropped his bow, arrow careening harmlessly off a wall.

"Sum buck. Junk knife." Anuka swore, charging the Kobold.

The moment the Kobold recovered, Anuka rammed his shoulder into the thing's chest and rode him to the ground. They landed in a pile, flipping and twisting until Anuka ended up on top. He gave the Kobold a quick little punch to the face, mostly hitting its scaly snout, then rolled off to one side. Anuka sprang to his feet, looking for his knife. The Kobold scrambled away on his belly and Anuka saw his knife lying a few strides beyond the little creature's grasp.

Anuka leaped at the Kobold and drove his knee into its back, pinning it to the ground as it reached for his knife. The Kobold squealed as Anuka climbed over it and scooped up his blade. As he turned to make some holes in the Kobold, he was pelted by shards from an arrow that splintered on the ground in front of him. He jerked his head up and saw the other Kobold fumbling for another arrow. The bear had a pair of crooked little arrows sticking up from its haunches. Oblivious, it still fought against those vile dogs.

The Kobold nearest him tried to scramble away again. Anuka leaped on the creature and dropped a pair of heavy punches to the back of its head, his fist still holding the knife, and the scaly little creature lay still. Anuka slipped the knife away and sprinted for the abandoned bow just as another arrow skittered harmlessly by.

The bow must have been made from the most crooked stick on Dorwine, and the string was frayed and worn. *I've used worse,* he thought, though he couldn't think of when.

He scooped up one of the arrows spilling out of the unconscious Kobold's tiny quiver. Laying the arrow to the bow, Anuka drew the string back as hard as he dared and began scanning for his target.

The other Kobold must have realized what Anuka was about because he had taken shelter somewhere. Shooting around the bear and the two remaining dogs was going to be chore enough. If he had to keep an eye out for potshots, Anuka was likely to take an arrow the next time he poked his head up too high.

The bear had ripped the neck out of one of the dogs. It laid motionless in a pool of its own dark blood. Bear-Man, as Anuka was going to have to start calling Fish man, was also bleeding from a handful of wounds. The savage dogs were trying to flank him but the bear kept them in front of him.

Finally, one of the dogs came for the bear's side, teeth bared, and Anuka loosed his arrow. The pathetic little shaft whizzed harmlessly over the head of the dog, not even causing it to flinch. "Burning sun!" he cursed. You couldn't hit water from a boat with this thing. Seeing no other options, Anuka scooped up another arrow and started scanning for the other Kobold. Little chump was probably halfway to Marashaulithia by now. Another clear shot at a dog came up, so he took it. This time his arrow was true and the crooked shaft buried itself in the beast's flank. The dog flopped with a yelp and bit at the arrow. Bear-Man looked back at him with a look of gratitude on his face. That didn't make sense because, as far as Anuka knew, bears really couldn't be grateful. He would worry about that later. Just as Anuka looked around again for the Kobold, something struck him in the head and took him off his feet.

Blood pounded in Anuka's ears to the rhythm of his racing heart. He lifted his finger to feel his head. With a hiss, he quickly pulled them back. A glance at his fingers showed they were wet with blood. "Sum buck." He said. Fear and shock made his voice dry and strained. The wound stung like a hot poker up the nose but the cut didn't feel deep. Then terror gripped him as he had a horrible thought.

Flipping nimbly to his feet, he frantically looked around, hardly caring that another arrow might be headed his way. There it was, crumpled up against the wall near the door. He scurried over and gingerly scooped up his ruined hat with both hands. The arrow had torn a small hole in the front and messily ripped a gaping gash through to the back.

Anuka felt his face getting hotter. He couldn't see it but figured there was a red glow drifting off his skin like crimson mist. He slapped the once-fine hat back on his head, heedless of the pain, and turned toward the bloody fight. He spotted the little Kobold fumbling to put an arrow to his bow.

"You trouser stain!" Anuka screamed as he stalked toward the Kobold. "I stole that hat. From a slavin' pirate scum bag!" Wisps of smoke rolled out of his collar. He broke into a run as he yelled at the little Dragonoid. "You're one dead Sum Buck!"

Kelios felt like a hostage inside his own body. Only it wasn't his body. The first time the bear had come timidly. Like entering the home of a new acquaintance for the first time. This time, there was no trace of hesitation. The bear had made itself at home. Raw elation filled him, even as he fought for his life. In the first fight, his prey hadn't put up much resistance. Now he was swiping and biting and jumping at every turn just to keep these monstrosities from ripping him apart. And he loved it.

The thrill coursing through him was incredible but he was tiring. Moving such a large body took a lot of energy and he was leaking blood from a dozen bites or scratches. Master Kemthiss had taught Kelios that a host would survive if the guest body was slain. That was in regard to becoming a dolphin or a squid. Master Kemthiss had never seen a bear and Kelios didn't know if those lessons held true in this case. Another yelp from his left told him that the swat he had given the dog hadn't hurt it too badly. These beasts were smart. Smarter, Kelios supposed, than their mundane counterparts. They used the tactics of trained warriors and fought well together. At this rate, they would kill his guest, and likely he and Anuka would follow soon after. Anuka. Where was the little goblin? He prayed he wouldn't eat Anuka if the bear survived.

As if prompted, he could hear his friend cursing and yelling but couldn't spare a glance to check on him. He didn't need to. Anuka streaked past him, screaming at the Kobold who had released these hounds. Anuka was glowing red, a trail of steam following him as he leaped in the air and arced a dagger down on the Kobold.

Pain seared him and he roared. The moment of distraction had allowed one of the hounds to attack him from behind.

He felt the panic of the bear in his mind. It knew it was dying. Kelios remembered another of Master Kemthiss's lessons about who had control when a guest was visiting. If he continued to let the bear drive this fight they would both die. Kelios, like all servants of the Triton, was trained to fight with many weapons, and with none.

Kelios stood on his back legs like a man, his head nearly touching the high ceiling, and slid one clawed foot forward. Pivot foot. Then he smoothly slid the other in a short arc behind him with only the padding of his clawed foot on the smooth stone floor. Power foot, he thought.

The dogs stopped and stared in confusion. The one on his left had only one eye, the other socket a bloody mess. The beasts looked at one another. They stood two strides away, half the width of the room apart. As one they took a quick step each and launched themselves at Kelios. He pivoted to his right, out of the path of the dog on that side, and jumped to meet the other animal in midair. The mass of the bear was five times the dog and Kelios drove the creature onto the stone floor with all of his weight, crushing its ribs and spine like twigs. Aware of the other dog, Kelios sprang up as quickly as he could, just in time to see the remaining dog reverse its course and charge him.

Kelios timed his move as well as he could. The bear's body was new to him, but the bear was here, too. Inside his mind. As soon as the beast committed to his jump Kelios took a powerful step forward and drove all of his strength into an uppercut that slammed the airborne creature up, crushing it into the ceiling, then let it fall to the floor in a heap.

Bears weren't meant to punch, he realized belatedly and landed back on all fours with a sharp pain shooting up his forearm. Bones were broken, but he was alive.

"Sum. Buck." Anuka said. Kelios turned to see the goblin staring, mouth agape. He shook his head as he started wiping blood from his hands and knife blade. "Papa ain't gonna believe this. No way."

Kelios sniffed and whipped his head to and fro spraying the floor and wall with droplets of blood as he searched for more foes. The bear inside him, so full of rage and battle lust only moments before, now began to retreat from his mind. The battle was won and there were wounds to tend to. Kelios released his sagging grip on the bear and felt it slide down a long tunnel into the deep recesses of his mind. He gasped as the physical form of the creature shrank away, fading into his own slender body.

His arms shook with exhaustion as he collapsed to the stone floor, kneeling on all fours, heedless of the slick blood pooled around him. He barked a short laugh at the ludicrously macabre scene on the ceiling where he smashed the beast. Little crimson drops fell like gentle rain onto the stone. I did this, he thought. I wrought this violence. The thought was at once sickening and exhilarating.

All of his life he had practiced restraint in everything he did and said. He was Dulian, a royal servant, expected to be the quintessential example for his people. Every step of his life, every movement he made, was controlled by his parents and tutors, lest he falter in his service. When sharing the form of beasts of the Sea there had always been restraint and control. Taking the form of a beast was seldom done, only in dire need, and with great consideration. Tonight he had blown all of that out of the water.

Twice Kelios had given the reins of his consciousness to a savage beast and allowed it to run amok. In his heart, he felt shame. That he had betrayed his way of life, his family, and his people. From leagues away, he could feel the disappointed stare of his mother's huge, dark eyes. A glare, with the hint of a sneer, from his brother. Finally, his father would look at him and simply walk away.

Tonight, Kelios had chosen to forge his own path and defend his friend, his own way. He felt pride in doing so and was ready to accept the consequences. Kelios smiled despite his pain. He was his own man. And he was exhausted.

"Hey, bubby," Anuka called. "You're nasty, you know that?"

Wearily, Kelios propped his head up on one arm and looked at Anuka, who was also a bloody mess, but his red skin and clothes made it hard to tell. Anuka was right. He felt blood drying on his face, and his fingers felt sticky because of it.

"Why don't you go back and wash some of that off before we move on?" Anuka suggested more than asked.

Kelios nodded and slowly worked his way to standing on wobbly legs. "Will you be alright for a minute?"

As if to answer, Anuka bent over and slid a thin rapier from the slain Kobold's hanger and held it in front of his face.

"Ok, then." Kelios picked his way through the carnage of the room and went back to take a swim.

Chapter 18

The Burden of Compassion

He had enjoyed the cool if a bit murky, water for far too long. But he was clean and refreshed. Water always made Kelios feel like a new creature. When he stepped back into the room he discovered that Anuka had been busy.

The door to the kennel was open and the little goblin was rooting around in there. He tossed some clothing out into the room. When he emerged, he carried a wooden box. He kicked the clothes out of his way and sat the box down.

Anuka had laid the handful of tools he found in a neat row beside a small pile of ornate jewelry. There was an assortment of food that appeared suitable to eat. Kelios was impressed. This little goblin was a fount of surprises. Kelios cautiously upgraded his opinion of his companion.

"What is all this?" Kelios asked, gesturing broadly.

Anuka shrugged. "I don't know. Lookin' for treasure. Found a bunch of junk."

Anuka wasn't wrong. Most of this stuff, save the food, was useless to them. Kelios gestured questioningly toward the food and Anuka shrugged again.

"Go for it, if you're brave enough to eat Kobold grub," Anuka said, grinning.

Kelios sat down, folded his legs under him, and began to inspect the food.

"I reckon that for a fella that can turn into a bear..." Anuka paused to gauge Kelios's reaction, "eating Kobold food is no big adventure."

Kelios sighed and gestured for Anuka to sit. "Come, eat some of this awful food, and ask your questions."

Eying Kelios warily, Anuka sat across the neat little pile of food from the Triton and considered his words.

"So. You some kind of devil or something?"

Kelios chuckled, shaking his head. "No, friend. I'm no devil. I am Seaborne, as you say. I suppose I am also Fish Man. But my people are known as Tritons, which means guardian in the common Draconic. My people are servants of Rathune, an old god lost to history."

"Rathune? Tritons. Man, I have no clue what you're talking about! One minute you're Fish Man, the next you're Bear Man. What am I supposed to think?"

Kelios considered the strange goblin. "The ocean is filled with a multitude of horrible things. They claw out of the muck or even slip into our world from another. Long ago, after the First Judgment, my people swore allegiance to the Judge of this world, who your people once called Rathune, to guard his seas and to answer when he beckons. This oath is to last for all of time."

Anuka opened his mouth but Kelios stayed him with an upraised hand.

"For our service, some of my people were given a taste of Rathune's essence. Some of his power. We have been faithful guardians of this power for centuries. Some of those chosen for service are given the gift of Becoming. We can link with a creature and assume its form, for a time. That is what I am."

Anuka poked out his lower lip and raised one eyebrow thoughtfully. "So, you come from a group of people who live in the ocean and can turn into bears? Makes perfect sense!" Anuka declared tossing his hands in the air.

Kelios sighed and bowed his head. *Just when I was ready to place faith in him.* When he looked up, Anuka was grinning stupidly, a piece of dried meat trapped between his near-perfect teeth. Kelios just shook his head. Anuka understood more than he let on. Always.

They ate in companionable silence for a while, Kelios tearing into the food with enthusiasm until noise outside the room got their attention. Anuka had shut the door while Kelios was swimming so the sound was somewhat muffled. The two stood and gingerly crept toward the door the first Kobold had gone through.

"You got another bear in there?" Anuka asked, gesturing at Kelios's chest with his head.

Kelios shook his head. As tired as he was, Kelios was amazed he could still walk. To change again so soon might fracture his body or even his mind beyond return.

"Ok, then. The old-fashioned way." Anuka slid his knife from his belt and gestured at the door handle.

Kelios slowly turned the metal handle and the door opened with a faint creak. He flinched at the sound but Anuka moved silently through the door as soon as it was open wide enough. *More guts than brains,* Kelios thought, and then promptly followed the goblin.

⚬

Ember's nose twitched when the door leading out of the prisoner's chamber opened once more. Was it the slaver returning? Had Jhaldus come back to remove any witnesses? Mostly, Ember hoped it was the nasty little Kobolds bringing the day's meal.

Instead, a most curious creature poked his head, and his knife, into the room. Sparkling little eyes swept the room. It was a goblin. Or at least part goblin. The height and shape were correct; Goblin's heads were way too large for their bodies. But the color of this one was wrong; this creature was red! *Fascinating*, Ember thought. Not only red but distinctly so. He may even be glowing. *So curious.*

The tiny goblinoid crept into the room and twitched at the sight of the captives. No doubt he saw the humans first, or perhaps the elven lady. Ember wondered if she really was a lady. His Elvish was poor but he had gathered that some of the things she had said were quite lewd. Ember's eyes widened when the next figure stepped into the dim torchlight of their cell. A Triton...Or would they be called Seaborne in this region? And a Regal, judging by how he carried himself. *Surely they are here to save us all!* His heart thumped in his chest at the possibility. They must be warned about Jhaldus and his group.

The Seaborne man recognized the peril of the prisoners immediately and went quickly to their aid. The goblin had some skill in skullduggery and began working to open the locks. He easily had each unlocked in short order.

It seemed their rescuers had killed or driven off the little Kobolds that brought them food. That would explain the lack of keys for the doors. The Goblin freed Offund and the blue-skinned Triton saw to the little man. The small lock picker stepped up to Ember's cell and peered at him through the bars.

"What are you supposed to be?" the little red creature asked, his hands on his hips.

"I am Ember. My kind are called Malkin. Or Cat Man, if you prefer. Or occasionally Felinominis, by the more educated. Mostly I am called a host of names unfit to repeat, by those less educated." The wide-eyed stare from the little goblin spurred Ember to continue. "I am a traveler and a scholar. And you, unless I miss my guess, are Filgenium."

"I'm a what?" the goblin asked incredulously.

"One of your parents was not a Goblin but resides primarily on a world of fire. Filgenium have red skin like yours, possess otherworldly beauty, and use a strange type of magic."

Anger, confusion, and shock wrestled across the goblin's face. Then Ember grinned and said, "You, my new friend, are Son of Djinn."

"Anuka!" Kelios was yelling at him. "Put that away." Fish Man left the little hairy Nob he'd been talking to and stalked over to him.

"What are you doing? You are supposed to be freeing the prisoners."

"Sum Buck called my mama something...weird." *Little worm*. Some lines you don't cross. Speaking ill of a man's mother tops that list.

Kelios stared at Cat Thing. *He would see the right of it. Sum Buck.*

"Greetings. I am called Kelios." He tried to push Anuka aside and extended a hand through the bars.

Being in the middle of a good mad, he wouldn't be shoved aside so easily. Anuka did his best to stand his ground.

"Greetings, Kelios. I am Ember." The Malkin placed the opened palm of his right hand on his left breast and bowed a shallow bow from the waist.

The Seaborne's eyebrows shot up, but he regained his composure and returned the strange bow.

"What are you two up to? Look Bear -er- Fish Man, you can't trust this guy. He might know how to dance but he's a spy. I'm sure of it."

Kelios aimed a confused look at Anuka. "A spy? For whom?"

Anuka didn't know who, so he made something up. "Some Dragon, I'd guess. Let's leave him here. We've done plenty of rescuing for today. He'll just slow us down."

Kelios stared at Anuka as if the goblin had just sprouted eyestalks. "What is wrong with you? Get him out of there."

Fine, Anuka thought. *He'll be easier to kill outside of the cage.* Grumbling under his breath all the while, Anuka got the metal tool he had scavenged from the Kobold's things and used it to work the lock.

"I did not mean to offend you, friend." The mangy cat said.

Anuka was wishing they hadn't killed all of those dogs. That would teach this mouthy kitty cat who was boss. He fumbled the tool and it clanged to the floor. He fixed an accusatory look on Cat Man. *It was unnatural for a cat to speak,* Anuka thought.

"I meant no insult to your mother, I assure you. It is fascinating to meet you. Your mother-" Ember paused when Anuka jerked up and fixed a dangerous look on him. "Your mother was an amazing person, I imagine. Her kind are known as the most elegant and regal of all aliens to this world."

Anuka didn't understand any of that, but it didn't sound half bad. The truth was, Anuka knew very little of his mother. It wasn't weird to him that his mother and her handmaidens were red-skinned, twice as tall as his dad, and shot fire out of their hands. He had assumed everyone's mother could do that. As an adult, he started to understand that his childhood was a little peculiar. Once or twice Anuka had tried to ask his Papa some questions, but all he would say was, "Son, your mama was Queen of Fire and my heart." Or "Your mama was hot!" Nothing of substance, really, but true nonetheless.

The idea that this overgrown kitten knew something about his mother that Anuka didn't frustrated him. Maybe he'd let him live for a while. Perhaps he could even learn some things that might help piece his memories together.

The lock shifted with a muted clank and Anuka pulled the door open. He stood staring at Ember for a long moment before making a decision. "Ok. You get to live."

⚬

Kelios watched the prisoners pick through the clothes and food Anuka had scavenged. They were in a far corner of the room, separate from the others. Anuka motioned him to come closer, so he squatted down on his haunches and met Anuka's eye.

"How we gonna get them out of here? I can't hide em' under my shirt, bubby." Anuka asked, miming stuffing things under his shirt, as though Kelios needed a visual.

Kelios saw the problem pretty clearly. The human men were sailors and would be easily recognized. The others were as odd a sight as he and Anuka.

"I don't know. But we can't leave them here. That is the end of the discussion." Kelios said sternly.

Anuka held up his hands defensively. "I didn't say to leave them here. Just that we can't take them with us."

Kelios sighed and gave Anuka a sidelong look. "That's the same thing."

"What is the big Silver gonna say if we show up with a bunch of refugees?" Anuka asked. "Some of them are slaves, as in other people's property."

Anuka was correct but abandoning these people was not right. "We will take them to Celebris and let him decide." Kelios hoped he sounded more convincing than he felt.

The goblin sighed and tossed up his hands. "Fine. Whatever. If we don't get killed by angry drunks, and the guards don't stop us, we'll see what the mighty Silver dragon wants to do."

"The Silver has a reputation for fairness that resonates even to the bottom of the ocean. Celebris will know what to do." Kelios said.

"You show me the world's least stinky turd and I still won't pick it up. You can't trust any of the Dragons. They are all the same, no matter what color their scales are. I've seen them. My Papa dealt with them. They're concerned about one thing only: Dragons."

"What other choice do we have?" Kelios said, realizing that he had raised his voice more than he had intended. Primal rage still simmered under the surface of his emotions. He and Anuka glanced at the prisoners. Kelios saw fear and uncertainty on their faces. Turning back to Anuka, Kelios said in a quieter, more controlled voice. "What other options do these people have? I know you like to live freely and do what you want when you want and that's fine. But we are responsible for these people, like it or not. You are going to have to learn to trust the authorities for once."

Anuka stared up at Kelios, his eyes rimmed in fire. "Fine. But don't come crying to me if the noble DragonMan decides to sell them--and us--to Bog!"

"We're going to find a ship," said one of the human brothers, "We have means."

"And we have obligations." The other human said. The two exchanged a look that communicated a great deal.

"Thank you." Said the younger of the two men.

"Yes. Thank you," agreed the other man.

"Ok, great. If we don't get killed in the first five minutes, we'll drop you off wherever you like!" Anuka said, storming off. He headed toward the door beyond the cells.

Kelios gathered the prisoners, a half dozen total, and followed Anuka. Beyond the doors was an earthen hallway. At the end of the corridor, the Malkin pointed out a trap door overhead that led up into the tavern. Kelios caught Crenthys's scent and understood why as they climbed up into the room where Crenthys had met Jhaldus. Ember had helped Kelios figure out that the slaver aboard The *Brinery* and the DragonsBlood dealer Crenthys met with were the same person. Kelios was grateful that he hadn't smelled blood nor was there any other indication that she had been harmed. Still, he worried for her and didn't understand where she could have gone. *Celebris would have answers*, he thought.

Sensation was returning to Crenthys's legs and arms. Jhaldus saw her flexing her hands and had the DragonMan bind her wrists. She almost wished the feeling hadn't started to return yet. The biting wind had caused her shivers to return and everything she could feel ached and cramped from the tight quarters of the boat. Nearly an hour had passed since they'd left Usban and, judging by the preparations the small crew now made, she guessed that they were near their destination.

Overhead she saw craggy cliffs silhouetted against the pale moon as they passed on her left side. They were still traveling south along the coast as far as she could tell. Knowing which way they were going wouldn't help her much, but it gave her something to think about.

The stars winked out one by one and the jarring of the boat smoothed to a gentle glide. Sound changed too. The churning of the waves faded and was replaced by the sounds of the oars cutting the water and distant splashes that echoed in the darkness. One of the two men rowing fished a torch out from somewhere and handed it to Pazzix. The DragonMan spit fire on it and lit it with practiced ease. When it flared to life he passed it back and the man placed it in a sconce at the prow of the boat. Once her eyes adjusted to the new light she saw a rough stone ceiling passing overhead. Water dripped from a dozen or so points and made little splashing sounds all around them.

The man at the front of the boat hopped into the water and began dragging the vessel ashore. The boat crunched to a halt on the rocky bottom and the DragonMan stepped into the shallow water to help pull the boat more fully onto the shore. A pair of massive scaly hands plucked Crenthys out of the boat. The DragonMan tried to stand her up, but her legs buckled. He caught her and, with a curse, took her in his arms again.

"Gently, friend. Please." Jhaldus chided in passable High Draconic.

"You isn't expected, Elf." Croaked a strained voice from someone Crenthys couldn't see.

She saw Jhaldus turn to regard the speaker. "Peace, Rythrax, I come bearing gifts."

"He won't be pleased, slaver." the voice replied. The speaker sounded as if he had a mouth full of rocks and a rope drawn about his throat.

"We shall see!" Jhaldus hissed.

Then a third voice joined, smooth as silk and calm as a summer breeze. "Peace, indeed."

Jhaldus straightened and the stress in the air deflated.

"You both are right. I don't like surprises, but I am always curious to see what gifts Jhaldus brings me."

Crenthys recognized the voice from somewhere. She turned her head toward the voice and stared wide-eyed at the newcomer. Her heart sank.

Smiling warmly at Crenthys, Wave gave a deep bow.

Chapter 19

Dragon Games

A nuka felt like he had back when he was a kid and he had been caught burning things. Sweating about his punishment while his tutors found mama. He hated that feeling. Their group was crowded into the lavish great room of the Inn where the Silver was staying. He and Kelios waited to see Celebris while the famished slaves gobbled up the cakes put out for the guests.

What am I even doing here? He had gotten all emotional and agreed to help Kelios find Crenthys. That was stupid. It was time for him to get going before everything caught up to him. He needed to get moving and find papa. *Then what?* Most likely Anuka would find him drunk in a ditch. At least they could wiggle out from under the Dragons.

But what would happen to Crenthys and Kelios? More importantly, *why do I still care?* He did care. Anuka had never needed anyone. He'd been taking care of Papa and himself since his mom died and they had gotten along just fine. He'd never had a friend unless you counted Rigby the Bard. So probably no.

Wave finally came downstairs and insisted on hearing the report first. After Anuka and Kelios explained the situation to Wave. The sea elf decided to break the news to Celebris himself. He took the pair of them upstairs to the Silver's room and laid out the details gently to the DragonMan.

The roar was impressive. Anuka was pretty sure he was around twenty years old and he'd been yelled at plenty. Never before had he legitimately thought he would be roasted on the spot. *Good job, Wave.* The sea elf had disappeared shortly after, leaving them to fend for themselves with the angry DragonMan.

The Silver paced back and forth, the floorboards groaning with each thundering step. The DragonMan faced them again after thinking of another thing to yell about. "Do you have any idea the position you've put me in?" Spittle flew liberally in bursts as Celebris raged. "I've spent my day humbly making assurances to the priests of the Black DragonLord. Humans, no less!" he said as if that explained everything.

Anuka didn't know what the big deal was. It was one stupid tavern. They didn't even burn the place down. This was why he never got tangled up in politics. Too many things to keep up with that made somebody mad. Anuka preferred to make people mad across the board. He was judicious that way.

"What am I supposed to do with half a dozen refugees? This Jhaldus has Caustimis's favor, don't you doubt it. And you snuck into his place of business, killed his retainers, and stole his property."

Caustimis was Bog's real name, Anuka guessed.

"We could not leave them locked in that dungeon. They are people, not property." Kelios made the statement pleadingly, but Anuka heard the edge to the words.

Somehow, Celebris loomed even taller and looked down at Kelios. He was going to get torched. Kelios was fried fish.

Instead, Celebris said more calmly, "To you and I they are. To Caustimis, they are property. Everything is property to him. A slave's mark is a formality. He will take this affront personally and the rift between him and my master will grow. Relations between the Silver Dragons and the Black Dragons are tenuous. Upsetting that delicate balance could result in a disaster. Possibly even open a war. *That* is what is at stake here."

Anuka had never seen a Dragon afraid before but he could sense fear in Celebris. Maybe he wasn't afraid for himself, but when talking about his master's pain Anuka could hear genuine hurt in his words. He almost felt pity for the creature. Almost.

Dragons were schemers above all else. Anuka knew that first hand. This one, so noble and honorable, was no different. Their loyalties lay with Dragons, Dragon Servants, and then everyone else, in that order. Semantics aside, Celebris would probably value Bog's life over Anuka's or his friends. Time to get some real answers.

"But if we find evidence against Apostate then none of that will matter, right?" Anuka asked.

The question seemed to surprise the Silver. He looked at Anuka. A flash of uncertainty darted across his scale-covered face.

"That is correct. When you find the evidence to implicate those rebels, much will be forgiven." Celebris opened his mouth to say more but closed it again.

"So as long as everything ties up neatly, we're all in the clear?" Anuka asked, gesturing his open palms in front of him like that made perfect sense.

Celebris did not answer.

"Where did they take Crenthys?"

Kelios looked sharply at the goblin. "Anuka."

His tiny raised hand silenced Kelios, for now. Anuka continued, "You know where these Blood Letters are."

"Blood Letters?" Celebris asked.

"Yeah. That's what I'm calling them. You know, they're leeching the Dragons. Blood Letters. Never mind. You know they aren't Apostate. Not officially, at least."

"You don't know what you are talking about," Celebris said with a growl.

"Usually not. But I know people, or in this case, Dragons. Bog cares about coin and only coin. Look at this dump." Anuka gestured around him. "This city. It's people. Everything is carefully designed to keep the coin flowing. If someone shows up dumping DragonsBlood on Bog's streets he's gonna be there to mop it up and make a profit from it."

Again, Celebris did not answer. That was fine with Anuka. He was just warming up.

"So you aren't here to solve a crime. You aren't even here to reprimand Bog for ignoring these Blood Letters. You aren't demanding to know where these Blood Letters are. In fact, I would wager that Bog called you here under an agreement to pin this whole thing on Apostate. By the time you got here, he'd figured out how to profit from this mess. And now, Bog doesn't want you to crush his revenue stream. Lots of raw DragonsBlood is getting passed around? Poor people can get their fix cheap and the dregs among his slaves die and are swept away. His alchemists will make a fortune turning it into Tor knows what. Now, which parts did I get wrong?"

The Silver's nostrils flexed and flared but Anuka saw guilt in those eyes. "You see much, Fire Blood. Much, but not all."

Fire Blood? What was that? Anuka was tired of people calling him names but he wanted to hear the DragonMan out.

The DragonMan worked his jaw like he'd found a fish bone and was about to spit it out. Finally, he said, "These people began selling Blood and Caustimis grew concerned that he would be blamed. His relations with my Master, Mistress Shimmer, have always been poor and she could make his life on the Council of Wyrms very unpleasant. So he investigated, eventually finding out who was involved. He decided he could make more profit from allowing them to continue selling illegal DragonsBlood. Enough profit that he was willing to risk upsetting the Dragon Council."

"What?" Kelios said incredulously.

"Freaking knew it. Dragons..." Anuka said shaking his head.

"When the DragonsBlood was discovered by the Council, Bog was called to account. Mistress Shimmer agreed to help Caustimis end the problem in a way that benefited everyone."

"Every Dragon, you mean," Anuka said.

Celebris ignored the comment. "I do know where the Blood Letters are, if not who they are, but I can do nothing to stop them. If I send my men to shut them down, I violate Caustimis's right of territory. Caustimis will not send his own men because he is still profiting from these miscreants."

"So you hired us." Kelios breathed.

"Enslaved. He enslaved us, remember?" Anuka provided.

"I had hoped you would come to agree with my assertions that Apostate was involved and implicate them. A small price for your freedom."

"Ya, implicate innocent people," Anuka said snidely.

"They are rebels!" Celebris roared. "They erode the civil structure that keeps these lands from falling into chaos. You may not like being ruled by DragonKind, but without us, the whole world crumbles. Be grateful. The edges of the grace I have afforded you are fraying."

⸺⬥⸺

Scaled-covered Sum Buck. Anuka opened his mouth to jam his boot inside when the door burst open. Everyone, Celebris included, was startled as Wave stepped in and bowed.

"Apologies, my Lord." Wave said, rising. "I was detained by some nasty business. Some sort of disturbance roused the guard." Wave looked right at Anuka and Kelios, but mostly Anuka when he mentioned the disturbance. "Travel within the city has been made difficult."

Who did he think he was? Bootlick shows up smelling like the ocean and acting all glib. *Did Wave go have a swim while he and Kelios got their tongue lashing?* Anuka smiled and was about to resume his questions.

Kelios beat him to it. "Where have they taken Crenthys?" It was a good question so Anuka held back.

The massive silver DragonMan flexed his jaw muscles as if chewing a tough bit of grisly meat. His expression could pickle honey. Anuka knew the creature carried a lot of responsibility but that's what he deserved for playing god. *What would I do if the fate of the world was on my back?* Run. That's what smart men did. Let fate sort out the world's problems.

Celebris exhaled briskly through his nose. Anuka thought he saw a puff of smoke trail from each nostril, which reminded him that they were dealing with a DragonMan.

"There is a cove barely a league south of the City. The rebels are there. I believe they are the ones who took your friend."

Wave looked up at the DragonMan. "Master?" he said, concern in his voice.

"No, Wave. I must accelerate my plans. Too much innocent blood has been spilled." He looked back at Anuka "I can provide you a boat and a man to navigate for you."

"What about loaning a couple of your big ugly dudes with all the muscles?" Anuka asked.

"No, he cannot." Wave replied hotly. "He is getting more involved than is advisable already." Some of his vitriol seemed directed at Celebris.

"Good thing I didn't ask you, then," Anuka said, taking a step towards the Sea Elf.

"He is right. I cannot assist you with more than I have promised. Too much is at stake." Celebris said, forestalling an escalation in the argument.

Anuka expected nothing less. Dragons and their games.

"How many men are in this band of rebels?" Kelios asked. The Triton seemed to be standing a little straighter than he had moments before. He seemed resolute. Great.

"Probably not less than ten. Perhaps as many as fifteen."

"Fifteen!?" Anuka said. "And you won't help? You both have sand between your ears if you think we're that stupid."

Wave's face turned a satisfying shade of purple and was working to form words that would surely slay Anuka.

Kelios simply said. "I will go. Anuka and I, and whomever of those we freed that are willing to face the danger. We will save Crenthys and find your evidence."

Now Kelios seemed to have taken on sand. Anuka hadn't survived his Papa's antics for twenty-some years just to get killed by some idiot pirates. He had to find Papa, get his ship back, and go enjoy life somewhere far away from Dragons.

"No," Anuka said a little more forcefully than he intended. Everyone looked at him and he suddenly felt very small. This had nothing to do with him. He forged on. "Forget this. I'm out."

"Anuka--" Kelios began.

"No, Kelios. I'm done. I've had my fill of Dragons. I'm sorry, bubby. I'm done." Anuka turned and pulled the door open. He had to leave before he changed his mind.

"Coward," Celebris growled. "Your father would be ashamed."

Anuka froze in his tracks. He slowly spun around and looked at the giant DragonMan. His mind was flooded with various ways that he could try and kill that big monster. A dagger in the eye would do it.

Or maybe the tip of his rapier rammed into his armpit would do the trick. No. It wasn't worth it. To the pits with all of them.

Anuka turned back around, walked through the door, and slammed it behind him.

⸺⬩◇⬩⸺

Kelios breathed a sigh of relief. It made him furious that Anuka would abandon them again, but it was hard to argue with his reasoning.

Anuka took some of the oppressive heat of the room with him when he left, but the tension still hung in the air like fog.

"Do you mean to continue your quest to save your friend and find my evidence?" The Silver asked, looking at Kelios.

"I do." There was no doubt in his heart, and speaking the words brought peace to his troubled mind. If Crenthys was alive she would need his help. The woman was strong in a way that Kelios didn't understand but she also needed him. He could feel it. He nodded to Wave and the Silver and said, "I will leave as soon as I can pack some things."

"That is well. I wish I was able to aid you more. Wave, see to his transportation and whatever weapons you can find." The Sea Elf left with a nod. Kelios turned to follow but the DragonMan said, "Wait."

"I do not know what you will discover when you find these Blood Letters." Celebris stopped like he wanted to say more.

"I understand," Kelios said. There was nothing else to say. Blood pounded in his ears as he felt the tendrils of fate drawing tight around him. He would succeed, or he would die. Either way, he finally felt like his own man. The larger hand of fate was upon him, upon them all, but at this moment he decided where his next step would fall. Mother was not here to scold him, nor father to judge him. His life was his own. He turned back toward the open door and took the next step toward a destiny of his own choosing.

Chapter 20

Into the Inferno

Anuka watched from the shadows of the nearby city wall as Kelios, Wave, and a handful of the freed prisoners poured out the front doors of the inn and strode down the sloping city street. Down to the water, no doubt. Down to save the Sea Elf girl. *Serves her right if she was dumb enough to get caught.* There was no conviction in the thought, however. Who knows what happened? If the freaky Dark Elf had her, she was done for. If the thugs selling illegal DragonsBlood had her she would soon be dead. If she was lucky. That's what happens when you mess around with Dragons.

He sighed as the last of the party passed out of the gate and into the next portion of the city. They would be fine. If they got into trouble, Kelios could just turn into a massive bear and eat their attackers. Crenthys was some kind of gypsy warrior. She would be fine. The weird talking Cat Man was going with them, too. They didn't need Anuka. His talents were needed elsewhere. He had to find his Papa, who did need him. Find his Papa, find his boat. He wasn't needed here. His skills had been a great help to Kelios and Crenthys. Now he was done. Anuka didn't believe any of that.

After he was sure Kelios and his party were well beyond the ward, Anuka pushed off the wall and moved through the opening into the lower part of the city. He needed something to drink and, even after he collected various coins and goods today, he couldn't afford to drink in the rich ward. The lower parts of the city offered much cheaper drinks. Besides, Anuka would need to see about passage out of this port quickly. He wasn't sure whether word about his work at the Lucky Toss had gotten around but he was pretty easy to pick out of a crowd.

He decided he needed to clear his mind so he started walking along the narrow grimy streets. It was dark and people congregated in small groups around fires for warmth and to cook. The evening breeze was cool. Anuka looked down a particularly desolate alleyway and saw a blazing fire raging a couple of blocks away. It was big enough that, at first glance, he thought a building was on fire. He lazily made his way toward the inferno.

It annoyed Anuka that he kept thinking about Kelios and Crenthys. They were grown-ups. They each had their own plans. That was clear. To Kelios, being noble was more important than being alive. What good is courage if you're dead? Anuka's Papa had always judged the value of something based on whether it could be eaten or not. That made sense. You can't eat courage.

Crenthys. She was up to something. Kelios didn't tell him much about her meeting with old contacts but Anuka read between the lines well. He could discern things that Fish Bear would never understand. Anuka had read her wrong on the *Sea Pocket*. That told him she was pretending to be someone she wasn't.

Anuka didn't notice the chatter until it stopped. A gaggle of part-humans huddled together around the large bonfire. They were all staring at him.

"Hey," Anuka said.

The people continued to stare at him.

"Nice fire. Very hot." What a stupid thing to say. He smiled his biggest smile then turned and stared at the raging fire. What were they burning? It felt good on his skin. The flames were hypnotic as they danced. Pops and cracks punctuated the night as Anuka stared, transfixed, at the flame. He was so engrossed in the inferno that he almost missed the gentle whisper of his name. He startled and looked around for the voice. Anuka didn't know any of the people around the fire.

"Anuka." The voice echoed again as he looked into the fire. The outline of a face appeared in the flames and Anuka's heart nearly stopped beating.

"Mama?"

Crenthys would have thumped Tamris bloody if someone hadn't beaten her to it. The woman's left eye was dark purple, bulging, and swollen shut. Her lip was split and she favored her right arm. She lay against a far corner of the room, staring at Crenthys with her good eye.

Crenthys sighed. The Helmer of Usban Port had always been the sensible one of them. Tam would be the former Helmer once Morglun heard about this mess. Tamris was wild but she had always tempered her wild streak enough to make good decisions when it really mattered. *What happened to her?* Crenthys wondered. She had hoped that her friend hadn't given her up to Jhaldus by choice. Her wounds indicated she hadn't, but Crenthys wasn't sure. The woman wore shame and guilt on her face like a veil.

Jhaldus wasn't a member of the Blood Letters, as Anuka called them. He did business with them, for sure. But the ambition and political intrigue weren't his style. As vile as the Dark Elf was, his motives were very simple to understand. Crenthys suspected something else was going on. Something she wasn't going to like.

Still staring at Crenthys, the battered Helmer said, "You gonn' kill me, Brinka?" The words were thick, forced from the woman's wounded mouth. Her voice sounded strained and dry.

With a casual coldness, Crenthys replied, "I may. I guess we'll see how this plays out."

As Crenthys's anger melted a bit, she noticed the others in the room. Two human girls clutched Tamris, both as torn and battered as The Helmer. Their hair color, style, and body shape suggested them to be sisters, though their face shapes were different. One girl had high cheekbones and a pointed chin. Her pale green eyes were full of fear. The other girl had a fuller, more rounded face that might have been kind once. The skinny mixed-blood sea elf boy who was with Tam the last time Cren had seen her was on the floor in the opposite corner of the room. He lay in an awkward position, unmoving.

Frowning, Crenthys folded her arms over her chest and blew out a sigh through her nose, "What did you do, Tam?"

The former Helmer swallowed, sniffed, and turned her gaze away from Crenthys. After a long moment, her head sagged to her shoulders. Trying not to move her busted mouth much she said, "I got ahead of myself. Tried to reach too far." Tears that the woman was too stubborn to let fall rimmed her eyes when she looked at Crenthys again. Crenthys returned the stare, allowing the silence to pass. She wasn't going to give Tam a pass this time.

Finally, Tamris shrugged and said, "Some men came 'round, askin' for me. They knew who I was. Who I *really* was. Helmer for Apostate and all. We talked and shared some drinks. They said they hated Dragons as much as Apostate. Only they intended to do something about it. I'd heard that kind of talk before, we all have, so I said I wasn't interested. They offered a stupid amount of money for a little information." Tamris looked at Crenthys but couldn't meet her hard stare this time. "So I told them some things. Things only someone with my connections would know."

This was worse than Crenthys thought. Initially, she thought the woman had simply betrayed her. If the woman had abused her position with Apostate and sold their secrets, the woman was as good as dead. Even if she managed to escape their captors, there was no place on Dorwine where she could hide from Apostate.

"What did you do, Tam?" Crenthys repeated, shock and accusation raising her voice a notch.

"I told them where they could get a Dragon egg," Tamris said. The tears she had been holding back trailed down her cheek.

"What?" Crenthys barked.

The tone and volume of Crenthys's voice snapped Tamris out of her tears and the battered woman turned a glare on Crenthys. Tam replied with a shout of her own. "I told them where to find the cursed thing! I wish I could have told them where all Dragon eggs are!" Tamris was trying to make her way to her feet but between her broken arm and the girls restraining her, pleading for her to calm down, she slumped back against the wall. "I told them to find it and make an omelet for all I cared. They paid me, Brinka. They made me a rich woman. Not all of us can just up and leave like you did. This was my way out. Out of the skulking, the hiding, the lying all the time. I'm... I'm just so tired." Tamris finally relented, her fury spent, and slumped forward. Soft sobs escaped her bloodied lips as the young girls attended her.

Seas, this was worse than she had imagined. Tamris had aided the kidnapping of a juvenile Dragon, a Bronze no less, from a secret hatchery. Apostate knew of many Dragon hatcheries. There were only so many places you could hide such a thing. Trading information and knowing what to watch for had led to the discovery of the hatcheries for almost every major color of Dragon. This information could be used as leverage to secure rights and freedoms that the Dragons had never afforded their subjects. In theory. As far as Crenthys knew, they had never actually used the information. Apostate certainly would never attack or rob a hatchery. To threaten and harass the Dragons was one thing, but to attack one was entirely another. They were still

Dragons. No one had ever fought a Dragon in recorded history. No man, no army, could match the raw power and potential destruction of one Dragon, let alone a coalition of them. Even without their magic, they were unbelievably strong. Since the Dragons hoarded all the magic of Dorwine, they could crush any resistance with barely a thought.

How had the Blood Letters taken a Dragon child without causing instant pandemonium? Those hatcheries were well hidden but also well guarded. Always. A horrible thought came to Crenthys. The muscles in her chest tightened and her heartbeat quickened.

"T-tam," she stammered. "Where did you send them?" Crenthys stepped towards the woman, knelt, and took her head in her hands. Shock washed over Tamris's face as Cren fixed a wide-eyed gaze on her. She ignored the protests of the young girls and put her face level with Tamris's.

"I-I" Tamris tried to say.

Crenthys shook her harder than she intended but the fist gripping her heart began to crush it. "Where?!" Crenthys yelled at the terrified woman.

"Scornrock. Scornrock Mountains. South of the Pelint Plains. The place Sheen abandoned."

Crenthys didn't remember releasing Tamris but faintly registered her cries of pain as the girls moved to attend her. The grip on her heart hadn't subsided. Rather it moved up her neck and clawed at her throat and left her gasping for air. She put her hand on the door to brace herself. Sweat suddenly broke out over her entire body. It felt cool on her flushed face and it evaporated quickly in the stream of air coming through the barred window in the door.

Like having a log laid on her chest, waves of pain wracked her. The accompanying mix of fear and elation crashed into her like waves rocking a boat in a storm. Someone she had buried long ago suddenly came back to life. The life she had spent a decade trying to run from had finally caught her.

She closed her eyes and breathed deeply through her nose. After several moments, she decided what had to be done. That clarity suffocated the panic she felt. Crenthys had to free the Dragon.

<hr>

"It's me, son." Said the reverberant voice of Anuka's mother from inside the raging bonfire.

A single tear tumbled out of his eye and sizzled as it trailed down his cheek. "Mama?" He said. He was surprised by how pitiful his voice sounded.

The confused wretches around the fire gaped at Anuka, but he barely noticed.

"Yes, my boy. Come. We haven't much time." The form in the fire beckoned him with arms that he alone could see. Every vision he'd had of his mother over the past decade involved images of her death replayed, to his horror. Part of him broke when he realized how desperate he was to see his mother again. He would willingly climb mountains, face down a Dragon, or even walk through fire.

He took two quick steps forward and was inside the raging inferno. The curious onlookers gasped and cried out as he passed into the flames.

Chapter 21

The Fire That Doesn't Burn

K elios and his small party journeyed south for about an hour when they discovered the hidden cove Celebris had told them of. Ember had seen a few other boats, similar in size to theirs, moored deeper in the channel so they had decided to disembark at the mouth and walk in. Ember had also proclaimed that he refused to get wet so Kelios was looking for a place to drag their little boat ashore so the Malkin could step onto dry land.

The cool seawater was refreshing to Kelios as he drug their small boat along the shallow mouth of the cove. He finally found a section deep enough to dock. A small waterfall had formed a plunge pool that allowed them to bring the side of the boat right up to the shore. As soon as Ember and the others stepped out, their guide, a thin, skittish human boy with a long neck, made a hasty retreat back to Usban Port.

Kelios accepted his pack from the younger of the two humans, who had come along after all, and slung it carefully over his back. Kelios was glad the brothers had decided to join their quest to save Crenthys. They said the business they had in the city could wait.

A part of him wondered how he wound up here. Just a day before he would never have had the courage to attempt a rescue mission for someone he hardly knew. He was a different Triton today. He could feel it in his bones. Maybe it was the bear lingering in his mind. Or maybe the bear had changed him forever. Either way, he waded through chilly water without reservation. The thrill of their mission invigorated him and he hardly recognized the man he had been the day before.

Sound carried well in this cavern. Kelios winced with each careless step the group took, jostling a stone or splashing a puddle. Ember picked his way lithely across the ground but the humans made way too much noise. As far as Kelios could see in the dark cavern, all of the shore was either jagged rock or thick layers of brittle rocks made smooth by the backwashed stream.

They crept slowly into the cavern in deep darkness, stumbling about, relying on Ember's feline eyes for sight. Finally, they saw a flickering orange glow lighting one side of the ravine. Ember scouted ahead, returned and reported he didn't hear anything, but saw evidence of people. They trudged on.

When they rounded a bend they indeed saw signs of people. They paused to look around. A small dock had been erected and was secured to the shore by metal spikes. There were crates and buckets strewn about the muddy shore. The faint smell of blood hung in the stagnant air. The metallic smell blended with the scent of brine unpleasantly. It smelled like the time he and his brother had happened upon the aftermath of a shark attack. Kelios felt his head begin to swim and realized the smell of blood in the air had caused the bear in him to stir. He disturbed some rocks, but quickly righted himself.

Ember gave him a flat look that made him feel like apologizing. Kelios shrugged instead and they kept walking slowly forward.

Kelios was exhausted already. To allow the bear to emerge again without rest would most likely have dire consequences. His two transformations earlier today had left him with a bone-deep weariness. And yet the bear still called to him. He wondered whether joining with the bear had been wise in the first place. He knew what his tutors would say.

Ember had picked his way ahead and paused at the dock to look more closely at the boats moored there. Kelios joined Ember on the dock and noticed the Malkin sniffing the air. Kelios smelled it too.

"Crenthys," Kelios said as loud as he dared. He was looking around as if he expected her to come strutting out to them. She didn't. She had been here not long ago. Ember had shared with the group what he had seen when Jhaldus and Pazzix passed through the dungeon with Crenthys in tow.

A motion caught his eye and he looked toward the cave ahead and saw the older of the human brothers signaling him. The others couldn't smell as well as he or Ember. Even if they had caught the scent they wouldn't know Crenthys's smell. Kelios quickly caught up to them and said in a hushed voice, "She is...they are here. Ember caught her scent." He decided it wise to keep his bear form a secret from as many people as possible.

Turning back, he saw that Ember was carefully picking his way up the mud-covered rock slope toward the scent. The Malkin stopped near them and stood pondering the mouth of the cave.

Ember said, gesturing, "Left, or right?"

Dull orange torchlight flickered off the gray stone walls of each corridor. The passage to the right was smaller and banked upward as it angled off to the right a few dozen strides in. The passage to the left was broader, the dirt of the floor was more traveled than the other. *That way then,* he told himself. "Left," Kelios said.

Without a word of reply, Ember crept that direction, adjusting his shoulder-slung pack as he did. The older of the brothers slid out the slender swords Wave had given him and followed Ember. The other unsheathed two short-handled cleaver knives from his belt and motioned for Kelios to go first.

He did, wishing he had a weapon of his own. He was trained to use a staff or a spear but had neither. Ember was well ahead so Kelios moved quickly ahead of the brother and did his best to keep quiet.

The fire didn't burn Anuka. He hadn't expected it to. It never had. Anuka was used to pretending to avoid the flame like everyone else did. Pretended to be burned when his hand carelessly rested on a hot stove. The truth was, deep down, Anuka knew that fire was his companion. He hadn't thought about these things because he thought all that died with his mother. Now here she stood.

It was dark even though Anuka and his mother stood in a ring of raging fire as tall as a coconut tree and about ten paces wide. It was real fire. Anuka felt the warmth but otherwise ignored the flames. All he saw was the lady in front of him. Anuka's head swam as parts of his memory, stomped down years ago, broke forth like water obliterating a dam. She was just the way he remembered her; Tall, likely taller than Kelios, with deep, blood-red skin the same color as his own. Jet black hair tumbled around her shoulders and down her back. Her outfit was all kinds of ridiculous. As a child, Anuka hadn't thought it weird that so much of her legs and chest showed around the skin-tight tunic and billowing blue-black skirt. Back then, she was just his mom. He hadn't realized how seductive her clothing was. Now it was kind of odd. Her eyes shone like the sun. Yellow, with no discernible pupil. Soft mist trailed from her exposed skin, giving her a mystic quality. If he had met this creature on the street, he would have turned and fled. She was both majestic and terrible. She was his mother.

"Mm," he said, unable to make the words. He cleared his throat and licked his lips. Lips that felt like they'd baked in the sun. He tried again. "Mama, I-."

Her smile broke his heart and his eyes burned from crying tears long withheld. In a flash, she had covered the few strides between them and scooped him into a crushing hug like he was a boy again. He grabbed at her neck and squeezed, a sound of exuberant elation escaping his lips.

The moment passed all too soon, and she set him on the ground. Then she shrunk.

Her body simply melted down to eye level with Anuka. His adult mind understood that she was a being of magic and strange power while his child's mind assumed her powers to be normal. She looked funny this size and he smiled. This moment wouldn't last forever, he knew, and he felt terror knowing that she might be taken from him again.

"Where did you go, Mama?" he blurted. "I thought...I thought you drowned."

"I know, my son, my beautiful boy, I know." Her voice sounded like a choir, so rich and full and melodious. With one hand she rubbed his cheek. "I was bound by a Duty, as I still am, that called me back. I am not of this world, Anuka. You know this. I came here for a holiday and met your father. He enchanted me and, for a time, I thought I could stay here forever. But when Duty sent for me, I was compelled to answer."

Anuka shook his head slowly. "What do you mean not your world? What duty is more important than your family?" Anuka paused before pressing on, "Than me?"

"Anuka, my son, listen to me. We haven't much time. My falling in love with your father, having you, loving you. These things were selfish indulgences. I am bound by a magic wrought of a different world. My people are created to serve, and we are bound by Duty. Duty is a being, not an ideal. When called upon, I cannot decline. I knew this, yet I chose to love anyway."

The twisting dagger in Anuka's heart must have shown on his face.

"I don't regret what I did, save for the pain I caused you and your father. It was unfair for you that I chose as I did, knowing I would one day be called again. My love for your crazy father captured me fully and I set aside the truth that I knew. For him. For you."

"This is why you pushed me so hard," Anuka whispered.

"Yes, my boy. Yes." Her face, though alien and angelic at once, smiled broadly at him. "I knew I would not be allowed to stay and I wanted you to be strong. I know some of what waits for you. Some of your future. To face it, you must be strong."

"I would rather have you, Mama, than to be strong."

She closed her eyes and barked out a cry that rent his tortured heart.

"There are dark things in our universe. Those of us gifted with power must face those dark things. No matter how badly I want to walk the dunes with you as I once did or read epic tales together long into the night, those things cannot be. My power binds me to Duty. As does yours, in a way."

He looked up at her face, wanting to flee, or scream, or grab onto her and never let her go.

"My power is in you, Anuka, and you have greatness before you. But this greatness is not for you. It is so others might have the things we cannot have."

"Love?" Anuka asked.

"Oh, my son!" she said, crushing him in another hug. Though she was almost a third her true height, her crushing strength was the same. After a moment she held him at arm's length, tears sizzling down her cheeks. "Never!" she explained. "We have loved enough for a lifetime. You, your father, and I. Though our time was short, we were blessed. There may be a day, when you come into your power, that you can come and join me in the Duty. Perhaps I can come to you again as time permits. For now, you are needed here. There are great evils on the horizon in Dorwine. Immediately, your friends are in danger. They need you. And after you help your friends..."

"Pops," Anuka said, half of his mouth frowning.

"Yes. My leaving broke your father. I told him of my Duty and of the day that might come, but he was not prepared. I have broken his heart. You, my sweet boy, must find him. And restore him. This world is going to need his brilliance."

"How? You kind of broke me, too." From the corners of his eyes, he saw the surrounding flames flare to greater heights in response to the ire that rose in him.

"No, my son. You are not broken. You have chosen to hide from what you do not wish to face."

The rebuke was a slap Anuka hadn't seen coming. The cool truth of her words doused his rising anger. The flames lessened as well. He had wasted his youth. He had gambled, cheated, stolen, and joked his way through the days since his mother had left. All the pain of her leaving had been tucked into a tiny room in Anuka's heart. Along with the pain, he had also hidden away the joy. The training for his future, he had tossed away. He recalled the words of his father from long ago, 'You will captain the most important vessel on the sea one day'.

"You aren't broken. You have just lost your way." She dropped her hands from his shoulders and stepped back to look at him. She smiled her motherly smile at him.

"You're leaving again, aren't you?" Anuka asked.

"No, son. This time you are leaving. You have a duty of your own that you are bound to. Go. Save your friends."

"I betrayed them, Mama. They are the only friends I've known and I deserted them." Anuka said glumly.

"Then go to them. Your actions will say to them what words cannot."

Anuka didn't want to go. The night was cold and he was ashamed of himself for leaving his friends. "Mama, can you promise that I will see you again?"

"No." She said and his face fell. She raised an index finger to forestall his argument and said, "You can see me again. But it is up to you. Grow, my son. Learn to keep your word and to become a man worthy of the trust of a nation. When your power is full you will be able to come to me. And I will try to bring you again to this place if I am able."

"I can come to where you are, someday?" he asked. She nodded.

"When I do, I'm gonna find that Sum Buck that took you away and POW! Right in the mouth!" Anuka made a wild uppercut swing in the air to punctuate his promise. His mother laughed.

"I shall tell your Uncle Zassi to watch his back. Goodbye, my son."

Anuka summoned all of his remaining courage and didn't let his lip quiver. "Goodbye, Mama."

The world around him blurred and swirled as he stepped backward out of the flames and into the cold streets of Usban Port. He ignored the gasps and curses as he stepped out of the flames and set off up the hill, back to the Silver, renewed with purpose. He had friends who needed saving.

———◆◆◆———

Time was melting away and Tabir knew it. He felt like sand slipping through the neck of an hourglass. *Rathune, help me,* he pleaded. The sense of foreboding he had known since stepping onto the *Sea Pocket* grew increasingly deeper. A sense of impending purpose gripped him. Like a sword longing for the hand of the master swordsman, Tabir felt the hand of his god poised over him.

It seemed a ridiculous notion as he ambled gingerly on sand-burned feet, wearing clothing made from scraps. But he knew in his heart that he would be delivered. With dishes from the evening meal cleaned and stored he shuffled contently back into the hovel that teemed with slaves.

Seeing the others settling onto their pallets on the floor for the evening pained him. He didn't know their fate and deliverance wasn't promised to them. From things he had overheard from guards and prospective slave owners, the city was in deep unrest. People were dying in droves and violence had erupted in small pockets throughout the city. Tabir was not surprised.

Seeing the demon aboard the *Brinery* had shocked him. He had prayed that he would never again see the like. Demons had taken his people and Rathune had destroyed them. Knowing that a demon walked the streets of Usban inside the body of a mortal filled Tabir with dread. Death and chaos would soon follow.

Tabir couldn't resist scanning the crowd for someone among this group of poor souls who may have taken a demonic spirit. That would explain the unrest in the city. The allure of power was too tempting for a happy man. A desperate man was doubly susceptible to the seduction of a demon's promise of power.

Tabir chided himself. His situation was bad enough without worrying about unseen demons. He considered his situation and his prospects seemed bleak. With a final glance at the departing burial boats, Tabir realized that he would do well to survive the next couple of days.

Anuka stared at the beautiful bone-handled dagger sticking up from the chest of the Silver DragonMan. Even crusted in dark red blood, Anuka recognized that dagger. *His* dagger.

"Dragonsbreath." He swore. "I'm in trouble."

It seemed unfair that, just when Anuka was coming to grips with his feelings and finally deciding to step up and be the hero he was destined to be, this would happen. It was selfish to think that way. He could be the poor sucker with steel jammed into his chest. Sighing, he stepped forward and reached for the hilt when a coarse voice from behind him rasped, "Don't!"

Anuka spun, his hand ready to throw the inferior knife blade when he saw the little half-sized man they had freed earlier, his head and one arm spilling out of a dresser drawer.

"Don't touch it. It's DragonsBlood. It will harm you."

Anuka slid the inferior knife back into its sheath and rushed to help the Nob. The left side of Offund's shirt was stained crimson and there was little color in his face.

"Offund, what happened?" He was proud of himself for remembering what Ember had called him, but he didn't have long to celebrate. The Nob toppled out of the drawer with a grunt. Anuka softened his fall a little but the Nob was heavier than he by a good bit.

"You okay?" Anuka asked and immediately felt stupid for it. Of course he wasn't okay.

"Wa---" Offund tried to say but was interrupted by a cough. The cough turned into a fit and he winced, putting a hand to his side. A hole in his shirt was soaked with dark blood. When the coughing fit passed he cleared his throat and looked determinedly at Anuka. "Wave. Wave did this."

Wave? That wormy little barnacle! He wasn't capable of something like this. It made no sense. Anuka reviewed the facts about the Sea Elf in his head. Wave was Bog's man. Literally, Bog owned him. If Celebris discovered that Bog was behind the Blood Letters then he would order the Silver dead. But that would directly implicate Bog. Bog wasn't stupid. What then? If Bog didn't order Wave to kill Celebris then who did? Who would want to stop the man hunting the Blood Letters? The Blood Letters would. "Sum Buck...Wave is one of the Blood Letters. Probably the leader of the Blood Letters." The idea seemed silly until Anuka heard himself say it out loud.

"He had help. There were others with him. One of them stabbed me." Offund tried to curl his head over to look at his wound but winced at the effort. "It isn't that bad. Just a lot of blood. I found the Elven lady. She lost so much blood..." Offund's voice trailed off as he squeezed his eyes tight and breathed slowly for a moment. "When the killers came looking for me I lay very still and they thought I was dead. I'm the only one left." The Nob's face contorted painfully and he wept.

Anuka supported the little man's big head and let him cry. *There would be a reckoning. Blood for blood.* But first, they had to get out of here. The city guards and Bog's priests and PeaceMen would be on this place like scales on a fish very soon.

"Offund, can you walk? At all?" Anuka asked.

Nodding, Offund tried to sit up. With a grunt and a little help from Anuka, he gained his feet. Tough little cuss. He was a little wobbly and still really pale but he would have to make do.

"Take your shirt off."

Offund fixed Anuka with a puzzled look.

"C'mon. We don't have time." Anuka said, helping Offund remove the shirt. With some quick knife work, the silky bed sheets were cut into strips. Anuka hastily wrapped the makeshift bandage around Offund's chest, under his arm. The wound was pretty bad and the little man had lost a lot of blood. Anuka was sure it was painful. He didn't like the idea of a mad escape with the little man but he knew he couldn't leave him behind. Anuka was trying to be a better goblin. As gracefully as he could manage, Anuka wrapped the bloodied shirt around his hand and wrenched the dagger free from Celebris's unmoving chest. "Sorry, pal," Anuka said as he wiped the dagger clean of DragonsBlood and stood. As he did, a folded envelope slid from the DragonMan's vest pocket. Anuka snatched it before it fell into the congealed pool of DragonsBlood on the floor.

The words on the envelope were in the High Draconic tongue but something about them gnawed at Anuka's mind. No time now. He stuck the envelope in his shoulder bag and turned to see Offund's head sagging wearily.

"Meet me downstairs," Anuka said before darting out of the room and down the hall to his quarters. By the time Offund had gingerly picked his way down the stairs Anuka caught up to him with some clothing. He draped a clean shirt over Offund's head and put a firm little dress hat on him. The hat had been swiped from the closet. Anuka took just a second to see how the hat fit him. Very nice. Anuka loved hats. On a whim, Anuka decided to buy them some time. He twisted the lock to the front door and snapped the little key off inside the lock.

"Let's get out of here," Anuka said, guiding Offund by the arm as quickly as he could move.

As they ducked out the back door they heard pounding on the front one. They heard boots and yelling from the main street as they exited onto the back alley. It was getting too late for people to be out and Anuka wished it wasn't so. They could get lost in a crowd. Two guys, half the size of a human, walking together down the street would be hard to miss on an empty night.

Where could they go? He had abandoned his only friends to their respective fates. *What a coward I am.* He thought back to his dad. Papa always had a saying or some piece of wisdom in times like these, and there had been plenty of times like these with Papa. The right one came to mind. Anuka knew them all. "Best thing to do in a pinch is make some friends, quick."

Lucky for him, Anuka knew a place where he could find a lot of friends. The unlikely pair of undersized heroes made their way toward the docks, sticking to the alleys and side roads.

Chapter 22

Faith

Tabir hadn't slept last night and tonight wasn't looking good either. Someone was weeping nearby, perhaps more than one. The smell of offal and vomit had been scrubbed off the slaves today but the hint of it hung in the air like the scent of a dead animal in the distance. The tiny room the slaves were currently in was only a little larger than the cargo hold they had been in aboard the *Brinery*. More and more slaves had trickled in over the past two days as ships had come and gone. Bodies were now packed in tight. The humid air in the room was as still as death. A few had even died. All of the slaves had been poked and prodded by potential buyers who had bribed the Holdmaster to let them have an early peek at the stock. Those found unappealing by the early shoppers had been culled from the herd. "The cost of doing business", one man had said after sending an elderly man to his death.

Tabir had helped where he could but refrained from using his Gift. Renewing someone's strength fully, or making a cut or bruise disappear, would bring too many questions. Then they all could die. His compassion had already earned him one beating and he didn't fancy another, let alone something worse. It was shameful how many times he had prayed for Rathune to give him the same renewal that his Gift could give to others. Tabir had repented each time but his resolve was wavering.

Mighty Rathune, he prayed, *I can ask nothing of you. I am nothing. There is no good way in me. Thank you for teaching me patience. You have given me no reasons to doubt you, but I am weak. Teach my heart faith, according to your will. I wait for your provision, exalted one. Thank you.*

Tabir turned painfully from side to side, trying to get comfortable. Just as he settled down he locked eyes with a middle-aged human man who wasn't happy about Tabir's tossing and turning. From the look on his face, Tabir guessed he wasn't happy about anything. Who could blame him? Tabir turned onto his back in hopes of avoiding another beating. One per day was more than enough. He stared at the beams of the ceiling overhead. After a few moments, he lost interest in the ceiling and began to wonder what was in store for him. Things were bleak, but he had survived worse. Rathune had brought him through each of those trials and into something better than he could imagine.

He smiled, which reminded him of his swollen lip. He ran his tongue over the cuts where his lips had gotten smashed between fist and tooth. He whispered a prayer of thanks that he still had all his teeth. The cut was raw and tasted sharply of blood. The rest of his wounds weren't bad. The men had shifted from hitting his face to hitting him in places where bruises would be less visible.

He could still hear the soft muffled cries from nearby. Soon after, he heard what he'd been waiting for. The sonorous snores of the grumpy human reverberated through the small building. He carefully made his way to his feet and began picking his way toward the cries. If he could not find rest tonight he would bring comfort to some others.

⸺✦⸺

Around Anuka, empty crates that smelled like rotting fruit were piled about the sandy floor. The roof was thatched with straw and poorly covered. Anuka peered out from a gap in the wall of the reed shack. He was confident no one would be wandering by anytime soon.

Down the sloping beach about a hundred paces toward the dock, Anuka saw the slave huts they had seen on their way into Usban. They would be full now if his guess was right.

Behind him, Offund groaned so he turned to check on him. The little man rested on a stack of empty burlap sacks. Anuka wished they had a blanket to cover him with. Instead, there were just more of the dirty sacks. The night air was getting cool. Of course, getting too comfortable wasn't good either. If Offund drifted off to sleep he might not wake up. Anuka didn't know much about medicine but he knew a dying person when he saw one.

Resisting the huge yawn he felt coming on, he turned back to the gap in the wall and tried to spot something out of place. After scanning the camp a third time, he found what he was looking for. There, about ten steps away from the huts was a thick bamboo pole driven into the ground. A massive, fur-covered figure was seated on the ground, leaning against the pole with his hands behind his back.

"Welp, time to move," Anuka said. He turned back to Offund. "You stay put. I'm gonna get you some help."

Offund made a weak signal with his hand to indicate he understood.

Anuka hated lying to the little man. He deserved better. There was no help to be had for him. The best Anuka could hope for was to find a way to take him along on his suicidal plan for escape. But then what? Maybe it would be better for the little man to go to sleep and simply fade away. He hoped Offund didn't see the sadness in his eyes.

Anuka turned and, sticking to the shadows, picked his way down the beach.

Chapter 23

Answered Prayers

Everyone was sleeping. Well, resting, at least. *Everyone but me,* Tabir mused. He felt guilty about how bitter he felt. His head hurt and his eyes ached for sleep. From his kneeling position, he stretched upright and sat on his heels. *I am not sure if I can survive another night this way,* he silently prayed. When he closed his eyes for a brief rest he felt his head swimming and feared he might topple over on top of one of those sleeping around him. Noticing a slight change in the acoustics of the room, he stopped moving. He opened his eyes. In the doorway stood the red-skinned goblin from the *Sea Pocket.*

Silhouetted in the crooked doorway of the shack, thin light filtered around his small frame from a slow-burning lamp hung on a pole out in the courtyard. He looked like a fabled hero of old and Tabir couldn't help but smile. He whispered, *thank you, Father.*

The goblin beckoned him. Tabir carefully picked his way over, careful not to step on anyone. The goblin continued to beckon until Tabir squatted down to his level. Then he said in a whispered voice, "Hey. Do you remember me?"

Tabir smiled and nodded. Arrogant, foul-mouthed swindler. Now here he was, hopefully intending to rescue them. "I remember you, Anuka Sandbar."

"Well..." Anuka said with a smile. Still whispering, he said. "Good man. I promise to try and remember your name. If we live."

"I take it we are leaving?" Tabir asked.

"Yup. Can you get everyone up, quiet like?"

"I can. What is our plan?"

Anuka peeled his lips back and look chagrined. "Well, there is a plan. It's pretty stupid and kind of a secret. Okay, I'll tell you. We're going to storm the docks and steal a boat. Then leave."

Tabir swallowed hard. That wasn't very heroic. Tabir tried to keep a calm mask in place but was counting the ways the plan could, and likely would, go wrong. But when you're drowning, you don't turn your nose up at a leaky boat that happens by. Besides, this was no accident. He could trust the providence of Rathune.

"Sounds splendid," Tabir said.

"Ok, good. But you'd better hurry. It sounds like the other idiots aren't being so quiet." Anuka said. Then he turned and left.

Indeed, Tabir could hear others stirring outside of his shanty hut. Faith, Tabir reminded himself, was won in trials. And great faith in great trials. He started waking people up.

—◆—

The press of fear and excitement from the slaves was as real as the humidity in the muggy night air. Anuka peered over the short stone wall that served as a tide breaker, one of several built into the ground about two hundred strides from the docks. A handful of guards milled around. A handful of dock workers lazed about. A thin veil of mist drifted slowly over the hot sand as a cool ocean breeze wafted up the shore. Beyond it, Anuka saw the goal. As proud as the winner of a spitting contest, The *Brinery* bobbed lazily on the water, bucking gently against its moorings. She was the biggest vessel currently at port. He both wanted her and dreaded her.

People would die tonight. Some of them would be the underfed, untrained slaves crouching behind him watching for his signal. Some of them would be regular folk, just doing their job. But some of them would be Bog's people, and that made him smile grimly. If you worked for a Dragon you had to take whatever came with the territory. He found it funny that the principle applied so well to his situation. Choosing to follow Anuka would lead to the deaths of many of the slaves. The deaths couldn't be helped. If they were destined to die today, a death while fighting for your freedom was as good as Anuka could offer them. He would live, of course. His mama had said so.

The commotion behind him was building. That couldn't be helped either, he supposed. Instead of shushing them again, he jumped up on the little crenellation, pointed his rapier in the air, and cried, "To the *Brinery*!" Then he charged.

The roar from the slaves behind him was surprising in its volume and intensity. It spurred him on. He was within forty yards of the guards at the docks before they reacted. At first, they just stared in bewilderment. Slowly, realization dawned on the men as they discerned what the screaming crowd was about. The guard on the right bolted towards the docks, spraying sand as he went. The other reached for his bow.

Anuka reached the guard with the bow before he could aim his shot. With a swipe of his rapier, the man's bow was knocked aside and the arrow flew wildly over his head. A quick flash of his prized dagger opened the man's throat. He didn't dare stop. The wild mob of slaves was fast on his heels and he feared they might run him over in their panicked charge. Hopefully, someone would stop and take the fallen guards' weapons. They'd need them.

His eyes attuned to the night, Anuka saw people stirring farther down the dock as well as a couple of sailors on board the *Brinery*. The fleeing guard had a decent lead and Anuka's short legs meant he had no chance to overtake him. Once the man was out of the cumbersome sand and onto the wooden docks he gained speed. He clamored up the gangplank and onto the deck of The *Brinery*. *Sum Buck.*

Bows came up and Anuka tried to stop the charging slaves but no amount of shouting or pleading registered with the crazed mob. Not until the first two went down.

Long before they reached the gangplank two half-human male slaves went down, arrows sticking out of their chests. The next two died trying to duck for cover. A fifth of the slaves went down before they managed to scramble for cover behind barrels, crates, or wagons. Anuka poked his head around the side of a half-rotten crate to risk a glance at the deck of the *Brinery*. Three archers were combing the beach with their bows, arrows drawn, in search of a target. Before he ducked back behind the crate he saw three or four men with swords heading toward the gangplank.

A scream behind Anuka drew his attention up the beach where two more men with bows were taking up position near the slave quarters to pick them off from behind. They weren't pirates. Even from a hundred strides in the dark Anuka knew who these guys were. Bog's men. PeaceMen.

—⋯◆⋯—

No sooner had the cries of the dying men quieted them than they raised up again. Tabir crept to the door and opened it a crack. A tall figure in black leathers stood not five strides away with his back to the door of the slave quarters. He had five black arrows at the ready, each standing point first in the sand. He calmly searched for targets among the pinned-down slaves.

Tabir slid the door closed and leaned his back against the wall beside it. He squeezed his eyes shut so tightly it hurt. Unbidden, an image played out in his mind. He would open the door, take two steps, burst into a headlong roll, spring up and plant his dagger in the man's spine. Then he would spin to check his left while using the dying man as a shield from the other archer Tabir knew would be at his flank.

No! He screamed at the image. *No.* That was no longer who he was. Even if the need was dire he couldn't force himself to do those things again. Tabir was a mender, a bringer of light, a son of Rathune. He was no longer a warrior. He had vowed to never again take a man's life. Besides, he didn't even have a dagger.

"What is it?" said Offund, the question sounding like a croak. Tabir had been about to see to the man's wounds when the arrows started flying. He planned to heal the small man, with Rathune's blessing, and for the two of them to scurry aboard the ship once it had been taken. Offund would have to be sworn to secrecy, of course. The others would attribute the healing to Offund's unusual constitution and hope no one asked any questions. He could hide and pretend to heal naturally on the ship, then appear as good as new a few days later. That wasn't the best plan but Tabir still tried to balance healing those he could with avoiding death for using a power that didn't come from a Dragon.

Tabir went to Offund's side and put his thin hand on the small man's gray skin. His head was cool as a stone in a stream yet speckled with beads of sweat. "Our friends aren't doing well, I'm afraid," Tabir whispered grimly. He saw no point in lying to the man. Their fate was tied to that of the other slaves. "Sailors are raining arrows on them from the deck of the *Brinery* and now, it seems, two of Bog's PeaceMen are doing the same from outside our door."

Offund looked away from Tabir and stared at the ceiling. His pink tongue licked his parched lips, leaving a crimson stain behind.

When Offund looked back, Tabir saw there was a fire in those dark eyes and his jaw was clenched. "I can help them."

This poor man, Tabir thought. In his fittest state, he was half as tall as a regular man. Two hired killers stood between them and their friends. Offund was so brave.

The small man must have seen the doubt on Tabir's face and said with a growl, "I can help them!"

Tabir put a hand to the man's chest, partly to quiet him but also to keep Offund from rising.

Once back on the floor, the small man pounded his balled fist onto the wooden floor. There was little force behind the blow of frustration. He didn't have much strength left. Offund's breathing was uneasy. When he squeezed his eyes together a tear trailed from the corner of each. When Offund opened his eyes again Tabir didn't see defeat as he expected, he saw resignation.

"I am DragonBlooded," Offund said without looking at Tabir. The words echoed a defeat all their own yet they shocked Tabir. He may be an elf from a different land but was not ignorant of Dorwine. Offund was claiming to have Dragon ancestry. It was rare, but not unheard of, for Dragons to take mortal forms and mate. As often as not, the result was a horrid mutation that left the offspring insane or so weak it failed to survive a year. A few, however, were born as mortals and possessed some of the powers of the Dragon that sired them. This almost always included access to the Dragon's magic powered by their blood. Perhaps this is why Anuka was so keen on keeping the Nob alive. Maybe he knew Offund was DragonBlooded.

When Tabir didn't respond, Offund turned his head, looked at him, and continued. "I can do things. I can...hurt people. I know that I am dying but if you can move me to the door so I can see these PeaceMen I will use what's left of my blood to save our friends."

Tears filled Tabir's eyes and he was suddenly ashamed of his doubts. He laid one slender hand to rest on Offund's forehead and laid the other on his chest. "Rathune, be praised." He whispered.

Chapter 24

Hard Choices

Anuka knew his luck would fail him one day but he hadn't counted on it being the same day he decided to start caring about other people and generally being an adult. It made him doubt his newly adopted outlook on life. *What are our options?* Somebody had to get to the archers on the deck of the ship. First, they'd have to get past the Sum Bucks with swords and hope the other Sum Bucks with bows didn't shoot em' in the back.

He dropped to his belly though he wasn't sure why until he heard an arrow blast through the rotten crate in the space where his head had been a second ago. Maybe he had a little luck left. Or at least his instincts were good.

Papa would know what to do if he were here. And sober. *Stop it!* Anuka chided himself. That line of thinking wasn't going to help.

Suddenly the door to the nearest slave house burst open and a little feller that looked like Offund jumped out and shot something out of his hand at the closest archer. The man's back exploded into mist and he was blown off his feet. The other PeaceMan swung toward the little man and was set on fire by a three-foot-long streak of flame that came from Offund's outstretched hand. The screams of the archers got everyone's attention.

The Offund-shaped creature staggered around a bit. The skinny elf, Tabir, came out to help him. They quickly liberated the first dead

PeaceMan of his weapons and started picking their way down the beach.

It seemed that whatever Offund had done to Bog's enforcers had made the archers on the *Brinery* reconsider. A quick look around told Anuka the right of it, though. The sword-wielding sailors were stalking up the beach and the archers didn't want to hit their comrades. Anuka thought the men knew where he was hiding. Since his spot was the furthest down the beach, they would get to him first. At least he had weapons. The other slaves weren't so fortunate. He should have thought of that. No time now. Anuka could hear the men. It sounded like at least two of them. They were sneaking very poorly toward him. Each step they took made a soft whoosh sound in the sand. Timing their attacks to trap Anuka and finish him quickly, both men darted around the box and stabbed where Anuka had been hiding.

Just as he heard them move, Anuka had rolled back through the wood of the rotting crate, landing on his feet inside it. His chest tightened as his mind processed two sharp swords stabbing the ground where he had just been. *Life was about inches and seconds,* Papa had told him. Anuka didn't waste either. His mind was made up before the men had even gotten to him. With his right arm, he plunged his prized dagger forward and to the right. The blade point sunk to the bone of the man's thigh and he screamed in agony. The point of the dagger stuck a little in the man's leg bone as Anuka yanked it free. He kicked his way out of the crate and into the open. Anuka immediately stepped behind the box, spread his feet, and deftly flipped the long-bladed dagger over, carefully holding the sharp blade between thumb and forefinger.

With a cry, the uninjured man stomped around the box, stared at Anuka, then raised his worn, curved-bladed sword overhead for a cross-body swipe at Anuka's head.

The little goblin's prized dagger buried almost to the hilt in the man's gut before the swing fell. The man doubled over with a sharp cry, folding himself onto Anuka's dagger. The sword tumbled from his hand. Anuka scrambled forward to retrieve the sword, careful to steer clear of the gut-stabbed man's reach. He immediately spun and opened a cut on the man's back. The man screamed and flopped onto his side on the sand. Anuka's blood-covered dagger tumbled from the man's gut and fell to the sand where the man had been standing.

A yell from the first wounded man brought Anuka's attention around. The sailor limped toward him, his face screwed up with pain and anger, his own curved sword ready to strike.

Anuka was an excellent fencer and was very fast, but his luck against full-sized opponents was hit or miss. His superior speed wouldn't do much good in the slippery sand. Anuka brought his stolen saber up in a two-handed grip. That would be the only way he could block a blow from the enraged human. "Fine," Anuka said, "come on then, sea dog!"

The man suddenly lurched sideways several feet as he was tackled by a large roaring clump of fur. The giant Bull-man had rammed the unsuspecting sailor to the ground and simply broke him. He now lay in an unmoving pile a few strides away, his head twisted at a grotesque angle. Anuka was no expert on Bull-man expressions but this one seemed pretty pleased with himself. He snorted violently, sprayed snot out of fist-sized nostrils, and nodded at Anuka. It was like Bull-man was saying "no thanks needed, have some snot". The Minothos scooped up the dead man's sword, then stalked away.

Behind him, the other human groaned.

Anuka sighed, humanely put an end to the groaning man, and scurried after the Bull-man.

Kelios heard a gasp and looked up but not before stumbling into his companions who had stopped in front of him. They didn't look back to protest his clumsiness. They just stared into the massive natural cavern at the Dragon chained to the floor.

It was the most majestic creature he had ever seen. Yet, the state of it made his heart clench like a fist. The scent of blood that his inner bear had been following led here. There were no visible wounds on the creature but large metal devices connected to long tubing were strapped along the creature's body. The Dragon was no more than four full strides long. It slumped so fully into the floor that its back came just above Kelios's waist. Its leathery skin hung in mottled tan and rust-colored folds about its body. Skin that should have shimmered in the torchlight was dull and blotchy. Kelios tried to imagine the beast in flight, soaring high and sparkling in the sun's rays. He couldn't fathom it. "Does it yet live?" he asked, forcing his way through the crowd blocking the doorway. Reminding himself of the dangers of a Dragon, even one so small, his steps slowed and his confidence faltered as he neared it.

The Dragon's chest rose and fell. Kelios heard its labored breathing as he moved close enough to touch it. When his hand passed over the rough skin of its back, Kelios felt energy course through him, faint though it was. The thought of trying to link minds with this creature terrified him. Eyelids tacky with mucus slowly parted, revealing a dark reptilian eye peering at him. Then, as languidly as it had opened, the eyelids closed.

The creature flinched suddenly and panic jolted through Kelios. He looked around and saw Ember standing to his left inspecting the device that was draining blood from the dragon. Ember wore a look of chagrin on his feline face. The Dragon was bleeding, after all. Beneath each of the metal collars were patches of dark, sticky blood. Kelios noticed black patches on the floor where the creature's blood had dripped onto the stone and dried.

The Malkin said softly, "This is horrible. Who would do this?"

Kelios wondered the same thing. It seemed to him that it was unlikely Apostate was the culprit, based on the small amount he knew of the rebellious group. It didn't fit with their agenda. Besides, Crenthys was Apostate. She would never approve of this, no matter how much she hated Dragons.

Kelios looked again at the beast. It seemed a pale reflection of the majestic creatures he had read about in his studies. So dulled and muted was this poor being, Kelios couldn't even imagining it walking.

"We must free him," Ember said, bringing Kelios back to the moment. Ember's tone was both pleading and commanding. Kelios didn't disagree but they had to free Crenthys first.

"We will." Kelios made a point of meeting Ember's pained gaze with a resolute one. He hoped he showed more strength than he felt. "We'll save him, Ember. But we must find Crenthys first. Once we find and free her we will deal with those who have enslaved this poor creature. And we shall help him."

Ember seemed resigned but accepted his words. Kelios was glad. The Malkin seemed ready to begin freeing the creature immediately. He didn't want to deceive the Cat Man but was careful not to agree to free the Dragon. Not until they could ensure their safety. Injured, weakened, it was still a Dragon. Most creatures in such a state were more dangerous than usual.

He turned toward the doorway and noticed that the others were transfixed by the Dragon. They stood cautiously with their backs to the rough wall of the chamber. Each of them seemed to display the same great pity he and Ember shared. He marveled.

Most of these creatures had been slaves to Dragons all their lives, their families enslaved for dozens of generations. They worked tirelessly for the pleasure of the Dragons. Yet, here they stood, filled with compassion for a Dragon who suffered. Maybe it was the extremely pitiful nature of the majestic beast. Maybe they understood that a Dragon this size was likely no more than a child. Still, he marveled.

He was still marveling when a heavy crossbow appeared from the shadows of the doorway, the bolt tip pointed at his heart.

⸺ ◆ ⸺

Arrows blossomed from the deck of the *Brinery* again, as Anuka knew they would once the sailors had been dealt with. This time arrows were returned. At least two bows had been recovered and a couple of the slaves had enough skill to send the other archers scurrying for cover. Anuka's stomach tightened as another figure stepped up onto the deck. "Rollin' Seas. I should have killed that Sum Buck when I had the chance." There stood Captain Swet of the *Brinery*, minus his hat, the one Anuka was now wearing. His hair stood out wildly as he scanned the beach. Most of the slaves had taken cover again to avoid an arrow.

Now what? Anuka thought to himself. They had to get on that ship and somehow get it moving. He was pretty sure the Bull-man was a sailor but beyond that Anuka doubted any of the slaves had much experience manning a ship that size. Most of the crew of the *Sea Pocket* had been killed when the ship was captured. What would Papa do? Papa would talk his way out of this. By the end of the night, Papa and Captain Swet would be sharing a drink in a tavern somewhere. Anuka was good at talking people out of coin but he had no interest in bandying words with this infamous slaving monster. No time, either. His keen ears detected echoing sounds of alarm from farther up the hill. *Great.*

Some of the other slaves were starting to see it, too. Tabir and Offund knelt under cover twenty paces to his left. They were looking at him and whispering to one another. Anuka heard the Minothos snort from somewhere farther down the dock. He would have trouble hiding for long. Too big.

The flow of arrows slowed as targets and the supply of arrows became more scarce. Anuka suspected that Swet had told his men to wait for Bog and Brine's thugs to come. That's what he'd do, in Swet's position.

From his peripheral, he could see Tabir gesturing animatedly. He and Offund were motioning for Anuka to come to their position. Sure. I'll just dodge the arrows from both directions. No problem.

There was another figure huddled nearby that Anuka didn't know. Too many names and faces to keep up with! This was a slender human girl whose stare could melt a rock. She was holding the bow of the PeaceMan Offund had killed.

Hoping he hadn't misunderstood, Anuka swallowed the dry lump in this throat and looked toward the deck of the *Brinery*. Little had changed until the human girl's arrow thudded into the deck less than two paces in front of Swet. Anuka didn't hesitate. As soon as he saw the arrow he bolted, tiny legs eating the sandy space between him and his goal.

Anuka dove gracelessly into the sand behind Tabir and Offund, hearing the whistle of two arrows behind him as he did. He coughed and spluttered sand from his mouth as he was pulled roughly from the sand and deposited behind a stock of barrels. Another arrow whistled into the sand in front of the barrels they hid behind, spraying sand as it struck.

This is stupid, Anuka thought as he hacked and spit, almost to the point of retching, trying to expel the gritty sand from his mouth. He should have fled hours ago. Or hid. Seeing Mama had been too much. She got him all worked up about being a hero. Papa always said, "Women will make you do stupid stuff, son." He wasn't wrong.

It took him a moment to realize that someone was shaking him and yelling something at him. With a quick shake of his head, a handful of sand was flung from each ear.

"He can get you on the ship!"

It was the elf. Tabir. Anuka looked at him like he'd sprouted tentacles. "What?"

"Offund has...abilities. He can do things, Anuka." The words made more sense when his ears were full of sand.

"Anuka, my friend. I owe you my life. I want to repay you but you have to trust me." Offund didn't look crazy as he said the words, but a lot of crazy people didn't look crazy.

"Listen, to me," Offund continued, "We don't have much time, so you have to trust me." Anuka noticed that Offund was holding a long shard of broken glass in one hand like a knife. That did little to assuage his doubts. "I have inside me the Blood of Dragons. I was in that prison cell because Bog's priests discovered it and bought me just to kill me. If I can get you on that ship, and we can kill those archers, can you kill the Captain?"

Anuka looked at Offund as if searching for scales. Blood of a Dragon? That made no sense. Anuka had seen the little man punch holes in a PeaceMan and set another on fire just a few minutes ago. Somehow, the little man, who Anuka had left to die with Tabir, looked pretty strong just now. Maybe he was some kind of Dragon. Anuka thought of how the big human had changed into the DragonMan and nearly eaten him alive back at the Lucky Toss. Papa had told him that he would see things in the world that would melt his brains. That day had come, it would seem. *Drown it!* he thought. *Man's gotta die of something. May as well die trying to do something stupid and heroic.* Actually, papa would never say that. He must have come up with that on his own.

Offund opened his mouth to continue his argument but Anuka stopped him with an upraised hand. "Fine. Do it."

Tabir and Offund exchanged a glance.

"Put me on that ship, right behind Ol' Swet and I'll end him."

Anuka saw a flash of doubt cross Offund's face. Just a bit.

"I will open a hole in the air." Offund put up a hand to forestall Anuka's interrupting question. "Please, we have not time. I will explain later when we are safely heading for the Free Trade Isles. For now, you will see something like a curtain fall and a hole of blackness. When you see this, step in and be prepared to be on that ship."

Anuka rubbed at the dull pain over his left eye as he tried to make sense of Offund's words. Fine. Whatever. Anuka didn't know why a bird could fly, just that it did. He could trust Offund a little. "Sure. That sounds great. Hurry, before I lose my nerve."

Offund nodded and stood, pushing up the sleeves of his borrowed shirt. The little man looked at Swet and started to breathe very slowly. Anuka slid his dagger from its sheath and rolled the bone handle in his hands. His heart was pounding so hard he tried to do some slow breathing of his own. Without taking his gaze away from the ship, Offund raked the jagged glass along the meaty part of his forearm with a grunt. Then he held the shard of glass aloft with the other hand and Anuka saw blood staining the tip. Offund closed his eyes and brought his arm down in a broad arc in front of him. As he did, the air between them sounded like a sheet being ripped. A circle of blackness stood between them. It was like cutting a circle out of a portrait and looking at the unpainted side as it flopped down.

The blackness felt cold to Anuka, even from a couple of strides away. It seemed so wrong but it was exactly as Offund had described. His mind screamed for him to turn and make a break for the beach. To hide somewhere until this blew over, like he always did, and take a ship North in a few weeks. But he had promised Mama and he owed her this much. He sucked in a lung full of air and dove into the blackness.

He burst through the other side in midair, about the height of the bulwark, and landed with a thud on the deck of the *Brinery*. It wasn't a terrible distance to fall but he had imagined he would come out standing on the deck. Though a little stunned, he remembered the plan and jumped to his feet. His prized dagger had fallen from his hands as he instinctively used them to catch his unexpected fall. He scanned the deck for it.

Instead, he saw Captain Swet striding toward him, saber in hand.

Chapter 25

Acts of Desperation

Fighting had not been an option for Kelios and his band. Even if he could have gotten to the caramel-skinned man holding the crossbow before he loosed the bolt, the two still in the shadows would have killed him. And then there was the DragonMan.

Kelios and his party were now being led further down the poorly lit natural tunnel they had started down. Although the back of the DragonMan was exposed to Kelios as they walked, fighting was even less of an option now. Their hands had been bound and the crossbows were pointed at their backs. The red-scaled DragonMan was a head taller than Kelios, his head nearly scraping the rough stone ceiling of the narrow corridor they were traveling. So wide was the man at his shoulders that Kelios couldn't see around him on either side, despite being back-lit by a torch one of their captors carried. This was undoubtedly the same creature Anuka had encountered in the Lucky Toss, though seeing the chain armor stretched across his back and the arsenal of weapons hanging about him, the validity of Anuka's account of that encounter was questionable.

He pursed his lips and shook his head ruefully. If Crenthys yet lived, he was useless to her now. The mission to stop the Blood Letters was being shoved to the front of his mind by his inbred sense of duty, but he could scarcely consider that now. He was currently in no position to address either problem. *There is a way,* he reminded himself calmly. Like a handful of water tossed on a raging fire, the words did little to quiet his raging fears. They needed options.

The DragonMan--Ember had said his name was Pazzix--stepped into an open chamber and stopped suddenly. Craning his neck downward, the DragonMan inspected a ring of keys he pulled from his belt. He opened the massive lock hung about a thick metal slide lock and pulled open a heavy wooden door.

The odor of sweat and dank air oozed out of the room. Kelios felt a sharp poke at his back as the crossbowman urged him into the room. As Kelios entered he noted a sign above the door written in crude Low Draconic that read "Dragon Food".

Splendid, he thought.

⁓⊶◆⊷⁓

Crenthys heard the rattling on the other side of the door and steeled herself. If anyone short of the Red DragonMan opened that door she would make her move and escape. She flexed her hands into fists and crouched, ready to strike. The door swung open and Kelios walked in.

She could not have been more stunned if Morglun himself had walked in. Kelios should be long gone by now, far away from her troubles. This made no sense.

Kelios looked at her for a moment before averting his gaze and stepping to the side of the small chamber to allow a handful of strangers in behind him. She moved to follow Kelios as he filed into the back of the room near where Tamris and her girls huddled. He looked apologetic, and a little chagrined. Had he come here to rescue her? Somehow Wave's people must have captured him and brought him here. Who were these other people? She would have considered Kelios among those most likely to need rescuing. Yet here he stood. With a band of followers, no less.

The slam of the heavy door and the clank of the lock awakened her from her musings. Crenthys noticed that her mouth had been hanging open and that her hands were still fisted. The room had grown very quiet, pregnant with tension. She wanted to say something but couldn't lay hold of any of the thoughts swimming in her head long enough to spit one out.

"Hello." Crenthys jumped at the familiar voice coming from her left and near the door. She turned to regard the lanky Cat Man she had seen in Jhaldus's slave pens. He returned her regard curiously. "Pardon me. I am Ember. You must be Crenthys, unless I am mistaken. I have heard much about you from Kelios and Anuka." The creature bowed at the waist.

Crenthys turned to Kelios, who was staring at Ember with wide eyes. "Anuka? What does he have to do with any of this? And what are you doing here?" she asked.

Kelios looked at her but didn't answer right away. He seemed to be trying to decide which question to answer first.

"I found Akuna, well, he found me, shortly after you and I were separated." His pause at the last word didn't go unnoticed.

So the little goblin had a change of heart? If so..."Where is he, then?"

"He left. Again." Kelios said flatly.

As much as she expected. "Why are you here? Were you captured? Who are all these people?" Crenthys asked, gesturing to the newcomers.

Again, he didn't answer right away. "It's...complicated. We came to rescue you. These are my companions. Slaves we freed from Jhaldus's dungeon."

Rescue her? How did he know she needed rescuing? She remembered the people in the cages where she first saw Ember. It occurred to her that Kelios would have run straight back to the Silver as soon as they were separated. Had Augmaximitis known about Wave all along? That didn't seem to track. This was madness. Crenthys lined up her questions to pepper Kelios but before she could begin firing them she noticed a grave look on his face.

"Cren, do you know about the Dragon?" Kelios asked.

Her mouth sagged open again and the bottom fell out of her stomach.

"The one they are getting the DragonsBlood from. Well, the only one as far as I know. We've seen him." Kelios said.

Ember stepped up and stood by his side.

"Is he hurt? Do you know where they are keeping him?" Crenthys blurted the questions on top of one another.

"Yes, well, they have him hooked to some sort of device. They have been draining his blood to sell. We were captured before we could learn much, but he was alive when we left him, though barely."

Thank the seas! She thought. They had to get out of here. Panic twisted her stomach and she wondered how desperate she really was.

"How big is he?" she asked.

"Less than four strides, for a human of average height," Ember said without hesitation. Kelios and Crenthys looked at him. "You have to consider the height of the person making the strides, of course." Ember continued.

Crenthys looked at Kelios and asked, "Could he walk, or even fly?"

Kelios looked at Ember who pressed his lips together demurely and shrunk back a little. Kelios looked back at Crenthys and said, "No. At least I doubt it. He seemed very weak. And his wings may be tethered in some way."

That was bad. If they could free the Dragon, how would they get him out? How had they gotten him in? He might have been brought here before he hatched from his egg. That would be a problem.

Supposing they could even get out of this room. Then they would need a boat. A big boat.

"Where is your boat? How big is it?" Crenthys couldn't stop the tide of questions from pouring out.

Kelios put his hand on her arm and Crenthys's questions stopped like a skiff running aground. "We don't have a boat. The Silver told us where to go and had one of his men bring us here. But they left us. Cren, we didn't know we would find a Dragon here. I had planned to use the Blood Letter's boats. We came looking for *you*." Kelios drew nearer to Crenthys, his warm gaze intent, and lowered his voice. "*I* came looking for you."

Fear clawed at her gut as it dawned on her what he meant. She was not built to love. Morglun had loved her, or so he said. His profession, and the reciprocal feelings that profession stirred, are what caused her to flee to Usban. She had hoped she could avoid dealing with those emotions ever again. But here she was. Something on her face must have frightened Kelios.

"Cren, what's wrong? Say something." Kelios breathed, panic in his voice.

A dagger of reality burst the bubble she floated in. The baby Dragon. That was her mission now and nothing else mattered. Her heart ached as it broke a bit. She closed her eyes for a moment, then opened them again and looked at Kelios.

"No," she said breathlessly and drew her lips together, staving off tears that threatened to fall.

"No? No what?" Kelios's own words were hoarse like he'd gone days without water.

"Thank you for coming for me. But I can't love you, Kelios. I want to, but I can't."

Her words smashed Kelios like a falling tree. He worked his mouth but made no words. She pulled her arm free of his gentle grasp and held up her hand, forestalling him.

Crenthys forestalled him with a shake of her head. "You said yourself, you are practically married. Your father would never permit you to-"

"My father doesn't own me!" Kelios nearly roared, then composed himself quickly.

Crenthys was both surprised and proud of him. She had never seen such heat from him.

"I am sorry. Crenthys, I have let my family rule my life far too long. Even if I weren't an exile, the things that I've done in past days would put me far beyond their grace. I am choosing now. And I choose you."

Why was this so hard? She bit on her top lip and shook her head. "We can't, Kel. I can't."

"Why?" Kelios pleaded.

"Because she isn't like you, Triton." a voice from the other side of the door echoed.

Kelios and Crenthys jerked their heads toward the door where they saw Wave and Pazzix looking at them through the barred slot in the door.

The lock squealed and the DragonMan jerked the door open. Wave took a step inside and said, "She is a different animal altogether. Aren't you, Brinka?"

⸺◈⸺

Swet's saber thwacked into the deck where Anuka's head had just been. Unfortunately, he rolled in the opposite direction from his dagger. He whipped his rapier out with a metallic ring as Swet wrenched his blade with a grunt. He grinned as he took a casual step towards Anuka. "You have my hat," Swet said, pointing the tip of his saber at the hat on Anuka's head.

"Yeah? Well, I might just give it back. It's too big and it smells like a privy."

Swet lunged at Anuka with an overhand swipe... So quick was the strike that Anuka didn't have time to parry but dove to the deck as the blade whistled overhead.

That was too close. Even if Swet wasn't a fifty-year-old human with a gut like a seal, that strike would have impressed Anuka. As quickly as he had stepped into the strike, Swet was back in a swordsman stance. The old captain could strike or parry easily from that stance, and he had enough reach on Anuka that he could make slashes like that without ever being in real danger from Anuka's rapier. A smug, toothy grin split Swet's face.

Sum buck. The archers were back to harassing the slaves from their perch atop the deck of the *Brinery* and Swet was skilled and strong. Anuka wished for another flame-tossing half-man to pop up about right now. An idea suddenly came to Anuka that was so brilliant and stupid that he had to fight to keep the grin off his face. It must have touched his eyes because Swet looked at him curiously for a moment before darting forward with a sidelong swipe. Anuka was expecting it and ducked easily. The same couldn't be said for the reverse that Swet executed.

The second attack surprised Anuka and he nearly gasped aloud. Swet was quick and his swings moved in smooth, deadly arcs. Still off-balance from ducking the first blow Anuka thrust his rapier into the path of the saber deflecting it slightly upwards. The top half of his rapier blade got sheared off in the process.

Anuka pitched forward onto the deck and Swet lurched to the side. The hours of training and decades of fighting put Swet right back in the fight. He rode the moment of his temporary imbalance and followed that momentum into a spin that let him bring an overhand strike down on Anuka, aiming to split him in two.

Sensing the attack as Swet spun into it, Anuka hustled to get one foot under him and raised his small, broken, sword for one more parry.

Anuka turned the half-bladed rapier to catch Swet's strike at an angle. Sparks flew as the saber slid down the rapier blade and slammed into the broad pommel. It dented the handguard but stopped the blade less than a hand's breadth from Anuka's forehead. The edge of the blade creased the brim of his stolen hat.

Before Anuka could push away, Swet grabbed him with his free hand and, pulling him by his shirt, dragged him closer. The human grinned wickedly as his blade drew nearer to Anuka's face. The saber pushed the hat off Anuka's head a fraction of an inch at a time.

"This is my ship, slave," Swet growled, spraying Anuka's face with spittle that hissed into steam as it landed.

Swet barely noticed the wisps of smoke rising from Anuka's face. Though, for the first time, he did note the mischievous look in Anuka's eyes. Pushing against the man's crushing strength with all he had, Anuka said, "Maybe, but this is my hat!" On the final word, Anuka sprang up suddenly and raked his leg swiftly into Swet's groin.

The big human sucked in a breath but was too experienced a fighter to let a cheap shot do more than distract him momentarily. Luckily, that was all Anuka needed.

Anuka's well-placed kick caused Swet's grasp on Anuka to slacken. Anuka released his sword hilt with one tiny red hand and clamped that hand down on the dull side of the Swet's saber. The broken rapier clanged to the deck.

All of Anuka's sorrow and loss at his mama's death, the pain of abandonment by his father, the jeers and sneers of everyone Anuka had ever met over three feet tall raged in his tiny heart. Anuka poured all of that rage into Swet's blade. Blue flame erupted from Anuka's hand where it touched the sword.

Swet dropped the goblin and stood screaming, his eyes transfixed on the sword in his hand. It glowed a gradient of white and then orange. Smoke rolled up from Swet's hand and he belted a horrid wail just before the blade finally toppled from his hand onto the deck with a hiss. Breathing heavily, Swet stared in disbelief at his ruined hand. So horrified was he that he didn't notice Anuka scoop up his broken rapier and ram its jagged tip into his gut.

Swet fell to the deck in a heap. Anuka turned and scooped up Swet's melting saber before it burned the ship down. Already it had scored the deck and plumes of smoke were roiling up. Knowing it wouldn't hurt him, he held it a second. His mother's blood was to thank for that. Then he tossed the blade into the water where it splashed with an angry hiss.

Seeing both archers gaping at him, fumbling for arrows, he smiled. Casually, he scooped up his prized dagger and turned to greet them.

⁓◆⁓

Kelios tried to step protectively between Wave and Crenthys but staggered a bit. Crenthys grabbed him by his arm and steadied him. He wasn't fevered. His skin was smooth and cool just as she imagined it always was. Had her rejection injured him so severely that he could no longer walk? That was silly.

She saw Wave raise an eyebrow as she guided Kelios over to the two humans standing nearby. Then she turned to regard Wave. This might be their chance at escape. She did her best to drive away thoughts of her conversation with Kelios and put on a mask of stone for Wave.

"What do you want?" Crenthys asked, her contempt genuine. "Did you come here to gloat?"

"In part. I also came to confirm my suspicions about you. Which I have done."

"How did you get here so quickly?" Kelios asked, shaking free of the support the humans offered him. "You would have had to have left when we did, or shortly thereafter."

"He was here before you arrived," Crenthys said. She noted the befuddlement on Kelios's face.

Wave chuckled to himself and said, "I have tricks, Triton. Many tricks."

Crenthys noticed that Wave rubbed absentmindedly at a spot on his chest where something hung from a leather thong beneath his shirt.

"I didn't come here for your questions, Triton. I came for mine." Wave fixed Crenthys with a look and seemed to ponder what he would say. Still, he rubbed at the pendant hanging at his chest.

"Why have you come to Usban, Brinka? Did Morglun send you or is this simply a terrible twist of fate? Terrible, for you, that is." His smile was broad but held no mirth.

"Wave," she began, using the name he had taken though she was now certain who he was, "what have you done?" She strained to contain her outrage but it was no use. Her words were soaked in anger. "Kidnapping a Dragon? Draining its blood? This is not our way, Coryn."

"Do not call us that name!" Wave screamed, thrusting a bony finger in her face.

So sudden and intense was his rage that Crenthys felt he might grab a sword and start swinging it. The veins on his neck bulged. For an instant, his eyes darkened as if filled with blood. This was what she had seen him do on The *Brinery*, only worse now. She had hoped the use of his Apostate name would elicit a reaction. She hadn't expected such vitriol.

Wave quickly stepped back, sucking in air through flared nostrils and bowing his head with an exhale. He straightened the lapels of his traveling jacket and looked up, calm once again painted on his face. The veins of his neck had receded and his eyes returned to normal.

She had not seen that much emotion from Wave. Not even when they were stripped naked aboard The *Brinery*. And why had he said 'us'?

"I do not answer to you, nor do I answer to Morglun or his merry band of peaceful spies. No longer do I lick the boots of lesser men, or bow at the clawed feet of a Dragon. I've gotten what I've come for and done what I came to do. Coryn Osolar is dead. Tomorrow, Shimmer will come and set fire to the trash heap that is Usban and war will begin. First Bog and Shimmer, then the rest will join in. The Dragons will destroy one another and I will step in to pick up the pieces."

What was he talking about? He sounded mad. "Wave, what have you done?"

The sea elf's face twisted into a sneering smile. "I've done in a year what Apostate couldn't do in fifty. No shadow games. No back alley treaties or begging for scraps from the Dragons. Their time has come." Wave stopped and thoughtfully looked around at the other prisoners, his eyes resting on Kelios. But he directed his question at Crenthys. "Does your lover know who you are? Who you really are?"

Despite the crushing swell of terrible things Wave had just confessed to, Crenthys found herself wanting to deny that Kelios was her lover. Why did that matter? This was insanity. That half of what he'd said might be true made her mind numb with shock. Shimmer coming here? Impossible. Why would the Silver DragonLord attack a city controlled by the Black DragonLord? An uneasy feeling washed over Crenthys and she felt her mouth go dry.

"Where is the ambassador?" It was agony to ask but she had to know.

Wave's smile answered her question. "Puzzled it out, have you?" He rubbed at the bauble around his neck again and said, "I struck down the mighty Celebris Augmaximitis with the red goblin's dagger. The moment of his death pierced her like a spear, no doubt. If what they say is true, she felt it even as she was nestled in her mountain, leagues away. She will descend on Usban like lightning and turn the city to ash because everyone knows there is no pain like the pain a Dragon feels when her DragonMan is slain. Made with part of her own soul, there can be no pain greater than his death."

Crenthys was breathing so hard her chest burned and her balled fists shook at her sides. She clamped her mouth so tightly shut that her jaws ached. In the recesses of her mind, she heard a small voice crying out, pleading with her, but the words were lost in the white noise of her rage.

Coryn was taking great pleasure in her torment. "Unless," he continued, "it happened the other way around." He fanned his hands in front of him as if the thought had just occurred to him. "What would happen, do you suppose, to a DragonSpawn who watched as their maker was slain?"

With a primal scream that morphed into an ear-splitting roar, Crenthys changed. Her body rippled and doubled in size in the blink of an eye. Soft blue-green skin melted away, replaced by rough, leathery hide the color of tarnished bronze. She grew taller by a head and her beautiful half-elven face stretched and split into a reptilian head. A Dragon's head. Fingers and toes grew, terminating in long, hooked claws. Her shirt tore and fell away in tatters. Her pants simply burst apart as a long, spiny tail flopped onto the floor with a thump.

She lunged at Coryn but the sea elf was pulled out of reach and through the door by the Red DragonMan. The door slammed shut.

Ecstasy and exhaustion swept over Crenthys as she rammed into the door and bellowed another roar, pounding her scaly fist on the thick wooden frame. She slumped against the door, her head banging on the metal rim of the looking portal. Wearily, she squeezed her eyes shut and felt the sting of tears. This time she could not hold them.

Chapter 26

Captains and Consequences

The ugly turquoise vests on the pack of cudgel-toting thugs marked them as Brine's men. They would usually not have frightened Anuka, if not for their number. There looked to be at least thirty of the dirt lickers. Behind them jogged four of the black-clad archers like the ones who had harried them from the shore before Offund killed them; PeaceMen. Bog's assassins. Four! And that was the good news. An entourage of black-robed figures glided leisurely down the stone path leading to the docks. Four of those carried a platform between them, a bald human riding on it. He looked like he had been weaned on a pickle. A Blood Priest. One of Bog's magic users.

"Sum buck," Anuka said. Can I never catch a break? The last of the slaves clamored up the gangplank and two of them slid it on board and stowed it. Yeah, that'll stop em', he thought wryly. Anuka looked at the group of ruffians standing around the deck. They were all gaping at him. He sighed. With an experienced crew, a couple three ace archers, and a helmsman worth his weight in salt, they might escape. Maybe. These louts didn't know aft from a hole in the ground. He sighed again and turned to address his army.

"Alright, you soggy Sum Bucks! We need to bust out of here right now. Who has sailing experience?"

Three or four hands went up and the big bull fella nodded. His hands were busy holding a massive lantern post like a club. The lantern still dangled from the end so it looked like a giant morning star. Anuka sighed again.

"You," Anuka shouted at the plump, red-cheeked, human who had raised his hand. "Mainsail, take someone with you. Trim to twenty."

"Right, captain." Said the portly man as he grabbed the shirt of a scruffy mixed-blood lug and started towards the forecastle. He stopped suddenly, then doubled back and headed the right way. As he passed again he paused and asked apologetically, "Twenty, captain?"

Anuka resisted the urge to scream and held his arms as far apart as they would go. "About this much rope, chief."

"Right." The fat man nodded and trotted toward the mainsail.

"Do we need to man the oars, captain?"

"No oars, we're too close to shore." Anuka barked incredulously.

"Tug lines?"

"Well, that would help if we were docking. We are trying to leave! Stop trying to be helpful you maggots, and listen!" He spared a glance at the shore and saw the approaching guards were almost in bow range.

"Bovine!" Anuka yelled, pointing to the Minothos, "Put a pull on the kedge anchor!"

He clearly didn't like Anuka's name for him but stalked toward the capstan.

"You dogs," Anuka yelled at three men near him, causing them to jump, "cut the anchor lines. There should be six. The rest of you, get a weapon of some kind and get ready to fight. Be quick before that priest sets us on fire!" Anuka surveyed the men as they scurried about their duties. What was he doing? They were going to be killed and fed to the sea. He couldn't quell the nagging voice of his parents in his head.

"You were made for this. All of your life you have been preparing for this moment." The fiery image of his strong mother was etched in his mind.

"Boy, we've done so much with so little for so long, we can do almost anything with practically nothing!" Anuka chuckled at the memory of one of his Papa's favorite sayings. The sentiment was the same. He didn't want this. He wanted to be north where it got really hot, where there were no stupid Dragons, and where no one counted on him to not get them killed. Wishing would do him no good. He had to get to work.

"Offund!" Anuka shouted.

"What?" came the reply directly behind Anuka and he nearly pulled his dagger on the little man.

Anuka wasn't used to having other people his size around and kept overlooking him. "Can you magic these scum bags to the pit of Torment?" Anuka helpfully made little jerking motions with his hands, in case Offund didn't know what he meant.

"I...I don't know what I have left. They have a trained Blood Priest and a dung cart full of DragonsBlood, no doubt. I can try to buy us some time."

"Ok." Anuka tried not to sound disappointed. Offund stared toward the prow a moment, then turned back and asked, "How about a big gust of wind? Would that help?"

Anuka thought for a second and shook his head. "No. We are in shallow water. Wind like that might capsize us. We need something to push us from the bottom. Get us out of the mud."

Now Offund looked disappointed but there was no time for that.

Anuka turned and shouted, "Where are my archers?"

It was the best Anuka could have hoped for. They were pinned down pretty hard by Bog's archers and that priest was still setting up something. Offund had managed to scare the thugs with clubs away, for now. Besides being afraid, Anuka was tired. He had been up all night, running from guards, fighting, and swimming. He was tired. Offund had given him an idea about how they might escape but so far, that wasn't panning out. He just wanted to give up. Stand up, take an arrow to the heart, and be done. He knew he couldn't give up, though. With his luck, he'd take an arrow in the leg and wind up getting turned to stone and used as a fountain in Bog's castle. From where he lay on the deck, pressed against the bulwark, he looked around. There were a couple of men and women with arrows in them. Most of those were dead, though Tabir seemed to work miracles with the sick and injured. A priest is a good thing to have around, he mused.

"Captain!" Came the shout from his right and he saw the mouth breather who had helped trim the mainsail. He was clamoring out of the forecastle with a canister in each hand and a gap-toothed grin on his face. "I found em'!"

"Get down you lout!" Anuka shouted, just as an arrow caught the man in the middle of his chest. The big man staggered and fell on his back, the canisters rolling free of his hands.

Pandemonium broke out as crewmen started scurrying after the metal containers at the same time arrows sailed overhead or thudded into rigs or compartments. One canister rolled lazily towards Anuka and he scrambled after it on his belly. The real possibility of dying seemed to drive the casual thought of it from his mind. He gingerly scooped up the rolling metal tube and looked around to see Tabir cradling the other. He started to stand but thought better of it. Anuka gave the elf a nod and, surprisingly, the priest laid the canister on the hull and gave it a firm roll towards Anuka. As soon as it left his hand a stiff breeze caught the sail and the ship bucked in the water, the canister rolling back towards Tabir.

"We don't have time for this!" Anuka growled and scurried after the can on his fingers and toes like a crab. He snatched it up, then stood up about halfway and sprinted for the ladder. The wind buffeted his ears and he could vaguely hear muffled cries in the background. When he neared the stairs leading down he dropped onto his bottom and slid. His momentum carried him down the first three steps, then he leaped up and cleared the last four or five, landed with a slide, then sprinted to starboard. Within seconds he spotted what he was looking for.

Though he had asked repeatedly, Anuka hadn't gotten to operate one of these before. "Not a toy" or "too expensive to play with" was always the mantra of the gunner aboard his father's ship. Indeed, one shot from a DragonsBlood cannon was said to cost more than a month's pay for the whole crew. These were desperate times. Gunner would have to understand. Anuka grinned despite the screaming above deck and outside the porthole. Who knew what in Torment they were doing up there. Anuka knew how to load a cannon from watching others. He jammed the grapeshot in the aft cannon after deciding on a chain shot for the other one. Once done, he kicked the quoin pin in place to keep the cannon from moving much once fired. Ordinarily, you would want the cannon to rock a bit so it didn't throw your vessel off course but Anuka had other plans.

It didn't matter where he aimed the cannon, but he picked targets carefully, nonetheless. Anuka needed a kick to dislodge the ship from the shallow water around the docks. Standing behind the cannon looking for where powder should go, Anuka peeked into an open round slot roughly the size of the canisters. Shrugging he jammed the cylinder into the hole and pulled a lever down, which locked it in place.

He stood, hands on hips, staring at the cannon. "How do you light the Sum Buck?" The little door that locked the canister in place had a nipple poking up from the top. Looking around, Anuka saw a tiny, broad-nosed hammer hanging from a chain. *Ah,* he thought, picking up the hammer. He looked at the port side cannon. It was five strides away. He would have to be quick.

"Anuka!" came a cry from the stairs and Anuka nearly leaped out of his boots.

"In here!" He yelled, resisting the urge to launch a tirade lest his voice cracked from the strain.

Tabir appeared at the doorway, huffing. Sweat coursed down his dirty, bruised face that glowed orange from the torchlight.

"We are on fire!" Tabir blurted.

"What's on fire?" Anuka said, his voice cracking anyway.

"The sail. The big triangle-shaped one!"

"Sum buck." There wasn't anything he could do on the deck. If they got loose of the harbor they could run up another sail, or row out to sea. "Come here."

Anuka went back to the cannon, picked up the little hammer on a chain, and beckoned Tabir over. "You ever shoot a cannon?"

"No!" Tabir said incredulously.

"Well, you're gonna. I'll show you how to do it. Real simple. When I say 'go!' you smack this with the hammer, pretty hard." Anuka pointed at the little nipple sticking up. The look on Tabir's face didn't fill him with confidence. He pulled the elf over anyway and handed him the hammer. Tabir looked doubtfully at him, but Anuka ignored that. Best not to give him the chance to bail out now.

Anuka loaded the canister in the other cannon and primed it.

"Now, these are supposed to buck and carry on a bit, but I've battened them down. I've never shot this kind of cannon before so I don't know what it will do. It might break the rigging, it might explode. Who knows? Just don't stand behind it." Anuka said with a shrug. "Ready?"

"Explode? Anuka, no. Why is this cannon going to explode?"

Anuka grinned his biggest grin, the one that showed all of his perfect teeth, and said, "DragonsBlood." Then he drew back the hammer and yelled, "3, 2, 1, go!"

As the tiny hammer hit the nipple the world turned inside out. Immediately the huge ship listed to port and Anuka and Tabir were knocked off their feet. The flash of light was like putting the sun suddenly into a dark room. Anuka's vision went white and his ears rang like a bell. He opened his eyes and saw Tabir struggling to gain his feet. He was on his hands and knees feeling for the wall. The ship continued to rock back and forth. The last thing he remembered was the screams of the crew above deck.

———◆———

Anuka was cold. Cold and he seemed to be floating. But that wasn't right. He was sailing. Father had left Baranelrith two days ago and Anuka had gotten to come with him. His eyes were blurry but he was sure he was in his father's cabin, though it looked kind of plain. "Papa..." he croaked. He blinked his eyes and his head pounded. He was too young for strong drink, father would never allow it. Maybe he wasn't with his father. In a flash, it all came back to him. The cannon blossoming to life and hurling him to the deck replayed in his mind. He bolted upright.

Tabir was at his side. "Peace, Anuka. You are well." The elf laid an arm on Anuka's shoulder, but the goblin pulled away.

"What happened? Are we on fire?"

"No. The fire has been dealt with. Kikkabar is a capable sailor. We are well away."

"What's a Kikkabar?"

"Who. Kikkabar is the Minothos slave."

"The bull-man?" Anuka asked, his head still pounding.

"Yes, but I suggest you stop calling him that. He doesn't seem to care for it."

Anuka nodded absently. No way he would remember that name with this headache. "What happened?"

Tabir sat on a stool near Anuka's cot and, putting his hands in his lap, looked down at him. He seemed to be searching for the right words.

"Our aim was true, if you were aiming for Bog's priest, that is. One of the cannons hit him almost directly. The other...Well, after the cannon shot, and once the ship was righted, the soldiers gave up the fight."

Anuka winced. He felt...what? Guilt? Perhaps. It didn't make him happy to kill but sometimes it needed done. Bog's people, Brine's too, were not innocents. Soldiers or no, they were combatants. "Guards." Anuka corrected. "The Dragon lands have no standing armies. They were city guards and temple guards."

"Yes. Well, once the ship was righted they fled into the city. Kikkabar doesn't think they have the means to follow even if they desired. Much of the dock area was destroyed."

Anuka nodded some more. Then he looked at Tabir.

"Where are we going?" Anuka asked.

"I was hoping you could sort that out. The crew wants to go north, back to the Free Trades Isles."

"What? We just came from there! No. I've got stuff to do. I have to find my papa. He's south, not north!"

"And your friends?" Tabir asked with a look that felt suspiciously accusatory.

Sum Buck. His friends. Did he have friends? Crenthys and Kelios would certainly not consider him a friend. Not after he abandoned them. Twice. But he couldn't leave them to whatever that slug Wave had in mind for them. Being somebody's friend was easy when things were going well, he supposed. He sighed. "Fine. Let's go talk to the big Kick-a-choo bull-man." Anuka hopped off the cart and sauntered gingerly towards the door, leaving Tabir with his face in his hands.

Kick-in-the-pants looked like any other bully Anuka had met. Big. Hairy. Giant horns sticking out of his head. "Best to get this over with," he sighed. Anuka marched, head down, toward the Minothos when a cheer went up.

"Say hey fer Anuka, right?" a sailor yelled and a host responded, "Right!" Suddenly, there were pats on the back and cheers all around. One fellow tried to hug Anuka but the flash of his dagger blade held the man off.

Anuka finally wormed his way in front of the giant Minothos. One of his hooves was bigger around than Anuka's head. Anuka questioned his innate desire to start a fight that often led to great trouble. There was nowhere to run on a boat. Likely, he would end up in the drink. He felt a little stab of pain when he realized he didn't have any friends to stand with him. Well, the priest was with him, he thought, and maybe Offund. Pumping some steel into his spine, Anuka looked way up and regarded the bull-man.

"You live." Said the Minothos, his rumbling voice nearly rattling Anuka's teeth.

Kick-a-poo? Dang it. What was this thing's name?

"Yeah," Anuka said brilliantly. He hoped his voice didn't sound as stupid as he thought, but he was sure the bull-man knew it. Why was he so bad with names?

"Say, Kirr..."

"Kikkabar," Tabir whispered helpfully, from behind him.

"Kikkabar," Anuka said. "Where we headed?" His voice squeaked a little and didn't sound nearly as casual as he aimed for it to.

"North." The Minothos rumbled, "Crethos."

Anuka chewed on his bottom lip and nodded his head while looking around.

"How about we don't?" Anuka asked. Kikkabar just stared at him so Anuka continued. "I have business in the south. That's why I stole this ship in the first place."

"We stole this ship. The way south is shut. We have likely angered the Black god. He controls everything south. We go north."

"I'm not worried about Bog, or Brine, or Perdition." Anuka thumped his chest violently. "I am a free goblin. No Dragon rules me. Besides, I've been north. What I need is south."

Kikkabar looked away, out at the sea and said, "We go north."

"Listen here you mangy slab of beef. Turn this boat around or I'll open you from neck to nethers! Steaks for everybody."

Tabir jumped between Anuka and Kikkabar as the big Minothos stepped forward, fixing Anuka with a glare.

Anuka didn't remember drawing his dagger, but there he was, rolling it smoothly in his hand.

"Stop! We can't afford any more bloodshed!" Tabir looked between Anuka and Kikkabar until the Minothos seemed to relax just a bit. "Frankly, I am tired of tending the wounded."

Anuka still held his blade.

"You are outnumbered, goblin. The crew is with me." He was right and Anuka knew it. The posture of the crew said as much. Curse them all.

"If it weren't for me, every one of you Sum Bucks would still be in a box waiting to be sold as slaves. Every one of you!" Anuka's voice cracked on those last words. He knew it was pointless. "Just take me back. Or leave me on the beach somewhere and I'll make my own way." He couldn't help the sob from escaping as he spoke, his shoulders sagging.

The crew was silent and Anuka wished they weren't. He was ashamed of his tears. It would be better if they yelled at him, or kicked and spat at him. The silence hurt him more.

"What is so important that you would willingly face the wrath of a god?"

It was Kikkabar. Unless Anuka heard wrong, there was a note of sympathy in the thickly accented words.

"Everything." Said Anuka. It was the only word he could get out without bursting into tears like a child.

Another moment of quiet passed before Tabir spoke. "Anuka has lost his father." The goblin looked up at the elf, tears staining his cheeks. Tabir smiled back sadly as if to say, *Yes, I've been listening.* He continued. "His father is missing and the only friends he has in the world, his only help in finding his father, have been captured by a very bad man. They won't survive if they aren't rescued."

"The crew must go north. We are firm in this. We have decided. By right, this is your ship. There is no honor for us in stealing what is yours." The basso voice spoke the words with solemnity and resignation.

"You're right. I boarded the ship and killed its captain. The *Brinery* belongs to me." Anuka said.

Tabir looked at his feet at the mention of the captain.

"Keep the ship." Anuka went on, causing murmurs to ripple through the crew. "It means nothing to me without my papa. And without my friends. If you help me free my friends, and take us to the nearest port south of here, the ship is yours to do with as you wish. On my word as a...whatever I am."

Kikkabar looked around at the crew who mostly nodded their assent. With a nod of his own, the Minothos looked at Anuka and said, "On my honor. It will be so."

Chapter 27

Escaping the Truth

K elios tried to breathe but it wasn't working. His mind reeled with shock and he wasn't the only one. One of the girls supporting the woman with the broken arm fainted. Ember covered his eyes with his hands and made a hissing noise. The human brothers caught him when he tried, and failed, to become the bear. They let him go and guided him to rest against the wall. His own hands were shaking. So tired. Crenthys. She was like him. But totally different from him. What this her true form? If so, how could they ever...? He let the question die in his mind and moved carefully to her side.

"Crenthys." He said gently. She turned her head toward him a little but did not look up. "Crenthys, are you okay?"

"No, I am not okay." She said hoarsely, still not looking up. Her voice was so much bigger than before. More volume, more power. More pain. Undaunted, he stepped closer and put a hand on her back. She was now a head taller than him and much broader in the shoulders. She startled at his touch but slowly raised her scale-covered head and finally looked at him. Her look was meant to shock him into recoiling from her, he guessed, so he did not flinch. She was still beautiful. Was she a she? From his studies of Dorwine, he had read that DragonMen could not procreate. Their sex was a matter of preference on the part of their creator. He smiled sadly at her, not removing his hand.

Crenthys pushed herself off the door and stood to her full height. She looked down at Kelios with despair in her reptilian eyes.

"Kelios," she said, her voice musical. He had assumed her words would be garbled or thickly accented but she spoke with a smooth melody. "I have ruined everything."

"Why didn't you tell me?" Kelios asked.

Crenthys blinked slowly and exhaled a frustrated huff through her nose. "I could not. I am not supposed to exist."

Kelios shook his head. "I don't understand."

"My master, Belendurath, was slain. I should not have survived that." Crenthys said.

Behind Kelios, Ember gasped. "Sheen? Your creator was the Bronze Dragon called Sheen? That isn't even possible." Ember said. The Malkin had been invisible until the worst possible moment.

"I mean. You can't feel emotions like mortals. You can only love your Dragon. Which is why you should be..."

"Dead," Crenthys finished. "I don't understand it either, Ember. I am broken in a way that makes no sense. "

Kelios looked at the Malkin curiously.

Ember shrugged. "I read a lot. Dragon news is always written down."

Kelios turned back to Crenthys. "Cren, I still don't understand. You are Apostate. You hate dragons. But..."

"They don't hate Dragons. They hate how Dragons rule. Well, Apostate does. I hate them. All of them." She bowed her head and was silent. Kelios didn't press her. After a few moments, she looked back at him. Some of her despair had been replaced with anger.

"When...when Belendurath was killed, the Dragons left me. I was put out of my own palace. When I broke in to say my goodbyes, they tried to kill me. They said I would not survive a month and that I would probably go insane before I died. And that I would hurt people."

It was a generalization, Kelios knew, but the metallic Dragons were generally fair and honorable. This didn't make sense to him. The records his family had access to would need to be updated.

Crenthys continued, "I fled, staying as far away from Dragon keeps as I could manage. I couldn't use my status for any kind of help. Every time I did, a Dragon Hunter would find me, sent from the DragonLords. Kelios, I almost starved before someone found me and took me in. A human named Morglun gave me a place to stay and fed me. Eventually, after he had convinced the other leaders, he brought me to Apostate. It took years for me to be trusted, but they trained me and cared for me, despite what I was. When they discovered that I could morph into other forms, they put me to work. My first solo mission was to come here and find Coryn, and try to stop him. Only, we didn't know who he was, for sure. None of our group had ever met him in person. He was a valuable asset for many years but something changed him."

"It was the demon, I suppose." Ember offered off-handedly. Again, all eyes turned to the Malkin and he shrunk in on himself.

"Demon?" Crenthys asked.

"Well, yes, obviously." Ember looked from person to person but found no support, only blank looks. He sighed and smoothed back the hair on his face with the back of his hand. "All sentients -" Ember began, "all thinking creatures are souls."

"Have souls." Kelios corrected.

"No. That is modern teaching. We *are* souls, we *have* bodies. Our spirit was created by Rathune, our bodies designed by lesser gods. It's an important distinction. It's one of the reasons that no real scholar takes any of the Dragon churches seriously. It's an egregious-"

"Ember." Crenthys interrupted.

"Right," Ember said with a nod before returning to the topic. "These bodies hold our spirit like a melon in a basket. Only, there is room for more than one melon in our baskets, err, bodies." The look on Kelios's face suggested that he was forming a question so Ember hurried on. "We were created to live in a body alongside our Creator. Only, we denied him. He isn't with us. No, we don't have time for questions. We can discuss the finer points of theology later if we survive." Ember said, heading off another question. "Do you ever feel empty? Lonely in a room full of people?" Ember looked around, at the nods and shrugs. Kelios had never seen the Malkin so animated. His dark eyes twinkled. "This is because we aren't meant to be alone. In our bodies. It is confusing, I know, but it's essential to understanding what is wrong with Coryn. Recently, relatively speaking, within the last one hundred years or so, a group of elves began making contact with harsh spirits. Evil spirits. These spirits were in stasis with Keit and Tor, no, I said no questions. Anyway, these spirits spoke with these elves and began to teach them how they could invite them into their bodies. All of this is theoretical. I haven't yet found anyone to confirm it."

Kelios and Crenthys exchanged looks of wonder but both were intrigued by the Malkin's ramblings.

"Anyway," Ember continued, "These spirits offered the elves great powers if they could ride along with them. Put their melon in the elves' baskets. This gave these evil spirits much greater contact with the physical world. They truly did offer power, ancient power, to their new hosts, at a cost. Each time the host drew on the power of these spirits their own spirit's connection with their body weakened. The things I have read about this are why I believe this is what happened to Coryn. I mean, I thought he was just a troglodyte, but what you said about his sudden change confirms my suspicions."

The room was silent for a long time. Kelios looked at the door to make sure they weren't being spied on again. They were not. None of what Ember said lined up with what Kelios knew of this world. True, his people were technically not of this world, but some of this was hard to reconcile. Though some of it made sense.

"Ember, if what you say is true, what does that mean for us?" Kelios asked.

"Well, it means that Coryn is irredeemable. The host can, if given proper help, reject the evil spirit but why would they? They have access to power and they don't know they are hurting themselves. The elves who discovered this power were almost all destroyed. Rathune himself raised up a priest and made the ground swallow a whole city."

Silence lingered for a moment before Crenthys nodded. "So we have to kill Coryn?"

"Pretty much," Ember said.

Crenthys nodded. "Good. I think that might make me feel a little better."

Wow, Kelios thought. *That was dark.* "How are we going to get out of here?" He tried to lower his voice to a conspiratorially soft tone.

"I don't know," Crenthys growled.

"Well," Ember said sheepishly. "Crenthys isn't the only one of us with a terrible secret."

⁕

The Malkin was insane. That was the only answer that made sense to Crenthys.

"So you can do magic, like a Dragon. But you aren't DragonBlooded?" Kelios asked skeptically.

Ember huffed. "Yes. Blood is power. But the magic, as you call it, is really just the expressed power of Creation. Crenthys, when you morph into another creature, what do you think about?"

Crenthys shuffled uncomfortably and looked around at the others, who were listening with rapt attention. She cleared her throat. "Well, we are taught to fixate on certain symbols in our minds. Or sometimes to focus on an image of a symbol."

"Like these?" Ember said and used the palm of his hand to fan his arm hair up so it stood away from his skin. Crenthys looked closely and saw outlines of dark symbols scrawled up Ember's arm. He brushed the hair down and they disappeared.

"How is this possible?" Crenthys breathed.

"Secrets are only secrets until they aren't. At some point in history, these symbols were taught. Human priests have these. It's how they use this power."

"Yes, but they have access to DragonsBlood," Crenthys argued.

"Granted by their god or patron. My master in the Academy where I trained discovered that he could use this power by using a special alchemical formula to make a special kind of ink from DragonsBlood. These symbols, permanently etched into my skin, coupled with the blood of a Dragon, allow me to access this power."

"So, you need my blood?" Crenthys asked.

Ember sighed. "No, that won't work. It has to be pure DragonsBlood. Alchemy doesn't work with the blood of a DragonSpawn."

"So..." Kelios said, "What good does that do us? If you need real DragonsBlood how does this weird power help?"

Ember didn't say anything. He simply opened his other hand that had been locked in a fist. Covering his palm was dark, sticky blood from the baby Dragon.

Chapter 28

A Fools Hope

T his probably wasn't the stupidest thing Kelios had ever agreed to, but just now he couldn't think of anything to top it. Anuka likely had a litany of such events to pull from. Once everyone noticed that Crenthys was naked, they had pitched in and made a makeshift outfit for her. Now she stood with her back to the door and Ember nestled close to her chest in what looked like an embrace. His hand, the one not smeared with DragonsBlood, was aimed at the door beneath Crenthys's arm. The Malkin said he would shield them with a little magic and that would protect them somewhat. Kelios was not nearly as comfortable with this as Crenthys was. Indeed, a soft blue sheen of air hovered over the pair, easily visible in the mostly dark room. Ember was chanting to himself and holding his bloodied fist closed over a symbol on his right shoulder.

Crenthys fixed Kelios with a glare and, no matter how badly he wanted to look, he turned his back and covered his ears like the rest in the room had done. Kelios huddled down behind the three women, who Crenthys seemed to know, putting himself between them and the door. It seemed like they stayed clumped like that for a long time, it likely had only been a few minutes. Even with his palms pressed to his ears, he heard a cry from Ember that sounded quite feral, like a leviathan. Kelios heard a crack like a whip and he was suddenly bowled forward by a soft force of incredible strength. It was like being hit in the back with a pillow swung by a giant. The next thing he knew, he lay atop the women, and Ember was pressed against his back with Crenthys on top of him.

Kelios's ears rang, adding to his disorientation. He could feel Ember and Crenthys writhing on top of him, struggling to climb off. He wasn't having any luck pushing himself from the pile. The women he lay on top of were yelling and fighting violently to get him off them.

Crenthys finally got a hand on the wall and pushed off, dragging Ember with her. Kelios rolled to the side, landing painfully on one knee. He looked around and saw that two slivers of wood, each about the width of his hand, were all that was left of the door hanging on the twisted hinges. Splinters covered the floor of the room and down the hallway as far as he could see. Crenthys had dozens of tiny shards of wood stuck into her back, some of which bled a little. His head swam as he tried to stand. "We've got to get out of here." He tried to say but, since his ears still rang like the dinner bell on the *Sea Pocket*, he couldn't tell if he whispered the words or screamed them.

Crenthys grabbed him roughly and hauled him to his feet. *Seas she was strong!* He began helping others. If Kelios had known how powerful the blast was going to be he might have suggested waiting until Wave, Coryn, whatever he was called, was at the door again. He quickly glanced at Ember's hand and saw that most of the blood was either dried or gone and now thick, painful-looking blisters covered his palm where the blood had been. *We need to get to the water,* he thought. Pure DragonsBlood was toxic to most creatures, except Dragons, and Ember was favoring his hand. More reason to hurry.

The human brothers were out the door in a flash and returned shortly with a pair of lit torches. The plan was to get to the boat Coryn's people had used and trap them here, flee for Usban Port, and come back with authorities to rescue the Dragon. Kelios would have been more confident of the plans if Celebris wasn't dead and he knew which authorities could be trusted. Bog and his people would certainly want to avoid the wrath of the Silver DragonLord, but Kelios wasn't sure they could convince them of any of this. It was too far-fetched. He wasn't sure he believed it. Celebris had said that Bog knew of this operation but he hadn't said just how much the old Black Dragon knew.

Crenthys was a DragonSpawn. That was unbelievable even though his eyes confirmed it. *What would mother say now?* He thought with a chuckle. Did this change anything? He wasn't sure how he felt. An hour ago he had been willing to give up everything for her. What kind of future could they have? Besides, she had lied to him. Kelios shook his head to clear it and joined the others filing out the door. It didn't matter. She had made her feelings about him known.

He fell in line behind the three women and followed them as quietly as he could through the cool, stone cavern.

Crenthys felt like a blanket being pulled from all sides by excited children. At any moment she would fray and fly apart. Love. Attraction. Desire. These things were denied to her kind. She now stood as an abomination to her creation. She should not care what Kelios felt towards her. Yet... Kelios had stirred feelings in her she hadn't believed possible. And she had spurned him. After a decade of dealing with the loss of her creator, she learned she had a brother. Then she learned that he was being leeched to death. If they met the Red DragonMan in these dripping caverns they would all die, or she would die buying them time to get away. Then her brother would surely die. If they met Coryn . . .

The idea of killing Coryn excited her. That was a bit disturbing. She hated him for his betrayal, or maybe for his madness. She hated him because he knew her past and had revealed it to everyone. To Kelios. Mostly she hated him for hurting her brother. Crenthys supposed some part of her DragonSpawn nature included a protective instinct. It was powerful, whatever the source.

She abandoned those unhelpful thoughts and tried to focus on her brother. They came upon an opening to a cavern Crenthys recognized. She slowed but did not stop. They had come this way when she had arrived with Jhaldus. The scent of blood in the air made her hackles rise. She would come back for him. *They* would come back for him, Kelios had promised. Her hands shook by her sides and she balled them into tight fists. She ground her teeth together and took up a brisker pace.

The group slowed again a few minutes later. They came to the place where the cavern expanded and the two forks merged. The sounds of dripping water echoed off the rough chamber walls. Crenthys closed her eyes and opened her senses. She had been the half-elf for so long, she was no longer accustomed to the heightened senses she enjoyed in her true form. Everything was clearer. Though her elven ears were keen, she could now hear subtle things she otherwise would have missed. The scent of saltwater that previously melted into the background now hung heavy in the air. The mingled smells of blood and sweat were like the aftertaste of a bad swig of ale. As she concentrated on the information her bolstered senses took in, her mind filtered it.

Beyond the stink of unwashed flesh and Tamris's rotten breath - abusing Tent Weed had done that to her - Crenthys caught another scent. Her eyes popped open and she leaped forward just as a skinny half-elven girl stepped from the shadows, crossbow in hand.

"Ambush!" she yelled as she slammed into the surprised girl, using her momentum to smash her spiny forehead into the girl's thin nose, crushing it. As the girl fell back in pain, Crenthys wrenched the crossbow from her hands and raised it toward the other shooter that she guessed was hiding deeper in the shadows. She fired a bolt into his face without hesitation.

If they were quick, they may still be able to...

The thought died as she saw three more crossbows leveled at her. One of them was held by Coryn. He would not miss. The only weapon she had was the unloaded crossbow. In a surreal moment, she saw Coryn's eyes as he pondered her death. There was nothing she could do. She had only felt this hopeless one other time in her life. The day her Master was killed. Carefully she laid the crossbow down on the ground and kept her hands where they could be seen. Why didn't he just do it?

She heard a commotion behind her but didn't dare look. The Red. She hadn't seen him among the other of Coryn's people filing out of the darkness with weapons in hand. They were done.

You can't reason with a madman. If Ember was right, Coryn was worse than mad. He was possessed. She could stall. What else could she do? "Why are you doing this?" Crenthys asked. The question surprised her as much as it did Coryn. "Are you just so keen to watch the world burn around you?"

Coryn lowered his crossbow and looked at her. His eyes didn't hold much of the color she had seen earlier and no black veins were bulging atop his skin. Maybe she was talking to him, and not the evil spirit.

Coryn cocked one eyebrow and tilted his head to the side. Then he said, "Yes." He moved the crossbow to his other shoulder and shifted his feet. "Out of the ashes of Dorwine, a Dragon-free Dorwine, we will build a new nation."

"Who will be left? If you turn the Dragons against each other, we all die." She turned her hands out pleadingly.

"Not true." Coryn swung the heavy crossbow off his shoulder and began to pace. "I have learned things, Brinka. I can go where no one can find me. Take my people with me. Wait this whole thing out." He gestured with his hand but didn't look at her. "I am not alone in this. Do not fear." He stopped and smiled at her. "There will be plenty of us to rebuild. We will have the chance to forge our own cities, our own governments, our own races!" A touch of the wildness she had seen earlier seeped into Coryn as he got worked up. He stepped right up to her and said, "My people, the Sea Elves, will be just the Elves. We will be the only Elves left!" He smiled a big smile.

"You would sacrifice all of the people of this land? For that? You are mad."

He stepped closer, put his face right in front of hers and she feared he would attack her, though he was no longer holding any weapons. "*I'm* mad? Madness is living for a thousand years, worshiping those things, and living our whole existence for them! THAT is madness!" He stalked away and resumed his pacing. "Sometimes I think we're the only sane ones I know." He whispered as he paced away.

Crenthys chanced a glance over her shoulder and saw the Red DragonMan holding his shiny, long-bladed sword to Kelios's throat. Poor man. He would have been much better off had he never met her. She hated herself for that. Mostly she hated that she had other feelings brewing for him. It wasn't fair for either of them that she did. Now he would die never knowing how she really felt.

She felt anger rising from her gut like lava from a volcano. She spun back to where Coryn was muttering to himself. "What gives you the right?" she roared.

Her yell startled him from his mutterings and he snapped his head up. A mask of amusement grew on his face. "Why, I have all the power, love. This plan has been in the works for years. Every bow, every 'yes Master Dragon', every degrading, demeaning, tirade I've endured. They have all been for this moment." He gestured into the air with his hands.

"You think stealing a Dragon and selling its blood gives you power?" Her breathing was hard, and she had dropped her hands to her sides and formed them into fists. Coryn laughed.

He laughed hard for nearly a minute. So long did he laugh that Crenthys had trouble holding on to her anger. Instead, she was filled with confusion. *Had he cracked?*

When he stopped laughing and worked to catch his breath, tears were rolling from his eyes. "Who cares about DragonsBlood?"

He had to be mad. Best she could figure, he had made ten fortunes from the Blood they had sold. The fear that something even worse than the kidnapping was happening knotted her stomach.

"What are you talking about?" she asked cautiously.

Coryn pursed his lips before shrugging. "My people. His people." Coryn pointed over her shoulder at Kelios. "The blue-skinned Dwarves. What do we all have in common?"

It was clear after a moment that he was waiting for an answer. "Water breathing."

"Yes! Very close, at least. We make excellent underwater scavengers. Terrific slaves because of it." He gestured at his slave mark. "They catch us, or they buy us, and Brine brings us here to scour the ocean for baubles. Find something pretty or some long-lost magic item rumored to have been aboard one of the hundreds of ships to sink out on the seas. It turns out, some of those rumors are true." He shrugged and said, "Well, one is for sure." He flashed another half-crazed smile. "I found something, Brinka. Something so wondrous that I would sacrifice a thousand Usbans for it. I discovered where it was hidden and I came and took it! No Dragon can withstand me now!"

"What did you find, Coryn?"

"That..." he held up a finger and drew out his response, "I won't tell you. Some secrets are just too good. They don't even know." He chuckled, gesturing to the two Dwarves that flanked him, still aiming their crossbows in Crenthys's general direction.

They had to get away. He was going to kill them all, and her baby brother, too. She suddenly became overwhelmed with emotion.

"Coryn, please!" she cried stepping towards him, "You can kill me, kill us all, but please let my brother live. He is innocent."

Coryn's jaw slackened and his mouth fell open for a moment before another crazed grin covered his face. "In-credible! You didn't know the beast existed and now you act like his mother. What about the Triton? Are you willing to let him die?" He said, pointing over her shoulder.

She mumbled inaudibly through a sob.

He stepped closer and tilted an ear to hear. "What was that?"

She sniffed. "I. Said. Yes!" she screamed the last word and spun Coryn around, grabbing him in a headlock, and held his body in front of her as a shield.

The DragonMan increased his grip on Kelios's neck and squeezed when he saw Crenthys take hold of Wave. Colors swirled before his eyes. Even in the dimness of the cavern he reflexively grabbed at the iron grip. Kelios desperately wanted to help Crenthys but he knew he didn't have the strength to summon the bear. If it did come he wouldn't have the strength to send it back. That would be a disaster but no worse than his current situation.

The edges of his vision darkened and he felt his consciousness slipping away. Crenthys and Wave were arguing. The Red was yelling, too, but Kelios couldn't hear his words. It sounded like land folk talking underwater. His arm fell from the DragonMan's wrist and swung limply.

Suddenly, he crumpled to the ground and sputtered out a hoarse cough, gasping for air. Kelios was on the verge of vomiting as he tossed from side to side. The Red DragonMan stepped over him and marched briskly towards Crenthys. Finally, Kelios rolled to his side and saw the Red backhand Crenthys hard enough to knock her off her feet. He wanted to scream. He wanted to run to her aid and strike down the DragonMan. He hadn't the strength for any of those things.

Kelios felt someone put a boot on his arm and roughly roll him to his back, pointing a loaded crossbow at him. He lay on his back, arms and legs sprawled, staring at the rough gray stone ceiling as the orange torchlight danced across it. It was funny how it reminded him of the sea. He couldn't reconcile those days with this one. At home, he was spoon-fed his destiny each day. His whole life was charted out for him. Kelios realized that his people were so concerned with what would come next that they never were aware of the moment they were in. All the memories of his childhood were about honoring the family or doing your duty. There were no memories of enjoying the embrace of his mother or discussing something other than strategy or plans with his father. Even his relationship with his brother was a competition for love and respect. But it was all a lie.

Kelios would die here and all that talk of destiny would turn to dust. With all his heart he wanted to know how to just be in the moment. To savor it. It seemed so unfair. He squeezed his eyes shut and tried to push away the pain in his lungs, his neck, and his broken heart. He had followed his destiny so closely, had been the perfect son. Now destiny laughed at him.

In his mind, he felt the bear nuzzle his face. He sensed the creature's raw emotions tumbling about in its mind. There was sadness directed towards him. He sensed fear, also directed at Kelios. Finally, he sensed immense gratitude. Despite all that had happened to the poor creature, Kelios had shown her compassion where no others had. Questing forth with his mind, Kelios comforted the bear and wished her peace. Then the bear stepped over the threshold of Kelios's mind and took control.

———◆———

The ringing in Crenthys's ears was clearing, finally. She hadn't been hit that hard since...she couldn't recall ever being hit that hard. Her head swam as she tried to climb to her feet. She was aware of the Red standing over her with that long-bladed sword in his hand. *Seas*, had that been his backhand that struck her?

Her ploy had turned out the way most stupid ideas do. Now she felt the weight of reality threatening to break her back. The room still spun and she closed her eyes to clear it. The ringing was fading now, but she heard a churning noise, like maids churning butter. So odd, that sound.

The Red jerked his hand up to shield his face as a metallic ring resonated through the chamber. Crenthys looked up and saw shock on his face and a thumb-sized dent in his breastplate. She whipped her head back towards the water and heard, "Time to die you Sum Buck!"

She couldn't believe her eyes. Anuka was running up the shore towards them with a dozen of the oddest assortment of folks she could imagine, though she vaguely recognized some of them. A giant Minothos, one she was sure she recognized, ran right beside Anuka. Then she heard the roar.

The charge stopped and all eyes looked into the cavern. Kelios was melding into a giant bear right before their eyes, roaring all the while. Within seconds he filled the cavern with his furry bulk and simply swatted away the man aiming a crossbow at him like the man was no more than a bee.

"Bear Man!" Anuka yelled. Resuming his charge, he pumped his fist in the air and exclaimed, "Yeah baby!"

Chapter 29

Impossible Foes

Crenthys didn't understand what she saw. At once she felt joy, terror, and betrayal. Kelios had his own secrets, it seemed. The ease with which Kelios tore through Coryn's men made her heart sing. Pazzix backed up uncertainly as the bear mauled its way towards him. Still reeling somewhat but bolstered by the arrival of help, she stood and looked around for Coryn. He was gone.

That slippery eel! He had vanished in a second. At that moment Anuka stopped ten paces away, yanked back the string on his crossbow, and raised it to aim straight at her.

"Anuka, wait!" she plead.

He didn't lower the crossbow and his followers streamed past him to engage in fights with some of Coryn's men. Anuka lifted his head from the weapon's sight and cocked it to one side.

"Anuka, it's me, Crenthys!" she wanted desperately to show him something that would convince him but she had nothing. He was so dim-witted and thick-headed she would never convince him. "Put that thing down. We don't have time for this! Wave is escaping."

He lowered the crossbow then. "Crenthys?" He screwed his face up in confusion and looked her up and down. Then he put a hand on his hip and shook his head, huffing through his nose. "Am I the only person on this island that doesn't turn into something else?"

Part of her wanted to hug him, part of her wanted to break his neck. Before she could decide he jerked the crossbow back up, panic on his face. She dropped to the ground and Anuka fired. As soon as she heard the draconic swear she rolled gracelessly out of range of Pazzix's sword strike.

The Red was fleeing from Kelios and she had simply offered an opportunity for attack. The people Anuka brought weren't armed much better than her group and would provide little resistance to Pazzix.

A haunting series of growls and barks erupted from farther up the cave behind Kelios. Even the bear paused to look. The barks grew louder as they drew closer.

"Oh, seashells! Bubby, they got more dogs!" Anuka yelled and loaded his crossbow, pointing it generally in Kelios's direction. Now what?

A grin on the Red's face told her this was bad. She didn't know what to do. If Kelios was in danger, she should stay. But Coryn was escaping and she may never be this close to him again. Pazzix suddenly darted to the left and disappeared. Hidden passage!

"Anuka, c'mon. Kelios can handle this."

She saw the strain of decision on his face as well. Finally, he turned and handed his crossbow to a pale elf who just stared at it, then stalked up to the Minothos. "Look, buddy." Anuka told him, "These dogs are bad news. The bear," Anuka pointed at Kelios, "is on our side. Help him but be careful. Those dogs are nasty."

Anuka made to dart away but the Minothos grabbed his arm, "Where are you going?" the creature boomed incredulously.

"I got some Sum Bucks that need killed!"

That seemed to satisfy the Bull Man for he nodded and released Anuka. The little goblin slid out a dagger from somewhere and darted into a hard-to-see crevice in the wall that was only visible from a certain angle.

The gap was small. Crenthys wasn't sure how Pazzix had gotten through. It looked like part of the wall had been chipped away to make the space bigger but it was getting harder to tell as the passageway got darker. Goblins, or whatever Anuka was, must have better eyes than DragonKin. The only light was coming from Anuka's skin. He glowed a pale red that made him easy to pick out but probably didn't offer him much help to see.

Anuka was moving pretty quickly and she struggled to keep up. It dawned on her suddenly that she did not have a weapon. That was fine. If she caught Coryn she would rip him apart with her bare hands.

It was a good thing Anuka had a good lead on her, for she nearly bowled him over when he suddenly tucked into a roll, narrowly dodging the swipe of a long sword.

Placing her hands on the sides of the wall at the mouth of the crevice, she stopped herself before walking into a sword slice. She heard an angry cry and saw Anuka rolling again and Pazzix grabbing at a spot on his leg that suddenly blossomed red with blood.

In one smooth motion, Anuka rolled up on his feet and drew a short, double-edged blade with the hand opposite the dagger. "C'mon you big Sum Buck! The best part of you was left on the eggshell you hatched from!"

Crenthys looked around the room that the narrow passage had opened into. It was roughly oval-shaped and had two other passages on opposite sides of the room from her. Which one? *If I go the wrong way I'm as likely to have Coryn at my back with a dagger as I am to find him. Seas!* She cursed, looking about for a weapon. Anuka and Pazzix were circling one another in the middle of the room. Crenthys would have to cross that room and make a choice about which path to take. The choice was made for her.

There was a movement in the leftmost tunnel, her gaze drawn there just in time to see Coryn dart away. Making sure Pazzix's back was to her, she bolted across the room to the passage where Coryn went. Another roar bellowed from behind her that seemed to fill every chamber.

Tabir handed the crossbow to one of the other freed slaves and backed up against the wall. Four of the vilest dog-shaped creatures Tabir could imagine stalked into the broad hallway. The bear, who Anuka had said was his companion, Kelios, stood beside Kikkabar, who held a massive axe, ready to greet the dogs.

Offund stood against the wall at Tabir's side. The little man would be no good in a fight like this. It was too chaotic. His magic, what he had left, would be as likely to hurt one of their companions as one of their foes. The other slaves weren't faring well. Wave's men, or Jhaldus's, he couldn't be sure, all had proper weapons and seemed at least semi-competent in their use.

A part of him longed to fall in beside his companions and take up a blade but he could not. He would not. He had taken an oath to never slay another man and he meant to keep it. Should he live twice as long as any other elf he could never pay the debt for the blood he had already shed.

Still, it was difficult to watch his friends struggle. Most of them were not fighters or even seamen. They would be slaughtered if Tabir didn't find a way to help.

Across the hall, he saw a bunch of tools piled in a corner. One tool had a very long, wooden handle with a three-pronged fork on the end. He stared at it for a bit. It was torment. A stray strand of hair had fallen into his face and he absently blew it back. Sighing heavily through his nose, he bowed his head, closed his eyes, and prayed. *"I do as I can with what you give. Lead me. And forgive me."*

He drew his head up, sucked in air through his nose, and sprang off the wall. Most of the tools were propped against the wall with one end in a wooden box. Tabir snatched the over-long hay fork off the wall and looked at it. The tines were dark red, probably from blood. He glanced in the box and immediately saw what he needed. With three quick strikes the head of the hay fork came off and Tabir was left with a shaft of wood a little shorter than he was. He gripped it with two hands and prayed again for courage. Then he struck.

As familiar as a childhood home, the movements came to Tabir as his body remembered. Decades of training called long unused muscles to attention. He spun into the melee. A green-skinned humanoid was pressing one of the former slaves. With an uppercut swing, he swept the legs out from under him. Without slowing he arced the make-shift staff down in a reverse strike, connecting with the head of a dwarf with a scimitar, dropping him. His heart sank and he prayed that the man wasn't dead, but on he went. Two more foes went down before the tide turned and the enemies began to focus on him. His fellow former slaves took up the weapons of the four Tabir had ambushed and stood ready at his side. Their opponents seemed less confident now, and several broke away and ran.

Some fled toward the mayhem of claw and ax behind them as dog, bear, and bull did battle. Others made for the crack Anuka and his DragonSpawn friend had darted into. Tabir needed to decide quickly.

It was impossible to tell how the other fight was going. There was roaring and growling and blood was everywhere. None of them had any business trying to step into that nightmare. Tabir nodded for Offund to follow him and he slipped off into the crack. A fool on a fool's errand.

Kelios had never simultaneously held this much joy and terror. The bear moved apart from his control. It wasn't even listening to his suggestions anymore, as far as Kelios could tell. A part of him didn't care. His mind was so weary he could barely follow the fight. He blessed Rathune for the bull-man and vowed to learn his name if they survived. That seemed a small chance. Even if the bear killed the dogs, there was a good chance it would turn on the Minothos. Kelios did not have the energy to control the beast. All he wanted to do was to lie down and sleep for two or three days. Or forever. Seas, but he couldn't think straight.

In the first fight, he'd felt like a man in a bear costume. Now he felt like a flea on its back. So small. So weak. The only thing keeping him awake was the mental imagery of what would happen after the fight. Each possibility was worse than the one before it. He saw himself, the bear, attacking his companions. Killing them. He imagined the hopeless look on Crenthys's face as she and Anuka killed him. Or worse, failed in the attempt.

He would sooner allow one of the dogs at his throat. A touch of his faith in the idea of destiny had been restored and he didn't want to let go of that. He was just...so...tired.

The Red was no former fencer gone to seed as Swet had been. This was a nightmare from the pits of Torment in scaly flesh. With a sword. And a metal breastplate. They paced around each other like dancers but Anuka saw no hesitation in the DragonMan's eyes. He was just waiting for Anuka to move. But Anuka was out of moves.

Sum Buck's arms were as long as he was, the sword blade longer! Anuka did not doubt the strength in his bulging arms, each as big around as Anuka's head. Oh well, he had to try something.

"You ain't still mad about all those Dragon jokes, are you?" Anuka asked. "You have to admit, some of that was pretty funny."

No reaction. Anuka lunged suddenly, aiming his sword strike for the DragonMan's heart. The big Red batted the sword away swiftly but did not press the attack. He brought the big sword back up to a guard position and continued to stare at Anuka.

Real fear began to squeeze at Anuka's tiny heart. He couldn't beat this thing. The best he could do was stall, but for what? Unless Kelios somehow got the bear through the crack none of them could match the Red. Even Crenthys would likely be useless against this thing. Some DragonSpawn were made to be emissaries or representatives for their Dragon. This DragonMan was bred and trained to kill. The fear in Anuka's gut must have leaked onto this face because the DragonMan grinned. It looked hideous on him and made Anuka feel even worse.

The Red stepped forward suddenly with one foot and pivoted into an expert cut at Anuka's head. Oh boy.

Anuka put all of his strength in batting the weapon aside. The impact with that massive blade rang like a bell and sent a shower of sparks up, nearly taking the weapon from his hand. Before he could roll away the DragonMan launched his giant foot into Anuka's chest.

Anuka tried to block that, or at least make him pay for it, with his dagger hand, but the blade raked across the thick sole of his scaly foot, barely drawing blood. Anuka launched through the air and smashed into the wall four strides away. The only miracle bigger than Anuka not dropping his weapons was him not gutting himself with them as he fell. With his arms holding his weapons away from his body, he slammed face-first into the stone and did not move.

Crenthys knew Coryn was likely aware that she was following and would have a trap ready but she didn't care. She had to stop him. Where could he go? The thought came suddenly and she slowed her frantic chase. They were on an island. There were twenty of her allies in the hallway. Coryn couldn't escape. This realization made her more cautious. She moved deliberately, listening and sniffing the air before moving.

This hallway was untouched by pickax or chisel but was much wider. The floor was wet and she could see the reflection of the dim torch behind her shining in a few small puddles. They must be moving down, below the level of the ocean. The path ahead was very dark and she smelled the acrid odor of smoke and oil. Coryn extinguished the torch ahead of her. Crafty little eel. He was a Sea Elf, as true-blooded as could be found, and had eyes that were made for the pitch black of deep water. He would have no problem navigating the darkness. For her, it was not the same. And this soon after her transformation, she could not use magic. Also, it had been so long since she had accessed that power she wasn't sure it would ever work again.

Crenthys moved to her left and felt for the wall. She continued slowly, moving into the darkness. With her hands she felt the wall about head height, searching for the torch in hopes that he may have replaced it after he put it out. Instead, she found an empty sconce. She was tempted to double back and retrieve a torch. Crenthys listened very carefully but couldn't hear anything apart from water dripping in the distance.

With a sigh, she turned around and went back to the nearest torch. She grabbed it and returned to following Coryn. No more than twenty steps beyond where she had turned back for the torch, she saw a wooden door at the end of the hall. It was slightly ajar. *This is it.* She felt it in her bones. No light came from within the room. Slowly, she moved toward the door and peered in through the crack. She saw nothing. The quiet made her tremble. Gathering her courage, she drew in a deep breath, then with all her strength, kicked the door open and bolted into the room.

The door banged hard against the stone wall behind it. Coryn sat on a simple cot against the wall opposite the door. He looked unperturbed by her abrupt entry. He had one leg folded over the other and wore a strange device on his face. It looked like an eye patch with a piece of ruby-colored glass instead of a patch. The eye behind it was magnified and looked eerie. "Hello, Brinka."

Crenthys realized that she was holding the torch like a sword and that she was still panting. Standing straight, she tossed the torch to the floor and stalked towards Coryn. She had to hurt him. She needed to make him pay. He had to live, however, and be hauled back before the leaders of Apostate. Then let the Dragons have what was left.

Coryn's mouth was drawn into a tight frown and his brow was furrowed to a "V" shape, but he did not move. When Crenthys got within a stride of him, Coryn lifted his hand, made a fist, and yanked his hand down. Crenthys's world exploded with pain and her legs gave out beneath her. She collapsed into a pile and struggled to get enough breath to scream. Coryn uncrossed his legs, stood, brushed his vest, and stared at Crenthys, smiling. "It is always best to hold the advantage. Failing that, cheat."

Chapter 30

Little Man

"You cut me." The Red said incredulously as he loomed over Anuka.

He looked up at the DragonMan and tried to give him a hateful look but his face hurt too badly. Anuka could feel his left eye swelling shut and he tasted blood in his mouth. That was the problem with having thirty perfect pointed teeth. He wanted to sink them all into the DragonMan's calf but doubted he could get through that tough hide. From a sitting position, the Red was enormous. Very little of the light from the torch in the sconce behind the beast reached Anuka, so vast was the DragonMan's shadow.

Craning his neck, Anuka looked the Red in the face. "What're you lookin' at?"

The DragonMan chuckled. "So small. So alone." His face was cast in shadow but Anuka could imagine the grin. "I must see to bigger problems." The slight emphasis on bigger was evident despite the thick accent. Sum Buck. Anuka intended to make a hole in this snake with legs before he went down. Where could he put the hole? The light changed slightly and Anuka smiled.

"Go ahead, cut me down, and limp after your master like a good little dog." Anuka sneered and prayed his guesses were right.

The Red suddenly looked less pleased with himself.

"If you hurry, he might let you wash his back or braid his hair." Anuka taunted.

The DragonMan shuffled his feet a bit and adjusted his grip on the long sword.

"You two looked close. You let him play with your tail?"

Taking his sword in one hand, the DragonMan twisted to his right and drew back his killing stroke. Anuka made ready to put up an impossible parry. Then came a loud whistle and crack.

The DragonMan cried out and spun clumsily around reaching for his already injured leg. As he moved, Anuka saw the silhouette of a lithe elven figure twirling a shovel handle over his head and stepping into a guard position. The priest. *Sum Buck.*

Anuka waited for the Red to attack Tabir before leaping to his feet and bringing his small weapons to the ready.

The big creature leveled a two-handed swipe expertly at Tabir's head. The agile elf stepped aside instead of trying to parry. Anuka moved in for a stab with his saber. The DragonMan shifted his weight and swiped his tail as soon as he made the sword strike, anticipating Anuka's attack from behind. Anuka flattened himself to the ground to avoid the tail and had to roll immediately to avoid being stomped on.

To his surprise, Tabir didn't hesitate. He brought another swipe of his staff at the Red's head. The DragonMan batted the attack aside and sheared off a couple of inches of Tabir's staff, making a spear out of it. Tabir spun away and again assumed a guard position. Anuka was too busy trying to gain his feet to be much good.

It would have been nice if the Red was perturbed by his assailants, but he looked perfectly calm and in control. If he was as patient as he seemed, Tabir and Anuka would eventually defeat themselves by making a mistake or running out of weapons. A dagger throw was a great way to end a fight, but it would have to be perfect. This creature was too tall. Anuka feared he couldn't hit anything vital, even with a perfect throw. Tabir's face was placid but Anuka saw tension under that facade. Where had Tabir learned to fight? He was pretty good for a skinny little elf.

Out of the corner of his eye, Anuka caught movement from Offund standing at the mouth of the crevice that opened into the room. The poor little fellow didn't even have a weapon. He looked pretty pitiful, too. Probably wanting to help, but knowing he couldn't. Yeah, Anuka felt that way sometimes. He hoped the little man could get away.

The DragonMan suddenly lurched for Tabir. The elf immediately moved as the DragonMan did. It was another big swipe. Anuka thought that was a stupid move for the big swordsman. He saw the ruse just as Tabir turned to dodge the swing and his heart sank. The Red cut his attack short, pivoted on his power leg, and snapped a savage kick into Tabir's exposed hip, launching him three strides away.

Before Tabir landed, the DragonMan stalked back toward Anuka. The torchlight flickered across the creature's face and Anuka wished it hadn't. He didn't see fury on the Red's face. Just the placidity of a man determined to finish a job.

⸺◆⸺

A sharp pain awakened Kelios abruptly and he was instantly aware that one of the dogs had the bear's neck in its powerful jaws. The bear's life was slipping away and Kelios felt its terror as his own.

Frantically, Kelios tried to regain control from the bear. This was difficult because it had little strength left. There was a shocking amount of blood on the floor and walls. He saw the Minothos lying on his back with his massive arms and legs locked desperately around one of the hellish dogs. He was doing his best to hold the beast. The blood coating its fur made that a difficult chore as the two writhed on the ground. The Minothos was trying to get his arm around the slippery beast's neck.

Kelios could not help his ally. The dog he fought was smashed between the wall and his bulk. Stubbornly the dog held on. Kelios tried to make the bear roll or grind the dog harder into the wall, but it was no use. He was just too weak. Pride welled up in Kelios when he considered the valiant fight the bear had made, the sacrifice it had made for him. From the time he was a small boy, he had been taught not to form a strong emotional bond with his guest because losing them could be deadly to the host. He supposed that made sense but even so, he loved the bear. The bear didn't need his permission to go but he gave it. They both were too weak for a contest of wills and he had no right to ask the bear to stay.

The change was much faster than Kelios imagined it would be. In moments the bear was gone and he lay face-down in a sea of blood. Footsteps and shouts behind him reminded him they weren't the only ones here. It sounded like men with swords had come to finish off the dogs. He wanted to thank them or help them. Instead, he closed his eyes and whispered his gratitude to the bear who had saved him, again.

⸻ ◆ ⸻

Everything in Crenthys's body hurt. Every muscle was so tight it might rip. Air came in quick gasps. She lay on her side curled up, muscles spasming.

Coryn knelt and looked her in the eyes but she couldn't focus on anything but the pain. And then it stopped.

She rasped out a weak screech and was disgusted that it sounded like gratitude. She was thankful the pain ended. Panic rose again a moment later when she tried to move and discovered that she could not. She felt like she was back in Jhaldus's boat. Helpless.

"Now that we understand one another," Coryn said without expression, "I hope you will appreciate the gravity of my discovery." The Sea Elf tapped at the contraption covering his eye. "This is what I came for, Brinka." He stood and casually stuffed items into a bag on his cot.

"It seems that in a bygone era there were others who found submitting to the Dragons distasteful." He slung the pack over his shoulder, turned, and looked down at her. "Dragons haven't always held all the power, all the magic. I'll be honest, I wasn't completely sure this would work on you. You aren't a real Dragon, after all."

Her heart pounding, Crenthys strained against the unseen force that held her fast. It was much worse than the poison Jhaldus had used. It had limits, a soft edge. This power was like a wall you couldn't push against. It was ethereal, yet unmoving.

"I haven't figured out how to kill a Dragon with the device's power yet, but I will. I am sure I could make you kill yourself. Even compared to your baby brother your will is very weak."

Coryn walked away, though it sounded like he was putting other things in his bag.

"Your friends will be heading this way soon if Pazzix or Jhaldus's pets haven't killed them yet, so I must be on my way."

Crenthys saw his finely booted feet and he squatted down again, much closer this time. "Sadly, I don't have time to experiment. So I will do this the old-fashioned way." He slid a short-bladed single-edged sword from a glossy wooden sheath.

<hr>

Anuka saw Tabir regaining his feet but was too far away to help. Anuka's skin glowed red and wisps of steam and smoke trailed up from his clothing in various places. He tossed his shoulder bag aside to keep from getting tangled in it.

The DragonMan stopped a few paces short of Anuka and drew in a massive breath. Uh oh.

Pazzix unleashed the most profound belch Anuka had ever heard. Grik the six-fingered Orc would have to lay down his title as Bastion of Belch before the Red. Anuka found that thought amusing in the split second before his clothes caught on fire.

Anuka was aware of the heat and his mind was trained to react to fire like a normal person. So he writhed and screamed as the DragonMan blasted Anuka with DragonsBreath. Smoke burned Anuka's nose as his belongings were incinerated. The rapier he filched from The *Brinery*, his new clothes, and his stolen hat floated away in little motes of ash.

When the torrent of flame abated, Anuka lay very still. The DragonMan panted nearby. Anuka cracked one eyelid and looked around. He saw his prized bone-handled dagger lying nearby, unharmed. He smiled.

The DragonMan uttered something in Draconic that sounded like a horrid swear. I need to learn that one, he thought. Anuka opened both eyes slowly, blinking away ash and grime, and stared at the Red.

"What manner of creature are you?" The DragonMan barked in disbelief.

Anuka queued up a solid retort but held it. Behind the DragonMan, Anuka saw Offund standing with his little arms spread, blue light building in his fists. Anuka started to laugh. He snorted once and his laugh became an uncontrollable guffaw.

The big Red craned his neck to look over his shoulder while keeping a guarded eye on Anuka. He saw Offund.

His eyes closed, a bluish-white light emanated from the little man's hands. Tabir was on his feet again and looked at the space between the DragonMan and Offund but didn't move.

"What are you playing at, Little Man?" the DragonMan said in his basso voice.

Offund's head snapped up and his eyes popped open, glowing with light. "You never get to call me 'Little Man' again!"

The DragonMan made a leaping charge at Offund that was terrifyingly quick for a creature so large, but Offund flung his hands out at the Red with a scream. An arc of lightning leaped from Offund's hands, striking the airborne DragonMan in the center of his chest plate. His metal chest plate. A crack like a giant whip sounded and the DragonMan was blasted backward. His body immediately went rigid and smacked into the stone wall opposite Offund. He fell to the floor with a thud. A second flash rippled through the room and washed over Tabir and Anuka.

Anuka felt like strings were tied on every finger and toe, his knees and elbows, and to the roots of his hair, and every single one was simultaneously jerked tight. He slumped over onto his side and jerked as the imaginary strings were pulled again and again.

When the spasms stopped and he unclenched his jaw he felt like he had just swum ten miles through thick mud. Everything ached and his smaller muscles were still spasming.

Incredibly, the DragonMan lay groaning and straining to sit like a turtle stuck on its back.

"Nope," Anuka growled as he rolled onto his hands and feet, then scrambled toward the prone DragonMan. The stench of the creature reached Anuka well before he got near enough to touch it. Smoke puffed out from under the plate armor and a savage burn arced up the Red's face. His massive clawed hands were curled up unnaturally.

Anuka reached the DragonMan and touched his plate gently to make sure it wasn't still charged up. Satisfied, he propped himself up on the DragonMan's chest, supporting himself with one hand, drawing his dagger with the other.

The DragonMan raised his head with some effort and looked at Anuka. "Kill me and my patron will search every grain of sand for you. She will flay the skin from your bones and feed it in strips to her young! And as you die-" his words cut off as Anuka drove his beautiful bone-handled dagger down into the Red's neck with both hands, the blade's second DragonSpawn kill in one day.

Chapter 31

Grab the Dragon on Our Way Out

A commotion awakened Kelios into a foggy state. It was a mixture of chattering voices and odd sensations tumbling about in his mind. He tried to recall where he was. He remembered the bear. A valiant friend he was glad for. He was vaguely aware that Crenthys had followed Anuka in a chase for Wave. No, Coryn. That was his true name. *It was best to be proper when able*, his mother had told him. Now he was in water up to his neck. Or was it blood?

That unsettling thought sobered him and he blinked his heavy eyelids open. He was in a stone trough filled with water. He sat up the best he could and saw that he was in the Dragon's prison cell. Someone had stuck him in the Dragon's drinking dish. He tried to say something but the words sounded unintelligible. His mouth was so dry, his tongue hurt and was swollen. He must have bitten it. Licking his lips he tried again to speak but couldn't overcome the volume of chatter in the room.

Finally, Ember noticed him and picked his way over to him.

"Don't strain yourself. Are you a full druid, or just a changeling?" Ember asked.

"Druid." Kelios managed. How did Ember know? Thinking too hard made his head pound angrily.

"I thought as much. I also thought the water would do you good. Don't worry, it is clean water. I have food for you as well."

"Than-Than..."

"You are welcome. And thank you. You and Kikkabar saved us."

Kelios submerged his head under the water and opened his gills, drinking deeply of the water. Refreshed, he resurfaced and asked, "How is he?"

The pained expression on Ember's feline face said much.

"The other members of Anuka's crew say that Tabir has some skill at medicine. Let's pray it is more than that." Ember propped an elbow on his belly and tented his hand under his chin thoughtfully. "There are a staggering number of surprises in this small band. It's fascinating, really. Things are happening that have never happened in recorded history . . ."

"What are you doing?" asked Kelios.

The Malkin was quiet for a while and Kelios thought he hadn't heard. Then Ember snapped back to the moment. "Oh. Well. We are trying to figure out how to get this Dragon out of this room. He seems to have grown a bit since he was brought here, despite his...poor diet." The Malkin shivered. Given what the placard over the door of their cell read, Kelios could imagine why.

"Can it walk?" Kelios asked.

"Perhaps. The bigger issue is the leaching system they have concocted. We don't know how to remove it without-" Ember looked over his shoulder at the Dragon and lowered his voice to a whisper, "without bleeding the poor thing to death."

That was a problem. He tried to think of a solution but was just too tired.

Ember acknowledged this and bade him eat and rest. Kelios was inclined not to argue. He couldn't do anything else.

Crenthys saw the blade of the short sword as it cleared the scabbard. He likely wanted to hurt her as badly as she wanted to hurt him. She felt her insides convulse at that thought. *Had all of his dealings with Apostate been a means to an end?* Her eyes burned and watered from being unable to even blink. If she were able to move at all Coryn would have seen her trembling. A silver lining.

Coryn stood suddenly and Crenthys heard, "You Sum Buck!" The voice was rough and he was panting, but it was definitely Anuka. That blessed, annoying little creature.

"An elf, an imp, and a goblin enter a room. That has the makings of a bad joke." Coryn said with a sardonic sneer.

The shuffling of feet from the doorway made Coryn move, and then Crenthys was standing. Her arms and legs moved but not of her own volition. Suddenly, she stood as a shield in front of Coryn. A keen pain burned at her neck and she saw the slender sword pressed to her throat. "Take care, Goblin. Lest someone winds up hurt."

Anuka stood holding a beautiful dagger in one hand. He was naked, again. The elf was holding...a shovel handle? "Hey! Don't do something stupid. You're fit'n to die. No way around that. It's just a matter of whether you die cleanly or end up roasted like your big Red friend." Anuka spat at that last bit.

"Don't flatter yourself, goblin. I've done what I came to do. Usban will burn and war won't be far behind. And I got what I came for." Crenthys couldn't see his grin but heard it in his voice.

"After I make a couple of holes in your neck, that won't matter much to you," Anuka said.

Crenthys's arms fanned out to the sides and Coryn stepped back.

"Your threats are hollow, little goblin, but I do find you very amusing. Why are you naked?"

Anuka likely couldn't see much of Coryn. He slid slowly to one side. The goblin was flipping his dagger end over end and catching the glittering blade smoothly in his tiny hand.

"Alas, my time has come to depart. I hope we meet again An-" Coryn stopped when he noticed Anuka had sprung to the side. He was just in Crenthys's peripheral vision. With a flourish, Coryn drug his hand through the air in a wide arc, and the space in front of him flapped down like a curtain. Cold wind and snow blew in from the hole he had cut but he didn't slow. When the hole was made he moved smoothly toward it.

Anuka let his dagger fly as soon as Coryn started moving. There was a sudden cry from Coryn, then he was gone. The cold and snow stopped as abruptly as it had come. Crenthys pitched forward, suddenly in control of her body again, and only just managed to keep from toppling over. She looked quickly around the room for any sign of Coryn. Instead, she saw a slack-jawed Anuka cry, "My dagger!" He spun around, looking dumbstruck, and said, "Sum Buck..."

⚬

"I had him! I had him! I had him!" Anuka growled aloud, his skin glowing bright red. *I may have still hit him.* The throw was true and he had knocked something loose. "Sum Buck is right," he mumbled as he looked around on the floor for the thing he knew he saw fall from Coryn.

"Anuka!" the bronze-colored DragonMan, err Woman, err DragonSpawn, yelled.

"What?" he replied with a bit more snap than he meant. He had just found his prized dagger again!

Not satisfied with the amount of attention she was getting from Anuka, she picked him up by his shoulders until he was looking into her wild eyes.

"Where is Kelios?" she asked.

"I don't know. It isn't my turn to watch him. Put me down."

She did. Then she stalked out of the room. Eventually, Tabir and Offund followed slowly in her wake. Offund had passed out after he fried the big Red Sum Buck and was still shaky. The Elf was limping, complaining of broken ribs.

Anuka sighed heavily and looked more slowly around the room. Then he saw it.

Under the cot the Sea Elf had used for a bed, all the way against the wall was something shiny. Stretching his short arms, Anuka fished it out. It was smooth, as big around as the cork on a keg, as thick as his thumb, and round like a medallion. It looked like some kind of glass. It was pretty dark but the little disk reflected the poor light from the sputtering torch in the corner of the room. Anuka smacked it really hard on the stone floor three or four times. Not glass.

It wasn't even scratched. Ruby? He sauntered down the dark hallway back to the room where he had fought the Red. A torch hung on a sconce producing a strong, flickering light. Anuka held the little circle of ruby up to his eye and peered through it. He saw a different world.

Everything was brighter and had much greater detail. He had expected the lens to paint everything red but it didn't. Everything glowed in its natural color. Just much brighter. The pool of blood under the body of the fallen DragonMan glistened like chainmail in the sun. The DragonMan, too, looked very different. Although Anuka saw the beast as it was, he also saw him as something different. His mind couldn't describe it in a way that made sense. Instead of just a dead body, Anuka looked at the Red's corpse and saw something he could use. Instinctively, he reached out with his mind and slipped inside the dead creature's corpse.

Suddenly, he could feel that the body was dead. It could no longer hold the spirit that once lived in it. It was like putting on a DragonMan costume. He commanded the corpse to raise his arm and it moved as commanded. Instantly, Anuka was back in his own mind. He gasped and jerked the disk away from his eye. The arm had moved. Anuka understood that, if he wished, he could make the body do whatever he wanted. It would get up and walk, dance a jig, or even fight for him. The thought was horrifying. Anuka rolled the ruby disk over in his hands and stared at it. He hurriedly retrieved his shoulder bag and stuffed the ruby inside and took off after his friends. Anuka couldn't shake the eerie feeling that he was carrying something both awesome and terrible.

⸺◆⸺

The next Kelios knew, his hair was being brushed out of his face. He hadn't really been sleeping, only resting his eyes. It was for this reason that he came awake much more quickly. He jumped when he saw the face of a DragonSpawn looking down at him.

"Crenthys," he said, apologetically. "I-I'm sorry. I was..." He smiled at her and she returned the smile. "I'm sorry. It will take some time to get used to you like this." Kelios motioned at her with his head.

"No, Kelios. I should be sorry. I should have told you about this." Crenthys said.

Kelios was silent. He didn't disagree with her and wanted to hear what else she had to say.

She continued resignedly. "I don't trust anyone. Not even myself. I'm changing, Kelios, and I shouldn't be. It isn't natural. Since my master died, my anchor is gone and I don't know what is happening to me. I'm not officially on a mission for Apostate. I may not even be considered a member any longer." The words seemed to hurt Crenthys as she forced them out. She closed her eyes and exhaled before continuing. "I started having feelings for Morglun, the man who brought me into Apostate, and I got scared. So I ran away. I thought that getting away from Morglun would keep me from changing, but it hasn't. It's so confusing and it hurts so much."

"I know," Kelios said smiling, "it's called growing up."

Crenthys barked a laugh that was part sob. "Well, I don't like it."

Kelios didn't know what to say. He was changing, too. All that he had known, everything safe, was gone.

"Ember says that he has never even heard of a DragonSpawn surviving what I did. So I am making it up as I go. Part of me wants to run again. I'm afraid I won't survive these feelings."

Kelios saw her eyes were glassy with unshed tears. He put his hand on hers. "Is there another part?" He asked.

Crenthys barked out another laugh. "Yes. And that part of me wants to snatch you out of that water and carry you to this beautiful place I know. It is the most beautiful little grove that is nearly impossible to get to if you don't fly. And it's covered with the most beautiful red flowers, and it..." Her smile was radiant as she stared wistfully into the distance.

Kelios thought he was beginning to understand her subtleties if only a little. When she looked back at him she was still smiling, but he thought he saw some sadness in her eyes. He felt it, too.

He reached a heavy arm up out of the water and laid it on the rough hide of her face. She leaned into the touch and closed her eyes.

"I need time to figure things out. Things are changing too fast." Crenthys said softly.

Kelios had expected as much. He wasn't sure what he thought about her change.

In the background, Kelios heard a familiar voice say, "I can hit that! I'll blow the top right off of that!" Anuka was about to blow something up.

———◦———

Anuka pushed up the sleeves of his new shirt and pretended to listen to Ember explain how blowing a hole in the roof was likely to kill the Dragon and that it would be in poor taste to do so. He heard the word DragonsBlood. Blah, blah, blah. Tabir's grim explanation of how Wave had a Demon inside him, whatever that was, and how he used a Dragon's Claw to cut reality and step into another place made no sense. Sum Buck cheated. Now they had to deal with the Dragon. He would have to worry about Wave later. By the looks of it, this thing wasn't going to survive the night. The kindest thing to do was...*Seashells and sunburns! What was the Elf doing?*

Tabir appeared to be hugging the Dragon and had his head lying on its neck. It looked like he was talking to it. He stood up suddenly, looking pale. Really pale. Like fresh sheets. But he also looked determined. He turned around and said, "I need everyone to leave."

Crenthys, who was canoodling with Fish Man over by the drinking hole, came to her feet like an arrow from a bow. *Great.* Anuka had seen that look before. He moved to intercept her before she did something they'd all regret. Kelios jumped out of the drinking bowl and followed Crenthys.

"I mean him no harm. In fact, I aim to aid him, if I can." Tabir said, his voice lacking sense or reason. A little fear wouldn't hurt him. Anuka recognized it when someone was about to do something reckless.

"Crenthys, stop. Look, you can trust him. I trust him." Anuka said.

"I don't trust you!" Crenthys yelled in Anuka's face. "You betrayed Kelios and me. Then, when he trusted you again, you betrayed Kelios a second time!"

"Oh yeah? Looks like I was the smart one. You turned out to be a Dragon!" Anuka said the last word like the vilest sailor's swear. He hadn't wanted to get into this but she pushed him. "You know who trusts a Dragon? A FOOL! Look around you. How many of these people, who traded their blood to save yours, have any love for Dragons? You wanna know why they are here? Why they agreed to come south and save your hide instead of going north to save theirs?

Because I asked them to." The words seemed to melt a bit of Crenthys's anger but Anuka wasn't ready to stop just yet. "Yes I betrayed you. I turned my back on both of you. Before today, I didn't know what a friend was. Maybe I still don't. But today I learned that a friend is someone who may not always be there but, when things are really bad, they show up."

Anuka saw Kelios's glare soften a little. The Triton unfolded his arms, stepped forward and put a hand on each of their shoulders. Crenthys looked at him, and then at Anuka. His anger spent, Anuka sighed. "I know I'm a lousy friend. But apart from Fish Face, I'm all you've got." He couldn't keep the toothy grin from his face and was relieved to see Crenthys smile a tiny bit. Then she put a heavy, scaly hand on his shoulder and he knew that was as close to an apology as he would get from the stubborn woman.

"Ok, then. What's the plan?" Anuka said rubbing his hands together.

Chapter 32

Trust

"I don't understand, Tabir," Crenthys said.

"I know. And I'm sorry time doesn't afford an explanation. Later, when there is time, I will try to explain it to you. Right now I need you to trust me."

Crenthys dipped her head.

"Excuse me," Ember offered meekly with a rub of his hand over one ear. "Have you seen the Minothos, Kikkabar, walking around?"

"I have," Crenthys said.

"After fighting those Dragon Dogs-that is what I am calling them," he raised a finger at Tabir to forestall his objection, Ember turned back to Crenthys. "Afterward, he lay in a pool of his blood in much worse shape than Kelios. Tabir...helped him. And now he is sound enough to walk."

Crenthys squinted her eyes together and tilted her head to one side, looking at Tabir. "How?"

Smiling warmly, the pale Elf laid his hands on her arm comfortingly, "Faith."

"But I have none of that," Crenthys said, her jaw set, her look serious.

"Few do. I, by Rathune's grace, have faith enough for all of us."

Motioning toward the Dragon, Crenthys's voice sounded tired and pitiful, despite her stoic mask, "He is my family. All I have left. Can you swear to me you'll bring him no further harm?"

"That, I can swear. But you need to leave. This will be strange, at least. Likely, it will be dangerous."

Anuka and Kelios stood, waiting by the contraption that still impaled the Young Dragon. Ember led a reluctant Crenthys away and cleared the room of the rest of its occupants.

This is the most reckless thing I have ever done, Tabir thought to himself. Given what he had been a part of today that was a significant thought. *Anuka is a bad influence on me.* He had learned years ago that bringing Rathune's blessing came at a cost. The exchange seemed cruel at times, trading his life for the life of another. I suppose this is why the Elves are so long-lived. Tabir's people were meant to be a priesthood that exchanged their long lives for the well-being of the short-lived races. This was a trade he would make for as long as he could. Already he showed, and felt, signs of old age that he shouldn't exhibit for another four or five centuries. He had never seen an elf die of old age and he knew of elves who claimed to have lived before Dragons were made.

It was settled. There was no point debating it any longer. He would die healing someone one day. Maybe today. He was okay with that. He was already living on borrowed time he didn't deserve. Rathune should have destroyed him for his crimes ages ago.

"We're ready, bubby. You sure you can...you sure this is a good idea?" Anuka asked. The little red goblin never failed to amaze Tabir, for better or worse. He gathered his courage and said as clearly as he could manage, "Yes, Anuka. When I signal you, remove the device. It should look like a spear if my guess is right. Be as careful as you can. And then run."

Tabir walked determinedly to the Dragon's head. "Poor creature," Tabir said, stroking its long neck, "you don't even have a name yet." Then he closed his eyes and began praying in Elvish:

"I can't understand why you allow me to live. At every turn, I have wronged you, yet you lavish mercy upon me. I have taken life and deserve to die, yet you bless me. Even as I stand in the center of such blessings which I cannot comprehend, I doubt. Forgive me, my Master. Let me do your work. Let me minister your mercy. Let me show your grace. And may no glory fall on me. This creature can offer you nothing. His life is yours. I ask for your mercy that I might stand in his place. My life, to him, to your eternal glory."

Lifting one trembling hand from the Dragon's neck he signaled to Anuka and Kelios. He never opened his eyes but heard the horrible sounds of the gruesome work his friends did. In his heart, he felt the Dragon's pain. His fear. His approaching death. He heard his friends fleeing and released the building tide of warm power he felt washing over him. In Tabir's mind, he saw himself as a thimble and the Dragon as a bucket. Tabir began to pour power from the thimble into the bucket and it began to fill.

It was agony and ecstasy. At once he felt Rathune's alien strength enter his being and mingle with his essence before both were ripped from him and fed to the Dragon. As quickly as he was empty, he was being filled again. It was like drowning from too much air.

The smallest part of his mind was aware that he was screaming and clawing desperately to keep ahold of the Dragon. He slipped, then, into that place he had touched before. He saw seven balls of blue and green arrayed in a perfect ring. Each spun in its own circle while the whole chain rotated together like a great wheel. In the middle of the ring was something that Tabir could not look at. It was Rathune, or his glory, perhaps. Tabir knew that to look upon it would mean death.

Suddenly, Tabir was ripped from that place of wonder and he gasped a breath of air, the first in a long moment. All of him ached like he had been pressed by a heavy rock or beaten with reeds. It was the same every time he exchanged with someone. It was the same with

Kikkabar, though it had never been so strong as it was in this moment. Tabir felt as if a brisk breeze could carry him away. His hands moved slowly and he toppled backward before he could react. He landed painfully on his back and looked up to see the Dragon was awake and looking hungrily at him.

Sum Buck, Anuka thought, seeing the Dragon just stand right up. It no longer looked weak or near death. Mostly, it looked hungry. Before he knew what he was doing, Anuka deftly slipped the ruby eye from his pack and into his pocket, took a few steps into the room, and waved his hands to get the beast's attention. It turned its gaze slowly toward him. "Tabir," Anuka said out of the corner of his mouth, "Get outta here." Then over his shoulder, he added, "Rest of you Sum Bucks stay back unless you want to get roasted!" He smiled at the Dragon all the while and was relieved when he saw Tabir scrambling away like a deer on cobblestones. "Kelios," Anuka barked out of the side of his mouth, "hold this for me." Anuka slipped his bag off his shoulder and tossed it behind him. Someone must have caught it because he didn't hear the bag hit the ground. He had bigger problems to worry about anyway.

DragonFire was magical fire, whatever that meant, and would probably, according to Ember, kill Anuka the same as it would anything else. DragonMan's fire was different, according to Fur Ball. The stupid cat didn't know everything. His heart clenched tight in his chest nonetheless and the thin line of drool pouring out one side of the Dragon's mouth suddenly concerned him a great deal. It was time to test the ruby's power.

Anuka quickly glanced over his shoulder to make sure he was alone, then deftly slipped the disk out of his pocket and placed the artifact over his eye. He held it in place between his eyebrow and lower eye socket. It was uncomfortable but he wanted his hands to be visible. If Crenthys saw what he was doing she would kill him. No passionate speech would save him.

When he looked through the Ruby Eye everything looked different once again. The Dragon stared at him dumbly, the look of hunger replaced by calm placidity. The Dragon looked different, too.

Anuka could see every bone and every organ. He saw and knew so much it hurt his brain. The Dragon's blood, dark, thin and cold, moved rhythmically throughout its long body, passing through four organs in the center of its chest, each the size of one of Anuka's feet. He saw a series of bags that Anuka knew were its stomachs. He saw which one caused the beast to belch forth gouts of fire. Anuka felt his scalp tingling as if the knowledge burgeoning in his mind was making his brain grow like a moistened sponge. The Dragon awaited his command, Anuka realized. He also realized that this was how Wave had controlled the Dragon. And Crenthys. The thought made his stomach turn.

He was not Wave, but Coryn, or whatever the sea elf called himself. Anuka didn't want to hurt the Dragon. He just wanted to get out of here. Besides, he had at least two Dragons after him now, maybe four if you considered Brine a real Dragon, and he didn't want to add Crenthys's name to that list.

Anuka looked around the room for something useful.

"Anuka, what are you doing?" it sounded like Crenthys but her voice had changed since she grew a foot taller and was covered in scales.

"Making friends. Be quiet before you get us all killed!" Anuka hoped that was enough to buy him some time. He didn't want her to know that he had found Coryn's Ruby, or what he was up to. When he focused his eye a certain way the color of everything changed. He knew what the colors meant. Temperature. The cooler things were blues and greens, the hotter things were reds, oranges, and yellows.

His skin practically glowed red. He looked at the ceiling and all around the chamber until he saw what he hoped he would see.

A fissure ran down the back wall that was pale blue. A thin stream of water trickled down the crack making a small puddle at the back of the room. Anuka sighed. This was his worst idea yet.

—◦—

Kelios stood holding Crenthys's hand, as much a means of restraint as an act of affection, in the massive cavern near where Anuka's crew had moored their boat. All of the former slaves and crewmen stood lined up together along the wall behind him, murmuring.

They heard grunts and the rustling of scales coming from the Dragon's cell. Crenthys looked at him and he saw fear in her eyes. Kelios had never seen Crenthys fear anything. It was a selfless fear. She feared for her brother. That term still was a stumbling block to him. Was the Dragon really her brother? He would think on that later.

Kelios squeezed her hand firmly, "We have to trust Anuka. He somehow seems to have things under control."

She smiled, and at that moment Anuka yelled, "Let 'er rip you big Sum Buck!" Her face fell. A roar of wind and fire blasted out of the mouth of the prison room, bright orange light bathing the hallway outside the door. A wall of stinging heat smacked those standing in the hallway and they all cried out. It became very hard to breathe. Most everyone dropped to their bellies on the rough wet stone and covered their faces. Crenthys, alone, stood erect in the face of the heated wind that buffeted her. She had her eyes closed and looked quite peaceful. The use of a Dragon's Magic awakened more of her true self each time she experienced its use.

At least now Kelios understood why Anuka had asked him to hold his bag. He truly hoped that his small friend knew what he was doing and was well.

"Hahahahahahaha!" Anuka cackled from the room. Kelios figured he was being burned alive and enjoying it. He sprang to his feet and was only a step ahead of Crenthys at moving toward the door.

"Don't come in here!" Anuka yelled and the pair of them stopped halfway to the door. Crenthys, he could tell, paused hesitantly and was on the verge of ignoring the command. "A lot of stuff is on fire in here and I'm naked again!"

Kelios and Crenthys exchanged incredulous looks.

"Um, everything went well. Meet us on the ship!" Anuka cried out.

Crenthys bolted forward then and Kelios hustled to keep up. They got to the door and confirmed what Anuka said to be true. Everything in the room not made of stone, and some things that were, either smoldered or were still on fire. The floor outside the door of the room was burning his feet through the soles of his boots. The door was on fire as well.

They stood watching, dumbfounded, as a naked Anuka walked up the back of the Dragon, then the Dragon stepped out a large, fire wrought hole in the back wall of the cavern.

"Sum Buck," Crenthys said as she and Kelios watched them disappear into the night.

"That doesn't make sense." Ember was saying.

"No, it doesn't." Crenthys agreed. No sense at all. Dragons did not suffer riders except on the rarest of occasions. The first decade of a Dragon's life is an incredibly feral and dangerous time. Young Dragons tend to eat and destroy whatever they want. It is only the patient instruction of a much larger Dragon that brings them to heel.

The last of the others had climbed into a boat, leaving only her. She took the hand Kelios offered and stepped into the small boat, grateful this boat wasn't very full. Still, her weight made the boat dip and rock. As a prim half-elven maid that would have embarrassed her.

In truth, she did feel her cheeks color a bit but was sure no one noticed. A part of her wished she was that wisp of a girl again so she might lean back onto Kelios's chest and try to relax. It was insane for her to feel this way. All of her emotions were so strong and wild. She was like a teenage human girl. Besides, she couldn't afford to relax now. Crenthys had lived her most recent years searching for a purpose worth living for. That had ended when she learned of her brother. Now the task of caring for him would require all of her attention. She had to return her brother to his people. Her heart ached when she thought of the torture he had endured in his short life, and that feeling quickly turned to rage. Once her brother was back with the Dragons she would find Coryn and gut him.

It seemed like it took ages to exit the tunnel in the small boats, but once they cleared the cave, the outline of the *Brinery* was silhouetted against a giant moon. She saw her brother perched on the deck of the ship. It was difficult to restrain herself from taking the oars out of Kelios's hands and blasting through the water to her brother's side. Closing her eyes, she breathed deeply and drank in the brine scent of the sea. Anything was better than the metallic smell of the blood of the slain, mixed with the blood of her brother, hanging in the dank air.

Moments crept by as they inched toward the ship. Since their boat was the last to leave the cave, they were the last to arrive at the anchored ship. She was first out of their boat. The massive hand of the Minothos was offered to aid her up the gangplank onto the deck, though she didn't need the help. Crenthys offered a nod of thanks and took the hand anyway. She nearly leaped aboard the ship. It was strange to see the metal breastplate and greatsword, both looted from Pazzix, on the Minothos. The spoils of war, she thought. For some reason, she felt like those should remain in DragonKin hands, but she dismissed the thought when she saw her brother curled up on the deck asleep. Anuka sat nearby, leaning on the mainstay. Thankfully, the goblin had found yet another shirt. This one hung loosely from his tiny frame.

Without preamble, Crenthys promptly picked Anuka up and wrapped him in a hug. The goblin's eyes popped open and he started to protest. Before he could say more than a couple "Sum Bucks" she held him at arm's length and said, "Thank you, Anuka. Thank you for saving my brother. I'm sorry I doubted you."

Anuka looked chagrined and, for the first time, didn't know what to say. She put him down gently and moved to where her brother slept. He looked whole, and well. Tabir must be thanked, as well. Her baby brother looked so content in his sleep. It would be selfish to wake him for her own peace of mind. Anuka wandered off murmuring to himself and Crenthys nestled in against the young Dragon. There were plenty of capable hands aboard the ship and she knew little of sailing anyway. The steady rhythm of her brother's breathing quickly put her to sleep.

•

Kelios smiled to see Crenthys take her place with the young Dragon. He was her people, he reminded himself. *Was that how it had to be? Were those her people, while his people lived in the ocean? Could there never be an 'our people'?* Ember had said that DragonSpawn could not mate. But Crenthys was different from other DragonKin in other ways. The logical part of his mind said there was no point in a romantic relationship. But his heart, undeterred even in the cold face of logic, felt otherwise. He had always been proud of not being governed by his passions, but since coming to the surface, he had known passion so deep, he could never have fathomed. He still blamed the bear for the change in his demeanor. Besides, Ember had been wrong about DragonFire harming Anuka.

Kelios was so weary. His head felt as if it might burst open. If he was smart, he would sidle up next to Crenthys and join her in some peaceful rest. But he decided to avoid doing so until he could sort out his feelings for her. She had said she needed space and he intended to give it.

There was a commotion on the port side and he saw a few of the former slaves laughing and pointing to something in the water. Kelios stepped to the bulwark and peered into the water at a pod of dolphins swimming close alongside the ship. They were breaking the surface and falling to the back of the pack in turns. There were six, as best he could tell. This was an ill omen. It seemed to the crew that the creatures were entertaining them but Kelios felt the dolphins' stress.

Quickly, Kelios stripped down to only his pants.

"Who do we pay for the show?" Anuka asked from nearby.

Kelios looked at him and must have given away how he felt because the smile melted from Anuka's face.

"What's wrong, Fish Man?" Anuka said.

"I don't know. I aim to find out." With his boots discarded, Kelios dove into the water among the dolphins.

The impact and sudden chill of the water were refreshing and some of Kelios's weariness faded into the background. Kelios made the familiar change without hesitation. He knew what it would cost him. His long form shrank and contorted, morphing into the smooth rubbery skin of the dolphins. This had been one of the first forms he had learned as a youth. It was also his favorite. He was grateful that the memories that washed over him were of swimming with schools of these peaceful creatures and not the terrors of his tyrannical family.

Instead of kicking to the surface, he dove deeper and easily kept pace with the ship that was just making its turn to exit the cove. He felt so free and happy. Murder, injury and heartbreak seemed distant things as his mind melded with the dolphins in the pod. They were anxious and wanted him to see why.

He looked around at what his brothers were pointing out. What he saw was astonishing. The mouth of the cove was filled with sea life, and all headed deeper into the cove. They were fleeing something.

Kelios spoke with fish via telepathic images in his mind. These creatures were terrified. Something dangerous was just beyond the mouth of the cove. Kelios knew all of the types of creatures that lived in these waters and could only think of one that would frighten so many others. He gave his weary mind more fully to the connection with the dolphins. He saw what they had seen.

Despite his fatigue, Kelios reverted to his natural form. He was able to climb the rigging of the *Brinery* until he was close enough for Kikkabar to hoist him to the deck.

"What'd them dolphins say, bubby?" Anuka asked as Kelios lay panting on the deck.

"They said," Kelios said between breaths, "That Brine is waiting for us."

Chapter 33

It's Just a Dragon

Well, that was quick. Anuka knew he would have Dragon troubles soon but he was at least expecting to live the night. He was the hero of the Fareth Tore Enclave, mighty pirate captain, heir to the *Flat Bottomed Girl*. But he wasn't a Dragon fighter. That was considerably outside of his skill set.

"We can broadside and hit him with the DragonBloods!" One of the crewmen suggested.

"Yeah, and he would yell 'ouch' and then set our boat on fire." Another replied wryly.

"Actually," Ember chimed in, "Brine isn't a true Dragon and doesn't have fire. He is a Wyrm, technically. Instead of fire, he belches forth boiling saltwater." When Ember saw the looks the gathered crowd was giving him, he wilted. "Which, I suppose, is at least as bad as fire." The Malkin slowly turned back to the animated conversation he and Offund had been having.

"Cannons won't work. We have no gunner. None of you could hit water if you fell off the boat. Besides, skinny is right, I don't know if a hit from the DBs would kill Brine. Have you seen that Sum Buck?" He shuddered. Anuka knew that wasn't the news they hoped to hear from their fearless leader but he didn't want to lie to them.

Anuka looked at Crenthys, who had awakened from an enjoyable nap to join them, but she didn't offer any useful suggestions.

"Kel, could you convince a bunch of whales to distract Brine while we sneak out onto the ocean?" Anuka asked, but Kelios was already shaking his head.

"No. Even if I could convince them, I would not ask them to sacrifice themselves for us."

Anuka sighed. They were just fish. The silence was thick as a Dragon's skull as everyone thought and prayed. He had survived so much in the past couple of days and he didn't want to die. He had just found another hat. There was so much to live for.

"Ember and I might have an idea," Offund suggested sheepishly. Everyone turned to look at him and he didn't wilt. He put some steel in his spine and looked around.

"It is a dangerous plan, and a lot of things could go wrong," Offund said.

"Those are my favorite plans!" Anuka said, actually feeling the cheer his voice held.

"Shut up, Anuka." Crenthys chided him, "Offund, go on."

Man, she was cranky when she didn't get her nap in.

Offund laid out their plan and Anuka agreed, it was crazy. Crazy was okay, but he didn't think this one would work.

Soon they all stood crowded together at the bow, all except those who were needed on the riggings. When that was explained, Crenthys joined the Minothos, lending her great strength to the Bull-Man for the quick turn. Crenthys didn't want to witness what Offund had in mind, Anuka guessed. It required using some of the DragonsBlood they found in the captain's quarters. Blood Anuka assumed came from her 'brother'.

The crew looked pretty scared. "Lighten up men, there are worse ways to die than on the sea."

"Dying is dying. Ain't no good way to do it, right?" One of the crew said and several responded with, "Right."

"Not true," Anuka said. "My papa always said when he went, he wanted to be beaten to death by thirty jealous husbands."

That brought a round of muffled chuckles.

"Seriously, I know a lot of you have been told to put your faith in the Dragons, but I think we all see where that gets us. My friend Tabir here seems to think that he has reconnected with our long-lost Creator. Maybe he's right. I don't know what to put my faith in. I just know that with all the dung that's been flying the last few days, I'm lucky to be here. It's hard not to believe that something, whatever it may be, is moving pieces around. Today, things have gone our way. Hold onto that." That elicited some nods and Anuka saw some of the crew relax a little. He had no clue where that came from. He generally just made stuff up as he went along and it rarely turned out that good.

Tabir was smiling at him. A bird call made him look up and he saw a young boy in the crow's nest making hand signals. Turn coming. Get down. Hold Fast. Shut up. Anuka nodded and moved to take his place in the crow's nest once the boy was safely down. The baby Dragon was awake now and Anuka rubbed at the Ruby Eye through his shirt pocket but did not take it out. He had already used it to convince 'little brother' to be still while they tried their escape. If he kept using it he was sure to get caught.

Offund and Ember stood holding hands, looking out over the sea as it passed quickly beneath them. That was weird to Anuka, but whatever. He knew nothing of magic, or Cat People, or Nobs for that matter. They were heading partly windward and the chill of the pre-dawn air cut them like knives. Ember took his free hand and dipped a white cloth into the jar of DragonsBlood Kelios held for him. He smeared the nasty-looking stuff on one of the weird tattoos on his right hip.

Suddenly, Anuka felt a rush of warm air settle on his skin like dew. Everyone must have felt it because they looked around like a bunch of idiots. Anuka only noticed them because he was observant. Not because he was looking around like an idiot. Like a curtain of smoke, a dense fog began to rise off the water. It was incredible to see from atop the main stay. The fog was as wide as Anuka could see in every direction and quickly covered the ship. Anuka clenched up and tried not to panic. He wasn't really afraid of heights but he wasn't thrilled that there was fathomless water beneath the veil of fog. In the silence, he heard panting and figured Ember was about to hack up a hair ball or something. "Now." Ember croaked.

Anuka heard a faint, lonesome whistle in the distance and suddenly felt a stiff breeze from behind that nearly took his new hat off. The fog curled up and blew away from the ship, rolling like the tide going out. Anuka whistled his response to the call, relaying the message to those below him nearer the back of the ship.

Anuka's keen eyes had won him the lookout spot. He could see the sweat dripping from the conjoined hands of Ember and Offund as they stood on the prow of the ship. Anuka thought that was gross. Both of them were panting and the Nob was sweating like a smuggler in the port master's office. The half-sized man's over-large shirt was drenched.

Ember had dropped the bloodied cloth at some point and held out his hand for another. Kelios gave him one. Ember dipped it into the jar and repeated the process. This went on for several minutes. Anuka realized that the wind Offund was making had them headed leeward now and Kikkabar was busy adjusting the sails accordingly.

Soon Anuka saw the outlines of the shore on both sides of the ship. The turn would be soon. "Places, everybody," Anuka signaled with a low whistle, and people moved.

They had battened and lashed down everything they could on the starboard side and everyone not on a line was hunkered down. Kikkabar and Crenthys were busy on the main pull. It was weird looking down on the tops of their heads. He looked at his friends and was glad. Maybe he was seeing them for the last time. Even if they survived the evil pseudo-Dragon, Anuka had promised the ship to Kikkabar. Oh well. Come easy, go easy. He got to work.

Anuka saw the faintest glow of sunrise in the distance. The timing was going to be close. The plan was to slingshot around the mouth of the cove under the cover of the fog Ember and Offund were creating. Anuka's eyes stung from fatigue and he blinked to clear them. He hadn't slept in days and his body would soon launch a rebellion. *After this, I'll either sleep for a couple of days or forever.*

Anuka gave another whistle and Kikkabar gave a low grunt and a massive heave on the ropes he was manning. As soon as they finished the pull, Crenthys tugged her lines and Kikkabar took up the slack. The massive ship dipped to port and the mainsail snapped tight as the vessel began its turn. The shore on the East side of the cove made a needlepoint. They were attempting to whip around that as tightly as possible to avoid attracting Brine's attention.

Anuka felt the tug on his body as the starboard side of the ship rose and the port side dipped. He held onto the rigging they had secured to the bulwark with all of his strength. The mainstay creaked and groaned but was holding together so far.

Kikkabar kept looking up at the Nest for instructions. Anuka gave the sign. Rivers of sweat ran down the Minothos's face and chest. "Reverse. To port." He growled as quietly as could be expected. This was the tricky part. Cren and Kikkabar switched sides and those hunkered down on the starboard side suddenly scurried to the port side. The weight shift wasn't much but they were pulling such a tight turn every bit helped.

Anuka felt like he was back on the *Sea Pocket* when she was sinking. This ship wasn't sinking, he reminded himself. And he wasn't going to drown. He grasped the rigging in the crow's nest as tightly as he could and braced his feet in the stirrups.

With another great groan, the ship teetered and bobbed until it righted itself. Kikkabar and Crenthys tied off their leads and slumped to the deck. Anuka sighed. Looking over their heads, to the East, he saw the sun as it crested the horizon. It was beautiful. Then a geyser exploded from the water on the port side and a massive, turquoise figure snaked up with alarming speed. Anuka looked into the hate-filled eyes of Brine.

⸻⸺◆⸺⸻

A tidal wave crashed onto the deck and nearly swept the handful of crew overboard. Had Crenthys and Kikkabar not been ensconced in the rigging of the sails they would have been washed away.

Tabir greedily sucked in a lungful of air as he fought to keep his grasp on the battened cargo. He glanced around and saw Offund prone, unmoving across the stairs to the forecastle. The crew had tied a rope around his waist in case the use of magic knocked him out. Something had. That rope was all that was keeping the Nob from being washed overboard.

The dark tattoos on Ember's skin stood out behind his drenched fur as he tried to claw his way to a nearby rail. He did not look happy.

An epithet from Anuka drew Tabir's eyes up. He couldn't see the goblin but saw the Wyrm clearly for the first time. As the *Brinery* rocked violently to and fro in the wake of the mighty Sea Dragon, Brine stared down at the crew.

Tabir felt like the snack of Brine's choosing. From the corner of his eye, he saw Kelios rise gingerly to his feet, whaling javelin in hand. Brine noticed the Triton and turned his focus on him.

Brine cracked open his maw, revealing rows of sharp teeth each as long as Tabir's forearm.

Kelios was murmuring something in a language Tabir didn't know as he adjusted his grip on the javelin.

"Kelios!" Crenthys cried from where she fought to untangle herself. The Wyrm ignored the cry as it waited for the boat's swaying to slow so it could strike. Then a dagger struck, pommel first, right in the Sea Dragon's eye.

The beast recoiled quickly causing another upheaval that sent the *Brinery* into turmoil.

"You greasy Sum Buck!" Anuka yelled from atop the crow's nest. "Eat me you oversized tapeworm!"

The Sea Dragon slowly peeled back his eyelid to reveal an uninjured eyeball. The dagger had only startled it. The beast's full attention was back on Anuka. Tabir knew what had to be done.

"Kelios!" he screamed over the tumult around him. When the Triton looked to him, Tabir continued, "Come with me!", then darted below deck.

——◦——

This was new territory for Anuka. A level of crazy he had never before imagined. If word got back to Rigby, the bard would write an epic poem in honor of the day Anuka was steam-boiled by a pseudo-dragon.

He knew he hadn't hurt the Dragon. The cheap dagger didn't even land right but he had the thing's attention. Anuka didn't remember the last thing he had eaten but whatever it was threatened to pass out of him when the Wyrm turned its hideous gaze on him.

Its eyes shone like sapphires that glowed with an angry light. Broad slits long enough for Anuka to lie down in angled up each side of its angular nose. They flared as the beast bore into Anuka with its hateful glare. Scales hung from its chin in a massive 'V' shape making a long, pointed beard.

The size of this thing boggled Anuka's mind. He had seen drawings before and had even caught a glimpse of the old Wyrm cresting the water far away during one of his voyages. Nothing prepared him for the reality of the Sea Dragon in person. It knuckled the eye Anuka had hit with the back of a massive webbed hand. Brine could simply seize the *Brinery* with his massive hands and snap it like a twig. Anuka imagined that the beast intended to preserve the vessel that was named for him, and that he likely owned, but not the persons aboard it. Maybe he could exploit that somehow.

As the Sea Dragon began filling its lungs with air in a prelude to using its breath weapon, Anuka guessed that wouldn't be the case.

Crenthys finally untangled herself from the lines that secured the mast. Kelios and Tabir had gone below deck with haste. She was torn between following them and rushing to her brother's side.

The baby Dragon was looking at Brine with interest. He seemed not to know what to make of the Wyrm. Brine would not let the Dragon survive this attack.

Kikkabar broke loose of his ropes with a grunt and slid his newly acquired greatsword from its scabbard. Slowly he stalked toward the port side of the ship as it continued to rock in Brine's second wake.

What could they do? None of them had a weapon suitable to fight such a foe. It would be decades before her brother could challenge the Sea Snake, as her people called Brine. Even then a true Dragon would likely find a fight with a Wyrm as old and cunning as Brine to be a challenge.

She would fight. Judging by the Minothos, they all would fight. Arrows were being fit to short bows by those who had regained their wits. So be it. Her determination faltered slightly as Brine drew in air and began to super heat it.

Anuka hadn't remembered putting his hand in his pocket or slipping the ruby up to his eye. When the world went red around him he was surprised.

The gem thrummed with power as it sat against the skin around his eye. The ruby had worked against Crenthys. It had worked against the baby Dragon. Anuka prayed it would affect the not-Dragon in the same way. It didn't.

The power of the Ruby Eye told Anuka's goblin brain everything about this creature in an instant. It was as much a Dragon as a chicken was a bird. Same basic design, totally different function. Brine could never fly. He also lacked the physical make-up of a Dragon internally. His breath weapon was simply water boiling in a stomach-like sack that he would vomit onto a target. Very inelegant. Brine wasn't capable of speech and didn't seem as intelligent as the baby Bronze Dragon.

Anuka also saw his limitations. He couldn't control Brine's mind as he had the baby Dragon. Nor could he control its body as Wave had Crenthys'. But he could make it hurt.

The parts of Brine that were Dragon-like were at Anuka's command. One slender heart pumped blood quickly through Brine's body and into his tail. Anuka squeezed it with his mind and Brine screamed, bellowing his torrent of boiling salt water into the air, and began to writhe in the water.

The spray of water fell over Anuka but didn't harm him. Without the force of the blast it didn't burn him any more than a campfire would.

For the third time, the *Brinery* was tossed about in the wake of the massive flailing Dragon. Anuka didn't think he could kill the Dragon this way. He was doing more harm than good as indicated by the screams from the deck. At least one crew member had been tossed overboard.

Anuka released the Dragon's heart and it spun in a circle in the deep ocean water. He could feel the anguish in the Wyrm and also felt the rage building within it. Brine coiled in the water like a snake. Anuka realized that the Sea Dragon intended to leap onto the deck, smashing the *Brinery* to splinters.

Desperately, Anuka grasped at the Wyrm's physical systems searching for a way to stop it. With a shard of power from his mind, Anuka stabbed at a cluster of nerves in the Sea Dragon's back just as it sprang out of the water.

He had been too late. Brine was gliding through the air on target to crash onto the deck of the *Brinery*.

"Now!" Tabir screamed as he felt the *Brinery* roll to Starboard at a terrifying angle.

Beside him, Kelios smashed the little hammer down exactly where Tabir had instructed him. The DragonsBlood cannon roared with a deafening report.

Tabir had secured the cannon to the ship the way he and Anuka had done in Usban. It almost killed them all.

The recoil from the cannon drove the ship down so deep into the ocean that water flooded their compartment through the holes where the cannons protruded from the port side of the ship.

He couldn't see where their shot had gone but clearly heard the inhuman screams of Brine as the beast cascaded towards them.

Crenthys had no explanation for the odd behavior of the Sea Dragon. Whatever Anuka had said or done had hurt the Wyrm and it lashed back with incredible violence. As the *Brinery* pitched backward as if to brace for Brine's impact an unmistakable cannon report pierced the sea-sprayed air.

Crenthys dug her claws deep into the wood of the smaller mast she clung to. Just as the *Brinery* was driven down by the cannon blast she saw the cannon shot tear a hole through Brine's chest.

The momentum of the great Sea Snake was arrested as it doubled over and plunged back into the sea. As it fell, its tail whipped violently through the air, severing the mainstay just below the crow's nest.

She saw Anuka tumble out of the little basket and into the sea. *Bloody waters!* She thought, scrambling to her feet. When she got to the rail, she scanned for the little goblin but he was nowhere to be seen. The emotions that had been flaring so wildly within her threatened to undo her as she scanned the sea. Anuka had been so brave and had likely saved them all. It was unfair for him to suffer the worst sort of death he could imagine. The death his mother had suffered.

"We have no time to mourn," bellowed the deep voice of the Minothos as he put a hoof on the rail and launched himself into the water.

Brine slowly churned in the water below and she realized what he had meant. They still had a Dragon to kill.

⸺◦⸺

Kelios tumbled like a fish in a barrel. When he finally stopped, he struck hard against the wall behind him as the tilt of the ship temporarily made that wall the floor.

With a groan, he rolled to his hands and knees, then stood. Tabir was in no better shape but waved him off before Kelios could move to attend him.

Taking the steps three at a time, Kelios raced onto the deck. The swaying of the ship was slowing and he found the deck mostly empty. *Where was Crenthys?* Yells and splashes drew his attention and he raced to the rail. The Minothos and Crenthys were sitting on the back of the floating body of Brine. Kikkabar stabbed downward into the Wyrm's scale-covered back with a grunt. Crenthys held on with one hand and raked a deep gash with her other clawed hand.

"Crenthys!" he called down.

She looked up from her grim work and yelled, "Anuka," while pointing to her right with a gore-covered claw.

Without undressing, Kelios dove into the cool water and shifted to the form of a dolphin. He searched frantically for his companion in the water, now stained pink by Dragon's blood.

⸻ ❖ ⸻

"Sum Buck," Anuka screamed as he kicked and thrashed. The harder he fought to keep his head above water the harder it became. He felt panic as his arms grew harder to move. It seemed like he was made of lead. His last desperate kick had barely brought his head out of the water. The next one didn't.

Drowning seemed the worst thing that could happen to a person. It had haunted Anuka his entire life. Now, as his last precious air bubbles squeezed between his lips he knew peace. It would be moments now. Then no more struggling. No more pain. No more missing Mama or worrying about Papa. Crenthys and Kelios had each other.

He wouldn't get to see Mama again. There hadn't been time to find his power. Whatever that meant. As he sank deeper and the light above faded, all Anuka wanted was to see Mama one more time.

His legs buckled as he felt his feet hit the bottom of the sea.

⸻ ❖ ⸻

Crenthys lay panting on the sinking Wyrm as Kikkabar struggled to put his long-bladed sword back in its scabbard. The Minothos tumbled into the water and swam toward the ship.

No Kelios yet. And no Anuka. A lone sob wracked her chest before she slid off the dead Sea Snake's back and followed the Minothos. Anuka's death seemed so pointless. Crenthys' tears mingled with the seawater as she swam. She crashed into Kikkabar's back and the Minothos roared a bellow that startled her.

Springing from the water, she looked up at the bull-man who was clinging to the side of the ship with one hand and pumping a fist with the other. She looked out over the water in time to see a long gray dolphin crest the water with the limp form of Anuka on its back.

Kikkabar pulled the little goblin from Kelios's back. Anuka spit water and croaked, "I rode a dolphin you big ugly Sum Buck."

⸺◆⸺

After a heated debate, Kikkabar and the officers he had appointed finally agreed that they could not go north. Not yet. A plume of smoke rising from the north told them that Coryn's prediction of a burning Usban was probably true. With Bog likely in an acrimonious state they could not go north. So south it was. At least until they could make port and get some information.

Rest had done them all good but everyone prowled the deck for a day or so pacing with nervous energy. Anuka had found some decent mead in a barrel and was having some for breakfast. Seemed a reasonable way to celebrate another day of life. Crenthys and Kelios sat together, deep in discussion, near the bow of the ship. Anuka realized he was thankful for them. He had friends. He couldn't wait to tell Mama about his new friends, and Papa if he ever found him. That reminded him of something, so he sat his wooden mug on the deck between his feet and pulled the letter from his shoulder bag. He replaced his hat and turned the letter over a few times before opening it. He didn't want to bother his new friends, but this couldn't wait. He scooped up his mug in one hand, the letter in the other, and moved to the bow. Anuka plopped down by his friends and handed the letter to Crenthys.

"What is this?" She asked suspiciously.

"Read it. Please. I think my Papa wrote it." Anuka said.

She looked the letter over and then looked up at Anuka. He waved his hand encouragingly. She began to read:

Master Celebris Augmaximitis,

Forgive my boldness. I am Captain Attakah Sandbar, formerly of the Axefaced Dolphin, in service to Lord Triseth Valanir, Lord of the Sea, ESQ, and presently aboard my own vessel in deep Southern waters. We have a mutual acquaintance in Scribe, Book Master, and Terrible Card Player Xonan Whireenpaup. The miserly one-eyed gnome owes me a debt which he can detail to you at his discretion.

RE: The business at hand - I have a son who, after the fashion of most fathers, I suppose, I am quite proud of. He is heir to all I own, including my most prized possession; my ship. I have left information for young Anuka to come and join me post haste and take my place as Cpt. of my ship but he has been delayed. My son is inexperienced as a sailor. He is also terribly afraid of water and may be on fire when you find him. Despite all of this, I believe he will make a fine captain and I would see him join me soon.

Some of the company I have been forced to keep has made conditions unfavorable for me and I would have my son, whom I trust, at my side.

Of you, Most Shiny and Well-Scaled sir, I ask a small favor. I have heard that your vessel may carry you to the Eastern shores of Dorwine into the territory of Brine the Maldavien. If, during your stay, you can find a vessel called The Sea Pocket, seize it, and sink it.

I understand that this is a peculiar request, but it is my desire to expedite Anuka's voyage south and I fear he has taken to frivolity. My son, should he be aboard, needs be taken captive by whatever means are available, along with any companions that you deem would be suitable for him on his journey south. The plan I have diagrammed will benefit at least six parties; Yourself (and your illustrious Master) as my son will prove an excellent investigator suitable for your needs in Usban, those opposing the slave trade, the many victims of The Sea Pocket, those enemies and victims of Capt. Swet, Anuka, and Myself.

Along with this letter I have enclosed a note, redeemable in Usban Port, as a tribute to the Mighty Shimmer. Once Anuka has resolved your riddle, please speed him Southward with great haste. I have left other clues for him to follow as I fear to say overmuch in this letter concerning my whereabouts.

Yours,

Cpt. Attakah Sandbar

The three shared a stunned look and said in unison, "Sum Buck!"

The End

Split the Party

They had been watching the Dragon circle toward them for a quarter-hour.

Of the half-dozen Dragons that want me dead, which one is this? Anuka wondered.

"I think it is a Brass Dragon," Offund said, peering through a lens he had found somewhere.

"Give me that," Crenthys demanded and he did so without further prompting. She brought the tube up to her eye and steadied it carefully. Her breath caught. "It is a Bronze."

"Bronze? Thems your people, right?" Anuka asked.

"Right," she confirmed absently.

"Well, what do they want?"

"The Dragon, I would imagine." Ember offered helpfully.

The Dragon, still unnamed at Crenthys' insistence, looked miserable lying under a series of thick blankets suspended by various rigging to provide it shade. Apparently, being born in a cave made it hard to adapt to direct sunlight.

"Here we go," Anuka announced as the Dragon swooped toward the water, arced its wings to stop its descent, and then flapped them to hover about twenty feet above the water. A man dove from its back and began to swim towards the *Brinery*.

"Well. Wasn't expecting that." Anuka commented.

Bows were fetched and loaded and the general mood on deck was anxious. Tabir borrowed the looking glass from Crenthys and looked at the stranger. He gasped, then his face split into a grin that took over his whole face. He absently handed the glass to Offund who quietly stuck it back in a pocket of the voluminous shirt he wore.

The swimmer stopped near where the ship had dropped anchor and yelled up to the people congregated on the deck.

"Ahoy, I am Coltimar, emissary of Lord Dovondes the Benevolent, or Burnish, as he is called. Permission to come aboard."

"Big sucker. What do you think Kikkabar?" Anuka asked. The Minothos grunted.

"Of course he can come aboard. He is one of my oldest friends. Put away your bows." Tabir chided the archers and they reluctantly complied. A ladder made of rope was dropped into the water and the man, a human with short black hair, grabbed the ladder and scurried up it like a cat.

"Sum Buck," Anuka said, clearly impressed when Coltimar planted his bare feet on the deck. He wasn't big, he was massive. Only Kikkabar was taller, and not by a great deal. He wore a billowy white shirt that clung to him, revealing bulging muscles. He was handed a towel and commenced drying himself. Tabir had been hugging him for a time before he seemed to notice. Finally, he took the Elf by the arms and smiled a smile of pure joy.

"Tabir! Praise to the Prime! I wasn't sure when I would see you again. You-" Concern replaced elation when he inspected Tabir more carefully. It seemed like the human was buying a horse. Anuka expected he'd demand to see his teeth next. "What have you done? You look horrid!"

"It is good to see you, too, old friend." Some of Tabir's mirth was gone as well, but he still seemed happy to see the man.

In a low voice, the human said, "Did you heal an entire village? We've talked about this, at length."

"Coltimar, please. Can we continue this age-old argument another time?" Tabir said as calmly as he knew how.

"Of course," he conceded, "Where are my manners? Who is the captain of this vessel?"

All heads turned to Kikkabar and he raised a finger in the air.

"I am grateful that you would have me. My friend and I," Coltimar pointed to the circling Dragon, "Have come a long way."

Introductions were made and Coltimar was offered food and drink but he seemed keen to get to the business at hand.

"Tabir?" Coltimar said, nodding toward the baby Dragon who was looking on with interest.

The small group walked to where the baby Dragon rested and Coltimar inspected it much the same way he had inspected Tabir. He spent some time looking at the beast's side when he looked up sharply at Tabir. "Is this who you healed?"

Tabir looked at his feet.

"Seas...you could have killed yourself. You-" Coltimar stopped himself and looked around. "Can he fly?"

"Little bit," Anuka said clearing his throat. He dug at one ear with a pointed finger and took interest in something in another direction. "We went for a little ride."

"Coltimar," Crenthys said, "where do you intend to take him?"

"Lady," Coltimar said with a small bow, "Do you know him? I mean, is he..."

"He is my brother. My patron, called Sheen, was...was slain. We are her orphans."

Coltimar was silent for a few moments. "I am sorry. Are you well?"

"I have been well cared for. This child is my responsibility until a proper mother can be found." Crenthys's tone was firm.

"I understand. I intend to take him home." Coltimar said.

Anuka understood that he didn't want everybody to know where the Dragons live. *Whatever. Who cared anyway?* Anuka wasn't expecting to receive a dinner invitation.

"You can come along, of course. You are all the family he has now," Coltimar said.

It's what Crenthys was asking for but she seemed stunned that he agreed.

"I would, of course, be honored to join you, Crenthys. If that can be arranged." Ember said. He fidgeted with his clothing but managed not to dip his head or fade into the crowd as he usually did.

Crenthys looked at Coltimar who pursed his lips into a thoughtful frown. "I suppose that could be arranged. Will anyone else be joining us?"

"Not me. No offense, Cren. I'm on a mission." Anuka said. The need to find his father burned inside him. It was like an itch he couldn't scratch. He really hoped he didn't hurt Crenthys's feelings but he couldn't wait any longer to find Paps.

"I am with him," Offund said as he stepped up beside Anuka.

Well, that was sweet, Anuka thought.

Crenthys looked at Kelios and he looked back at her. *Gross,* Anuka thought.

"I also must accompany Anuka," Kelios said. He held himself straight-backed, his head high.

For about half a second Crenthys looked like she got zapped by Offund's lightning. She recovered quickly and gave him a firm nod. It seemed like she and Kelios had a lot to discuss. Anuka was glad they weren't going to break into it right here in front of everyone.

"Ember, Crenthys, and I then," Tabir said with a nod of finality.

"Excellent. Let us make preparations and be on our way," Coltimar said.

A half an hour later, Anuka stood on the deck flanked by Offund and Kelios, watching the Dragons fade off into the horizon. Fish Man looked sad. He and Crenthys had a hearty row in the Forecastle. As loud as they were, they might as well have gone for it on the deck. They settled whatever it was and now she was riding a Dragon to some mountain castle.

Offund looked like a lost man searching for his soul. There was more to the little guy than Anuka imagined.

Anuka hoped to see Crenthys again someday. Seeing the Cat Man wouldn't be the worst thing to happen, either. They were four days from Riverbreach where they intended to put in. Then Anuka would head for the swamp for the next clue to lead him to his papa. For once, it seemed like everything might work out after all.

Second Chance

S wet planted an elbow in the wet sand and vomited another mouthful of salt water onto the beach. He tried to climb another step up the shore to get beyond the pull of the tide washing over him but couldn't move another inch. Instead, he collapsed to his back where he lay panting. The star-pocked sky was as black as pitch.

Why do I yet live? Swet wondered as another series of coughs racked his exhausted body. When the fit subsided he lay back on the sand as another wave washed up the beach. He could remember the little red goblin burning him somehow. Then he remembered the explosion of pain as a blade was rammed into his gut. Men had grabbed him roughly and tossed him overboard to drown. But something had happened before he was cast into the sea.

Swet remembered the form of a pale, lithe High Elf looming over him, his worried face captured in the light of a torch. *What had he said?*

"You are a wicked man, Swet. You deserve to die alone and in pain. But Rathune is mercy. So I must be mercy." Then the elf placed a hand on Swet's chest and murmured, "My blood, for your life. My life, for your wounds." A light as bright as ten suns exploded in his sight and his body felt like it had been submerged in an icy ocean. Then the elf staggered away, leaving him on the deck of the Brinery.

Swet remembered the rough hands and the shock of the cool water as he was tossed overboard. He wasn't dead, so he swam. He kicked and fought the salty sea until the yelling and cursing of dying men was a distant thing. Now he lay here on the beach rubbing his smooth skin on a belly that had been ravaged by steel. His shirt still bore the holes from the weapon and the stains of his blood. The place in his hand where he expected to find seared flesh was whole. *How?*

A figure stood over Swet and he cried out. He tried to roll away but the man was suddenly kneeling then and placed a hand on Swet's chest holding him in place. That hand may as well have been a barrel of rocks. Try as he may, Swet couldn't move.

"What is this? Who are you?" Swet demanded. His fear lent him strength but he still could not move.

"You are not worthy of my name. This is another chance for you, given freely by Tabir, son of Leofir." The voice was calm but rumbled like a distant storm. Long wavy hair hung about his placid face.

Not worthy? Swet cursed and bashed at the arm that held him pressed to the sand. "Do you know who I am?"

"The man, Onan Swet. Thief. Liar. Murderer. Adulterer. Rapist. Justly sentenced to die, mercifully rescued by a child of the Revered."

Swet's outrage faded at the man's words. In the pale moonlight, Onan could see the man's fathomless eyes searching him. "Who are you to so accuse me?" Swet asked the question but immediately regretted it. His racing mind told him that he didn't want to know.

"Rachinda. Leeli. Varinel. Sofee. Kanri. Myellan."

Those names! How does he know those names? "St-stop. Stop it!"

The man stopped speaking, letting a name die on his lips. "Do you deny me, now, Onan Swet?"

Those were women he... Indignation tried to well up and defend himself but a strong emotion swept those thoughts away: shame.

"Shall I list the men you have murdered?" The man asked, his face a mask of serenity covering the face of an executioner.

"No. Please..." Swet felt completely naked before this man. *He knows my life. Does he know my thoughts, as well?* That thought made him shiver.

"You are a creature unfit to utter the name of the elf Tabir, son of Leofir, let alone of his Master. But I have been compelled to tell you these things that your life may be redeemed. Tabir, son of Leofir, spent years of his life in exchange for yours. Because you live, Tabir's life will be shortened. There can be no life without the remission of guilt. Tabir has paid your debts, Onan Swet. I beseech you to take the man Onan Swet and drown him in the sea. Then rise with a new name. Go forth a new creature. Live your second life, not to your glory, but to the glory of he who made Tabir capable of offering that life to you. His name is unknowable. Your kind calls him Rathune."

With those words, the man was standing. Swet didn't see him stand up. He simply was standing. Staring down at Swet that man seemed on the verge of taking back his words and crushing him into the sand. Instead, he said, "I will be watching you." Then he was gone.

The man who was once Onan Swet lay panting in the sand thinking for the first time of the consequences of the life he had lived. He began to weep.

About Author

Jack Adkins has been spinning tales for over thirty years. He is a seasoned veteran of Dungeons and Dragons, Top Secret, Vampire, MechWarrior, and almost every RPG in between. Jack has finally gotten around to sharing his unique humor and imaginative stories with the world. Before he began writing novels, Jack enjoyed building lightsabers with his four boys, moving props and equipment for the Marching Band, and studying Reformation Era Christian Theology. In his spare time, Jack has built a twenty-four-year IT career.

You can visit Jack's website to explore more of his writing, check out his Bad Book Reviews (not bad books, just bad reviews), or contact him.

https://authorjackadkins.com.

Also By